"T... ... ...n Uskevren
journeyed north to the Tangled Trees. He met an elf
woman—a wild elf of the forest—and . . . lay with her.
A year later he returned, and found that she had given
birth to his child.

"I was raised in his house, in Sembia,
but now I have returned. I am looking for…"
She paused, unsure for a moment how to continue.
"For my roots. My . . . family."

The elf's eyes had grown wider as Larajin spoke.
Suddenly, in one swift motion, she lowered her bow.
She pressed both hands against her heart,
palms to her chest and bowed.

DIVIDED HEART.
UNSWERVING STRENGTH.

"I should have paid more heed to the goddess's sign.
Perhaps then I would have recognized you," she said
as she straightened, "but it's little wonder that I didn't.
You and your brother are as different as day and night."

SEMBIA:
GATEWAY TO THE REALMS

HEIRS OF PROPHECY

SEMBIA

GATEWAY TO THE REALMS

BOOK
V

LISA SMEDMAN

Sembia: Gateway to the Realms, Book V
Heirs of Prophecy

©2002 Wizards of the Coast, Inc.

Cover art by Raymond Swanland
Map by Dennis Kauth
First Printing: June 2002
This Edition First Printing: July 2007

9 8 7 6 5 4 3 2 1

ISBN: 978-0-7869-4290-9
620-95956740-001-EN

U.S., CANADA,   EUROPEAN HEADQUARTERS
ASIA, PACIFIC, & LATIN AMERICA   Hasbro UK Ltd
Wizards of the Coast, Inc.   Caswell Way
P.O. Box 707   Newport, Gwent NP9 0YH
Renton, WA 98057-0707   GREAT BRITAIN
+1-800-324-6496   Save this address for your records.

Visit our web site at www.wizards.com

PROLOGUE

The Year of Wild Magic (1372 DR)

Crowned by the horns of a rising crescent moon, the stone stood in the forest, dappled with shadow and enfolded deep in the whispers and creaks of trees moving in the wind. Four times the height of a person and wider than extended arms could reach, it had been hewn from a single slab of gray granite, then polished by ancient crafters until it was as smooth and glossy as the surface of a still lake.

A solitary figure kneeled before the stone, his knees and bare feet denting the loamy ground. Dressed in short leather breeches with fringe at the knees and a leather vest tooled in an oak-leaf pattern, he held a bow, the ends of which had been carved in the shape of acorns. The fingers and thumb that gripped that bow were dark, though the hand itself was no ruddier than was usual for his race.

The figure's dark auburn hair was pulled back in a single braid, revealing sharply pointed ears, the left one pierced near its tip with a length of gilded bone. The elf's face was long and narrow with almond-shaped eyes, and framed by bangs that hung in a series of tiny fringelike braids. A small black feather was woven into the tip of each braid and fluttered against his forehead in the wind. At his throat was a glint of gold: a ring that hung on a leather thong.

With his free hand he reached out, touching the stone with slender fingers. As they rested upon its surface, moonlight revealed the delicate tracery of ink on skin that made the digits appear darker than the rest of his hand. A single, broad line had been tattooed along the back of each finger, another along the thumb. Smaller lines feathered out from these root lines, giving his digits the appearance of dark quills.

Feather-fingers moved upon the Standing Stone, tracing the words that had been inscribed upon it more than thirteen centuries before. Twining around the base of the stone like a vine around a tree, the inscription—written in Espruar, the flowing script of the elves—commemorated the ancient pact between Cormanthor and the humans of the Dales.

The kneeling figure whispered it aloud, from memory. "For thus have the humans of the East solemnly sworn: No axe shall fell the Forest, nor road cross it, nor settlement or farm reduce it, nor invasion claim it, so long as there are elves in this Wood. In return, the Elven Court grants the humans from the East full title to the lands surrounding Cormanthor, to tend and sow as they will. Let this stone stand as a permanent monument to this our solemn pact. For so long as the friendship and trust between our two races endures, so long this stone shall . . ."

Where the final word should have been was only a dark, empty space. The flowing script vanished into a split in the stone. More than four fingers wide at the base, the crevice rapidly narrowed, but a thin crack continued up the front of the monument, marring its smooth surface.

Tracing this crack with a fingertip, the elf slowly stood. The line ended at a point even with his heart.

The elf drew a bone-handled knife from the belt at his waist and tested its tempered steel against a smooth section of stone. Metal grated against granite once, twice, thrice, eventually etching a faint line. Lowering his knife, the elf peered at the scratch he'd made, watching as it began to glow with a faint, silver light. As the wound in the stone healed itself, the elf slowly nodded. The magic of the Standing Stone was still intact.

Movement at the base of the monument caught the elf's eye. Sheathing his dagger, he kneeled swiftly. He reached into the crack in the stone with a slender finger and felt something round and rough that had an opening in its side. After a moment, he recognized it as a carefully woven ball of twigs and leaves: a hidden nest. The crack must have been there for some time, perhaps a month or more.

Gently probing inside the nest, his fingertips brushed against the soft back of a tiny bird with an upturned tail—a wren—who protested the intrusion with a sharp peck of her beak. Ignoring the warning, the elf quested further. Inside the nest were two tiny eggs, tucked under the wren's downy chest. A third egg, pushed to one side of the nest, was cold.

Dead?

The elf closed his eyes and turned his head, seeking out the direction of the breeze by its feel against his skin and the flutter of the feathers in his bangs. He whispered a prayer, letting the wind take his words. A moment later, the sound of a distant flute blew back on the wind. He inhaled sharply, taking it into his lungs, then concentrated its energy from lung to heart to veins to fingertips. Slowly, the egg grew warm under his touch. When it was the same temperature as the others, he nudged it back under the wren's warm chest.

The elf withdrew his hand, then stood. He turned away from the stone to peer through the darkened wood. No more than a few dozen paces from where he stood was a gap in the forest—the wide, bare slash that was Rauthauvyr's Road. It was a wound in the forest that was growing wider, becoming more putrid, with each passing day.

As the clouds overhead thickened, the elf scowled. The Elven Court of years long past was wrong to have capitulated to the humans of the south, to have allowed the trees to be felled and the road to be built, breaking the sacred pact. It was a wonder that the stone had not split then, with the first stroke of the axe.

He spat. If he had been born five centuries earlier . . .

But he had not.

For four hundred and fifty years, human feet had stamped along that road, tramping through the Vale of Lost Voices and troubling the sacred sleep of those laid to rest between the roots of the mighty oaks.

A blight was spreading along that road, destroying the forest to either side and worming its way deeper into the wood with each passing day. Like fleas on a dog the blight must have been carried by humans.

It had to be stopped.

Trees creaked against one another as the wind picked up, and clouds scudded across the face of the moon, throwing stone and elf into shadow. Closer to the road, one of the blighted trees groaned as it was bent by the wind, then it cracked and came crashing down in a tangle of broken limbs. After a silence that stretched for a heartbeat or two, thunder grumbled in the sky to the east. The clouds overhead thickened, and the first drops of rain began to fall.

The elf turned his face up to the heavens, allowing the tears of the Leaflord to mingle with the tears flowing from his own eyes.

"These humans," he vowed, in a voice as twisted as a gnarled tree root. "They will pay for what they have done."

He slung his bow over his shoulder and squatted beside the stone, thrusting hands out to either side. A faint tingle began at his splayed fingers, and a shivery chill rushed up his arms. The transformation began. Tattooed fingers flattened and became feathers, arms elongated, changed articulation, and grew into wings. Vest and breeches turned into a covering of sleek black feathers. As the elf's head grew rounder and his nose and lips hardened into a beak, his body shrank, continuing the shift until he stood on three-toed feet.

Shaking the rain from his feathers, the elf-become-crow gave a single loud caw. A heartbeat later, the cry was echoed by a bright flash of lightning.

The crow launched itself into the air, circled the Standing Stone once, then winged its way to the southeast through darkening skies.

CHAPTER 1

Larajin stared at the face that looked up at her from the pages of the leather-bound book she held in her lap. The woodcut image, printed more than a century before, showed a wild elf with a long, narrow face and high forehead. Tucked behind his pointed ears were braids tied with bits of bone and feather. Feral, almond-shaped eyes glared above cheeks tattooed with thick, black lines.

Bare-chested and clad only in rough leather breeches, the elf stood in a forest, surrounded by the trunks of massive trees, thick ferns hiding all but the top of his fringed moccasins. He gripped a knife with a hilt made from a deer's hoof in one hand, a short bow in the other. Underneath the illustration was the caption: *Wild Elf Warrior of the Tangled Trees*.

Larajin ran a finger along the top of her own ear. It was smooth and round—a legacy of her human father, Master Thamalon Uskevren the Elder. From her mother—a "wild elf" of the Tangled Trees—Larajin had inherited her rust-colored hair, slim build, and impulsive nature.

What had her mother been like? Beautiful, certainly, to have lured the master's affections away from his wife. Well respected by her people, Habrith had said, but Habrith—who was like an aunt to Larajin—had refused to tell her more. She said only that Larajin would find out on her own in due time, when the moment had ripened.

Larajin knew she would one day travel to the Tangled Trees, but something was holding her back. It was fear, perhaps, or the comforts of Stormweather Towers, or the fact that the few Elvish words she'd managed to glean from dusty old tomes would not enable her to make her complicated story understood.

A thud startled Larajin out of her reverie. She peered around the high back of the armchair in which she sat, thinking that someone had entered the library—that she was about to be caught handling the master's precious tomes. She saw with relief that the door to the library was still closed and realized the noise had just been a book falling over on one of the shelves. From elsewhere in Stormweather Towers came the sound of raised voices, but in the hall outside the library, all was quiet.

On the carpet at her feet, a tressym sighed contentedly, eyes closed. The catlike creature sat like a sphinx, forepaws extended and wings tucked tightly against her back. Even folded flat, the wings were exquisitely beautiful. Unfolded, they rivaled a peacock's feathers, with spots of brilliant turquoise, vibrant yellow, and ruby red, all edged in tabby-stripe black.

As if sensing Larajin looking at her, the tressym opened luminous golden eyes and inclined her head.

Brrow? she asked quizzically.

Larajin bent down to stroke silky, blue-gray fur. As always, she was amazed at how the tressym trusted her. Anyone else foolish enough to try to pat the creature would have had her hand shredded by those sharp claws.

"You shouldn't be here," she chided. "You're a wild creature— you should have flown back to wherever you came from, after I healed you. Why do you keep sneaking into Stormweather Towers? Don't you know your being here is dangerous—for both of us?"

The only answer was a rumbling purr. The tressym closed her eyes and in a moment was fast asleep.

Larajin settled back into the armchair and turned the page, wrinkling her nose at the musty smell of age-spotted paper and old leather. The book was a history of the founding of Sembia, an unfortunately rather dry account of what must in fact have been truly heroic events. Larajin would liked to have learned more, for example, about the great clash between humans and elves at Singing Arrows in the year 884 DR. What had prompted the historians to give such a bloody battle so poetic a name? Also given short shrift was the visit to the Elven Court of Sembia's first Overmaster, Rauthauvyr the Raven, in 913. Instead of describing elven customs, the author dwelled interminably on arcane legal arguments about whether or not Sembia had the right to construct a road.

There was one tantalizing detail, however. A footnote at the bottom of a page containing a list of the members of the council noted that these were not the "true names" of the elves. It added that every elf was given both a true name and a common name by his parents on the day that he was born.

Larajin had been named by her adoptive human mother, the servant Shonri Wellrun. Now she wondered—had the elf woman who died giving birth to her twenty-five years ago lived long enough to give her daughter a true name?

Lost in thought, Larajin heard the tressym hiss, but she paid it no heed, assuming the creature was reacting to something in a dream. A long shadow fell across the pages, and a hand reached down and jerked the book out of her lap, causing Larajin to shriek in alarm.

"This is the final stone, girl," a deep voice growled.

Blushing furiously, Larajin looked up into the stern face of her nemesis: Erevis Cale, head servant and butler to the house of Uskevren. Tall and implacable as a tower, he glared down at her, a terrible wrath in his deep-shadowed eyes. The sleeves of his gray shirt were smudged with what must have been soot, judging by the strong odor of smoke that clung to him, and there was a small cut on his bald scalp, as if he'd banged his head on something.

"B-but, Sir," she sputtered, "it's long past dark, and my chores are done. I know that's a rare and valuable book, but I took great care with it and didn't bend any—"

"And what of the tallow you were melting on the stove?"

The quiet words stopped her cold, more than any shouted rebuke might have done. Her eyes widened as she remembered the last task she'd been assigned that evening: softening tallow for the servants who topped up the lamps in the evening. Despite the close summer warmth of the library, her stomach felt like sharp icicles had suddenly sprouted inside it. A question rose in her mind, one she dared not whisper aloud: How much of the kitchen had been burned?

Behind Cale, the tressym launched herself into the air, seeking the safety of the rafters. For the first time since the creature had followed Larajin back to Stormweather Towers, some eighteen months before, the butler ignored the fact that it had once again crept indoors. Instead he merely stared at Larajin, his lips pressed together in a thin line.

"Get up," he ordered. "This time the master himself will deal with you."

As she was marched to the door, Larajin heard him add, under his breath, "And this time, by the gods, I'll finally be rid of you."

The hallway to the master's study had never seemed so long. Steered by Cale's heavy hand on her shoulder, Larajin dragged her feet along the plush carpet, unwilling to face the disappointment she knew she would see in the master's eyes. Gilt-framed portraits of the Uskevren ancestors glared down at her from either side, and a suit of plate mail holding an axe stood as if waiting for Larajin to place her neck on the chopping block.

From behind the heavy oak door of the master's study came the murmurs of two voices. As Larajin and Cale approached, the door opened. Through it came one of the kitchen staff—Aileen, a girl with wispy blonde hair who hid a shrewish disposition behind pretty smiles—carrying an empty decanter. She wore the formal Uskevren servant's uniform: a white dress slashed with blue, and a gold vest and turban bearing the Uskevren crest with its horse-at-anchor design. Tiny silver bells sewn onto her turban tinkled as she stopped short, obviously surprised to find Cale and Larajin in the hallway.

Larajin was suddenly aware that she had mislaid part of her uniform—again. Her own turban was lying forgotten in the library, and her long hair hung uncombed and tousled about her shoulders. Aileen noted this with a quick glance and crinkled her nose.

Aileen had halted with one hand still on the door behind her, which remained open a finger's width.

"The master has a visitor, Sir," she told Cale in a mincing voice. "He instructed that . . ."

Her eye fell on Larajin's shoulder, and the sooty mark Cale's hand had left there. Her lips twitched into a smirk.

"The master instructed that whoever caused the fire atop the stove be brought to him straight away."

Larajin turned to Cale to protest, but her words died on her lips when she saw the hard gleam in his eyes. He either couldn't see that Aileen was ensuring that the master would deal with Larajin more harshly after being interrupted, or he didn't care.

As Aileen scurried away down the hallway, Cale marched

Larajin to the study. As his hand fell on the door latch, a snatch of conversation came from behind the door.

". . . such drastic measures," the master was saying. "Surely the Merchant Council must realize the reaction this will prompt. It came as no small surprise to me that the Hulorn encouraged this folly."

Cale paused, obviously reconsidering the wisdom of an interruption. As a frown creased his brow, Larajin allowed herself a tentative shred of hope. Perhaps the butler would be forced to wait until morning to bring her to the master. By then, both their tempers might cool.

From the study came a second male voice, this one with a slight wheeze to it.

"The Hulorn was not the only one to cast a vote in favor. The council will stand behind its decision, come what may. Your opinion is that of the minority—even the Overmaster recognizes the necessity of responding to the attacks with swords, not words. The Dales have declared themselves neutral, and Cormyr has shown no interest in the squabble."

The voice paused, then added in a seductive tone, "Thamalon, I hope you will give this matter careful thought. This may provide Sembia's only chance to push the Red Plumes north. It may even provide an excuse to march on Hillsfar itself—an opportunity you've long been waiting for, or so I'm told."

The master's voice grew thoughtful. "We shall see."

From inside the study came the clink of a glass being set upon a metal tray. It was followed an instant later by the rustle of robes and the *thunk* of a staff against the floor as someone approached the door. Cale's hand dropped from the latch, and he moved away from the door, pulling Larajin with him as he made room for the departing visitor.

As the door swung open, Larajin's eyes widened in alarm. The master's visitor was a tall, dark-skinned man wearing smoke-gray hose and a doublet with crimson-slashed sleeves. Perhaps fifty years of age, he had eyes that glittered like polished jet, dark, wavy hair, and a neatly trimmed beard that was no more than a thin line framing his jaw and chin—a Sembian affectation he had adopted, together with the doublet, since the last time Larajin had seen him. He leaned on a knotted bloodwood staff studded with dark thorns that had been pushed point-first into its blood-colored wood like tacks, forming a spiral design. A halo of upturned thorns crowned the top.

A tiny corner of Larajin's mind screamed at her to drop her eyes, as Erevis Cale was doing, to play the part of servant, to avoid drawing attention to herself. Instead she stared, mesmerized, at the staff. She had seen first-hand the deadly black bolts of magical energy that staff could produce, had watched in horror as they reduced a wild elf to a smoking husk in the Hunting Garden—and all because Larajin had seen what the Hulorn had done to himself with his foul magic.

Please, Goddess, don't let him recognize me, Larajin silently prayed, dropping her eyes at last and staring hard at the carpet. I'm a servant, only a servant. Invisible and silent.

If only she had stopped a moment to put her turban on. Perhaps he would not recognize her, even with her hair unbound. She'd been wearing different clothes then, had . . .

The Hulorn's wizard paused, directly in front of her. Ice flowed through her blood as his gaze slithered down, then up her body, coming to rest on her face.

"You look familiar to me, girl," he wheezed. "Do I know you?"

Somehow, Larajin found her voice. "I do not think so, sir. I'm just a servant. Perhaps you saw me waiting tables, during a previous visit to Stormweather Towers."

"This is my first visit to your master's house."

"Or you might have seen me on the streets or in the market," Larajin quickly added. "I'm often sent to do the shopping."

The wizard's eyes grew bored. "Perhaps that was it," he agreed.

Inwardly, Larajin sighed with relief as the wizard turned to leave, but just then, a familiar sound echoed down the hall.

Mrrow?

The tressym padded out of the open library door, into the hallway. Head turning, she looked in Larajin's direction—and her ears flattened as she spotted the wizard. Baring her teeth in a hiss, she backed slowly away, then suddenly spun and leaped into flight, her brilliant wings flapping furiously. Landing delicately on a window ledge, she batted at the latch with a paw, opened the window with a shove of her head, then disappeared through it.

Erevis Cale muttered, "That's enough of you, cat."

He strode down the hall to snap the window shut.

Larajin froze, unable to speak, as the wizard turned back to her with narrowed eyes. He tipped his staff until the head of it was under her chin. Its thorns pricked her skin, causing her to flinch and jerk her head up.

Recognition burned in the wizard's eyes as they met hers.

"Does your master treat you well?" he asked in a whisper. "Would you like to come and serve the Hulorn, instead? Perhaps you could feed his pets."

Larajin's mind flew back to the rats she'd encountered in the sewers under the Hulorn's Hunting Garden. Misshapen monstrosities, they'd been altered by the Hulorn's dark magic to grow hooves, wings, horns—even a tiny human head. Larajin shuddered at the memory of their sharp teeth worrying her flesh. She'd fought them off once—and didn't want to face them again. The Hulorn's wizard was subtly letting her know what her fate would be, now that he knew who she was.

"Sir, I . . ." was all she could manage in response. Gods, was this all she could do—cower before him, meek as a mouse? At last she found her voice. "My master is too fond of me. I am like a daughter to him. He would never allow—"

"A pity," the wizard answered, withdrawing his staff from under her chin. "You seem like a good servant—one who knows the value of being seen and not heard." His voice dropped. "Of course, there are other, more certain ways to ensure silence, aren't there?"

He turned away with a chuckle as Erevis Cale strode back to where Larajin stood. Cale gave the wizard a sharp look, and followed him with his eyes as the wizard made his way down the hall.

A moment later, the master appeared in the doorway. He appeared not to have overheard the exchange and merely nodded at the departing wizard's back.

"Erevis," he said, "please see Master Drakkar to the door."

Cale glanced up sharply at this command, then turned and walked smoothly down the hall. The moment he was out of sight, the master said, "Larajin, a word if you please."

Still shaking from her brush with the wizard, Larajin immediately launched into a defense of her actions. Now, more than ever, she needed the master's goodwill.

"Master Thamalon," she said, "I only meant to leave the tallow untended for a moment. The fire in the stove had burned down to coals. I didn't realize it would—"

The master held up a hand, demanding silence. Deep green eyes blazed down at her from under a thick crop of wavy, snow-white hair. Surprisingly, though the conversation Larajin had just overheard seemed like a matter of state, the master was casually dressed, wearing a doublet with solid sleeves and soft leather house shoes over plain white hose. He'd obviously not been expecting a visitor so late at night. He closed the door of the study, then turned and spoke in a stern voice.

"Larajin, I would ask that you refrain, in the future, from describing my affections for you in the terms you used tonight."

Braced as she was for a reprimand about the kitchen fire, Larajin was surprised by his words.

"Master, I don't—"

"You don't understand? No, I suppose not. I shall have to put it plainly, then. I am asking that you not, at any time or in any company—noble or common—describe my feelings toward you as being like that of a father for a daughter. People might draw . . . the wrong conclusions." Heavy eyebrows frowning, he let his eyes bore into hers. "Do you understand me now?"

Biting her tongue, Larajin nodded. She understood all too well. Since that day last winter when Habrith had revealed that Thamalon Uskevren was Larajin's father, Larajin had kept this secret close to her heart—like the obedient servant she had been raised to be. The only one she had confided in, so far, was Talbot.

She'd tried to summon up the courage to tell the master that she knew that he was her father, but whenever she'd been about to speak, the words fled from her lips. Now she could see the response they would have incurred. Not what she'd prayed for—acceptance and acknowledgement—but anger. The last thing the master wanted was to acknowledge the fact that he had sired a child on a wild elf of the Tangled Trees. Larajin was nothing more than an embarrassment to him. She was a thorn he deliberately pricked himself with, day in and day out, by keeping her as a servant—a reminder of something in himself that he abhorred.

The master accepted her silent reply with a nod, probably not even seeing the anger that was starting to smolder inside her. His lips parted, as if he were about to add something more, but whatever he was going to say was interrupted by a knock at the study door.

"Yes?" he asked.

The door opened, and Erevis Cale stepped into the study with a bow.

"Master Drakkar has departed Stormweather Towers," he announced. "I'll ensure that the driver of his carriage gets a good tip."

"Very good, Cale."

Larajin had heard master and butler use this code in the past, and understood what it meant. Cale had just assured the master that Drakkar's movements would be noted and reported. The master's suspicions about the wizard would do her little good. She could hardly tell him about Drakkar attacking her in the Hunting Garden without bringing up her wild elf heritage and with it, Thamalon Uskevren's indiscretion. After his stern warning never to even allude to this secret, she could hardly turn to him for help.

She would have to seek help elsewhere. Now that Drakkar knew who she was, Stormweather Towers was no longer a safe haven. She had to leave Selgaunt, and as soon as possible.

She dropped her eyes to the carpet as Cale folded his arms across his chest and scowled at her.

"Now then, Larajin," he began. "There is the matter of the fire atop the stove—a fire that could have spread to the rest of the kitchen, had it not been spotted—and the disciplinary action to be taken." He turned to the master, and added, "In light of the gravity of the error, I would suggest, Master Thamalon, that—"

The master sighed, and once again held up his hand. Cale fell into an obedient silence.

"I think we'll keep her away from the kitchen for the next little while," the master said. "Perhaps getting her out from underfoot will give you some relief. Assign her to serve in young Thamalon's tallhouse for the next month, and see how she fares there. As her punishment for causing a fire that could have burned Stormweather Towers to the ground, had it spread beyond the stove, Larajin is to immediately undertake the task of cleaning the mess in the kitchen. She is not to stop nor rest until the stove is returned to full working order and the pots are gleaming. She must do this alone, without assistance from any of the staff."

This last was directed at Larajin, who was meant to quail under the imagined enormity of the task, but her mind was on more pressing concerns—like whether the Hulorn's men would arrest her the next time she ventured out onto the streets.

"Master Thamalon, I must protest," Cale sputtered. "The punishment is not severe enough. I would suggest—"

"Erevis Cale," the master said. "I am not interested in hearing your suggestions."

Larajin blinked in surprise. In all her years at Stormweather Towers, she had never heard the master use that tone with Cale. For the first time in memory, he was speaking to his butler as a servant.

Cale's face flushed, but he held his tongue. "As you wish, Master."

His eyes, however, spoke volumes as he turned to Larajin.

"Kitchen," he spat. "Now!"

Larajin studied her reflection in the mirror in Mistress Thazienne's bedroom. The emerald-green gown she wore was stiff with gold embroidery and seed pearls, its sleeves tight to the elbow and flaring with slashes of white from elbow to shoulder. The bodice was high and thrusting, the hemline low.

The gown was Thazienne's, the color designed to complement her sea-green eyes. It was a little long on Larajin—a good thing, since it hid the serviceable leather boots she was wearing—and a little loose in the bodice. With a bit of padding, it fit her well enough.

She'd tucked her hair up into a bun, and covered it with an elaborate cap hung with lace and trailing peacock feathers. Looking in the mirror, the only thing that gave her disguise away was her work-roughened hands, the nails still black with soot. Otherwise, she looked like her half-sister. It ought to work. The gods only knew how many times Thazienne had disguised herself as Larajin, when she wanted to creep about the city in the guise of a common servant.

She yawned, then stretched to ease the aching muscles

in her neck and back. She'd spent long hours scrubbing the kitchen, under Erevis Cale's baleful glare. She was exhausted, but she couldn't afford to sleep—she had to get away from the city first.

Cracking open the door to Thazienne's room, she made sure the hallway was clear. She picked up the leather bag she'd packed for her journey and slung its strap over her shoulder. She'd raided the pantry after she finished cleaning the kitchen, and had filled the bag with enough food to see her through the next few days. The bag also held a kitchen knife, candles, flint and steel for kindling a fire, a light summer blanket, and a change of clothes.

Also inside the bag, tied into a handkerchief, were the few coins she'd been able to save over the years: mostly pennies and a handful of silver ravens. She hoped they'd be enough for a seat on a carriage to the neighboring city of Ordulin—perhaps even as far as Essembra.

She crept down the darkened hallway to Tal's bedroom and slipped a folded letter under his door. She'd left a similar letter for her adoptive parents in the stables, where her father would find it in the morning. Their letter had been vague, saying only that she was in danger, and had to leave Selgaunt for a time—that she would send word to them later. She told her parents they shouldn't worry; she was going to a place where she would be under the goddess's protection. It wasn't exactly a lie. Her destination—the Tangled Trees—was watched over by Hanali Celanil.

Her parents, however, would assume that she meant the goddess Sune and that she was traveling to the House of Firehair—Sune's temple in the city of Daerlun. When they reported their daughter's sudden and seemingly inexplicable departure to the master, he would no doubt send agents after Larajin—and they would head west. Drakkar, if he followed them, would be thrown off the scent.

The letter she'd slipped under Tal's door included more detail than the one she'd left for her parents. She'd included a description of her encounter with the Hulorn's wizard, whom she now was able to put a name to. Tal knew about Larajin's earlier brush with Drakkar in the Hunting Garden. He would understand the threat, why she needed to leave—and the need for secrecy.

Making her way through the wide halls to Stormweather Towers's grand front entrance—if Drakkar did have men watching the house, they'd probably be expecting her to slip out through the servants' door at the rear—she peered out a leaded-glass window at the darkened street. The time was halfway between midnight and dawn. At that hour, Sarn Street was virtually deserted. A boy walking on stilts tended the street lanterns, trimming their wicks and topping up their oil, and a solitary carriage clattered past on a side road, but the tallhouses that lined the street were, for the most part, dark and silent.

She was just about to open the door when the gleam of metal in a doorway across the street gave her pause. The lantern boy noticed it, too. He bent at the waist to peer down into the doorway, then straightened and moved away at a rapid clip. Inside the doorway, a figure shifted. It was a man clad entirely in black but with a helm that caught the lantern light. He was a member of the city guard.

Larajin had been right. The Hulorn's men were watching Stormweather Towers. They must have expected her to try to slip away, perhaps even counted on it. That way, she could simply be made to disappear, and Master Thamalon would never be the wiser about who took her or why. The gods only knew how many of the guard were out there, waiting and watching. Larajin wasn't going to make it on her own—even in disguise. She needed help.

She was only an initiate of the goddess Sune, not even a real cleric, and what little she knew of Hanali Celanil's worship was entirely self-taught from tomes in the master's library that had been written by human authors who hadn't been initiated into the goddess's mysteries, but perhaps . . .

Reaching into her bag, she pulled out a heart-shaped locket. It was made of cheap metal, probably brass, that had been burnished to look like gold. Most of the finish had rubbed off long ago, and the original chain was long gone. Larajin had replaced it with a short circle of red embroidery thread, just wide enough to slip over her hand. She'd paid only a few pennies for the trinket, which she'd found in a peddler's stall in the market. Its value to her, however, was immeasurable—not because of the locket itself but because of what it held.

Larajin lifted the locket to her nose. From within came a faint, floral scent, as fresh as the day she'd placed the petal inside the heart. She knew that if she opened the locket, the petal would still be a bright red, flecked with gold.

The flower from which it had come—known as Sune's Kisses to humans, and Hanali's Heart to the elves—was sacred to both goddesses. Drawing its scent into her lungs, Larajin released it in the form of a whispered prayer.

"Sune and Hanali Celanil, hear my plea and shield me from my enemies. Cloak me with your breath, and make my footsteps as light as a lover's whispers."

The locket in her hand grew warm. From inside her clenched fingers came a faint red glow: the sign of magic at work. Thankful that her prayers had been answered—by Sune, it would seem, since the floral scent that accompanied Hanali Celanil's blessing was absent—Larajin slipped the string of the locket around her wrist.

She squared her shoulders and opened the door, trusting in the goddess to protect her. Even so, her heart was pounding in her throat as she descended the front steps that led to the street.

The air had a thick quality to it. A mist that glittered as though it were flecked with droplets of gold formed whorls and eddies in the street, obscuring the tallhouses on either side. Across the street, the guard stepped out of the doorway and squinted. He raised a hand, prodding the air ahead of him like a blind man, and took a hesitant step into the swirling fog.

"Hey, lads, look sharp!" he called out. "Something's up."

Larajin smiled. She could see him, but he, it seemed, could not see her. Gathering up her gown so it wouldn't rustle, she crept up Sarn Street on tiptoe, barely daring to breathe. Cloaked in the magical fog, she was all but invisible to the guard who was bounding up the front steps of Stormweather Towers, tripping in his haste to block the door. She was likewise unseen by the guard at the corner, and a third, who had been approaching down the cross street, only to be confronted by a cloud of golden mist. The latter drew his sword, and used it like a cane to probe the air ahead—a cane with a deadly point. He cocked his head as Larajin's boots made a faint scuffing sound on the cobblestones, and he turned in her direction.

Larajin froze, watching with wide eyes as he moved toward her. If she kept utterly still, he might pass by her, allowing her to slip away. He came closer, sword probing, until he was within a pace of where she stood, then he walked by, continuing up the street toward the corner.

Then, like a man suddenly remembering something, he stopped. Larajin heard him sniff.

Too late, she realized that Thazienne's gown was thick with perfume. In another instant, the guard would find her. Larajin did the only thing she could think of—she turned quickly in place and began walking toward Sarn Street, then deliberately blundered into the guard.

"Hey there!" he exclaimed, grabbing her shoulder. He leaned closer, and peered at her face through the swirling fog. "Who are you, woman?"

Remembering whom she was impersonating, Larajin squared her shoulders and gave the man a haughty glare.

" 'W-woman?'" she sputtered. "That's 'Mistress,' if you please."

As she spoke, she glanced out of the corner of her eye. The other guards were still somewhere around the corner on Sarn

Street, lost in the gold-flecked fog. She prayed that the man's startled question hadn't been loud enough for them to hear.

"Ah ... Mistress, then," he said, nodding at her gown. Close enough to see her now, his eyes missed nothing—not the heavy bag over Larajin's shoulder, nor the toe of the boot that was peeking out from under her hem. His eyes narrowed. "What urgent business compels you out of your home and onto the streets this late at night?"

Larajin stared at him for a long, silent moment, imitating the way Thazienne had once stared down a young serving girl who had caught her climbing out a window late at night. The serving girl—Larajin—never reported it to the master.

"I am returning to Stormweather Towers after a ... liaison," she said, falling into a flawless imitation of noble speech. "The business I was about was legal and therefore none of your concern. I am Mistress Thazienne of House Uskevren, and when my father hears how you roughly accosted me and tore my sleeve, he will be sorely displeased. You can imagine what conclusions he will draw and what reports will reach the Hulorn's ears."

As she spoke, she grabbed a handful of slashed sleeve and yanked on it just enough to cause a small rip. The soldier's eyes widened at the sound of tearing cloth, and he took a step back. He bowed, sweeping a hand in the direction of Stormweather Towers.

"Mistress, I beg your pardon. Please proceed."

As haughtily as she could, Larajin swept by him, her gown rustling. After a few steps, a quick glimpse behind assured her that the guard could no longer see her. Immediately she gathered the skirts of the gown, turned silently around, and tiptoed past him—giving him a wide berth, so he wouldn't smell the perfume this time.

When she was certain she'd left the guard well behind, she broke into a jog, then a run. As she ran, she tried to decide which way she should go. The High Bridge lay to the north, along Galogar's Ride. It was the only way out of the city for travelers bound for Ordulin, but Larajin could hardly head there. In another moment the guards would realize they'd been duped and would start searching for a "noblewoman" in a green gown. She needed somewhere close, somewhere she could change into a different disguise.

Habrith's bakery was just a few blocks away.

As she hurried there, Larajin chided herself for not thinking of Habrith earlier. Not only was the baker someone she could trust, she also knew the route to the Tangled Trees. It had been Habrith who set up the trading mission that took Master Thamalon there twenty-five years before. Larajin suspected that Habrith had made the journey more recently than that, as well. More than once, over the years that Larajin had known her, the baker had left her shop in the hands of apprentices who were able to say only that their mistress was "on a journey to the north."

With luck, Larajin might even be able to persuade Habrith to accompany her. If not, Habrith would at least be able to provide her with a fresh disguise and tell her how to reach the Tangled Trees—and what to expect when she got there.

Habrith's bakery was certain to be open, even at so early an hour. Bakers were early risers who began work while the rest of the city still slept, so that their loaves would be ready at dawn. Habrith was a perfectionist, who liked to supervise the baking herself. Her loaves might look simple, but the exotic mix of ingredients that flavored them demanded absolute precision in measuring—something her newest apprentice was still struggling to learn.

As Larajin rounded the corner onto Larawkan Lane, the smells of yeast and baking bread drifted down the road toward her. Mixed with them was the sour smell of the dung that a street sweeper was pushing to the side of the road with his broom. Larajin passed the front of the shop, which had a closed sign on its door and its curtains drawn, and turned into the alley that led to the delivery door at the rear.

She'd no sooner stepped out of the street light than she

heard a faint noise on the rooftop to her left. It sounded like a foot scuffing against roof tiles. Larajin caught a glimpse of what might have been a person crouching. She flattened herself against the wall and tried to decide what to do. Run the last few strides to Habrith's back door, and risk being taken down from behind? Or stay with her back to the wall, and attempt another spell?

Before she could begin her prayer, something hurtled down from the rooftop. Larajin spun to meet it, then heard a familiar sound.

Brrow?

The tressym landed in the alley and stared at Larajin with eyes that were twin pools of reflective gold, her head cocked slightly to the side. She folded her wings and padded toward Larajin, then butted her head into Larajin's leg through the stiff fabric of the gown, purring loudly. The tressym sat down and looked up, as if expecting to be scratched under the chin.

Her heart still pounding, Larajin let out a heavy sigh. Instead of patting the tressym, she flicked both hands at her.

"Shoo! You already got me into enough trouble tonight. Go away!"

The tressym's ears swiveled back, but she refused to budge.

Larajin didn't appreciate the tressym following her. She could ruin any disguise Larajin might adopt with one affectionate rub against her leg. Larajin might as well wave a banner with her name on it over her head. If the tressym hadn't been sacred to Hanali Celanil, Larajin might have tried to cast some sort of spell upon the creature.

A door opened behind her, spilling light into the alley. The scent of baking bread wafted out, making her mouth water. From inside came the clatter of pans and the squeaking of a water pump.

"Larajin—is that you?" an older woman called. "By the gods, it is—and in a noble's gown! What brings you to my shop in the middle of the night? Is something wrong? Are you in danger?"

Embarrassed at having her disguise seen through so easily, Larajin turned to face Habrith. The baker was in her late sixties, older than Larajin's adoptive mother, but unlike Shonri Wellrun, she was hale and hearty for her age. Her face was wrinkled, but her dark brown hair, bound in a simple braid down her back, had yet to see a single strand of gray. A large apron covered her clothes. Against it, on a thong around her neck, hung a silver pendant in the shape of a crescent moon.

"You know me too well, Habrith," Larajin answered, "and you're right, I am in trouble. The wizard I told you about—the one who attacked me in the Hulorn's Hunting Garden a year and a half ago—has discovered who I am and where I live. He's threatened to . . . to 'silence' me." She swallowed nervously and glanced up and down the alley, then shifted the strap of her bag slightly. It was biting into her shoulder. "The Hulorn's men are looking for me even now. I need to leave Selgaunt as quickly and as quietly as possible."

Thankfully, Habrith didn't argue, though her forehead crinkled with concern.

"I knew this time would come," she said quietly. "Where do you intend to go?"

"North, to the Tangled Trees."

That got a nod of approval.

"I don't know how to get there or how to introduce myself to the elves," Larajin continued. "I thought you could help."

Habrith glanced at the tressym, which was rubbing back and forth against Larajin's legs, rustling the fabric of her dress.

"Isn't that the creature you rescued from the Hunting Garden? Are you taking her with you?"

"Not if I can help it."

That brought a wry smile to Habrith's lips. "I see. I think the tressym might have other ideas."

Larajin dropped her voice, even though the tressym was just an animal and couldn't possibly understand her words. "Perhaps you might offer her a bowl of cream in a room without windows and a lock on the door . . ."

As Habrith started to chuckle, the rubbing against Larajin's ankles suddenly stopped. Larajin looked down—just in time to see the tressym stalking away down the alley. An instant later she spread her wings and launched herself into the night. Larajin watched her disappear behind the rooftops.

Habrith shrugged, then gestured with a flour-dusted hand. "Come inside."

Larajin followed her into the delivery room of the bakery, piled high with sacks of flour and barrels of fresh milk. Habrith closed and latched the door, then pitched her voice low so the apprentices in the next room wouldn't hear her.

"Tell me, Larajin, have you scattered starlight upon the Pool of Reflection?"

"Habrith! Do you serve the Lady of Love also?"

The baker chuckled, and shook her head.

"Then how do you know about the first initiation ritual?"

Habrith smiled. "You've obviously taken it, then. That's good. It means you can wear the crimson robes."

Larajin absently fingered her heart-shaped locket, which was hanging against her palm. She'd taken her vows and pledged her love to Sune and had received formal training in those few spells the goddess had already seen fit to bestow upon her—simple healing, charms, and commands, and the obscuring mist she had just conjured up—but had yet to don a cleric's robes. She'd been hesitant to commit herself fully to just the one goddess, lest Hanali Celanil become jealous. She wondered if Habrith was suggesting she become a full-fledged cleric of Sune and take shelter in the temple, turning her back on the elf goddess.

"It won't work," she said, thinking out loud. "I can't hide inside the temple for the rest of my life."

"How about just until dawn, then?"

That brought Larajin up short. "What do you mean?"

"A Heartwarder from the temple in Ordulin has been visiting our local temple for the past tenday," Habrith said. "She returns to Ordulin this morning, accompanied by four novices who will serve in that temple. One more novice wouldn't be noticed by the city guard, and even if she was—and was recognized—the guard wouldn't dare risk the wrath of the goddess by interfering with a Heartwarder."

Larajin smiled. It would work—she was certain of it. She was as good as out of Selgaunt.

"Once you get to Ordulin, there's a tailor I know who can help you," Habrith continued. "He's a half-elf, himself. He can give you the name of an elf in Essembra who can guide you to the Tangled Trees."

"Could you . . . accompany me yourself?" Larajin asked hesitantly. "At least as far as Ordulin?"

Habrith shook her head. "There's too much to attend to here in Selgaunt."

"The new apprentice, you mean?"

That brought a twinkle to the older woman's eyes. "Not exactly—let's just say I'm making sure the bread is buttered on the correct side, and leave it at that."

Larajin wondered what Habrith meant by that, but she knew better than to ask. Habrith often spoke in riddles, using plain language only when it suited her.

Habrith paused. Her eyes grew worried, and she fingered the pendant at her throat.

"I'm glad you came to me before leaving, Larajin. It's a dangerous time to be journeying north. The Heartwarder will see you safely to Ordulin, but once you pass there, you'll fare better under our protection."

Exhausted at having been up all night scrubbing the kitchen, Larajin took a moment to register this remark.

"Under whose protection?" she asked at last.

Habrith's voice dropped to a whisper. She touched the

pendant at her throat and asked, "Would you recognize this symbol, if the harp was still there?"

Larajin blinked in surprise as she realized what Habrith was referring to. The pendant, which Larajin had assumed was merely decorative, had a rough patch along the inside of the crescent where another portion of the design had broken away. Put a harp at the center of the crescent moon, and it became much more. It became the symbol of the Harpers, a vast network of clerics, rangers, and bards who worked silently and secretly to thwart the plans of unscrupulous mortals and evil gods alike. Larajin had been right—Habrith was no mere baker.

Larajin chastised herself for being such a fool. Why hadn't she made the connection before? Then she realized the answer. Habrith seemed so innocuous, so nondescript, not a noble or a cleric but a baker, a common tradeswoman. She was widely traveled, it was true, but those travels could be explained as nothing more than trips to gather the spices and herbs that flavored her breads. All the while, she must have been secretly carrying out other, more pressing missions.

Habrith watched the understanding grow in Larajin's eyes, and smiled. "There is more I could tell you about the Tangled Trees, Larajin, and about yourself, but that would just complicate things. You know what I always say."

Larajin nodded, and recited Habrith's favorite saying. "Simplest is best, and all ingredients in balance."

"Exactly," Habrith agreed. "Some things in life turn out better if allowed to come to fullness on their own time, like rising bread. I can tell you this, however. When you reach the Tangled Trees, you will be more than welcome. The forest elves have a surprise in store for you."

"What is it?" Larajin asked.

Habrith held up a hand, and quoted her other favorite saying. "All in due time, and not a moment before." She winked. "You'll find out, soon enough."

CHAPTER 2

Leifander wheeled high above the forest, peering down at the caravan that was slowly making its way north along Rauthauvyr's Road. He counted six wagons, a dozen teamsters, and nearly two dozen soldiers. All were human, carrying both crossbows and swords, and clad in chain-mail armor that winked red in the sun.

Their numbers were greater than expected: The humans below outnumbered the elves awaiting them two to one and were better armed than the elves had guessed they would be. When the caravan reached the spot where the elves were hiding, everything would depend upon the advantage of surprise. Thankfully, Doriantha had chosen the ambush site well.

Winging his way north again, Leifander flew to his appointed place: a tall oak that had somehow retained many of its leaves, despite the blight that surrounded it. He landed on a sturdy branch, then shifted back into elf form.

Glancing down through the branches, he could only just make out the dozen wood elves who waited for his signal. Clad in brown leather, they matched the colors of the forest, with faces browned by the sun and hair that ranged from grass-yellow blond to autumn red. The bright steel of their swords had been dulled with a rubbing of soot, and their arrows were fletched with plain brown feathers, instead of the brightly colored fletching the elves normally favored. All trace of personal ornamentation had been set aside in preparation for the ambush. Gone were the brightly polished bell-beads and colorful feathers they normally adorned their braids with. Such vanities had no place where the tinkle of a bell or the flash of a yellow feather could give the ambush away. The elves' sole decoration was the black ink that had been needled into the flesh of their cheeks and chins. The tattoos helped to camouflage them, allowing their faces to blend with the shadows of the forest.

Doriantha, leader of the troop, peered up at Leifander from the elves' hiding place across the road. She moved a slender hand in a complex gesture, asking a silent question. Leifander answered with hand signals of his own, indicating the strength of the human warriors and the distance the caravan had yet to travel: less than a mile.

Doriantha's pale brown eyes sparkled, and her lips twitched into a feral grin. From Leifander's position high in the tree, the tattoo on her face looked like a solid line of black across her nose and cheeks, but in fact it was an intricate band of knotwork that continued under her hair and above her pointed ears, forming a sacred circle. Lean muscles flexing, she tested the draw of her bow, sighting down an imaginary arrow. In that moment, with the sunlight slanting through the trees behind her, with the hood of her cloak thrown back and her long sun-bleached braid draped over her shoulder, she looked as magnificent as the Great Archer.

Realizing he had blasphemed, Leifander touched a forefinger to his lips then smacked it against his open palm to negate his silent words. Comparing a mere mortal to a god—even a mortal as vibrant as Doriantha—might cause the Great Archer to withdraw his favor from the day's deed.

It was hard to imagine the elves' arrows missing their mark, however, when they had the forest on their side. The road below held a carefully concealed trap: a thick growth of choke creeper that had grown across it in long, snaking coils. The trap had been constructed earlier that morning, just before dawn. With Doriantha directing them, sword in hand in case the powerful vines entwined any of her troop, the elves had carefully raked dirt over the choke creeper, hiding it from view.

The carnivorous vine would be the elves' ally in the ambush that was to come. When the soldiers marching in front of the caravan trod upon it, the hawk-swift vine would lash them to the spot, making them perfect targets for elven arrows. The humans would then have a choice. They could either throw down their weapons and allow their caravan to be inspected for evidence that it was carrying the blight, or they could be slaughtered to the last man.

As he waited for the caravan to reach the ambush point, Leifander savored the warm caress of the morning sun. Tired from the night's flight through the forest, he let his eyes close. He listened to the rustle of the leaves around him and the creaking of trees in the wind, and felt the flutter against his forehead of the feathers twined into his bangs: the feathers of his totem animal, the crow, which allowed him to work his magic. Something tickled the back of his bare foot—a spider. Without conscious thought he adjusted his stance as the branch swayed in the warm wind from the south.

Eyes closed, he could almost convince himself that the forest was as it had always been. Instead of the smells of growing leaves, ripening acorns and sun-warmed moss, though, his nose caught an acrid odor, like that of seared grass. It was not the smoky-sweet smell of ash, but something harsher, closer to the stench of sulfuric mud.

Opening his eyes, he fingered one of the leaves on the branch above. It should have been two handspans wide, with delicately scalloped edges, a rich, dark green. Instead it was yellowed and crumpled, spotted with dark gray patches that tore like wet paper and left a stinging, oily film on Leifander's fingers.

Wiping his hand clean on his leather breeches, Leifander shifted his attention to the trunk. It too was spotted, its bark shriveled and splitting open. The moss that clung to it was as dry and dead as the whiskers on a corpse. Like so many of the trees in the Vale of Lost Voices, this oak was dying. It seemed strange to see it bathed in morning sunlight, with a clear blue sky above. Surely the Leaflord should have been weeping at the sight.

As recently as two months before—the month of Mirtul—trees and underbrush had crowded Rauthauvyr's Road on either side. With the month of Flamerule only a few days old, most of the trees had lost their leaves. It was less than three tendays before Midsummer, and the bushes below should have been heavy with berries, but they looked instead like winter-blasted sticks. The ferns that had dotted the road were a shriveled, gray mush beside the wagon ruts.

Leifander shaded his eyes and intently scanned the road. The wagons had yet to come into sight. They were hidden not only by a bend in the road but also by the morning mist, which instead of burning off under the rising sun seemed to be thickening below.

A fluttering of wings announced the arrival of a thrush. Leifander glanced up at it, then ignored it, but the bird seemed intent upon catching his attention. It flew straight at him, beating its wings in his face and plucking at his hair with its feet. Leifander tried to wave it away, but the bird was insistent.

"What?" he asked in exasperation, tearing his eyes away from the road.

As the bird settled on the branch above Leifander, a chorus of excited cheeping revealed the location of a hidden nest. Two downy heads thrust out of a tangle of twigs and grass, beaks open wide. Born and reared in this ruined wood, the nestlings were scrawny, and they chirped with a ravenous insistence.

"Ah," he said to the mother bird, understanding at last. "Your children are hungry. Perhaps I can help."

After a moment's search, he located the spider that had tickled his foot and killed it with a quick squeeze of his fingers. Placing it delicately between his lips, he leaned toward the nest. He let one of the nestlings pluck a portion of the spider from his lips, then repeated the process with the second bird.

The mother thrush seemed unsatisfied, however. She continued to flutter around Leifander's head a moment more, as if recognizing in him a crow that might rob her nest of its young. With an indignant flick of her tail, she flew away.

Leifander resumed his survey of the road below. The caravan had not yet appeared, but it would not be long now. He needed to . . .

Leifander felt the scratch of tiny claws against his fingers. Looking down, he saw that the larger of the two nestlings had clambered out of the nest and was climbing onto his hand. It perched there, flapping its wings for balance. It seemed poised to burst into flight at any moment.

"Are you ready to leave the nest, little one?" Leifander asked it in a soft voice as he lifted it to eye level. "What is so important, that you must be about it at once?"

The nestling tilted its head, regarding Leifander with glossy black eyes. Wind rustled through the trees, fluttering what leaves remained. The shifting branches dappled the bird with flashes of sunlight and shadow, causing the nestling's feathers to change from amber-brown to black-brown and back again in rapid succession. For several heartbeats, Leifander held his breath, convinced that something much greater than the nestling was regarding him through its eyes. Then the breeze stilled and the feathers, pooled in leaf-shade, returned to a solid, dull brown.

Chuckling at his own conceit—surely the Winged Mother had better things to do than look down upon one of her fledgling priests—Leifander bobbed his hand up and down. The nestling responded with a flutter of wings.

"Go on then—try out those wings of yours," he said, casting the young bird into the air.

He winced as the bird faltered, remembering his own first flight, not so very long ago. Given his youth, he was fortunate to already be an accomplished skinwalker—most elves did not master it until they had reached their first half-century and were well into adolescence. Leifander, however, had matured more quickly than his peers and had been rewarded when Doriantha had chosen him as a scout for this patrol.

Watching the nestling, Leifander smiled as it at last found its wings, flapping its way back up from a plunge that had carried it nearly to the ground. Seeking a clear space in which to fly, the bird winged its way along the road.

Returning to his survey of the road to the south, Leifander saw that the human caravan had drawn into sight. He cawed once to alert those below to its progress, then sought out the nestling again, enjoying its first flight.

The bird swooped low over the ground—too low—and a section of the buried choke creeper lashed out from under the soil. Beating its wings furiously, the nestling rose into the air, barely avoiding the vine's leafy grip. As the bird fluttered gamely on up the road, toward a thicker patch of morning mist, the choke creeper followed it, uncoiling from the soil like an awakening snake.

Leifander cursed silently. Much of the choke creeper now lay visible on the road, twining sinuously as it quested for its prey.

He glanced in Doriantha's direction, but it seemed that she had not yet noticed the hole that had suddenly been torn in her plan. Even though the caravan would not arrive for a few moments yet, the elves could not simply rake soil over the vine again—not now that the sun was up. The ambush was ruined—and all because of Leifander. He glared down at the nestling, wishing he had never launched it into flight.

Something was wrong. The young thrush was no longer winging its way steadily through the air—as soon as it had entered the thicker patch of mist, it seemed to forget how to fly. Peeping shrilly, it beat its wings in a frenzy, at the same time spiraling off to the side. Its wings stopped beating, and the nestling fell to the ground like a stone.

Leifander blinked, at first not believing what he had just seen. The thicker patch of mist drifted over the twisting tangle of choke creeper, and every bit of greenery on it wilted. The choke creeper sagged to the ground, like a taut rope suddenly gone limp.

The mist drifted silently on, toward the wood elves' hiding place.

A frightened caw burst from Leifander's mouth before he found the words to warn those below. "The mist!" he croaked, rising to a standing position and cupping a hand to his mouth. "Doriantha, beware! That thicker patch of mist, not more than ten paces to your left—it has the power to kill!"

Although startled, Doriantha reacted quickly, signaling a retreat. As one, the troop of elves scrambled to their feet and began to melt away into the forest.

Leifander, watching from the safety of the trees above, breathed a sigh of relief and thanked the Winged Mother for her warning. The ambush was spoiled. The elves would have to regroup in the forest and fight another day, but—Aerdrie Faenya be praised—Doriantha and her troop had been spared from that mist, whatever it might be.

Leifander closed his eyes and stroked the glossy black feathers in his braids, summoning up the strength of the crow. As he finished shifting, a cry from below warned him that something had gone wrong. Opening his eyes, Leifander cocked his head to peer down at the ground. He spotted the problem in an instant: one of the elves—Jornel, a copper-haired youth whose face was tattooed below the eyes with raindrops, making it look as though he were perpetually weeping—had failed to move away from the ambush point. From his vantage point, Leifander could see that one of Jornel's legs had become entangled in a strand of choke creeper that must have quested in his direction after being awakened by the nestling. Jornel slashed furiously at the vine with his sword, but even as he did, a second strand sprang up and caught his wrist. Held fast, he yanked at it in a futile effort to free himself, eyes bulging in horror as the mist drifted toward him.

Doriantha, signaling urgently for the other elves to stay hidden in the woods, slung her bow over one shoulder and doubled back at the run. She drew her sword to hack at the creeper, but it was clear she would not free Jornel in time. Already the deadly white mist was lapping at him like a sickly smelling, cloying tide.

The vine that held Jornel wilted and went slack, then the mist engulfed him. Doubled over, retching, he tried to stagger out of the mist, but the choke creeper still entangling him slowed him down. Dragging the limp vines behind him, he managed only a few stumbling steps before sagging to the ground, coughing violently.

Leifander saw in an instant what needed to be done. As Doriantha backed away from the approaching mist, he hurled himself into a steep dive. He held his breath as he plunged into the clammy mist and landed next to Jornel.

Using his beak, he seized a loop of the vine that was twined around Jornel's wrist, then leaped into the air, flapping his wings hard. Pain seared his lungs as he took an inadvertent breath, and he could feel the foul-smelling mist eating at the tips of his feathers. His eyes stung, and his vision blurred.

Weakened by the mist, the vine tore free from Jornel's arm. Dropping the foul-tasting vine, Leifander winged his way out of the mist and took a deep breath of clean air, his feathers and skin still burning from the mist's corrosive touch.

His effort, however, had been in vain. Jornel's leg was still tangled in the vine. His skin was blistering, and a bloody foam bubbled at his lips.

While the other elves watched, uncertain, Doriantha took a deep breath, then leaped into the mist. Blisters erupted on her skin as she untwined the last strand of vine from Jornel's leg and dragged him clear of the mist. Two of her troop ran forward, one to pick the injured elf up, the other to lend his shoulder to Doriantha as she staggered away, coughing violently.

The rumbling squeak of wagon wheels grew louder as the elves took cover in the forest. Leifander climbed to treetop level, still wheezing from the foul mist that had seared his throat and lungs. He circled above the road, squinting down with blurry eyes at the caravan. The soldiers accompanying it seemed oblivious to the retreating elves—and to the mist that lay in their path, no more than a hundred paces ahead. Would they blunder into it and be killed?

Curious despite the ache that gripped his lungs, Leifander watched as a strange thing happened. From somewhere within the mist came the sound of a whistle. Hearing it, the sergeant leading the soldiers raised a hand in the air. Teamsters reined in their beasts, and the caravan drew to a halt.

As if blown by an sudden wind, the mist drifted away into the forest, leaving a wilted mush of vegetation on the road. After a moment or two, a row of dark spots crossed this area. Footprints.

The footprints paused in one spot, forming an overlapping cluster next to a thick strand of the dead choke creeper. A section of the tangled vines moved slightly, as if nudged by a foot.

A heartbeat later, a man dropped the spell that had been

cloaking him from sight. Human, perhaps sixty years of age with pale wispy hair over a bulging forehead and soft, fleshy arms, he wore a yellow vest and hose that gave his skin a sickly complexion. Gold rings glittered on every finger of his right hand. His left hand held a slender wand that looked as though it had been carved of bone. Tendrils of white mist drifted from the wand's tip, which was set with a single black pearl.

A silver whistle hung from a chain around the man's neck. He raised it to his lips and blew. Back at the caravan, the sergeant's hand went down, and soldiers and beasts resumed their trudge forward along the road.

Leifander glared down at the man holding the wand, anger burning bright in his breast as he realized he was looking at the origin of the blight that was consuming the forest. Like a nut and its shell, the pieces now fit. This was why the blight had centered itself upon the road. The caravaners had enlisted the aid of a wizard, one who was using destructive magic to clear Rauthauvyr's Road of the choke creeper that had become so prevalent in the forest. Only humans would be stupid and selfish enough to unleash forces that destroyed not just the creeper but the forest itself.

As if sensing Leifander's glare, the wizard looked up. His eyes fixed on the crow circling overhead, and the fingers of his right hand twitched. Did he recognize this "crow" for what it truly was? Did the raising of his hand mean he was about to cast a spell?

If so, Leifander would never escape in time. Instead of fleeing, he did the unexpected. He tucked in his wings and dived. Pulling up at the last instant, he beat his wings in the wizard's face, raking the man's fleshy cheek with his talons.

Cursing, the wizard reacted instinctively, raising his wand to beat Leifander off.

He'd done exactly as Leifander had hoped.

Twisting, Leifander wrapped his talons around the wand. It felt spongy and slick, like a bone slimed by rot, but the wand was solid at its core. Throwing himself backward, wings beating furiously, he tore it from the wizard's grip.

As the wizard began chanting in a strange, garbled tongue, Leifander realized his folly. Not only had he announced himself as something other than a crow, with his strange, uncrowlike actions, but he had placed himself too close to the wizard for escape.

An arrow shot out of the woods ahead, whispering past Leifander, then another arrow, and another. More than one thudded harmlessly into the ground, or caught in the branches of a tree before reaching the road—but the distraction gave Leifander the chance he needed to escape. Instead of casting a spell at Leifander, the wizard halted his incantation in mid-phrase and began another. The air in front of him shimmered, obscuring him from sight. An instant later an arrow hit this sparkling wall of force—and exploded with a crackling release of energy into a thousand harmless slivers.

As yet more arrows sang out of the woods, shattering on the wizard's spell-shield, he blew on his whistle to summon the soldiers from the caravan. The hail of arrows stopped abruptly as the elves, seeing Leifander enter the safety of the trees, retreated into the woods.

Still clutching the wand in one foot, Leifander winged his way after them.

From high in the forest, drifting down from leaves dappled by moonlight, came the sound of chanting voices. Leifander kneeled at the base of the tree from which they originated, an oak so old that its trunk was as wide as extended arms could span, with pale gray bark that looked silver in the bright moonlight. High above its thickly leafed, spreading branches, a near-full moon crept to its zenith against a star-speckled sky.

Doriantha kneeled beside Leifander, also awaiting the summons from those above. In the days that had followed the abortive ambush on the caravan, Leifander had used his magic to heal the blisters on her arms and face, and to heal his own wounds. Now all that remained were a few faint pink scars.

The wand that Leifander had yanked from the wizard's grasp lay between them on the forest floor. It had been wrapped in rabbit skin, the soft fur turned inward to protect it from the rigors of their journey through the woods. During the days it took Leifander and Doriantha to respond to the summons from the Circle of the Emerald Leaves, the bone had lost its sponginess and turned hard and brittle, and the pearl at its tip had lost its sheen. Yet the wand still stank of the foul mist it had produced.

Above, the chanting stopped, then a single female voice rang out. "Doriantha of the Tangled Trees, rise up, and meet our sacred circle."

Picking up the fur-wrapped wand, Doriantha rose to her feet. She glanced down at Leifander, still kneeling, who returned her terse nod. Then she reached with her free hand for the trunk of the Moontouch Oak. A branch appeared, pale and insubstantial as moonlight, and she grasped it. Another moonbeam bent and met the trunk near the ground, forming a second branch, and on this she placed her foot. She climbed, using the branches that appeared in a rising spiral around the oak's trunk, each one disappearing after her foot had left it.

Waiting his turn as voices murmured above, Leifander wondered why the Circle of the Emerald Leaves had included him in their summons. Both he and Doriantha had already related the full story of their aborted ambush to the elves' High Council, but perhaps the druids wanted to hear the tale themselves. Perhaps they felt there was some detail that only they could coax out of the pair, some thread of information that the High Council had overlooked.

A short time later, a rustling above announced Doriantha's descent. When she reached the ground, she appeared puzzled.

"Strange," she muttered. "They didn't want to know anything more about the wizard or the wand. Instead they asked me about you."

Leifander's eyebrows knitted together in a frown. "About my part in the ambush, you mean?"

"Yes . . . and no. They told me about your . . ." She hesitated, then seemed to change her mind. "They asked if I had noticed any omens or signs that—"

Before Doriantha could finish her whispered answer, the voice called out once more from the leaves above. "Leifander of the Tangled Trees, rise up, and meet our sacred circle."

Springing nervously to his feet, Leifander waited as moonbeams coalesced into a spiral of branches around the Moontouch Oak's trunk. He gave Doriantha one last look, and his courage nearly faltered as he saw the tense, expectant expression on her face, then he climbed.

Despite the warm summer air, the moonbeam branches felt as cool as a mountain stream under Leifander's bare hands and feet. He followed their course, climbing in a spiral around the trunk until branches completely obscured the ground below. The murmurs of voices overhead led him to a spot perhaps fifteen or twenty times his height above the ground. He peeked up through a hole in the center of a platform that surrounded the trunk of the oak—a platform made of floating leaves, their scalloped edges knitted together to form a soft green carpet.

On it stood the druids of the Circle of the Emerald Leaves: six elves, three male and three female, all elders with deeply lined faces and silver-white hair. Five were moon elves with lighter skin; the sixth was a forest elf with skin a healthier tree-bark color, her cheeks tattooed in a pattern reminiscent of branches.

Leifander knew all of their names by rote, despite the fact that he had never met them face-to-face. Ruithlana was the youngest of the elders, with hair cascading from a gold clip and one eyebrow permanently arched, as if he were about to ask a question. Klanthir the Learned stood stroking his chin with a slender hand, eyebrows frowning beneath a high forehead. Horthlorin wore his hair loose about his shoulders and had eyes that were a rich, forest green.

The three women who balanced the sacred circle included Quinstrella, who had milk-white hair cut high above her ears; the much older looking Bhanilthra, who leaned on a walking stick made of gilded, sacred oak; and the forest elf Rylith.

The five moon elves wore leaf-green hose and boots, and soft shirts whose fabric rustled like leaves in a faintly stirring wind, but Rylith instead wore a serviceable pair of leather breeches and vest. All of the druids had a band of silver oak leaves twined in their hair, and wore cloaks woven from brilliant, fall-colored leaves that somehow had not dried and crumbled—magic must have been sustaining them.

The wand Leifander had taken from the wizard was nowhere to be seen.

As he climbed onto the platform, marveling at the springy bounce of the carpet of leaves underfoot, Leifander wondered which of the druids he should bow to first. Ranged in a circle around the platform as they were, if he bowed to one it would mean turning his back on at least one of the others.

Rylith solved the problem by walking forward and taking Leifander's hand. Shocked by so intimate a gesture from a powerful druid hundreds of years his elder, Leifander fumbled his way through a bow. As he rose, Rylith shifted her grip to his chin, turning his face for the others to see.

"His eyes," she said. "See their color? They are hazel—it will be as the legends foretold."

The others crowded close, solemn faces nodding. Leifander felt uncomfortable under their scrutiny. Yes, his eyes were a strange color, but he'd thought it merely an oddity.

Rylith released his chin. Her dark eyes bored into his and she asked, "Have you ever wondered, child, who your father was?"

Leifander tried to speak but could find no words that

seemed suitable. Instead he nodded. He had wondered—every day of his life.

"Your father was a great man," she continued. "He was a friend to the Harpers, a man who tried to bring humans to appreciate and value the Tangled Trees. Sadly, he did not succeed, but he left his legacy among us: you."

Leifander stood silent and trembling, like a bird startled by a sudden noise but uncertain which way to fly.

"Who . . ." He faltered, then tried again. "Who was he?"

He waited for the answer, afraid to breathe. To the best of his knowledge, his mother had never revealed the name of the man who had sired him, even to her closest kin. Indeed, she had left him little at all, aside from the ring that hung at his throat—a ring they said she had been wearing at the time of her death.

The family who had raised Leifander had always shrugged when he asked them who his father had been. Over the years, he'd gradually stopped asking. Now the questions rekindled inside him, burning brighter than ever before.

"There is someone who can tell you who your father is—even introduce you to him," Rylith said at last.

As he realized that Rylith had spoken of his father in the present tense, Leifander's heart leaped with joy. His father was still alive!

"That man is Thamalon Uskevren," Rylith said at last.

Leifander frowned, puzzled. The name meant nothing to him. It sounded foreign. He tried it on his tongue. "Tham-a-lon Usk-ev-ren. Is he a high elf—one of those who departed for Evermeet—is that where my father lives?"

Rylith shook her head. "Thamalon Uskevren is not a high elf," she said. "Nor a moon elf, nor one of the woods. He is human. He hails from the city of Selgaunt, in the realm of Sembia."

Leifander's puzzled frown deepened. "Does my father also live . . . among humans?" The last word hung bitter on his lips.

Rylith nodded, then quickly turned to one of the other druids. Taking his cue, Klanthir the Learned cleared his throat. Slender fingers gripped the edges of his cloak, hands resting against his chest as he assumed the posture of a speaker of the High Council.

"We commend you, Leifander of the Tangled Trees, for your brave rescue of your companion on Rauthauvyr's Road and your daring attack on the wizard whose evil magic was blighting the wood. You proved the High Council correct in our assumption that the depredations upon our wood were caused by human hands. More than that, you have laid the blame squarely at Sembia's doorstep."

Sembia? That was the name of the realm from which the man they said knew his father hailed.

"That's good, isn't it?" Leifander asked tentatively. "Now we know the name of our enemy. We know which caravans to strike."

In his heart, though, he didn't care which of the caravaners died. They were all human and equally deserving of the elves' wrath.

Klanthir sighed. "If only it were merely a matter of striking caravans. . . . Now that the Council knows who perpetrated this blight, they are speaking of war. If it comes to that, the balance will be forever tipped, and in a direction not in our favor. Long gone is the glory of Cormanthor and Myth Drannor. Though we hold the wood still, we are a scattered people. A war against Sembia will be a war we cannot win."

"Not so!" Leifander cried, unable to contain himself. "We may be outnumbered, but one elf is a match for any four humans. They will never take our wood! We know it too well. On our home ground we cannot fail."

"That is so," Klanthir agreed, "but the wizard you met cannot be the only one working magic along Rauthauvyr's Road. So great is the destruction—so widely are the seeds of the blight scattered—that one wand could not have sown them all."

"There is yet time for us to act," Rylith added. "The man

I spoke of earlier—Thamalon Uskevren—is the head of a powerful merchant family. His voice speaks loudly in the Sembian council. If he could be persuaded to counsel against rash action, a war might yet be averted."

With a sinking feeling in his heart—for he could guess the answer—Leifander asked, "What is my part in this?"

"Go to the city of Selgaunt, and find Thamalon Uskevren," Rylith said. "Speak to him. Remind him of the love he once had for . . . the Tangled Trees. Plead with him to steer Sembia toward a course of action that will placate the High Council—one that will heal the rift between elf and man."

"I have never been to a human city," Leifander said. "I couldn't . . ."

It was a half-hearted protest. Already his mind was turning over the possibilities. He would deliver his message to Thamalon Uskevren, then press the human for information about his father, insist that he arrange a meeting between father and son.

"Don't worry," Rylith said with a twinkle in her eye. "Selgaunt is not far—as the crow flies. Now listen closely, while I relate what you are to say."

CHAPTER 3

Larajin kneeled on a carpet of fragrant rose petals, her reflection rippling in the pool beside her. The cleric who kneeled in front of her rinsed his brush in the water, scattering flakes of gold, then dipped it again into a pot. Concentrating on Larajin's bared midriff, he applied moistened gilt paste to her skin with delicate, tickling strokes, marking her as one of the novices who would be traveling to the temple in Ordulin.

The temple of Sune was tranquil at this hour of the morning, filled with the soothing sounds of fountains and harmonious voices chanting the Song of Sunrise under the direction of the Heartwarder. The clerics stood in a group on the other side of the sacred pond, arms stretched to the skies, moving slowly in perfect unison through the ritual exercises that accompanied the song. Closer at hand, flowers, kissed by the first pink rays of the sun, slowly opened their blossoms, while brilliant yellow songbirds flitted from branch to branch amidst the topiary.

In this peaceful setting, Larajin could almost forget the fact that a powerful wizard wanted her dead; the Hulorn's men were no doubt scouring the streets outside even now, searching for her. Exhausted from having been up all night, she sighed, wishing that she could lie down beside the pool and be lulled into a peaceful slumber.

When she'd arrived at the temple just before dawn, it hadn't seemed to matter that she was no more than an initiate. While Habrith had a quiet word with the temple's Heartwarder, the clerics had welcomed her, given her their blessings, and clothed her in Sune's vestments: a crimson robe, cut to reveal her midriff, sandals embossed with Sune's winking eye, and a red silk scarf to tie back her hair. They had noticed the locket at her wrist and recognized it for what it was—a devotion to Hanali Celanil—but had just smiled, and commented that it must be difficult to serve two goddesses who were rivals for the same heart.

Yes, Larajin thought, she could happily tarry here forever, safely hidden within these walls. She looked up, and saw the tressym perched on the wall above, intent upon the songbirds. Larajin shook her head, willing the creature to go away. She didn't think the clerics would react kindly to having their songbirds being killed and eaten. The tressym leaped into the air and dived into the courtyard. Larajin tensed—but the tressym bypassed the songbirds, instead gliding to a graceful landing beside the sacred pool.

The tressym bent to sniff the water, then began lapping delicately. Once she finished her drink, she stretched with catlike grace, extended one brilliant wing, and preened red and turquoise feathers with long, sure strokes of her tongue.

"She's a beauty," the young cleric said, pausing in his art to admire the tressym. "Is she yours?"

"*She* seems to think so," Larajin quipped. "Or perhaps she thinks that I am hers."

The cleric laughed. Auburn-haired and long-lashed, he wore the garb of the temple: tight-fitting crimson hose capped by a padded codpiece, and a crimson shirt whose short sleeves revealed finely chiseled muscles. The shirt ended well above his midriff, exposing the deep red lines tattooed into his flesh: the pattern of Sune's lips, symbolically pressed against his belly in a sacred kiss.

He dabbed his brush back in the pot, and paused a moment before continuing his work. "Will your journey be a lengthy one, Mistress?"

Larajin did not know how to answer him. She was about to leave behind everything she knew and everyone she loved. Would she find protection among the wild elves of the Tangled Trees? More than that, would she find family, a new home?

"Mine will be a long journey," she told the cleric, the exhaustion of not having slept making her words heavy. "One I may be on for the rest of my life."

The cleric applied one last tickling brush stroke, then regarded the finished work appreciatively.

"Indeed? Then may Sune watch over and protect you for all of the days of your journey . . . and all the days of your life." He brushed his lips against her midriff, sealing his design with a kiss.

Larajin flushed as the warmth of his lips spread up and down her body. The blush spread to her very toes and fingertips—which, she saw, were surrounded by a faint red aura—and prickled through her scalp. When the magic that had accompanied the blessing took hold, it left her feeling rested and refreshed.

"Thank you," she whispered.

"My pleasure, Mistress." He gathered up his brushes and pot of gilt paste. "I hope to see you again, should your journey at last come to an end."

Larajin's eyes lingered on the cleric as he departed the

courtyard—he was *very* good looking, even for one of Sune's chosen.

She rose and cast a pebble into the pool and watched as ripples spread across it. No answer was given to her silent question. Perhaps even the goddess did not know what Larajin would find amidst the Tangled Trees. Unless the answer was the thing that was reflected in the pool: herself.

Bending, Larajin dipped her fingers in the water, lost in thought. The tressym butted up against her, and, remembering that the creature was the one who had alerted Drakkar, Larajin flicked wet fingers at the winged cat. The tressym flattened her ears and gave an indignant hiss, then launched herself into the sky.

Larajin watched her go, shaking her head. She'd tried to slip away from Habrith's bakery without being followed, but somehow the tressym had found her. It seemed Larajin could no more leave the little creature behind than she could escape her own shadow. At least the tressym had the good sense not to pad along behind Larajin like a dog, as she'd made her way to the temple. Instead she'd kept her distance, flitting along from rooftop to rooftop, up where few noticed her.

While she waited for the Heartwarder and her clerics to finish their ritual—they'd be setting out as soon as the Song of Sunrise ended—Larajin stared out through the courtyard's gate at the street, which was just starting to fill with carriages and passersby. One of them stopped at the gate, and peered in through the wrought iron. For a moment Larajin thought it was one of the guard—that she'd been spotted—then a familiar voice shouted her name.

Realizing it was Tal, she hurried toward the gate, gesturing frantically for him to be quiet. At the same time, she silently cursed. She'd hoped that Tal would sleep until well after she was gone. He'd obviously awakened earlier than usual, found her note, and assumed that she wouldn't leave the city without paying her respects at the temple. Had Drakkar guessed the same?

Larajin opened the gate and all but yanked Tal inside the courtyard. She shut it hurriedly, then dragged him into the shadow of the wall, where they couldn't be seen from the street. They stopped beside a pile of bags and crates the clerics would take with them on their journey to Ordulin.

Tal looked as though he'd left the house hurriedly. His doublet was only half buttoned, his hair was uncombed, and a shadow of stubble covered his heavy jaw. He carried a small leather pouch in one hand and a cloth-wrapped object the size of a candlestick in the other. The latter he held in a peculiar fashion, arm extended to keep it at arm's length from himself.

"Larajin," he panted, a worried look in his eye. "I'm so glad I found you. Are you really leaving Selgaunt? These are dangerous times to be traveling."

Larajin nodded. "I have to, Tal. Drakkar—"

"I want to come with you . . ." Tal said in a husky voice, then, before Larajin could protest, he added, "but I can't. The Merchant Council is agitating for war against the elves. If it comes, I'm to serve in a company under Master Ferrick. Leaving now would be seen as desertion—as cowardice. I just wish . . ."

Larajin, horrified by the prospect of war engulfing the lands to the north—lands through which she was about to travel—could only stare at Tal.

Misinterpreting her look, he hastily added, "Don't worry, Larajin. The elves are only half the soldiers that we are. They're too simple to understand the tactics of battle. If it does come to war, we'll squash those savages in a tenday. I'll march home again without a scratch."

Larajin said nothing. In his usual blundering way, Tal had insulted her without realizing it, not understanding that Larajin had been born to a mother who was a "savage" and therefore "simple."

The leather pouch clinked as he thrust it into Larajin's

hands. "There's twelve fivestars and nearly a hundred ravens in there—all I could scrape together at a moment's notice. That should help you along."

It was an incredible sum. "Tal, I can't—"

Tal waved her protest away. "Yes, you can."

Thanking him with a silent nod, Larajin found her bag and tucked the pouch inside it.

"I've brought something for you to protect yourself with," Tal continued. "Here."

He held out the cloth-swaddled bundle. Taking it, Larajin noted that it was heavy. She unwrapped the cloth and saw a dagger, its pommel embossed with the Uskevren family crest. Sliding it out of its sheath revealed a brightly polished silver blade with a strange glyph engraved upon it.

"It's magic," Tal said in a hushed voice, as if afraid his words would activate it. "If you say *'illunathros'* while holding it, the blade will glow with the brightness of a torch. It may also have other magical properties, but I don't know what . . ." He hastily amended whatever it was he'd been about to say. "I, uh . . . haven't used it that much, so I'm not sure what they are."

Larajin saw a twinge of guilt in his eye. She refrained from asking whom he'd stolen the dagger from. By the crest on its pommel, she could guess.

"You're too generous, Tal. I'll never be able to repay you."

Out in the street, a member of the city guard called the All's Well. Larajin glanced nervously at the gate, even though she knew the guard couldn't see in to where they were standing. Across the courtyard, the sound of singing stopped, as the Song of Sunrise ended.

"I have to go," she whispered. "The clerics I'll be traveling with are leaving now."

Tal's eyes ranged up and down the crimson vestments Larajin was wearing and lingered on the freshly painted eye of Sune upon her midriff.

Hesitantly, he asked, "You're not just . . . making this up as an excuse to follow some cleric on a quest, are you?"

Larajin's anger flared at his over-protectiveness, but then she realized he was only asking because he cared. Tal wasn't the one who had sent men after her to force her back to the city, when she'd tried to follow Diurgo Karn on his abortive pilgrimage to Lake Sember eighteen months past. Despite Tal's animosity with the Karn family and his own personal dislike for Diurgo, he had defended Larajin's right to follow the dictates of her heart—and of her budding religion. It had earned him stony silence from his father for several days afterward.

"Nothing like that, Tal. The Hulorn's wizard really did recognize me. The danger's real enough."

"Where are you going?" he asked.

"North, to Ordulin," she answered, giving him a partial truth.

"Ordulin?" Tal gaped. "Why there? That's where our armies will be mobilizing, if war comes. It's no place for—" He paused abruptly at the look Larajin gave him, then changed his approach. "Why not go to ground here, in the temple, and let me deal with the Hulorn's men? Wouldn't that be safer?"

"Tal," she said carefully, "I can't tell you exactly where I'm going, or why, except to say that I feel the goddess calling me. There are some secrets that have to be kept, even from . . ." She paused, choosing her words more carefully. "Some secrets that can't be shared, even between a brother and sister. Can you understand that?"

To her surprise, he nodded. "I suppose we all have secrets," he muttered.

His gaze shifted to something behind her. Turning, Larajin saw the Heartwarder and four novices heading toward them. She gave his arm a squeeze.

"I love you, Tal. If it comes to war, take care of yourself."

"You too," he said gruffly, then he turned and left through the gate, without looking back.

As the clerics shouldered their luggage, chattering brightly about the five-day carriage ride that lay ahead of them, Larajin's thoughts were grave. She'd known there was tension between Sembia and the elves to the north. She'd heard of caravans being attacked—had known that this was not the best time to be traveling to the Tangled Trees—but she hadn't realized that Sembia was on the verge of war. If it came to that, the Tangled Trees wouldn't just be a strange and foreign land, it would be behind enemy lines.

Larajin made her way through the streets of Ordulin, navigating by three buildings at the city's center that rose above all the rest: the Great Hall where the Merchant Council sat, with its gilded dome that shone golden in the late afternoon sun; the crenellated Tower of the Guards that housed the city's soldiers; and the so-called Guarded Gate—in actuality, an enormous stone-walled and column-fronted warehouse that housed the Sembian mint. Just beyond them lay the Trader's Quarter, starting point for the caravans that fanned north, east, south, and west through Sembia, carrying the goods of Ordulin's many merchants.

Though Ordulin was smaller than Selgaunt, its streets were more crowded. Nobles rode past in gilded carriages, with servants holding parasols to shade them from the blaze of the sun. Merchants in elaborately patterned hose and quilted doublets walked the streets, their only concession to the muggy heat being their lace-sleeved shirts, designed to allow the non-existent breezes through. The common laborers had no such pretensions. A gang of stonemasons setting the foundations of a house sweated bare-chested in the heat, while serving women gathering water from a well in the street splashed water onto their reddened faces and bare arms.

High overhead, the tressym wheeled and circled, occasionally disappearing from sight behind a building. So far, no one had noticed her, perhaps thinking her a hawk or an eagle. Larajin hoped it stayed that way.

Throughout the five-day journey to Ordulin, Larajin had remained in the crimson vestments of Sune, but now she wore what she thought of as her "adventuring garb": serviceable boots, her trouser-skirt, and a lightweight shirt. She still wore the crimson scarf of Sune in her hair, however, and the brass heart hung from her wrist. She might be trying to look nondescript, to blend in, but she would not forsake her devotions to the goddesses—both of them.

As she walked along, Larajin's ears were filled with the noise of the streets: the clatter of carriage wheels on cobblestones, the calls of merchants from their shops, and the clip-clop of horse's hooves. She stopped to ask a driver who was lounging on his carriage, waiting for his master, the way to Thread Street, the four-block-long collection of tailor's shops where Habrith's friend had his shop. The driver pointed at the next street and indicated she should turn the corner to the right. Thanking him, Larajin walked in that direction.

As she drew closer to the corner, she could hear a commotion. There was laughter and shouting . . . and the sound of heavy thuds and breaking glass.

Rounding the corner, she saw a knot of people at the side of the road, in front of one of the tailor shops. Its window had been smashed, and a burly man was kicking the front door with a heavy boot. The door crashed open, and the crowd surged inside. A moment later, several heavy bolts of cloth came flying out through the broken window. Laughing, the people outside scooped them up and staggered away down the street, carrying as many as they could under their arms. In front of the shop, two women each grabbed an end of the same bolt of cloth—a green fabric heavily embroidered with the outline of gold leaves—and began squabbling over it like a pair of angry chickens.

Shocked, Larajin realized these people were looting the shop. She looked around, searching for the city watch. She spotted three of them just up the street, lounging on their horses. Not one of the chain-mailed guards made a move for the bow at his pommel, however, or for the mace that hung from his belt. Instead one pointed at the looters, and the other two chuckled.

As she skirted around the mob, crossing to the other side of the road, Larajin noticed a symbol, painted on the door of the looted shop in a blaze of red: a vertical oval, with triangles jutting out of the top of it, like a face with horns. She wondered what it signified. Surely not a symbol of disease, with all of those people so willingly entering the shop. Perhaps the tailor had been convicted of a crime, and this was his punishment?

From inside the shop came the sound of blows and grunts of pain. Larajin hesitated, wondering if she should intervene, then she reminded herself that this was not her quarrel—that she was a stranger in Ordulin with trouble enough of her own. She didn't need to go shouldering someone else's burden, especially if the recipient of the mob's wrath was a criminal. Wincing, she tore herself away. She'd come back to Thread Street later, when the commotion had died down, and seek out the Harper agent.

She strode instead toward the Trader's Quarter, which lay just ahead. The smell of manure, hay, and axle grease assaulted her nose as she walked through an arched gate into a wide plaza fronted on all four sides by enormous stables. At its center was a notice board; on it was a document bearing the same symbol Larajin had seen on the tailor shop the mob had just looted. Curious, she decided to take a closer look.

She wove through the crowd of people and horses, sidestepping piles of dung that dotted the cobblestones. The notice bearing the horned oval turned out to be an official proclamation—one that sent a chill through Larajin as she read it, despite the heat of the sun on her shoulders. It reminded the citizens of Ordulin that the ten-year-old ban prohibiting elves from entering Sembia was still in effect. Not only that, but the ban now had been extended to half-elves, as well.

Dated less than a tenday ago, the proclamation ordered all

half-elves living in Ordulin to leave the city immediately or face retribution at the point of a sword. It further ordered that all homes and businesses belonging to half-elves were to be marked with a sign warning the citizens of Ordulin against doing business with the enemy. An example of the symbol used to designate the property to be confiscated was printed at the bottom of the notice. It was a crude representation of an elf's face—an oval with pointed, triangular ears.

Sickened, Larajin turned away from the notice board. She realized now that the tailor she'd heard being beaten inside his shop hadn't committed any crime, other than being born a half-elf. He was probably the man Habrith had told her to contact. Only an agent of the Harpers would tarry so long in a city that was hostile to his race. Was it too late to run back and offer him whatever healing she could—or had the mob that had looted his shop also carried him away . . . even killed him?

Larajin nervously fingered an ear. Were people looking at her, noticing her too-slim build? If the scales of fate had tipped only slightly differently, giving her the pointed ears of her mother's race, Larajin could have been the one receiving that beating.

In one corner of the plaza, a dozen men in civilian clothes practiced with pikes, taking turns thrusting at a wooden dummy under the eye of a member of the town guard. They were the militia, no doubt only recently mobilized. Larajin once again was confronted by the oval-and-triangles symbol. This time, it had been painted on the practice dummy.

Ordulin no longer felt like a safe haven. She was in as much danger there as she had been in Selgaunt. She needed to leave the city as soon as possible, to keep moving north. She'd have to try to find the Harper agent in Essembra on her own.

She scanned the notice board, looking for a suitable caravan, but while the notices advertised caravans bound for Yhaunn, for Highmoon, to Archenbridge, and back south to

Selgaunt, the only caravans bound for Essembra had departed more than a tenday ago.

"Looking for a caravan, Mistress? Where to? If it's north, I c'n help you."

Larajin could smell the man before she turned around. His breath had the fetid odor of a bad tooth, and his appearance matched the smell. His hose had a tear in the knee, and his leather doublet was stained under the arms. One hand rested on the hilt of a sword, which hung in a rust-spotted scabbard at his hip. The man's scalp was shaved but he wore his beard long. Flecks of what must have been his lunch still clung to it. His eyes kept darting to the money pouch that hung from Larajin's belt. One cheek puckered as he sucked on his bad tooth.

Larajin wanted nothing to do with him, but she did want to find out more about any caravan headed north—if one existed. The fact that no such caravan was advertised on the notice board made her wary. She wasn't going to venture down any back alleys with this lout. She rested a hand casually on the dagger she'd belted at her hip.

"North to where?" she asked him.

"To Featherdale and Essembra, and, if luck holds, all the way to Hillsfar. It'll prob'ly be the last one heading north 'fore the road closes. We'll have to wait out the war in Hillsfar—not that I mind."

Larajin looked him in the eye. "How do you know about this caravan?" she asked. "It's not posted on the board—and you're no trader."

He guffawed, and Larajin winced at the smell.

"Course it's not posted! You want some halfie reading it and telling his savage cousins in the trees we're coming through?" He shook his head. "You got one thing right, though, I'm no trader. I'm a sellsword. Name's Enik."

He waited for Larajin to volunteer her name. When she didn't, he shrugged and continued, "I been hired to protect the caravan." He stroked the hilt of his sword. "You come north with us, and me and my steel will be what's standing between you and them wild elves, missy."

Larajin didn't like the way he was rubbing the hilt of his sword. It was all too suggestive of something else. Still, it wouldn't hurt to see if this caravan really existed. If it was the only one headed north, it might be her only chance to reach the Tangled Trees. From her readings of the Master's books, she knew they lay more than one hundred and fifty miles to the north. She could hardly travel all that distance on foot.

This man was only a sellsword and as such could be expected to be rough and unsavory. She could at least see if the traders driving the caravan were decent folk.

"Where is the caravan assembling, and when?"

Enik gave her a twisted grin, still sucking his bad tooth. "That'll cost you a raven. Fer all I know, you're a halfie spy."

Larajin froze, feeling the blood drain from her face. He hadn't guessed that . . .

No, he hadn't. Enik, still grinning, gave her a broad wink. He hadn't spotted the elf blood in her, after all. It had just been his idea of a joke.

"Tell you what," Larajin said carefully. "You give me the information, and when it's proved to be accurate, you'll get your raven—but not until we're under way. Deal?"

Enik sucked on his tooth, considering it.

"All right." He pointed at a warehouse just beyond one of the arches leading out of the plaza and said, "The caravan is loading its cargo of wine there, at the Foxmantle warehouse. They'll be at it all night. Come first light, it's away. You want to be on one of the wagons, you meet me there just before dawn."

Larajin nodded. If what Enik was saying was true about this being a Foxmantle caravan, things were looking up. The Fox-mantles might be loud and brash, their wild young daughters prone to scandalously foolish exploits, but the family was a firm friend and ally to the Uskevren—they were people Larajin could trust. All she had to do was show the head driver the dagger with the Uskevren crest on it and claim to be Mistress Thazienne. With luck, he wouldn't have met Thazienne, and she'd have nothing to worry about.

She eyed Enik. Nothing, that was, except making sure this lout didn't try anything during the journey north, but the dagger would also see to that.

She nodded to him, patting the money pouch at her hip. "Dawn it is, then, at the Foxmantle warehouse," she said. "I'll see you there."

She kept the smile on her face as she watched him leave but let it drop the moment he was out of sight. Making her way out of the plaza, she took a circular route through the side streets that would lead her to the Foxmantle warehouse. She wasn't going to go trustingly to meet a lout like Enik in the murky light of dawn, down some back alley behind a warehouse. Instead she'd make her own arrangements with the caravan's head driver while the wagons were being loaded. If she liked what she saw, she'd arrange for her passage north—and worry about traveling with Enik later.

Larajin coughed as a tendril of mist drifted back down the road toward the caravan, stinging her lungs. Beside her, on the driver's seat of the lead wagon, Dray Foxmantle dabbed a monogrammed handkerchief to his eye.

"Gods curse that fool of a wizard," he muttered. "Why couldn't he have waited until there was a wind to blow the stuff away?"

Still in his early twenties—about Larajin's age—Dray was blessed with perfectly straight teeth and dark hair that hung in tight spirals to his shoulders. His beard was trimmed to a thin line that exactly traced the bottom of his jaw, in the prevailing fashion, and a heavy gold hoop hung from one ear. He wore the family blue and purple, and a silver ring on the little finger of his left hand that bore the Foxmantle crest: three diamond-pupiled eyes, set in a diagonal line.

Dray had been flirting with Larajin ever since the caravan departed from Ordulin eight days ago, telling her how pretty she was—ignoring the fact that the long, hot journey had left her dusty and sweaty. Truth be told, she didn't mind the flattery, though she wondered if much of it wasn't business, rather than pleasure. Dray kept hinting, with every second breath, about a possible merger of the Foxmantle and Uskevren vineyards.

Still, she enjoyed his company. He was playful and fun and was blessed with a beautiful singing voice, as she'd found out one night around the campfire when he broke out his mandolin and sang a ballad for her. He would have made an ideal candidate for Sune's priesthood. He even reminded her, a little, of Diurgo.

Now, however, he seemed oblivious to the possible danger of the wizard's magical conjuring. Larajin peered nervously at the thick mist that swirled above the road a short distance ahead, hoping Klarsh knew what he was doing. The caravan had stopped—for the third time this day—so the wizard could clear away some choke creeper that had grown across the road. Even though Klarsh was well ahead of their wagon, Larajin felt nervous. The trees on either side of Rauthauvyr's Road were enormous, forming what felt like a steep-walled canyon to either side, and the underbrush on the forest floor was thick—too thick to pass through at anything but a struggling walk. If the poisonous mist spread beyond the wizard's control, the caravan drivers, soldiers—and Larajin—would all be killed.

Behind them, five other wagons had also pulled to a halt. The horses hitched to them snorted and pawed at the road, nostrils flaring and ears flicking nervously in response to the acrid smell of the magical mist. The drivers called out to soothe them, occasionally tugging on the reins to restrain a team as it tried to jerk a wagon forward, causing its cargo of wine bottles to rattle and clink inside their wooden cases.

The two dozen sellswords hired to protect the caravan lounged on either side of the road, glancing at the forest only every now and then. Like Enik, they were a scruffy-looking lot—tough enough and well armed, but not nearly as disciplined as Larajin would have liked. She supposed that, with nearly all of the able-bodied fighters in Ordulin being conscripted into the militia, these were the only men Dray could find.

They were nominally under the leadership of Paltar, a capable-looking man in his late fifties with iron-gray hair and eyes to match. Walking with a slight limp that he'd gained earlier in his career as a soldier, he glared at the sellswords, tersely ordering them to keep an eye on the forest, but was answered only by grunts and shrugs. Paltar kept glancing back at Dray, as if waiting for a supporting word, but none was forthcoming.

Enik—whom the men did listen to, when they were of a mind to—strode toward where Larajin and Dray sat, wiping a trickle of sweat from his forehead. Sunlight glinted off a gold ring on his little finger, which seemed to be a new addition to his otherwise scruffy wardrobe since their departure from Ordulin. As he stared up at Dray, she noted that he had none of the traditional deference that a hireling normally displayed in the presence of a noble. Instead he met Dray's eye directly, cheek puckering as he sucked his tooth.

"Sun's hot, and it's been a thirsty march," Enik said. "How about we open a couple of bottles from the cargo and slake our thirst?"

Dray opened his mouth as if about to protest, but then his eyes got a dreamy, faraway look. He licked dry lips, and nodded.

Paltar, having overheard the exchange, strode forward. "That's not a good idea, my lord," he told Dray. Eyes narrowing, he gave Enik a sideways look. "The men should stay sharp. We've still got a way to—"

Dray cut him short. "Don't be silly, Paltar," he said. "In this heat I'd like a drop myself." He turned to Enik, and with an exaggerated wink, added, "No more than a bottle between every two men. I expect you to stay sharp."

Enik touched his forefinger to one eyelid—obviously a signal his men understood, for they were on their feet in an instant, crowding around the back of the last wagon in line. Boards creaked as a crate was opened and corks popped, and the sellswords were tilting bottles to the sky, Adam's apples bobbing as they gulped down the wine.

Shaking his head and muttering curses under his breath, Paltar let his hand drift toward the hilt of his sword. A moment later, when Enik wrapped an arm around his shoulder and murmured in his ear, he nodded, and a slow smile spread across his face. Letting Enik lead him, he made his way back to the last wagon, ignoring the questioning looks the drivers gave him.

As Enik threw a leering grin back over his shoulder at Larajin, Dray reached into one of the crates behind him and pulled out a slender blue bottle that bore an elaborate label.

"Ice wine," he told Larajin. "The finest the Foxmantle vineyards has to offer, from the pick of last year's crop. Very expensive—which is why I insisted on driving this wagon myself. The other wagons all carry lesser vintages. Would you do me the honor of sharing a bottle with me, Thazienne?"

Larajin was still watching the sellswords at the back of the caravan. They'd passed a bottle forward to the driver of the rear wagon, and seemed to each have a bottle to themselves. Paltar was drinking and laughing with the rest of them, one arm draped around Enik's shoulder.

"Dray," she cautioned as he popped the cork of the bottle in his hand. "They're drinking more than you permitted."

He glanced back briefly, then shrugged. "So they are. Even so, they're still more than a match for elves. And don't forget, we have Klarsh with us."

He peered ahead, trying to spot the wizard through the

thick white mist, then he glanced up at the sun, noting its position in the sky.

"We should reach Essembra well before evening," he said, "and I don't anticipate any trouble along the way. All of the attacks have been on the stretch of road north of town. We'll be perfectly safe, even with a tipsy guard. Let them have their fun."

Larajin knew nothing about soldiering, but she didn't think it prudent for the sellswords to be letting down their guard within the wood, even in an area that was supposedly safe. When Dray offered the bottle to her, she declined it with a slight shake of her head. She peered into his eyes. Even though he'd drunk only a little wine, they had a dreamy, glazed look.

"Dray," she said carefully, "it looked as though you were going to tell Enik that his men couldn't have any wine. What changed your mind?"

Dray shrugged again and took a pull from the bottle. "Delicious!" he pronounced. "I'll have to commend our vintners." Then he seemed to remember Larajin's question. "Oh, yes. Enik. He seems like a good fellow. I like him."

The vagueness of his reply clinched it. Dray might be foolhardy—taking a caravan north when war was imminent proved that much—but he wasn't stupid. Enik must have used magic on Dray, to convince him that he was harmless. Some sort of spell, no doubt, or that ring.

Now that she thought about it, Larajin could remember several times in the last few days when Dray or Paltar had been about to reprimand one of the sellswords, only to change his mind at a word from Enik. Larajin shuddered, thankful that Enik hadn't tried using the ring's magic on her. Or maybe he had tried, and one of the goddesses had been watching over Larajin.

In any case, she didn't like the look Enik had just given her as he tipped back his wine. Three of the five drivers had tied off their reins and joined the sellswords near the rear wagon. Larajin was suddenly very aware that she was the only woman among more than a dozen men, all of them rapidly getting drunk—and all of them capable of being magically compelled to do whatever Enik wanted them to. Maybe she should just strike off through the woods on her own and hope for the best.

"These woods used to be part of Cormanthor, didn't they?" she asked Dray.

He nodded.

"I've heard of a place called the Tangled Trees, where the wild elves are said to live. How close is it—are we under any danger of attack?"

Dray waved a hand at the forest to their right. "It's somewhere in that direction, but don't worry, Thazienne, my dear," he reassured her, patting her hand. "It's deep within the forest, at least three days' march from here. The wild elves shy away from the road. We've nothing to fear from them."

Larajin squinted ahead into the mist and saw that it was thinning. The wizard must have completed his task. A breeze that was probably magical, given the muggy stillness of the air elsewhere in the wood, was blowing the last of the mist into the woods at the side of the road.

"I'm going ahead to talk to Klarsh," she told Dray. She jerked a thumb in the direction of the sellswords. "I think you'd better see to them. If you don't, they'll drink all of your cargo."

Dray swallowed the last of the ice wine and laid the empty bottle on the floor at his feet.

"I suppose you're right," he said with a sigh. "It is time we got moving, anyhow. I'd like to get to Essembra in time for a hot meal and a bath, to wash the dust from my hair."

He tied off the reins and climbed down from the wagon. As he walked away, Larajin reached for her bag. Holding it in front of her body, she chose her moment carefully—when Dray was busy shaking a finger at a bored-looking Enik—and slipped down from the wagon. She jogged up the road, keeping the wagon between herself and the men, hoping that Enik would be too busy working his magic on Dray and Paltar to notice. She felt guilty abandoning them—both seemed like decent men—but sticking around seemed like a bad idea. She might be able to counter a simple charm, but she didn't know any spells that would protect her from more than a dozen drunken men.

Hopefully, it would be some time before anyone noticed she was gone. It would take Dray some time to get the caravan moving again—especially if Enik "persuaded" him to join in another round of wine. By the time they looked around, she would be well into the woods. The only problem was that she had to get far ahead of the wizard before entering the forest. His magical wind had rather quickly blown the mist to either side of the road. Slow to dissipate, it clung between the trees in wispy patches, drifting to a halt when the breeze Klarsh had summoned was gone.

The area that had been cleared lay just ahead of where Dray had halted his wagon, an expanse of putrefying vegetation that befouled the road and spread several paces beyond it, into the woods. The larger trees to either side of the road were still whole, but their trunks were blistered and cracked where the magical mist had washed over them like a roiling tide.

Larajin rounded a bend in the road and breathed a sigh of relief, realizing that she was hidden from Enik's sight. A patch of blighted vines squished under the soft leather of her boots, lending a foul odor to the air,. She nearly stepped on a dead mouse that had been caught by the mist. It lay on its back, limbs contorted and mouth gaping wide. She kneeled for a moment to offer up a quick prayer for its soul, passing her hand once over its tiny corpse—then winced as a wisp of mist that still clung to the ground stung her skin.

Stealing a glance at the treetops, she was relieved to see a familiar flash of turquoise some distance behind where the caravan had stopped. The tressym had stayed well away from the mist, thank the goddess.

A pace or two ahead, Klarsh stood with hands on hips,

surveying the damage his wand had wrought. He was an older man, with thinning gray hair and a hard, clean-shaven face that would have looked more at home on a soldier. He wore a robe of heavy black wool, despite the heat of the day, with the sleeves rolled up. Despite the mist that had swirled around him moments ago, he breathed easily. Larajin, on the other hand, felt her eyes watering.

"Klarsh," she called. "I need to relieve myself. I'm just going a little ahead, to find a spot in the forest that's—"

"Quiet, girl," he hissed.

His attention had shifted to something at the edge of the road. Without another word, he strode toward the base of an ancient, enormous oak. He spent several moments inspecting peculiar scratches on its trunk, then bent down and pulled a small knife from a sheath at his hip. He thrust the blade into the soil, scooping up dirt as if he were using a spoon. When he stood he began chanting a spell, holding the knife out in front of him, blade level with the ground.

Larajin, fearful that the magical mist was about to boil across the road a second time, began backing hurriedly away. Before she had taken two steps, Klarsh flicked his knife, sending a scattering of dirt flying from the blade. He continued chanting, and a moment later his spell took effect. The ground beneath the tree began to buckle and heave, like waves on the sea. As the motion of the ground grew ever more frantic the oak leaned, groaned, leaned some more . . . and its roots tore free of the soil. It fell, splintering smaller trees like twigs and slamming into the ground with a crash that knocked Larajin to her hands and knees. Several lesser crashes followed, as smaller trees dominoed in its wake, then all was silent.

As Larajin clambered, shaking, to her feet, wiping the stinging sludge from her hands, all she could do was thank the goddess that the oak hadn't fallen in her direction. The trunk of the tree—as wide across as a stable door—would have crushed her like an ant.

"Wh-what are you doing?" she sputtered at Klarsh, shock

causing her to momentarily overlook the fact that she was shouting at a powerful wizard. "I might have been killed!"

He ignored her, and strode over to the hole the oak's ruptured roots had torn in the ground. The wizard bent down, and pulled from the hole something that looked like a tarnished bowl, holding it by the golden knob that protruded from the bottom of it. He turned it in his hands, so the knob was at the top, and shook it gently. A round white object fell out and landed at Klarsh's feet. It was a skull.

Shocked, Larajin realized that this was not a bowl that Klarsh held but a helm, its silver tarnished and black from long years of lying under the ground. Only the crest at the top of the helm—a knob of gold as thick as her thumb—had survived intact. More gold glinted in the ruptured ground at Klarsh's feet.

Larajin heard the sound of running footsteps behind her. A moment later the sellswords appeared, Enik in the lead and spluttering curses.

"What in the Nine Hells . . ."

A feral smile spread across Enik's face as he saw what Klarsh held. He strode forward and plucked the helm from the wizard and juggled it gleefully in one hand.

"Well done, Klarsh—well done, indeed." He turned to show it to the other sellswords. "Didn't I tell you the Vale of Lost Voices would give up its dead? All we had to do was find one of the tombs. We're rich, boys. Rich!"

Whoops and cheers greeted this pronouncement. A moment later they turned to cautious, surly looks as Dray jogged up the road.

Despite the fact that he was a Foxmantle, Dray wasn't quite as stupid as Larajin had supposed. As soon as he saw the overturned tree and Enik holding the dirt-encrusted helm, his eyes widened in alarm.

"Put that back," he ordered. "That's an elven burial you're disturbing. It isn't right."

Paltar appeared a moment later, sword in hand. "What's going on here?" he demanded.

Enik squared off with Paltar, tossing the helm to one of his men and letting his hand hover near the hilt of his sword. Instead of drawing it, however, he spoke in a soft voice.

"Now, now, Paltar, there's no need to draw steel. We're all friends here, and friends share. You'd like to be a wealthy man, wouldn't you?"

Paltar paused, blinked, then slowly lowered his sword. At a gesture from Enik, one of the sellswords stepped forward, yanked the sword from his hand, and danced back out of reach. Two others grabbed Paltar's arms with rough hands, and a fourth held a dagger to his throat.

Dray, slower to react, was even easier to subdue.

"Not a noise—from either of you," Enik told them.

He gestured a second time, and six of his men turned and jogged back toward the wagons, a purposeful look in their eyes.

Larajin could only stare, dumbfounded by the realization that the events that were unfolding must have been carefully planned, long in advance. That same realization was slower in coming to Dray. He struggled in the grip of the two ruffians who held him, tearing his shirt.

"Klarsh! Do something!" Dray shouted. "They're thieves—stop them!"

Klarsh smiled. "I think not. I'd like to receive my share."

Enik guffawed and sucked on his tooth, considering the struggling Dray. "He'll fetch a good ransom." His eyes turned to Larajin and he said, "As will she. House Uskevren will pay handsomely for the return of its wayward daughter, I warrant, and we'll be safe in Hillsfar, with a war to prevent anyone from reaching us."

Still chuckling, he strode toward her.

Paltar, who had been quiet, began to struggle. He was rewarded with a stab in the throat. A rush of blood sprayed the face of the sellsword with the knife. Cursing, the man finished the job, slamming the hilt of his sword onto Paltar's head and knocking him down. The old soldier was dead before he hit the ground, the flow of blood from his neck no longer pulsing.

Dray sagged between the two men who held him, looking like he was about to faint.

Larajin backed cautiously away, knowing that she had to act. Quickly, she whispered a prayer. She was rewarded an instant later with the floral fragrance of Sune's Kisses. She thrust out a hand, palm-first, at Enik, and uttered the one-word command that would trigger her spell.

"Flee!"

Enik jerked to a halt, one foot dangling above the ground in mid-step. For a moment, his eyes widened in fear. He half-turned to flee—then shook his head, like a man awakening from a dream.

He drew his sword and danced back a step, shouting over his shoulder, "Watch it, lads, she's got spells. Klarsh! Do something."

With a sinking heart, Larajin realized her magic had not been powerful enough to subdue the brigand. Was his will really that strong—or had she done something to displease the goddesses?

No time to wonder about that now. Klarsh had already begun muttering a spell. Determined to go down fighting, Larajin drew the magic dagger Tal had given her and assumed one of the fighting postures he'd taught her. Enik looked scornfully at her and laughed. As he started to speak, Larajin steeled herself, trying to close her mind to the magic she was certain was about to be unleashed upon her.

"Hey, now, missy," Enik said in a low voice. "Have you forgotten that old Enik's your pal? Why don't you give me that pretty little dagger before you hurt your—"

A hissing noise, like the switch of a whip through the air, cut off his words. Enik's expression changed, his eyes widening and his jaw dropping open. For a moment, Larajin thought something had gone wrong with his spell, then she realized that that other objects were whistling through the air all around her.

Arrows.

Enik looked stupidly down at the bloody barb of the arrow protruding from his chest, let his breath out in a bubbling sigh, and collapsed to the ground. Behind him, the other sellswords cursed, drawing their swords and whirling to face the threat. The wizard hurriedly cast a spell, and disappeared with a soft *pop*.

Larajin saw slender shapes flitting through the woods and caught a glimpse of a tattooed face. Elves!

Whirling, she clutched her bag to her chest, uncertain which way to run. From behind her came the screams of men and the whinnies of startled horses. The caravan was also under attack. She could hear arrows burying themselves in the sides of the wagons with harsh thuds.

She started to run up the road, but just ahead of her an arrow hit one of the brigands, causing him to howl in pain. Skidding to a stop, she decided to dash for the woods instead, but collided with Dray. He steadied her, then bent down and grabbed a sword from the lifeless hand of one of the brigands.

"Run!" he shouted. "I'll hold them back."

Before she could suggest that he, too, should run, an arrow struck Dray's arm. He doubled over in pain and nearly dropped the sword. A second arrow buried itself in the ground near his feet.

Seeing that it was hopeless to stand and fight, Larajin turned and did as Dray had bade her. She ran.

A driverless wagon thundered past, pulled by terrified horses. Larajin sprinted beside it, using it to shield herself from the elves' attack. Blighted vegetation cracked underfoot as she ran, and another arrow, fired under the wagon, narrowly missed her legs.

Realizing that she was still a target, she turned and sprinted for the woods on the side of the road opposite the one the arrows were coming from. Mist still hung in patches here and there between the trees. She zigzagged around it, fighting her way through the blight-slimed underbrush. Branches ripped her bag from her arms and tore open the mouth of her money pouch, spilling its coins. Larajin winced at their loss but kept running, one hand still clutching her dagger. She dodged around a tree, putting its massive trunk between herself and the elf archers.

Distracted by the screams of fighting men and a loud groan that might have been Dray's voice, she stumbled over a root, then recovered and ran on. Behind her, the curses and shouts were getting fainter—and fewer. A moment more, and they were replaced by silence, then came the sound of bottles being smashed.

Larajin ran on through the forest, angling north to parallel the road, all the while casting nervous glances over her shoulder. It sounded as though the elves were sacking the caravan—would that keep them so busy they would forget about pursuing her?

Out of the corner of her eye, Larajin saw something whipping up off the forest floor toward her—a rope? It coiled around her leg. Jerked to a sudden halt, she crashed to the ground, the wind knocked from her. A snare! The elves must have set a trap.

Her dagger lay beside her, where she'd dropped it. Head still spinning from her fall, Larajin groped for it, but as her fingers closed around the hilt, another snare whipped around her forearm, preventing her from using the dagger to cut herself free.

No—not a snare, she realized, looking down. That wasn't a rope around her arm; it was a leaf-covered vine. It looked like ivy, but it moved with a sinuous grace, and a purposefulness that suggested sentience. She realized that it must be the choke creeper the caravan drivers had spoken of it. This infestation was the reason the wizard was clearing the road.

She watched in horror as the loose ends of the vine coiled their way up her arm and leg like constricting snakes. Struggle as she might, she could not pull herself free. The vines were as strong as braided steel. More of them were questing blindly toward her, drawn by her frantic motions. She had blundered onto a wide patch of the creeper. The entire floor of the forest seemed to have come to life, to be reaching for her. Under that tangle of greenery, she could see the white of bones. She was not the first creature to have been caught in this trap.

Something tickled the back of her neck. Larajin jerked away, throwing herself violently to the side, but to no avail. One of the vines was around her neck. Larajin forced the fingers of her free hand under the vine, struggling to prevent it from crushing her throat, but this gave only momentary relief. Unable to rise, to flee, she wished now that an arrow had found her, instead. Knowing that she was about to die, she began choking out the words of a prayer.

As if in answer, an angry howl came from somewhere above. An instant later Larajin heard the fluttering of wings and saw the tressym swooping down through the trees.

"No," she choked out, as a strand of the vine rose into the air, questing for the tressym. "Don't . . ."

The vine around her neck tightened, forcing her fingers into her throat. Unable to speak, Larajin could only weep, certain that the tressym would be lashed from the sky.

But the tressym proved more agile than the questing vine. A leafy tendril caught and bent one of the feathers at the tressym's wingtip—but then she was swooping back up into the sky with powerful beats of her wings. She repeated the action, and with each dive and ascent more and more of the vines followed her—and Larajin found that her hand, which still held the dagger, was free.

She sat up, slashing at the vine around her throat. The sudden movement triggered the rest of the tangled mass, which rippled toward her, but the tressym had bought her the time she needed. With a single swift stroke of her dagger—whose magical blade parted the vine as easily as rotted twine—Larajin was free.

Scrambling to her feet, she leaped back from the tangle of

vines, onto a clear patch of ground. Sobbing with relief, she glanced up and saw the tressym perched safely on a branch, watching her with large, round eyes.

"Thank you, my little friend," Larajin said. "You and I are balanced now—one rescue for another. If that's why you've been following me all this time, consider your debt to me paid. You are free to go, but if you do decide to follow me farther, I think you should have a name. Certainly you've displayed a heart of gold today—and so, I grant you the name Goldheart."

She pointed the blade of her dagger at the tressym, like a king bestowing honors on a knight, then she bowed.

When she rose, Goldheart was gone. A single bent feather, fallen from her wing, drifted down through the branches. Larajin ran and caught it—then jumped back in alarm as a wild elf stepped out from behind the trunk of the tree in which Goldheart had been perched, bow at full draw and arrow nocked. Larajin thought about raising her dagger, then realized what a futile gesture that would be. If the elf had intended to shoot her, Larajin would be dead by now. Instead the archer just stared.

Larajin stared breathlessly back, incredulous to finally meet a wild elf, face-to-face. The woman's almond-shaped eyes were every bit as feral as the picture in Master Thamalon's book, and the black band tattooed across her nose and cheeks made her look fiercer still. Her long, blonde hair was drawn back in a ponytail, exposing the rest of the tattoo, which completed its circle of her scalp over her pointed ears. Her skin was a dusky brown—the same color as the tanned leather of her clothes. She wore rough breeches and a vest decorated with animal teeth that had been sewn onto it like buttons. Muscles bunched in her bare arms as she held her bow at full draw.

The irony of this meeting was not lost on Larajin. Rather than having to go looking for the wild elves of the Tangled Trees, they had come to her. Now, instead of introducing herself to them as kin, Larajin would be pleading her case as a captured enemy.

"I . . . elf-friend," she stuttered, using the few words of the wild elf tongue she had been able to glean from the books in the master's library. "I look . . . forest-mother from . . . trees-woven-into-trees . . ."

Wings fluttered above. The elf woman glanced up at Goldheart, but her arrow remained unwavering in its aim. The tressym circled once overhead, then turned and winged her way to the east.

"You must be blessed of the goddess, to have one of her favorites come to your aid," the elf said.

Startled, Larajin realized the woman had spoken in the common tongue. The words were heavily accented—and overlaid with the distinctive inflections of a Sembian. Larajin wondered who had taught her the language.

Larajin blurted out her explanation. "I pay homage to Hanali Celanil," she said, holding up her wrist to show the gilded heart that dangled there. "I am part elf myself. My mother was—"

A brief peal of laughter cut Larajin short. The elf had a skeptical, almost scornful expression on her face. Her eyes darted from Larajin's ears, to her hair, to her fair skin. She was believing none of it.

Behind the woman, from the direction of the road, came the sound of lilting voices. The elves had obviously completed their predation upon the caravan and now were breaking the eerie silence they had maintained throughout their attack. Larajin wondered if Dray had survived. She prayed that the elves had shown him mercy—and that they would extend that mercy to her. She decided to try a different approach.

Slowly, not wanting her movements to be misinterpreted, Larajin turned her dagger to show the elf its hilt. If this elf spoke Sembian-flavored Common, perhaps she knew a little of Sembia's geography—and politics. A member of a noble household might be deemed one worth keeping alive, worth ransoming.

"I am a member of a noble Sembian house," Larajin began. "My . . ." She hesitated, then decided there was no harm in telling the truth, so far from home. "My father is Thamalon Uskevren. This is his dagger. It bears our family crest."

Recognition flickered in the elf's eyes. She knew the master's name!

Larajin took a deep breath, hoping the elf would listen, this time.

"Twenty-six years ago, Thamalon Uskevren journeyed north to the Tangled Trees. He met an elf woman—a wild elf of the forest—and . . . lay with her. A year later he returned, and found that she had given birth to his child. She died during the birthing, and so I was given to my father. I was raised in his house, in Sembia, but now I have returned. I am looking for . . ." She paused, unsure for a moment how to continue. "For my roots. My . . . family."

She waited, praying the elf would believe her.

The elf's eyes had grown wider as Larajin spoke. Suddenly, in one swift motion, she lowered her bow. Removing her arrow, she slid it into the quiver at her hip. She pressed both hands against her heart, palms to her chest, and bowed.

"I should have paid more heed to the goddess's sign. Perhaps then I would have recognized you," she said as she straightened, "but it is little wonder that I didn't. You and your brother are as different as day and night."

"My brother?"

Before Larajin had a chance to ask more, the elven woman motioned for silence. Behind her, a dozen elves came running lightly through the wood. She turned quickly and signaled to them. They slowed their pace, at the same time lowering their weapons. The woman spoke to them in their own rapid tongue, pointing several times at Larajin, and once getting her to lift her hand and show the elves the tressym feather she was holding. There were mutters, at first, but then more than one of the elves began nodding.

The woman turned back to Larajin. "You will come with us, to the Tangled Trees," she said. "We will leave at once."

Larajin nodded, and allowed a smile of relief to creep to her lips. Silently she thanked the goddesses—first Hanali Celanil, then Sune—for watching over her. Despite the terrible fact that men had just fought and died on Rauthauvyr's Road, Larajin had survived, and would soon be on her way to the Tangled Trees. The goddesses seemed to be watching over her, after all.

CHAPTER 4

Leifander circled over the lights below, which were brighter than the glow from a thousand campfires. Even at this height the city assaulted his senses. The stink of dead fish, tar, and sewage rose from the harbor. Even in the depths of night, grunting laborers loaded cargo into ships, and carriages rattled through the streets, axles squealing. Lanterns burned on side streets where no one walked, and smoke smelling of cooking grease wafted out of chimneys, clogging the already humid air.

Leifander cocked his head, staring disdainfully down at the city. Humans were a wasteful, destructive race. How he yearned for the fresh green of trees that had stood for centuries, the quiet stillness of a forest glade under moonlight. He would be glad when this mission was done.

He finally spotted the building Rylith had described. Stormweather Towers was a massive stone structure topped with towers and turrets; it rose like a rocky spire out of a surrounding fringe of greenery far too symmetrical to ever be thought natural. Smaller buildings surrounded the main structure, marring the gardens with their ugly gray.

Lights burned in several of the rooms, and humans moved around inside, busy at a multitude of tasks. Several of the shuttered windows were open. The clatter of crockery and the harsh sounds of human voices drifted into the air. Leifander circled the building, glancing in through windows for the man he had been ordered to seek out. None of the people inside fitted the description he had been given: a man of sixty winters, with snow-white hair and heavy, dark eyebrows.

Uncertain how to present himself—Rylith had warned that elves were not welcome in Selgaunt—Leifander flapped his way to one of the second-story balconies and landed on its cool stone rail. The double doors that gave access to the balcony were open. Inside the room, he could see the dark shapes of a high four-poster bed with rumpled blankets, two armchairs, and a wardrobe. A small cabinet mounted on the wall behind the bed was fronted by two glass doors. Something amid the clutter of objects inside it glittered as it caught the faint light coming in through the balcony doors. Intrigued, Leifander cocked his head, staring at it.

A shudder coursed through him as he assumed elf form once more. Wings became arms, talons turned to bare feet, and feathers coalesced into a tooled leather vest and fringed trousers. A ridge of feathers along his back became a quiver, holding arrows and an unslung bow.

He hopped lightly down from the rail, arms still spread and fingers fluttering like feathers as he caught his balance. Cautiously, listening attentively to the faint noises coming through the door that led out of the room, he crept over to the bed.

Clambering up onto the rumpled blankets, he peered

inside the cabinet. The object that had caught his eye was a quill pen, the shaft of the feather gilded and set with a row of bright diamonds. It looked to be of elven make—perhaps even something that was sacred to the Winged Lady. What was it doing there, in a human home?

As he leaned to the side to get a better look at it, sparkles of red and blue fire danced in the depths of the gems. None of the other trinkets inside the cabinet—tiny gold bells, a silver dagger, ceramic statues, two gold rings, and an enameled locket—even came close to it in beauty.

Unable to resist, Leifander turned the latch on one of the cabinet doors. Something stung his finger, and he jerked his hand back. The cabinet door swung open. Leifander stared in surprise at shelves that had suddenly become empty.

A feeling of dizziness passed over him, then was gone. Leifander peered at his fingertip and saw a bead of dark blood welling there. Angrily, he shook it away, then felt inside the cabinet. The shelves were indeed empty—and though he could still see objects through the glass of the cabinet door that remained closed, his questing fingers found nothing but bare shelves. He had been fooled by an illusion—and, judging by the numbness of his punctured fingertip, nearly laid low by a trap.

Cursing all humans and their devious natures, he sprang down from the bed. In that same instant, the door began to open, spilling a crack of light into the room. Leifander hurried to the balcony, crouched there, and began the chant that would transform him back into a crow.

Before he could complete the spell, light washed over him, and a woman's voice hissed, "Ebeian! What took you so long? I was worried that . . . Oh! Who are you?"

Leifander shot a look over his shoulder, and saw a human holding a flickering lamp. She looked to be in her second decade of life, and had dark hair and eyes as green as the emerald that glittered in the ring on her finger. Dressed in tight, black leather pants and shirt, she was slender for a round-ear—and pretty, Leifander grudgingly admitted. A rapier hung at her hip, and the hilt of a dagger protruded from one boot. She made no move toward either weapon.

Leifander rose slowly to his feet, turning to face her.

"Did Ebeian send you?" she asked. "Is he in trouble? Did something go wrong?"

For a moment, Leifander considered trying to pass himself off as a friend of this Ebeian fellow, whoever that was, but he decided against trying to satisfy what was only idle curiosity. The schemes of humans were not his concern. More to the point, this woman seemed singularly unconcerned to have discovered a forest elf in her bedchamber. She might be the best one to ask where Thamalon Uskevren could be found.

"My name is Leifander," he said simply. "I am an elf of the Tangled Trees. I have come to speak with Thamalon Uskevren. I bring him a message."

"Do you, indeed?" she asked with an arched eyebrow. "So, messenger, do you always sneak in through second-story windows when delivering your messages—or do you sometimes knock at the front door?"

This woman was truly exasperating. "Will you show me to Thamalon Uskevren or not?"

She did not answer at once. Instead she hung her lantern on a long hook attached to the ceiling and pointedly glanced at the open cabinet above the bed. Leifander stiffened, but when she turned back to him, amusement sparkled in her eyes.

"I see you couldn't resist a little pilfering while you were waiting to deliver your message," she said, clucking her tongue in mock reproach. "It's lucky for you that you're an elf and immune to that drug—otherwise I'd have found you asleep on my bed. Exotic looking as you are, I'd have been forced to ravish you. As it is . . ."

She strode forward suddenly and planted a kiss on his lips. Startled, Leifander pushed her away. Were all human women so forward with strangers? He shook his head. It was time to get on with what he had come there to do.

"The message I bear is an urgent one," he told her. "I would deliver it at once."

"Give me your message, and I'll deliver it for you."

Leifander shook his head. "No. I must speak to Thamalon Uskevren in person . . . and in private."

A slight change in the woman's posture told Leifander that she had grown wary of him. "Why in private?" she asked. "So you can stick a dagger in his ribs?"

Leifander deliberately kept his hands away from the dagger at his hip. "You think me an assassin," he said bluntly. "I am not. I wish only to speak to Thamalon Uskevren about a political matter. The elves sent me because I have a . . . personal connection with him."

His explanation didn't help. Somehow he had compounded his earlier blunder. The woman's eyes narrowed with suspicion, and her hand came gently to rest upon the hilt of her rapier.

"You have no 'personal connection' with Thamalon Uskevren," she said, running the fingers of her free hand through her short hair in a nervous gesture. "If you did, you'd have known he was my father."

The rapier hissed out of its scabbard. "I think you *are* an assassin," she added in an icy voice.

Leifander raised his hands in what would seem a placating gesture. In fact, his fingers were already beginning to weave a spell. Before the woman could move to skewer him, he barked out three quick words in his own tongue. Sparks of magic energy crackled from his tattooed fingers—but instead of flying toward the woman's head, they struck an invisible shield and scattered in all directions. In the same instant, the ring on the woman's finger flared as its gem was illuminated from within. The woman stepped forward, and the tip of the rapier was at Leifander's throat. He swallowed carefully and held perfectly still. The woman had the poise and grace of someone who knew how to use a blade.

"I think I will take you to see my father," she said. "It

should prove an interesting diversion while I'm waiting for Ebeian. But I warn you: Make one move against him, and it will be your last."

The prick of the rapier against his back sent Leifander forward into a large room filled with foliage. Enormous ceramic pots crowded the floor, each planted with a small tree or flowering shrub. Smaller pots hung from the ceiling or sat on shelves, their greenery spilling down. A fountain in the middle of the room bubbled water into a trough that snaked its way across the floor between the pots. This artificial stream was filled with tiny, silver-blue fish. Banks of windows along the two outside walls of the room gave a view of the evening sky.

Leifander was surprised to see several plants he recognized—plants he had thought grew only in the shade of the Tangled Trees. Lady's Lace moss, Burlbush heavy with ripening nuts, a tangle of Honeyfruit vine, and the delicate white blossoms of the triple-leafed Lady's Promise. In the moist air scented with growing and blooming things, he felt a sudden pang of familiarity, then he reminded himself that this was all artificial—that humans must have stolen these plants from his forest and transplanted them to their stinking city. With an added snort of disgust, he noted tiny fingers of choke creeper growing out of three pots whose other seeds appeared to have sprouted and died. The human gardeners didn't even recognize a dangerous infestation when they saw one.

Through the greenery, Leifander could see a man dressed in knee-high boots, blue hose, and a gold doublet with sleeves slashed in blue and white. He stood in profile at one of the windows, the finger of one hand tapping his clean-shaven chin as he stared at the northern horizon with a troubled expression. He was taller than Leifander, but only of average height for a human, with a trim, muscular build. Had he been an elf, his white hair and slightly stooped posture would have caused Leifander to guess his age in the middle hundreds, but this was a human, to whom a single century comprised a lifetime. Leifander pitied their race. By the time he was this man's age, Leifander would still have the reflexes and appearance of a youth.

As if feeling Leifander's stare burning into him, the white-haired man turned. At the same time, a sharp pricking in Leifander's shoulder reminded him of the swordswoman at his back. He stepped forward briskly, and—in deference to the mission the druids had assigned him—placed a hand over his heart and gave the human at the window a courtly bow.

"Thamalon Uskevren, I presume?" he said in the common tongue.

"I am indeed he who bears that name."

Startled, Leifander looked up. Thamalon had spoken in the language of the forest elves—and not in the harsh, guttural accent humans normally mangled the language with. Instead, every syllable was perfect, articulated with flowing grace. Leifander wondered where and how Thamalon, a human of the south, had learned the tongue.

The sword pricked Leifander's back. "Well?" the woman demanded. "Are you going to introduce yourself? Let's hear this message that you snuck into Stormweather Towers to deliver."

Something flashed in Thamalon's deep green eyes—a warning to his daughter? One hand patted the air, instructing her to lower her rapier.

"A little less impetuosity, Thazienne, if you please," he said in the common tongue.

A moment later, Leifander heard steel slithering into a sheath behind him. The woman—Thazienne—stepped from behind him and stood to the side, malicious curiosity dancing in her eyes as she waited to hear what he had to say.

Leifander cleared his throat and held Thamalon's eye. He'd deliver his message quickly, then get on to the important part—asking this man for information about his father.

"My name is Leifander," he said in his own language. "I am an elf of the Tangled Trees. I bear a message from the Circle of the Emerald Leaves."

He paused, watching to see if Thamalon recognized the name. Thamalon nodded briefly. He did.

"The druids wish you to raise your voice in the Sembian council to state that the elves have attacked Sembia's caravans with good cause, to revenge the magical blight humans brought to the great wood. While most of the elves wish war, there are some . . . who will work for peace."

Thamalon's eyes bored into Leifander's. "But you're not one of them, hmm? You'd rather fight."

Leifander squared his shoulders. "I do as I am bid."

"Odd, that the druids would choose you to deliver their message. Are you certain there isn't another message you came to deliver, a message from . . . ?" Thamalon let his sentence trail off, turning it into a question.

Thazienne stood with arms folded across her chest. "Father! How can you listen to this nonsense? He's an assassin—or at the very least, a spy. I caught him in my room, creeping around in the dark."

Thamalon gave a barely audible sigh. "Hardly the first time a young rogue was found there," he muttered. His eyes, however, remained locked on Leifander's. "I'm waiting," he reminded the elf.

Leifander cleared his throat a second time. He decided to say as the druids had bade him, ask Thamalon for whatever information he could provide about his father, then be quit of this place.

"I am told, Thamalon Uskevren, that you have a fondness for the Tangled Trees. That you traveled there some years ago."

Thamalon's eyes brightened with anticipation. "Go on."

"While there, you had union with a woman of my people. That union produced a child."

Out of the corner of his eye, Leifander noted that Thazienne's mouth had dropped open. He hadn't realized that she understood the language of the forest elves—and neither had her father, from the startled look that Thamalon shot her.

Leifander kept an eye on Thamalon, watching for confirmation that the story the druids had told him was true. It came, in the form of a slowly creeping flush that spread upward from the collar of Thamalon's doublet, not quite reaching his cheeks. Thamalon's expression, however, remained utterly unchanging, as if his features had been set in wax.

"Go on," he repeated, this time in a voice crackling with tension. "You've come with a message from Larajin, haven't you? Is that where she's run to—the Tangled Trees? Is she safe—is she well?"

Puzzled, Leifander faltered to a halt. He'd spoken the words that Rylith had made him memorize—a message designed to play upon Thamalon's sympathies for the elves by reminding this human that he'd sired a half-elf child. That child, according to Rylith, lived in Selgaunt, and was named Larajin. It seemed this Larajin had flown from the nest. If Leifander revealed the fact that he knew nothing of her whereabouts, would Thamalon dismiss him without answering the questions that burned inside Leifander?

Thazienne ran fingers through her hair, then broke the strained silence with a question. "Father? Is what this wild elf's saying true? Is Larajin really your daughter?"

Thamalon closed his eyes for a moment, as if gathering strength. "I'm afraid she is." He shot Thazienne a look. "And you are to tell no one—not even your mother—what you have just heard. Am I understood?"

Thazienne started to arch a mocking eyebrow, then thought better of it. "All too well, Father," she said, struggling to keep a straight face. "These . . . impetuosities . . . do happen."

Thamalon glowered at her.

Leifander cleared his throat to remind them that he was still there.

"Sir," he said, "having delivered my message, I wish to speak to you about another matter. The druids told me that you know my father. He is an elf, living here in Selgaunt. I was hoping you could give me news of him."

Thamalon at last tore his eyes away from his daughter. "What is his name?"

Leifander blushed. "I . . . don't know." He reached inside his vest, feeling for his mother's ring. "The druids told me you would know him by his ring. He gave it to my mother, just before he left the Tangled Trees."

Thamalon stiffened as he glanced at the ring. His face blanched still further, and his voice grew strained when he asked, "What was your mother's name?"

"Trisdea. She was a priestess and warrior among her people. She died giving birth to—"

"Trisdea was also the name of Larajin's mother," Thamalon interrupted. "But that can't be. They said . . ." A troubled look came into his eyes. "How old are you?"

"Twenty-five."

Thazienne snorted. "The same age as Larajin? How convenient," she said, in a voice dripping with sarcasm. "Father, you can guess what's coming next. This elf is going to tell you some ridiculous story—that he's Larajin's twin, or something."

"No," Leifander protested. "My father was—"

"Then he'll try to claim his inheritance," Thazienne continued, "just like the last Uskevren 'heir' did. This fellow may have learned your dark secret, but whatever he says next will be lies and nonsense. He hasn't got a shred of proof that—"

Thamalon turned on his daughter, his voice pitched dangerously low. "Look there," he said, pointing a quivering finger at the ring that hung at Leifander's throat. "That ring. I was the man who gave it to his mother, twenty-five years ago, as a token of my affection. Leifander is indeed . . . my son."

Thazienne's mouth fell open in mute surprise. Her eyes darted from the ring to her father, then back to Leifander again. She gaped at him, as if seeing him for the first time. The shock she must have felt, however, was a pale shadow of Leifander's own.

"I'm no *human*!" he said, spitting out the word. "Nor even half-human. You're wrong!"

"I'm afraid not," said Thamalon. "Your story meshes with my own, like two hands folded together. I lay with Trisdea, and later, during my second visit to the Tangled Trees, learned that she had become pregnant by me. The elves told me that she died giving birth to that child—that although there was a cleric present at the birth, his magic could not save her. That her death was the will of the gods. They also told me she bore twins, but that only one lived. Now I see that they lied."

"Twins?" Leifander echoed.

Could it be true? He could feel his eyes widening. According to the ancient tales, twins were favored of the gods—twice blessed and destined for great and noble deeds.

He was too upset to say more. All he could do was stare at Thamalon. With a growing horror, he realized that what Thamalon was saying must indeed be true. Now Leifander knew why the druids had chosen him to convey their message, why they had said that by doing so, he would learn who his father was. They'd told him the truth, but now Leifander wished they hadn't. His father . . . a human? He couldn't believe it. He wouldn't believe it.

But part of him had already accepted this terrible fact. He thought back to the taunts he'd endured in his youth—taunts thrown at him by an elf many years his senior who had teased Leifander by calling him "round ears." At the time, he'd shrugged it off—his ears were as pointed as any other elf's—but Leifander's adoptive father had taken the incident more seriously, and had come to blows with the man. Later, when the fellow disappeared, there had been rumors that Leifander's father had killed him. At the time, Leifander had dismissed this as idle gossip, knowing there was nothing that could have prodded his father into so brutal an act.

He realized, now, that he'd been wrong. His adoptive father must have known all along that Leifander was indeed half-human. He'd killed the man to spare Leifander the shame of it.

A part of Leifander, however, still struggled with the revelation. How could he be part human? He had the look of a full-blood elf! Then he realized that subtle hints had been there, all along. He'd always been tall and somewhat heavyset for his age. His deep auburn hair was much darker than the autumn-leaf red of the other elves. Added all together, it seemed like damning evidence against him being a full-blooded elf.

He stared at Thamalon, searching for any resemblance, but just could not see it. Thamalon looked so human, and yet this man's blood flowed in his veins.

Human blood.

With that thought came a second realization, even more terrible than the first. If human blood flowed in Leifander's veins, that meant his life expectancy would be half what it should be—less than two hundred years. He stared at Thamalon with narrowed eyes, suddenly hating him.

Leifander started to turn, intending to stride back down the hall to the nearest balcony and fly off into the night, but Thamalon stepped forward and caught his arm. Though the fingers that gripped him were strong, the touch was a light one, imploring, rather than commanding.

"Please," Thamalon said. "Stay a little longer. I would like to speak with you further, my son."

Leifander tried in vain to keep from wincing at the word. "I must leave," he snapped. "Tonight."

"Must you?" Thamalon asked. "A pity. I'd have liked to have told you more about your mother."

Thazienne, having been roundly scolded, was keeping her silence, but her eyes spoke volumes. She shook her head, obviously still not believing a word of it.

Thamalon turned to her. "Please leave us, Thazienne. I

wish to speak to Leifander in private."

Thazienne opened her mouth to protest, then thought better of it. Lips pressed together in a tight, angry line, she turned on her heel and strode away.

Thamalon watched the door close behind her, then turned back to Leifander. His eyes lingered on the ring at Leifander's throat.

"I think there will be much for us to speak about," he said. "Did you know that your mother was a Harper?"

Surprised, Leifander shook his head. If it were true, not even the elves of the Tangled Trees had known it. What other surprises did this man have in store?

His curiosity piqued, he said grudgingly, "I'll stay . . . until I've heard you out, but then I must go."

"Fair enough," Thamalon said. He motioned to a bench under one of the windows. Leifander sat on it, on the far side from where Thamalon settled. Sire this man might be, but father? Never.

The older man looked off through the window at the stars, and absently tapped a finger against his chin, thinking.

"Well then," the human mused. "Where to begin?"

CHAPTER 5

Larajin followed the wild elves east through the forest. The route they took was a winding one, along game trails all but invisible to Larajin's eyes. Even before dusk fell, she was completely turned around. When the darkness became complete, she would have lost her way entirely, save for the firm grip Doriantha had on her elbow.

Larajin expected the elves to halt for the night, but they stopped only briefly to eat a few handfuls of dried berries and to drink from a stream. Then they journeyed on through the darkness, winding their way between the trees as if they had the eyesight of owls. Even Larajin, with her excellent night vision, was hard-pressed to keep up the pace.

By the time morning dawned, she was exhausted. Even if they had stopped long enough for her to perform the morning devotions, she would have been too tired to do them properly. She kept hoping that Doriantha would at last announce that they had reached the Tangled Trees, but the march east continued as the sun rose in the sky. The farther they got from Rauthauvyr's Road, the thicker the forest became. Larajin stumbled over roots and fought her way through prickling branches, skinning her hands and muddying the knees of her trouser skirt in scrambles up steep slopes.

The elves seemed unperturbed by the forest, moving through it with the quiet canniness of wild animals. Their bare feet skipped lightly across moss-slick stones that sent Larajin skidding into icy streams. They deftly avoided the broken branches of wind-fallen trees that snagged and tore Larajin's clothing and knew how to space themselves so that a branch bent by the elf ahead did not strike the person following.

After receiving yet another stinging slap in the face from the bent branch of a fir, Larajin wondered if the elves were deliberately leading her through the densest forest growth in an effort to test her ability to follow them. Resolving not to appear weak, she blinked the grit out of her eyes and stumbled stubbornly on, hot, sweaty, and footsore. More than once she heard low mutters from those ahead, always including a word that was spoken as though it were a curse—a word in the Elvish tongue she was coming to recognize—the word for human.

Larajin glanced up at the sky frequently, hoping to see Goldheart winging her way above the treetops. Once, she saw a flash of crimson and her heart leaped—until she realized that it was only the brilliant red plumage of a woodpecker. Reminding herself that she had released the tressym from any further obligation, Larajin eventually stopped looking for her. It was all she could do to keep her exhausted eyes open—and to watch for the next tree root.

When the elves paused at a stream to drink, Larajin noticed with dismay that sweat had long since washed away the gold eye the priest had painted on her midriff. She offered a quick prayer of apology to Sune, asking forgiveness for her disheveled condition, and another to Hanali Celanil. She'd had no opportunity to sing the Song of Sunrise that morning or pay reverent homage to the sunset the night before. Perhaps these transgressions were the reason Sune was ignoring her prayers. It was Hanali Celanil who answered. The air filled with the floral scent of Hanali's Heart, and Larajin's exhaustion floated away, the blisters on her feet closed, and the ache in her muscles eased.

Thankful for this boon, Larajin pulled the tressym's broken feather from the pocket of her shirt and cast it into the water, commending it to the goddess. The broken feather twirled a moment in a pool, flashing red and turquoise and yellow, then it was caught by the current and carried away.

The elves set out again a few moments later, bidding with curt gestures for Larajin to follow. They didn't seem to want her with them and did little enough to aid her but kept her in sight even so, as if worried she would become lost. They were probably just following Doriantha's orders, since none seemed inclined toward friendship. They spoke no Common and glared at Larajin with fierce looks when she tried to speak to them in the language of the wild elves. Even Doriantha said little, preferring to save her breath for the tromp through the woods.

Doriantha, however, did seem to care how Larajin was faring. From time to time she doubled back to point out the best path through a thicket or to lend a steadying hand as Larajin tried to cross a stream on a narrow log. When Larajin lagged behind, Doriantha appeared at her side, giving her a drink from her waterskin. Even so, the pace was so rapid that Larajin's strength began to flag once more as the afternoon wore on. With every step, she prayed it would be the last one necessary to take her to the Tangled Trees.

The elves seemed to be in a hurry to get there. Larajin could guess why. They feared retribution, once the humans discovered what they had done.

When they'd crossed Rauthauvyr's Road, Larajin had caught a glimpse of the aftermath of their attack on the caravan. It hadn't been a pretty sight. The elves had smashed the cargo and left the bodies strewn on the road for the crows to pick at. Larajin had nearly tripped over one sellsword whose body was so pincushioned with arrows that Larajin suspected the elves had used him for target practice as he lay dying. After that, she'd averted her eyes, not wanting to see any more bodies. She'd been glad once they were across the road and into the woods once more.

She'd felt no pity for the sellswords, only revulsion at the brutality of the elves' attack. The only one whose fate she cared about was Dray—the poor dupe. Not only had he fallen for Enik's ruse, he'd also had the misfortune to be in the wrong place at the wrong time. She hadn't seen his corpse as the elves hurried her across the road, but there was little hope that he had survived the attack.

She whispered a prayer for his soul, hoping whatever god he'd worshiped had taken pity on him. Dray was only a merchant; he hadn't deserved to be slaughtered with the rest of them. Once the Foxmantles learned of this atrocity their wrath would know no bounds. Not even the deepest shadows of the Tangled Trees would provide a hiding place for Doriantha and her band.

In contrast to their callous indifference toward the humans they had killed, the elves had shown a reverence for their own kind. Despite their rush to get away from the road, they had tarried long enough to gather up the bones and weapons from the tomb that Klarsh had unearthed. They packed these gruesome relics along with them still—probably carrying them home for reburial, Larajin guessed.

Struggling through the forest behind Doriantha, Larajin wondered if she was doing the right thing in following the elves. Doriantha's band had done Larajin a favor by saving her from Enik and his men, but that aid was only coincidental. What sort of reception would Larajin face once she reached the Tangled Trees? Judging by the attitudes of these elves, it wouldn't be the homecoming Larajin had naively imagined, back in the comfort of Stormweather Towers.

As darkness descended on the forest for the second time since their journey began, the elves at last stopped to make camp. They gathered clumps of pale green moss that hung from tree branches, long and lacy as an old man's beard, and formed it into nestlike pillows. They splashed their sweaty faces in a nearby stream, stretched their muscles, and ate a cold supper of leathery slabs of dried mushroom and a cold paste made by adding water to a powder of dried fish. Then they sank cross-legged onto the moss, weapons within hand's reach on the forest floor beside them, and sank into the meditative state unique to elves, known as the Reverie.

As Doriantha settled down beside her, Larajin fought to keep her eyes open just a little longer. A question burned inside her, one she'd been wanting the answer for ever since they'd set out but had no time to ask.

"Doriantha," she said, "you said I looked nothing like my brother. Did Mast—" She paused, and amended what she had been about to say. In the woods, she was a servant no longer, answerable only to herself. It didn't feel right using the title "master," anymore. "Did Thamalon the Younger or Talbot ever visit the Tangled Trees?"

Larajin could see little of Doriantha's face, save for the dark line of the tattoo across her nose and cheeks, and the glint of her eyes. It was impossible to tell what her expression was.

"The names you mention," Doriantha said quietly, "are these the children of Thamalon Uskevren?"

"Yes. He has two sons and a daughter."

"Full-blood human?"

"Yes, all three." Larajin yawned, blinking sleep-heavy eyes.

"They are only half-sister and half-brothers to you, then." Her voice dropped to a whisper. "No, I was speaking of your twin."

Exhausted as she was, it took Larajin a moment to fully appreciate what Doriantha had just said. When she did, she sat up, all thoughts of sleep having fled.

"I have a twin brother?" she exclaimed.

Rustling noises told her that she had disturbed some of the other elves with her outburst. She could see Doriantha shaking her head and gesturing for silence, but she didn't care. The news was amazing, almost impossible to believe. She wondered what her twin brother looked like. Was he, like her, struggling with the question of whether he was elf, or human, or something in-between? Or had he known of his mixed heritage all along?

A stray thought stopped her cold.

"Doriantha," she whispered. "Is my brother still alive?"

Doriantha glanced around. "Please—you must keep your voice low. Some of the others might understand what you say."

Larajin nodded, and Doriantha went on. "As far as I know, your twin is still alive. He was hale and hearty, when I last saw him several days ago."

"Where is he now?"

"As to that . . ." Doriantha paused, and in the starlit darkness, Larajin saw her shrug. "I only know that the druids sent him to do their bidding, far to the south."

"South? To the Dales—or do you mean Sembia? How long ago?"

Dread coursed through Larajin as she remembered the wild elves who had defended her eighteen months ago in the Hunting Garden. Had her twin brother also run afoul of Drakkar and been charred to a gruesome corpse by the wizard's dark magic?

Doriantha tilted her head back to peer up at the sky through the thick tangle of branches overhead.

"He left within the moon," she answered at last.

"Less than a month ago, you mean?"

Doriantha nodded, then added, "He didn't tell me his

destination. The druids forbade him to speak of it. You can, perhaps, think of a reason why."

After a moment's thought, Larajin guessed the answer: the impending war. Her twin brother had gone south to Sembia then, probably as a spy, since, like her, he could no doubt pass as fully human. She prayed that he hadn't ventured into Ordulin and been sniffed out and beaten by the mob.

She shook her head at the irony. All the while she had been heading north, to the Tangled Trees, her twin had been traveling in the other direction. For all she knew, they might have passed each other as strangers on Rauthauvyr's Road.

"Tell me more about my brother," she said. "What's his name? What does he look like?"

"His name is Leifander, and as I said before, he looks nothing like you. His hair is a similar color, but his eyes are a different shade of hazel. He's broad-shouldered, and tall, and looks . . . much more like the people of the forest."

"Was he raised by wild elves?" Larajin asked.

"He was."

Larajin nodded to herself. It made sense. Of course her twin would look more like a wild elf. If he had been raised among them, he would wear their clothes, style his hair the way they did, perhaps even have marked his face with those fearsome-looking tattoos.

"If the wild elves raised my brother then why . . . ?" Larajin paused, and cleared the catch in her throat with a soft cough. "Why was he kept and I given to my father?"

"From what I understand, that was a mistake. A woman of our people was found to wet-nurse your brother, but she didn't have milk enough for two infants, as well as her own. The human wet nurse was to have been only a temporary measure."

"Yet she became my mother," Larajin whispered. "Or rather, the woman who raised me. Her name is Shonri Wellrun."

Doriantha had paused to peer through the darkness at Larajin. "Perhaps it was not a misunderstanding on your father's part, after all," she mused. "Perhaps Thamalon Uskevren saw how human you looked and decided to keep you." She shrugged. "Whatever the reason, there are some who feel he committed a grievous sin. They believe that those who share a womb must never be sundered—that great ill comes of it. Of course, there are others who take a broader view, that your father was only playing his part in pushing the wheel of fate along its preordained path."

"What of our mother?" Larajin asked, uncomfortable with all this talk of destiny. "Tell me about her."

"Trisdea was a famous warrior. One of our most accomplished archers. At a young age—she was just seventy at the time—she distinguished herself at the battle of Singing Arrows. When the fletch tally was taken at the battle's end, her arrows were found to have felled nearly a hundred of the enemy."

Larajin listened with rapt attention. That battle, according to the history books, took place nearly five centuries ago. Doing a quick calculation, she realized that her mother had been more than five hundred years old when she'd given birth to her. For the first time, Larajin realized the implications of having elf blood in her veins. She herself might have a life span double that of a human: two centuries or more. She suddenly felt very young, indeed.

"What did Trisdea look like?"

"Her hair was copper-red, and she wore it loose upon her shoulders. Her eyes, brown. When she was angry, or in battle, they darkened to the color of smoldering coals. When she was in prayer, they grew lighter, to the shade of blond wood. She was quick in her movements and nimble with the bow, but her stubbornness would make a boulder look fickle."

Larajin thought her mother was everything she could have hoped for: noble, proud, and free—a wild elf, with windblown hair and tattooed cheeks.

"What else can you tell me about Trisdea? Did you know her well?"

"Everyone knew of her," Doriantha answered obliquely. "Trisdea was also renowned as a cleric—one might say infamous. She studied among the moon elves, and learned from them the worship of Angharradh of the three faces. That belief is rare in the Tangled Wood. We pay homage to each aspect separately, as a goddess in her own right." She raised a hand, and ticked off the goddesses on her fingers. "Hanali Celanil, who sent the tressym to aid you; Aerdrie Faenya, lady of air and wind; and Sehanine Moonbow, mistress of moonlight.

"Trisdea tried to persuade the elves of the Tangled Trees to worship all three goddesses in a single form but was not successful. Even her stature as a great warrior was not enough to sway our clerics. She clove to this notion stubbornly until the day she died, though she must have realized its futility. We wood elves worship in the old way and are slow to change."

Larajin nodded, realizing that she must have inherited her stubborn streak from her mother. Like Trisdea, who had refused to divide her devotions, instead worshiping three goddesses in a single, triune form, Larajin had chosen a difficult path. She balanced her devotions, giving praise in what she hoped was equal measure to both Sune and Hanali Celanil.

Having heard Doriantha's story, she now wondered if, like Angharradh, the two goddesses she had chosen to worship were a single whole—two sides of the same coin. One with a human face, the other with the face of an elf.

"Is my brother Leifander also a cleric?" she asked.

Doriantha nodded. "He pays homage to Aerdrie Faenya, queen of the winds. He's a skinwalker."

"What's that?"

"He can shift his form from elf to bird and back again."

Larajin nodded, savoring the wonder of it. She tried to imagine how riding the winds high above would feel but could not. If her twin could fly, no wonder she had not seen him on Rauthauvyr's Road. She said a quick prayer for his safety, bidding the goddesses to protect him on his journey south and his return to the Tangled Trees.

A realization came to her then. In five hundred years of adulthood, her elf mother could have given birth to many children.

"Do I have other brothers and sisters?" Breathlessly, she awaited the answer, imagining an entire clan of relatives waiting for her in the Tangled Trees, soon to be met.

"Only one," Doriantha answered. "A sister, who was born and grew old many years before you and Leifander came into this world. Her name was Somnilthra, and she was a great seer. She foretold many things during her time among us. She prophesied that Trisdea would die, were she to bear children again, and her prophesy rang true. Trisdea was much too old to be going through the rigors of childbirth—impossibly old to have become pregnant, some said. Somnilthra also foresaw—"

Doriantha stopped abruptly. Larajin waited, but the silence only lengthened.

"What?" she prompted at last.

"I am overstepping myself," Doriantha said. "I forget that some stories are not mine to tell. Suffice it to say that Trisdea did not heed her daughter's warning and now lies buried in the Vale of Lost Voices in a tomb befitting a warrior of her stature."

Larajin let this go without further comment. Instead, she mused over all she had just been told and started to see a pattern. Her mother worshiped the triune goddess, of whom Hanali Celanil, the goddess Larajin prayed to, was one aspect. Her brother Leifander worshiped a second aspect of the triune, the winged goddess Aerdrie Faenya, and Doriantha had said that their elder half-sister, Somnilthra, was a seer, gifted with foresight by the gods.

"Was Somnilthra a cleric, too?" Larajin asked.

Doriantha nodded. "She worshiped the Lunar Lady, goddess of dreams."

Larajin was puzzled for a moment. The elves seemed to have

a dozen different names for each god and goddess.

"Sehanine Moonbow?" she guessed.

"The same."

There it was: a pattern, woven into all four lives. A mother who worshiped three goddesses in one—and three children, each drawn to one of that goddess's aspects. What other strange and unseen patterns were the gods weaving through her life? Larajin could only wonder.

"You spoke of Somnilthra in the past tense," she added. "Is she dead?"

Doriantha placed a palm over her heart. "She has entered eternal Reverie. She dreams in Arvanaith."

Arvanaith. Larajin had read about it in one of the books in Stormweather Towers's library. It was said to be a final resting place—a heaven—that the souls of venerable elves slipped away to when their time on this earth was done. From all accounts—all of them hearsay, since the author of the book was human—Arvanaith was a beautiful place, a paradise where an aged soul prepared for its eventual return to this world. Larajin wondered if half-elves journeyed there too when they grew old and died. She prayed to Hanali Celanil that it was so.

Yawning, she fought to keep her eyes open. Wind sighed through the branches of the trees that sheltered them, carrying the scents of loam and leaves. The soft moss she lay upon was a welcoming pillow that beckoned her to sleep. Beside her, Doriantha had settled again on her own bed, her stories seemingly at an end.

"How far is it now to the Tangled Trees?" Larajin asked, stifling yet another yawn.

"If we rise at first light, we'll reach camp by tomorrow evening. Just in time for the Turning."

Larajin was too sleepy to ask what that was. Instead she sank onto her mossy bed and drifted into an exhausted sleep, dreaming of the mother and sister she had never met—and of the brother she hoped to meet someday soon.

❂ ❂ ❂ ❂ ❂

The first warning that they were approaching the elven camp came in the form of a snarl from the treetops, ahead and to the left. It was echoed a moment later by a loud *yeowl*, directly overhead. An enormous shape hurtled down through the tangle of branches, landing with feline grace no more than two paces ahead of Larajin. Round eyes glared at her, and sharp white teeth glinted in the moonlight as a giant lynx stared her down. Its tail lashed behind it as it growled and its ears were flat against its head. Suddenly wide awake, Larajin froze, barely daring to breathe.

Doriantha spoke a sharp word in the wild elves' tongue. Tail still lashing, the lynx gave Larajin one last baleful glare, then turned and padded obediently toward Doriantha. The elves behind Larajin laughed as Doriantha stroked the head of the lynx, which rubbed against her like a contented house cat. One of them nudged Larajin forward.

Angry at herself for being so frightened of what was obviously one of the wild elves' pets, Larajin stumbled forward on aching feet, following Doriantha and the lynx. Ahead in the forest, she could see the dark shapes of tents sprinkled among the trees. They were round and squat, like mushrooms. Under the thick canopy of branches their brown leather would have been invisible from the skies above. While most of the tents were silent and dark, Larajin could hear low voices murmuring inside one or two of those she passed by, and the occasional giggle or moan that made would have made her blush, had she not been so exhausted.

After walking for a few moments more, she saw a small tent up ahead that was illuminated from within. A single figure moved inside it, casting a dark shadow on its strangely mottled walls, which glowed a bright, translucent green.

As they drew nearer to this tent, Doriantha paused and spoke another command to the lynx. It turned and leaped into a tree, climbing swiftly up its trunk. One of the elves protested the lynx's departure, gesturing at Larajin, but Doriantha cut him off with a curt word. She spoke at length to the members of her patrol in their own language, and at last they grudgingly nodded their heads.

She turned then, to Larajin. "There is someone inside the tent who will want to meet you," she said quietly, "an important person, a druid of the Circle of Emerald Leaves. Please do not give the members of my patrol any cause for alarm."

Larajin glanced around her, and saw that several of Doriantha's band had their hands close to the hilts of their daggers. One had even unlimbered her bow and was silently stringing it. Larajin started to raise her hands to demonstrate that they were empty, then thought better of it. The locket that hung around her wrist could be as effective as any weapon, if the goddess so willed it. She didn't want to remind the elves of its presence.

Instead she nodded, and meekly followed Doriantha while the other elves waited behind. She could feel their suspicious eyes upon her back, all the way to the tent.

The mottled texture proved to be the result of the tent's construction. The walls were stitched together from hundreds of overlapping leaves of every shape and size. From within came the sound of a woman singing in the wild elves' tongue. Intrigued though Larajin was, exhaustion and the raw ache of her blistered feet made her wish that Doriantha had saved this introduction with whoever waited inside until morning.

Doriantha paused outside the tent and drummed her fingers against its taut leaf wall, then spoke a single word, "Rylith?"

It must have been the name of whoever was inside the tent, for the singing immediately stopped. Doriantha added something more, speaking quickly in the wild elves' tongue. Larajin heard her own name spoken by the person inside, then Leifander's. Doriantha shook her head and answered with an Elvish word Larajin understood: "No."

The singing began again, and suddenly an opening

appeared in its wall, just in front of where Doriantha stood. It was as if the leaves had blown away in the wind. Grasping Larajin's arm, Doriantha led her inside.

As they entered the tent, the wall of leaves became solid again behind them. Looking around, Larajin at first wondered if her mind was playing tricks on her. It was almost as if they were standing in a forest glen on a sunny day. Instead of bare earth, as she had expected, the floor of the tent was covered in thick, lush grass, trimmed as neatly as any carpet and sprinkled with miniature white daisies. Above, against the dome of the roof, the sun seemed to be shining. It took Larajin a moment of squinting to realize that the light must have been the result of a spell. A network of branches grew out of the ground and wove its way around the interior of the tent, forming shelves, a low bed, and a bench against its walls. This living furniture was dotted with bright green leaves and tiny yellow flowers, which gave off a sweet, citruslike smell.

Seated on the bench was an elf with gray hair and dark tree-branch tattoos on her cheeks and chin. A band of silver leaves in her hair glittered where the magical light struck it, and over her leather breeches and vest she wore a cloak that looked as though it had been woven from autumn leaves of red and orange and yellow.

The woman gave Larajin an intense, expectant look. "You are Trisdea's daughter?" she asked in fluent Common.

Larajin nodded.

The druid sighed. Larajin couldn't tell if the sound was one of relief—or something else. Was Rylith disappointed in what she saw? Had she expected Larajin to look more like an elf?

Doriantha placed both hands upon her chest, over her heart, and bowed low in the direction of the gray-haired woman. From the deference she paid Rylith, Larajin guessed that the druid was both important and powerful, perhaps as highly placed among her people as the Hulorn himself. Larajin, not wanting to insult her, imitated Doriantha's bow.

She must have done it wrong, for Rylith chuckled. She rose from her seat and strode to where Larajin stood, her leaf-cloak rustling. She bowed briefly in Doriantha's direction, then took Larajin's hands in hers.

"You have come at last," she said. "Welcome."

"Thank you," Larajin fumbled. "I am glad to have finally reached the Tangled Trees and found my . . . my mother's people. I hope I will be—"

"Welcome?" Rylith asked, as if reading Larajin's mind. The tattoos on her cheeks folded into grandmotherly wrinkles as she smiled. "Set your mind at ease, child. I will speak on your behalf."

Relief washed over Larajin as she met the gray-haired woman's eyes. Rylith had a presence that was at once calming—and commanding. If she told the elves of the Tangled Trees to welcome Larajin, so it would be.

Rylith said something to Doriantha, who nodded and picked up a small earthenware jar from one of the shelves. She passed this jug to Rylith, who unstoppered it and offered it to Larajin. The fruity smell of fermented berries rose from within. Larajin glanced down, and saw that the jar was filled with a blue-black liquid.

"A mild draught," Rylith said. "One that will help you to relax and to sleep. Your arrival is fortuitous. Tomorrow is the Turning, an important day among our people. The dance begins at dawn. I want you to be well rested. Until then," she added, glancing at Doriantha as she spoke, "I think Larajin should remain here with me, in my tent."

Doriantha nodded and returned Rylith's glance with a look bordering on relief. The warrior's shoulders, set so square a moment ago, at last relaxed. For the first time, Larajin realized that she'd made it as far as the Tangled Trees only thanks to Doriantha and was very thankful that Doriantha had been the first elf she'd met. Any of the other elves in the patrol would have taken one look at Larajin's too-human face, and feathered her with an arrow on the spot. Now, noticing the looks that Rylith and Doriantha exchanged, Larajin wondered what secret they shared.

"What's going to happen tomorrow?" Larajin asked.

Rylith nudged Larajin's hand, motioning for her to drink. "Trust in me," she said. "You've come too far not to. Tomorrow you'll get your answers."

Exhausted, aching in every muscle and nearly asleep on her feet, Larajin shrugged. What, really, did she have to fear? If the druid wanted to harm her, she could have done so long before now. The awe in which Doriantha regarded Rylith suggested that the druid's magic was strong. Larajin had no more reason to mistrust Rylith than she did to trust the elves of Doriantha's patrol who waited outside the tent with daggers and bows.

She nodded, and swallowed the liquid. It turned out to be as sweet as it smelled, though it burned like one of the Uskevren's strongest brandies. Wiping her lips with her hand, Larajin handed the jug back to Rylith. When she saw the blue-black stain the liquid had left across the back of her hand, she imagined her lips were a dark blue. The thought made her giggle and hiccup. As giggle and hiccup alternated, she became more relaxed. Doriantha disappeared somewhere into the distance, and Rylith's face and the walls of the tent began to blur, then soft, wrinkled hands were leading Larajin to bed.

Gratefully, she sank into the blankets, and nuzzled her face into the sweet-smelling blossoms that grew on the vine-woven bed.

Tomorrow, she told herself, echoing Rylith's words. I'll find my answers then.

Larajin squatted on the ground, surrounded by hundreds of elves who were drumming, feasting, and singing. They had gathered in a sun-dappled clearing in the forest, at the center of which was an ornately carved wooden pole. As thick as Larajin's waist and about one and a half times the height of an elf, the pole had been inscribed with Elvish runes that spiraled from the bottom to the top, which was carved in the shape of an acorn.

All around this pole, elves danced. Drums of every description guided their footsteps. Enormous hollow logs boomed low when struck with massive clubs by teams of drummers, taut-skinned drums clenched between knees were pounded with bare palms, dancing fingers tapped hand drums, and ornately carved hardwood sticks clicked together. The primitive music struck a chord deep in Larajin's soul. Excitement filled her as her heart kept pace with the frenzied rhythm.

The elves had been drumming and dancing since dawn, when a camp crier, perched high in a tree above, announced that the sun had crested the treetops. Now the sun was almost directly overhead, and they were hot, sweaty, and drooping, pausing only long enough to slake their thirst with large quaffs of nut-flavored ale that had been chilled in a shaded forest stream. Yet despite the growing heat of the day, the dancing and drumming continued without pause, fresh dancers springing to their feet to replace those who flagged.

Larajin watched, fascinated. The elves of the Tangled Trees looked just as savage as those portrayed in the master's books, but had a proud, noble quality about them that the engravings had failed to capture. Their tattooed faces, red-blond hair twisted with feathers and bones, bare feet, and rustic leather breeches and vests might give them a primitive appearance that would be scoffed at in fashion-conscious Selgaunt, but their dances were every bit as intricate as a quick-step quadrille or tarantella. The movements were physically demanding, suggestive of martial prowess—even the women's parts. Dancers hurtled into the air, propelled over the heads of their partners, spun furiously in a low squat that erupted into a sudden back flip, or leaped into the air, heels kicking high above their heads. Larajin was dizzy just watching.

Or perhaps it was the lingering effects of the draught Rylith had given her the night before, combined with the ale. She took another long swallow and wiped the foam from her lips, savoring the warm, muzzy glow the ale provided. With each sip, the world seemed somehow brighter, warmer, more welcoming. The ale was also helping to ease the ache in her legs and lower back left by the long march through the forest.

Every now and again, a wooden platter of food passed round from hand to hand, always finding its way to the spot where Larajin sat. She recognized none of the dishes but savored their exotic tastes. There were slices of sticky-sweet orange fruit, squares of roasted meat flavored with salt and the smoke of an open campfire, crisp curl-topped ferns cooked with pungent mushrooms, and brown bread crunchy with seeds and nuts. All of it had been prepared over simple cookfires inside the brown leather tents that surrounded the clearing.

Glancing over the heads of the dancers, Larajin caught sight of Rylith. The druid was walking around the pole in a slow circle that had begun in a crouch at dawn, fingers tracing the spiraling script. Several times, she glanced up at the acorn at the top of the pole—or perhaps to the sky above it—but most of the time her attention was on the ground. She seemed to be measuring the shadow cast by the pole. All morning it had been growing shorter until it was less than a palm's width long.

Nobody had taken the time yet to explain to Larajin what was going on, but she found that she didn't care. Rylith had indeed spoken to the elves, and as she'd promised, Larajin was a welcome guest. Even the elves of Doriantha's patrol, who had been so suspicious, had in the morning greeted Larajin with welcoming smiles.

Every elf Larajin had met that morning, in fact, had been overly attentive to her, greeting her with the same bow that Rylith had. They made sure her ale cup was full, and that the platters of food did not pass her by. The fierce challenges of the night before were gone, replaced by coy, curious glances.

No wonder, Larajin thought. The elves of the Tangled Trees received few human visitors and fewer still who claimed to have wild elf blood flowing in their veins. No, *forest* elf, Larajin corrected herself. That was what these people called themselves, and so should she. Though Larajin was willing to embrace them as kin, it would be another matter altogether to get them to see her in the same light. They were obviously still a bit wary of her completely human appearance—more than once, she caught them staring at her. Which was strange, since they shouldn't have been surprised by the way she looked, after having Leifander grow up among them.

Larajin returned her attention to the dancers. She longed to ask the elves next to her what the celebration was all about, but the few words of Forest Elf that she spoke had proved barely enough to do more than exchange names. All she could make out was that the dance had something to do with the sun and the year, which was either beginning or ending—or both. Perhaps it was a primitive version of the Midsummer Night celebrations she'd attended a year before in the temple of Sune. She wondered if it would end, like them, with couples slipping away to consummate their flirtations.

Between the throbbing drumbeats, Larajin heard a cry of pain, echoing out of the forest. Startled, she sprang to her feet and glanced around, thinking that someone had been injured, but an elf woman beside her shook her head and gestured for her to sit down again. The woman patted her stomach, then mimed holding a baby in her arms.

Larajin nodded, understanding. The cry was that of a woman in labor. Seating herself again, she wondered if she, too, had been born during a gathering like this, surrounded by enormous trees in a leaf-shadowed tent smelling of the moss that lined its floor, while outside, elves drummed and danced. It was a far cry from the formal halls of Stormweather Towers, where births took place in rooms with scrubbed stone floors, clean beds, and trained midwives.

Taking another sip of ale, Larajin basked in the warm glow it left her with and nodded in time with the music. Despite having been there less than a day, she was already coming to understand the forest elves. In just one morning she had learned the polite way to eat, with just her first two fingers and thumb instead of the whole hand. The elves had also taught her the proper way to greet a friend, with one hand on her heart. Especially honored guests were greeted with both hands—in the manner that Doriantha had bowed to Rylith. They had even suggested, tapping a finger against her cheek, that she adopt their custom by getting a facial tattoo. Giddy with ale, she was actually considering it.

Larajin nodded and smiled at the elves around her, thanking them for each new bit of lore. Despite the fact that they were instructing her in matters of formal etiquette—something Erevis Cale had tried to drum into her ever since she was born, much to her dislike—she felt at home there, a lost daughter returned to her roots. The forest elves were a strange and wild folk, to be sure, but being among them somehow felt . . . comfortable. Like her, they didn't worry about getting dirt on their knees or brambles in their hair.

Larajin shared their love of the forest and their delight at being surrounded by green and growing things. Having nothing but an open sky overhead made her feel free. She felt at home there—more than she ever had within the dusty confines of Stormweather Towers—and safe from Drakkar's threats. The forest elves had accepted her, would protect her.

Some of their customs were strange, but they fit her more comfortably than did a servant's quiet obedience. These people had a way of holding themselves, of walking and sitting, that mirrored her own. For the first time, her own mannerisms seemed natural. She missed Tal, and her friend Kremlar, and dear old Habrith, but in the Tangled Trees, she was among her own people. Here, at last, was a place she could call home.

As the sun climbed still higher in the sky, a patch of bright sunlight found her. Filtered through the branches though it was, the sunlight was hot on her shoulders and the crown of her head. Larajin rose to her knees, intending to shift to a patch of shade, when, as one, all of the drums stopped. She looked up, and saw Rylith standing rigidly at the center of the clearing, one hand extended overhead, face upturned and fingers splayed as she reached toward the sun. Around her, all of the dancers had sagged to the ground. They sat, panting, eyes locked on the druid.

As Rylith stood, stiff as a statue, a haze of heat formed in the air above her outstretched hand. Small as a clenched fist, confusing to the eye, the shimmer flickered rapidly back and forth between flame-white and shadow-black. At the same time, a beam of sunlight lanced straight down onto the pole while an ink-dark shadow seeped out from its base and began to creep upward in a slow spiral. Light and shadow met at the acorn atop the pole and crackled there with magical energy. Even though she sat a good distance away, Larajin's nose tickled, and the hair rose on the back of her neck. She felt as if a thunderstorm was crackling overhead, about to break over her.

A gasp whispered through the crowd when Rylith clenched her hand shut around the flickering heat haze. She lowered her hand to her chest, as if clutching something precious, then lifted it to her lips and whispered to it. Her gaze ranged over the assembled crowd, and as it lingered, then passed over each elf, he or she gasped expectantly, then gave a disappointed sigh.

Then the druid seemed to find what she had been searching for. She stared in Larajin's direction, and Larajin, still half sitting and half kneeling, twisted around to glance behind her. Several of the elves seated behind her were leaning forward expectantly, eyes locked on the druid. Their faces fell. Turning around again, Larajin saw that Rylith had moved away from the pole and had stepped to within a few paces of her. The druid gestured with her free hand for Larajin to rise.

Uncertain why she had been singled out, Larajin obeyed and found she was unsteady on her feet. With an effort, she regained her equilibrium. She didn't want to embarrass herself by falling over, not with the elves all around her looking up at her with expectant faces. Rylith stepped closer, and Larajin could hear the whirring of the magical energy the druid cupped in her hand. It was a high-pitched, fluttering noise, like the sound of a hummingbird's wings.

Rylith was speaking, addressing the crowd. The language of the forest elves flowed swiftly from her lips, as clear and high as a mountain stream or the ripple of a wind through the wood. Larajin caught only a word or two—her own name, and Leifander's, and the Elvish word for twins—then Rylith opened her hand. In one swift motion, before Larajin could jerk away, the druid threw the ball of magical energy. It shot forward with the speed of an arrow. In the instant that it entered her, Larajin saw a tiny white feather strike her chest, then flutter to the ground.

She gasped as sunlight flared in her eyes, washing her vision white. Waves of heat and cold gripped her body, which felt as though it was expanding, growing as large as the world itself. Thoughts whirled through her mind—a multitude of voices in three choruses: those who had died, those who yet lived, and those who had yet to be born. They had a message to impart, a message of hope and despair, joy and grief, urgings and warnings. A message she struggled to understand but could not, since it was being shouted in the Elvish and common tongues at once, each drowning the other out. The emotions behind the message, however, came through like breaking waves. The voices expected her to say something, do something, to *be* something.

Bobbing on the sea of human and elf faces was one she recognized. Tal. He stood amidst the throng, visible from the shoulders up, wearing chain mail over his shirt and an embroidered surcoat bearing the crest of House Uskevren.

There was something wrong about his face. His deep green eyes were staring, unfocused, and his dark hair was matted and wet on one side. Something seemed to be sticking out of it, just behind the right ear, as if a twig had been caught in his hair.

With a shudder of horror, Larajin realized that an arrow was sticking out of Tal's head, buried nearly to the fletching in a mat of blood-crusted hair.

He was dead.

The view shifted, drew back. Larajin saw hands bursting out of the earth like grasping vines, twining themselves around the ankles and calves of Tal and all those around him. The hands were dark, the color of earth, and had fingernails that flashed silver, like steel. They clawed at the flesh of those above, tearing deep gashes that wept a rain of blood onto the disturbed, heaving ground.

The elves and humans were still shouting at Larajin, calling to her, demanding she listen, imploring her to act. Unable to withstand the discordant chorus of voices that broke over her, one wave crashing in after the next, Larajin grabbed her ears with both hands and broke into a stumbling run. Somehow, despite her eyes being squeezed shut, she found her way through the elves in the clearing, running faster and faster through what must have been patches of sunlight and shadow. Blazing heat alternated with winter chill as darkness, light, darkness, then light flashed before her eyes. Something grabbed her from behind, and something else knocked against her legs, tripping her and toppling her to the ground.

She wept with relief as darkness finally claimed her.

Larajin woke to the patter of rain and the smell of wet leaves and soil. She lay on a bed of soft moss, covered by a light sheet, one hand outstretched. Cool, wet leather pressed against the back of her hand—the side of a tent.

It was too dark to see anything clearly. The walls of the tent were dark, and it had been pitched deep in the forest, with a tangle of branches shrouding it from what must be an overcast sky. The resulting gloom was as dark as a cave.

Larajin lay in the darkness, wondering what had happened. Her first thoughts were of Tal. Was he still alive? Had that truly been a vision of his death she'd seen? If so, when was it going to happen—now, or in the future? There was no way to know and little she could do to warn or protect Tal while she lay there in that tent, so far from home. The thought left her with a hollow in her stomach even deeper than her hunger pangs.

Hours must have passed since the celebration in the forest clearing. Had they carried her to this tent to recover from the druid's spell? Larajin was confused, groggy from her long sleep, hungry, and in need of relieving herself.

She sat up and located the faint line of gray that was the tent flap. Through it blew a cool breeze that smelled of rain. As she sat up and crawled toward the exit, something shifted. Larajin saw the dim outline of a creature, perched on the horizontal pole just above the tent flap, peering at her. Enormous round eyes gleamed in the darkness, then blinked. The creature shifted again, and Larajin heard a rustle of feathers.

"Goldheart?" she asked hopefully. She reached out in the darkness to stroke the tressym.

A loud hoot filled the tent, stopping her short. The creature unfolded its wings and flapped them once, warning her away. This was no tressym. It was an owl—an enormous one, as large as a hunting dog. It peered balefully at her, snapping its beak at her questing fingers. She pulled her hand back.

As the need to relieve herself grew more pressing, Larajin tried once again to crawl outside. The owl, however, beat its wings furiously and rose from its perch, raking the air in front of it with its talons and snapping its beak. Its message was unmistakable. It didn't want Larajin to leave the tent.

Warily, Larajin searched for another exit but found none.

She was frustrated and puzzled. Had this creature crept inside the tent while she lay sleeping? Or had one of the elves deliberately placed it there to prevent her from leaving? She had read in one of the books at Stormweather Towers that wood elves used owls as watchdogs.

Whatever the reason for it being there, the owl was clearly not going to let her get past it.

Feeling her way around the tent, she located a wooden bowl and dumped out the cold food that filled it. She used it to dig a hole and relieved herself, then covered the hole with earth and settled back onto her mossy bed, glaring at the owl. Whether the creature had been left there or crawled in on its own, she'd had enough of the thing.

"Hello!" she shouted in Common. "Rylith! Are you out there? What's going on?"

Lantern light flickered against the walls of the tent, and voices called out to one another in the elves' tongue. Then one side of the tent brightened. A moment later, moving shadows appeared and grew on its side.

The owl, which had returned to its perch, ruffled its wings a second time when the tent flap beside it opened. An elf poked his head through the entrance, peered at Larajin from under bangs that dripped with rainwater, and nodded when he saw she was awake. He said something to her in his own language, then switched to broken Common.

"You wait," he said. "Rylith gone."

"Where is she?" Larajin snapped.

"Travel to setting sun."

"She's journeyed west? Where to?"

The elf's only answer was a stony look. There were some questions, it seemed, he wouldn't answer.

Frustrated by his silence, Larajin chafed. She'd expected Rylith to come to the tent, to explain what had happened— what the purpose of her spell had been. Larajin felt no different than she had before, but the magical energy must have done something to her, had some lingering effect. She also wanted to ask Rylith what her vision had meant. Not the part about Tal dying—that was clear enough—but the multitude of voices shouting at her. Larajin didn't have the patience to just sit in this tent and wait. She'd have to find a way to get to Rylith, wherever she was. Perhaps Doriantha could help.

"What about Doriantha?" she asked the elf. "Is she here?"

He shook his head firmly. "No. Gone. Go fight."

"Has she gone to ambush another caravan?" Larajin asked hotly. "Wasn't killing Dray Foxmantle enough for her?"

That earned her a blank look. Larajin tried again, using simpler words. "Who does Doriantha fight?"

"Sembians," the elf said, then added, with a feral grin. "Now is war."

"War," Larajin echoed in a whisper.

That was it, then. The dam holding the mutual hostilities of the elves and the Sembians in check had finally broken. Was that why she'd seen an image of Tal's death? Was he marching, even now, toward a confrontation with the elf archer who would seal his doom?

And what would happen to her now? This elf didn't seem as friendly as the others had. Instead of smiling deferentially at her, he glowered. In fact, now that the glow of the ale—and whatever had been in that draught Rylith had given her—was gone, Larajin's certainty of her welcome was fading, fast. Had the elves only been pretending to accept her as one of their own? Had she just imagined their smiles?

For the first time since she'd set out on her journey to the Tangled Trees, Larajin realized the ramifications of her decision. The elves had seemed so benign, so welcoming, earlier in the day. Did they now see only her human features and consider her a prisoner of war?

She rose to her feet, keeping a wary eye on the owl. "When did Doriantha leave? Can I go to her?"

The elf shook his head. "No go. Stay. Wait. Leifander come.

Then you . . ." Unable to find the word in Common, he linked his fingers together. "Like so again. Prophecy time come, and gods take. All be good for forest elves."

Larajin didn't like the sound of that last part. What did he mean, exactly, by "gods take?" And what had he meant by that gesture? Larajin and her twin had been united that closely only once—in the womb. Did he mean they would be united again in death?

The elf stared at her a moment longer, then turned and stroked the owl. Seeing her chance, Larajin quickly whispered a prayer to Sune, pleading with the goddess to provide her with a spell. If she could command the elf to take the owl away with him, she might be able to slip out of the tent and find someone to help her, but though she prayed fervently, no answer came. There was no rush of magical energy, no red glow from the locket. Even the goddess had turned her back on Larajin.

The elf withdrew from the tent, leaving the owl. Defeated, Larajin turned her prayers toward Hanali Celanil, asking the goddess to fill with compassion the hearts of the elves who now held her prisoner.

As she finished her prayer, she sniffed the air. Was it only wishful thinking, or was there a faint scent of Hanali's Heart in the air? Would the elf goddess persuade her people to spare Larajin's life?

Time would tell.

CHAPTER 6

The sun was rising when Leifander at last flew away
from Stormweather Towers. He had sat with Thamalon Uskevren in the indoor garden throughout
the night, at first only grudgingly listening, then, as
Thamalon talked about Trisdea, gradually asking
more and more questions. The old man had managed to convince him that he too loved the Tangled
Trees—that his attempt to create a market for the
forest's wild nuts and fruits had been made with
the elves' welfare in mind. By the end of their talk,
Leifander was thinking that if he had to have been
sired by a human, he was glad that it had been
someone who could see the beauty of the forest
as clearly as any elf. When Thamalon tried to persuade him that there were other humans who felt
the same—who did not want war with the people

of the forest—Leifander had believed him.

Almost.

Angrily, Leifander shook his head. He flapped his wings harder, beating the weak notion from his mind with strong, sure strokes. Just because one human was benevolent toward the elves didn't mean the rest could be trusted, he reminded himself. Thamalon was an aberration: hardly representative of his race. Just look at the sprawling city below, at the people scurrying through it like ants. If their leaders told them to kill every last elf, they would do it without question.

As the pink rays of the sun slanted over the river, illuminating the walls and towers that surrounded the city, dark shapes began to rise into the air above a wide swath of greenery, itself enclosed by walls. Hearing the hoarse caws of his feathered kin, Leifander wheeled toward the flock. The crows—more than a hundred of them—were rising from their nesting place, a grove of trees beside a lake far too symmetrical to be natural. Now they were wheeling in the air above the lake, forming up for the flight to their daytime feeding grounds.

Leifander joined them, losing himself in their mid-air teasing and games. He tested his speed in a race against another young male, dived playfully at a female who avoided him with an adroit slip to the side, then found a strong current of salt-tanged air coming off the sea and showed off with a series of dives and loops that left the others croaking with envy. These birds were animals, not skinwalkers, but Leifander felt at home among them. They were his totem animal, their souls kindred to his own. Among them, he could lose himself in simple, mindless play. He could—

Flashes of sunlight from the ground below caught his eye. Wheeling in a tight circle, he passed over a wide, cobblestoned plaza a second time, and saw a group of several dozen archers beside caravan wagons, their brightly polished helmets reflecting the sun like mirrors. They looked as though they had lined up to receive rations—or perhaps a shipment of arms.

Curious, he dived from the flock for a closer look. It wouldn't hurt to do a bit of spying while he was there.

Settling onto the cool slate of a rooftop beside the plaza, Leifander hopped to the edge. From this vantage point two stories above the plaza, he could catch the scents of freshly sawn boards and the stink of the humans below, already sweating in their armor. The archers were carrying strung bows, and a few held quivers of arrows, but none had yet been nocked. Man-shaped targets—some made of wood, others sacks that had been stuffed with straw—lined two sides of the plaza, half hidden behind potted trees. Behind the targets, the ground floor windows of the shops had been closed and shuttered. Each of the streets leading to the plaza had been blocked by a wooden bar, beyond which a soldier stood guard. It looked as though the humans had assembled to practice their archery, but as yet the targets were unfeathered by arrows.

The four wagons were larger than those usually found in caravans and had been drawn up in a line. They looked newly made and were as yet unpainted. They were without horses, their traces and harnesses coiled in a heap in front of each wagon. Strangely, though, a driver sat in each wagon's seat, just ahead of the enclosed cargo area, holding the reins as if driving an invisible team.

A sergeant shouted orders, and the archer closest to the back of each wagon opened its rear doors. His curiosity fully aroused now, Leifander hopped sideways along the edge of the rooftop, trying to see inside. He had almost reached a good vantage point when he saw a flash of a mailed arm as one of the archers pointed him out. A heartbeat later, the archer beside him raised his bow and nocked an arrow.

Leifander hurled himself sideways, wings flapping, as the arrow skittered against the slate tile beside him, knocking loose a tile. As the archer below laughed and swiftly drew another arrow, he hopped back out of sight. They probably thought him nothing more than a crow—but that didn't mean they wouldn't skewer him with an arrow, just for sport.

Hopping across this rooftop to seek another, Leifander heard the sergeant shouting at his men to stop wasting their arrows, then voices arguing, pitched too low for him to make out the words. A moment later came an order to "mount up" followed by creaking noises below.

By the time he risked a peek down into the plaza again, all of the archers had disappeared. For a moment, Leifander wondered where they had gone but then saw the wagons shifting as the men inside them repositioned themselves. The sergeant walked from one wagon to the next, closing the rear doors, then strode out of the plaza at a brisk pace. From somewhere out of sight, came his shout: "Ready?"

The drivers stiffened in their seats. "Ready!" the lead one cried. "Ready!" the next called out, then the next, and the next.

The wagons ceased swaying and grew still. Soon the only sounds came from outside the plaza, the murmur of citizens going about their business, and the rumble of carts through the streets.

For several long moments, nothing happened. The drivers sat ready in their seats, hands occasionally flicking the reins. A whistle shrilled and as one, the drivers dropped the reins and lunged sideways on their seats, pushing hard on levers that Leifander assumed were brakes.

Hinges squealed and, with loud thumps and bangs, the sides of each wagon fell open, revealing a flat platform behind the driver's seat. Archers stood on it, facing outward, arrows nocked and bows at full draw. Taking only a heartbeat to aim, they loosed their arrows, which sang through the air toward the targets. They drew again, and shot, and again, and shot, filling the plaza with a deadly rain of arrows. Many struck the wooden walls or shutters of the buildings behind—but many more thudded into their targets. One of these, battered by a flurry of arrows, topped sideways and fell, like a man slowly dying. Others jerked and tore apart into sprays of straw. Only after each archer had shot an entire quiverful of arrows did the thrumming bows at last fall silent.

A whistle shrilled a second time, the archers lowered their empty bows, and the sergeant strode back into the plaza.

Leifander grimaced at he had just witnessed: a deadly trap that would take the forest elves completely by surprise—a trap that could be made even more deadly still if any of the hidden warriors were capable of wielding magic. The elves would come willingly to the bait, thinking the unguarded wagons soft and ripe, like jawa fruits ready to be plucked and peeled. When they attacked the "caravan," they would be cut down in droves.

Leifander crouched and spread his wings, preparing to take off from the rooftop. He needed to get back to the forest as quickly as he could, to warn the others. He—

Could not move. His body had become as rigid as a statue. He tried to draw in his wings, but though his muscles ached with the strain, not a single feather ruffled. His legs were likewise frozen in place, and though he continued breathing, his breath came short and shallow, drawn in and out of a chest that barely moved. With a rising panic, he realized he must be the victim of a spell.

He heard the scrape of a boot on the slate behind him and tried to cock his head but could not. Peripheral vision showed him the outline of a human climbing up from behind the peak of the roof and silhouetted against the morning sun, but the only detail he could make out was the fellow's raised hand. With a sinking heart, he realized he must be a wizard or cleric—one who had crept up on him and used a spell to immobilize him.

In the plaza below, the archers were pointing in his direction and talking in low voices. Cursing himself for a fool, Leifander realized that he had tarried there too long—that the humans must have been anticipating a spy. Whether they thought Leifander a wizard's familiar or knew that he was a shapeshifter didn't really matter. Either way, he had been caught and now would be executed. Worse yet, he had failed his people. If he didn't manage to warn the elves about what the wagons concealed, he wouldn't be the only one to die.

Darkness descended in the form of a large leather sack that engulfed him, then was drawn shut.

When Leifander regained his senses, he was still in darkness—in his elf form, lying naked on a cold stone floor. His body was bruised and aching, as though someone had taken the sack he'd been in and beaten it against the wall—though he doubted that even humans would be so stupid as to try to kill a spy before questioning him. No, the ache in his bones was probably the aftermath of the spell that had immobilized him.

Whatever had transpired after his capture on the rooftop, he had no clear memory of it, just a vague remembrance of the sack opening, of trying to fly free and being caught by strong hands, and of shifting into elf form to fight back against three powerfully muscled humans armed with clubs while a wizard stood by, leaning on a staff, and . . .

Leifander winced, and raised a hand to rub his temple. A chain rattled in the darkness, jerking his arm to a halt. Unable to reach his head, he gave up. He already knew what his questing fingers would find: a tender spot, and dried blood.

Cold bands on his other wrist and both ankles must be manacles. By the way the clanking of their chains filled the space, he knew he was in a small cell.

With that realization, claustrophobia overwhelmed him. Mind reeling, all he could do was sit and tremble. So used to the open skies above had he become that even the tents of his people seemed too close, too small. Now he was closed in, sealed into a cell, forgotten and left to rot—in a space no larger than a tomb. He was going to die there.

With an effort, he pulled his thoughts back from the brink

of the tunnel they were about to spiral down into. Concentrate, he told himself, steady your breathing—but it was difficult. He was woozy and thirsty and shivering from the cold that seeped into his very bones from the stone below. He still had his magic, though, and the manacles wouldn't hold him for long. He tucked his feet under him and eased his body into a squatting position.

Drawing a deep breath, he focused his will, initiating a shift. He imagined his outstretched, fluttering fingers as feathers, his nose and mouth as a beak, his body shrinking . . .

Nothing happened.

Concentration broken, Leifander squatted in the darkness, heart hammering inside his chest. Impossible! He jerked against the chains in frustration, lost his balance, and toppled to the floor.

Cold iron still clamped his wrists and ankles. Perhaps that was what was wrong—perhaps the manacles had been enchanted to prevent him from skinwalking. But as he rose to a squat once more, he realized the real reason. He could no longer feel bangs brushing against his forehead or the tickle of the feathers braided into them.

With a trembling hand, he reached up, at the same time bending his body and lowering his head. By straining, he could just reach his forehead. What he felt there nearly stopped his heart. All that remained of his bangs were several rough tufts of hair, hacked short just above the scalp. Shifting his hand to his ear, he felt an empty hole where the gilded bone should have been. His longer braid still hung down his back, but his captors had removed the crow feathers and bone earring that allowed him to work his magic.

For several long moments he forgot to breathe. Dizzy, he at last drew a shuddering breath, then he prayed.

"Winged Mother, Lady of the Air and Wind, hear my prayer," he cried out, his voice sounding thin and strained in the tiny space. "Do not forsake me. Peer down into this dark and terrible place, wherever it may be, and lend me your wings. Lift my spirit, mend my body, and soothe my soul."

From somewhere outside the cell came the sound of metal clinking against metal. Footsteps approached, and with them, a light that gradually limned a rectangular doorway. For a moment, a thin shaft of warm yellow light shone in through a keyhole, then it blinked out as a key was thrust into the lock. Metal grated as tumblers turned, and the door opened and light flooded into the room.

Blinded by the sudden rush of light, Leifander could make out little of the man who had opened the door. By squinting, he caught a glimpse of harsh features, blond hair and beard, and a mail shirt and helm. Behind the man was a narrow corridor, its far wall having at least two doors set with stout locks. The man nodded and called back over his shoulder to someone farther down the corridor.

"Looks like bird boy is awake," he growled. "Go tell Drakkar."

They dragged Leifander down a maze of hallways to a small room with windowless walls of damp stone, a low ceiling, and a floor stained with dark brown splotches. A human skull and some bones lay jumbled carelessly in a corner, gnawed clean save for a few jagged scraps of red and a patch of faded hair. The air smelled of sewage and decaying flesh, and the only illumination came from two oil lamps with wicks that needed trimming, set above each of the room's two exits. They filled the air with soot that roiled against the ceiling before disappearing out through a blackened ceramic pipe. From inside this ventilation pipe came a skittering noise like the scurrying of rodent feet.

While two men stood by with swords at his throat, a third—the blond guard—attached each of Leifander's manacles in turn to a metal bolt on the floor, forcing him into a spread-eagle position on his back.

When he was done, Leifander could barely move. Shivering with cold, all he could do was glare as the men taunted him, drawing the points of their swords slowly down his bare chest and stomach, then tarrying at his groin, threatening to emasculate him. He spat on the boots of the blond guard, defying him, and received a kick that made his ears ring and caused bright points of light to dance just in front of his eyes.

Leifander tensed, expecting further kicks, but instead the guards departed the way they had come; the closing door muffled their footsteps. Left to himself, Leifander struggled against the manacles in the futile hope that one of the bolts on the floor might prove loose. One was, but though he writhed like a snake, chafing wrists and ankles raw, he could neither tug it out nor slip his bonds.

Cursing, he regretted not having attacked the guards as they marched him at sword point down the short hallway. At least that would have been a quick death. Now he would reap the bitter rewards of cowardice.

A moment later, the room's second door opened. Through it stepped a monstrosity so disfigured that Leifander at first had trouble recognizing it as a man. It walked erect on two legs and wore purple hose and a black velvet doublet heavily embroidered with gold thread and studded with gems, but its head was horribly misshapen. The right side of the face looked human, aside from a single fang that curved over the mustached upper lip, but the left side was covered with a mass of black, serpentine scales, its eye bulging and pupil slitted. The hands were even worse. Emerging from the end of one sleeve was a birdlike talon, but with what looked like wriggling pink worms where the fingers should be. The other hand was human in shape but covered with a patchwork of fur, scale, and feathers. A heavy gold ring decorated one finger. The legs were strangely jointed, and while one foot was booted, the other was bare, ending in a cloven hoof. The man lurched into the room with a jerky, shuffling gait, his hoof clomping and booted foot twisting and dragging.

Behind him came a tall, dark-skinned man—fully human—wearing smoke-gray clothes. A thin line of beard framed his jaw, and his eyes glittered. He carried a knotted wooden staff into which thorns had been pressed, and upright thorns crowned its tip. He closed the door behind himself, then leaned on his staff, regarding Leifander with eyes utterly devoid of mercy.

"Is this the shapeshifter?" the deformed man asked.

"It is, Lord Mayor."

The first man cocked his half-serpent head and stared at Leifander through a slitted eye. "Fascinating." A human tongue flickered in and out through his lips, then he added, "Have him change, Drakkar."

The man with the staff—Drakkar—twitched his lips into the briefest of condescending smiles. "Lord Mayor, we have taken away his magic. With it, he would have escaped by now."

"What did he use, then? A wand? Or was it a ring, or a cloak?"

"None of those things, Lord Mayor." Drakkar gestured with his staff, indicating Leifander's forehead. "He used feathers woven into his hair and a bone."

Leifander jerked his head to the side, hiding his shame.

"Magical feathers?" the deformed man panted, his eyes glittering with desire.

"It would appear not, Lord Mayor. My spells could detect no glamor upon them, nor on the bone. The fellow must be a cleric of some heathen elf god. The feathers and bone were specific to his religion—useless to anyone else."

The human side of the mayor's face twisted into a pout, hiding his fang. "Talos take him, then!" he cursed. "He's of no use to me. Dispose of him."

Leifander flinched, waiting for the dark-skinned man to strike him with his staff, but Drakkar merely leaned upon it. "He is of use to me," he said softly. "This man was caught spying on our new war wagons. I would find out how much he has learned—and if there are other spies here in Selgaunt that we need to worry about. You will recall those wild elves that crept into the Hunting Garden last winter."

The mayor made a derisive noise—half snort, half hiss. "Do what you want, but be sure to kill him afterward," he ordered. He met and held Drakkar's eye a moment, then held up a malformed hand. "There are deeper secrets than your war wagons that need burying."

The Hulorn turned, fumbled the door open with awkward hands, and shambled from the room.

Leifander gave Drakkar a bold stare, making plain his defiance. He would not reveal a thing. If the torture became too much to bear, he would dash his head against the stone again and again until death claimed him. Indeed, there was little reason not to begin before the agony started. He whispered a prayer to the Winged Lady, imploring her to enfold his soul as it flew toward her, and lifted his head. But before he could begin, Drakkar kneeled swiftly by his side and grabbed his braid, yanking his head upward.

"None of that," he warned. "I want you alive and awake for a little while yet."

Still holding Leifander by the hair, he laid his staff on the floor, considered a moment, then plucked a thorn from it. Forcing Leifander's head to the side, he held it against the cold stone with one knee. From a pocket he pulled a wooden stick and used it to lever Leifander's mouth open, then he jammed the thorn into Leifander's tongue.

Drakkar released Leifander, stood, and began to chant.

Gagging, Leifander tried to force the thorn from his tongue but could not. He twisted his tongue this way and that, trying to scrape the thorn out with his teeth. He could feel its sting, could feel his tongue swelling from the injury done to it, but could no longer feel the thorn itself. It seemed to have vanished, deep inside his flesh.

Drakkar finished chanting and stared down at Leifander. "Where are you from, and when did you arrive in Selgaunt?"

he asked.

Leifander's mouth spoke of its own accord. "The Tangled Trees. Last night."

His eyes widened in alarm, as he realized that he was the victim of a spell that was compelling him not only to speak— but to speak the truth.

Drakkar nodded. "Why did you come to Selgaunt?"

"To deliver a message."

"From whom, and to whom?"

"From the druids of the Circle of Emerald Leaves. To Thamalon Uskevren."

"Why to him?"

"He is my father."

Drakkar's eyebrows raised. He glanced at Leifander's ears, at his tattooed face and asked, "What was the message?"

Leifander tried to clench his teeth shut or bite his traitorous tongue until his jaw ached, but it was no use. He answered every question the evil wizard asked, even giving the full strength of the wood elves' forces and naming the leaders of each patrol. Tears welled in his eyes and trickled down his temples, dripping onto the floor, and still his betrayal continued. Leifander was unable to consolidate his will enough to strike his head against the floor, unable to do anything but answer.

Drakkar paused, and for a moment Leifander thought the questions were over, then he spoke again, as if musing aloud. "Your forces are weak, then. The High Council must know that this is a war your people cannot win. I wonder—would the elves accept an offer of support, if one were forthcoming?"

It had been phrased as a question, and so Leifander was compelled to answer. "It would depend on who the offer was from."

Drakkar's lips twitched in the faintest sketch of a smile. "What if it came from Maalthiir, first lord of Hillsfar?"

This time, Leifander answered willingly, in a harsh voice. "Maalthiir!" he spat. "We'd rather accept the aid of a demon."

"And why is that?" Drakkar asked, unperturbed.

"He's banned all but humans from his city. Elves found within its walls are used as fodder for the gladiatorial games. The Red Plumes are known throughout the forest for the atrocities they commit. The council would never trust him. Never."

"What if such an alliance was the only way to save the forest?" Drakkar asked. "Pride can't harvest nuts from a blighted tree or shelter you from your enemies."

Leifander desperately wanted to say no, that the elves would fight to the last man, woman, and child, but he was haunted by the destruction the magical blight had already caused. He imagined elves standing homeless amid the skeletal trees of a destroyed wood.

"They . . . might," he conceded, "but I think . . . not."

"I see."

Drakkar sounded pleased. He'd obviously been fearing an elf alliance with the cities of the Moonsea. Leifander's rejection of any such notion had clearly set his mind at ease.

"This past winter, three wild elves appeared in Selgaunt in the Hulorn's hunting garden," he told Leifander. "Who were they, and why were they here?"

"I don't know."

The answer had been a truthful one, but Drakkar's eyes narrowed. He tried again. "You must," he growled. "They were protecting a girl—a human. A servant of the Uskevren house. Who is she?"

Once again, Leifander's tongue spoke the truth. "I don't know."

"Gods curse you!" Drakkar kicked Leifander in the ribs, making him wince, then a cunning look crept into his eye. "Let's see if you're lying," he spat. "Tell me, shapeshifter . . . what is your true name?"

"I . . . don't know," Leifander gasped. The kick must have cracked a rib. It hurt to breathe. "My mother died giving birth to me. If she gave me a true name, I don't know it."

Drakkar thought a moment, then tried again. "Do you know the true names of any of the elves of the High Council?"

Leifander fought the compulsion to speak as long as he could, but at last his answer burst forth. "Yes."

"Whose?"

"Lord Kierin of Deepingdale."

Drakkar's eyes gleamed. "What is his true name?"

"His true name . . . is . . ."

With a supreme effort of will, Leifander wrenched his head to the side, mashing his cheek into the cold stone as he spoke, slurring his words. He must not betray his adoptive father's sworn friend. He would not.

Drakkar bent over him, wrenching his head back. "Again. What is Lord Kierin's true name?"

This time, Leifander spoke clearly: "Sallal Lolthrailin."

"What does it mean?" Drakkar asked. "Tell me in the common tongue."

Weeping again, Leifander answered. "Keeper of the Wood."

"Well done," Drakkar said. "That should prove very useful."

He stroked a fingertip across Leifander's lips. A scent clung to the finger that was equal parts sweet cinnamon and something loathsome and rotting. It lingered on Leifander's lips, even after Drakkar drew his hand away.

Suddenly finding himself free from magical compulsion, Leifander wrenched his head to the side and spat away the taste. He turned the full force of his pent-up anger on Drakkar.

"May the Black Archer take you, and send swift arrows of vengeance to pierce you," he yelled. "May the Lady of Air and Wind buffet you with gales, and *break your bones!*"

Instead of trembling at the promised wrath of the gods, Drakkar gave a low chuckle and stared down at Leifander with flat, expressionless eyes.

"You'd better save your breath for a more useful invocation," he said. "One that protects you from rats."

Then, fingers caressing his staff as if they were reading a message in the pattern of the thorns, he chanted a brief spell. In the blink of an eye, he was gone—vanished from the room as if he had never been there.

A scuttling noise echoed out of the ventilation pipe overhead. Leifander glanced up—the opening of the pipe was directly over his naked chest. He saw two tiny human hands gripping the edge of the pipe. An instant later, two eyes that glistened with hunger stared down at him. Behind the rat-thing with human arms, other shapes jostled forward, eyes gleaming.

The first rat-thing leaped from the pipe. As it landed on Leifander's bare thigh and sank its fangs into his flesh, Leifander clenched his teeth against the pain, not permitting himself to make a noise, but as more of the vile creatures poured down from the pipe, landing on his naked body, he at last gave vent to his terror and screamed.

CHAPTER 7

Larajin awoke with a start to find a hand over her mouth. As her eyes flew open, she saw Rylith looking down at her. The druid raised a finger to her lips for silence. Larajin nodded, and the hand covering her mouth was withdrawn.

She sat up and glanced around the tent. The rain must have ended; hot sunlight filtered through the wet leather, which was steaming. Near the tent flap, the owl was asleep on its perch, ears twitching slightly with each rustle of Rylith's leaf cloak. Just outside the entrance, Larajin could hear two wood elves talking. Rylith cocked her head, listening, then pointed at Larajin and at herself, and jerked a thumb, indicating she'd come to take Larajin away.

Larajin stared at the druid, wondering how she'd managed to sneak past the guards and the owl. More to the point, what was she doing there? She was clearly at odds with the elves who were holding Larajin hostage—the need for silence told Larajin that much—but could Larajin trust her?

A section of Rylith's cloak rustled, seemingly of its own accord. Looking down, Larajin saw the cause. Golden eyes peered up at her as the tressym pushed its way past Rylith to nudge Larajin with its cheek. Goldheart turned and licked Rylith's hand and allowed the druid to stroke her head. Larajin could just hear her soft purring.

Larajin's mind was made up in an instant. If Goldheart trusted Rylith, so would she.

She pointed at the owl and in the direction the voices outside the tent were coming from, then shrugged a silent question. How were they possibly going to sneak past the guards outside?

Rylith winked, then drew a pouch from a pocket on the front of her vest. Loosening the thong that held it shut, she carefully began to pour out its contents: an orange-red powder that looked like ground crystal and smelled like tree sap. Goldheart watched intently, sniffed at the powder, then sneezed. As Larajin glanced in alarm at the owl—it didn't appear to have heard the faint noise and was still sleeping on its perch—Rylith scooped the tressym into her arms. She handed Goldheart to Larajin, then continued pouring the powder. When she was finished, a perfect circle had been traced on the ground between Larajin's bedding and the side of the tent.

Squatting just outside this circle of dust, Rylith held out a hand, and gestured for Larajin to join her. Tucking Goldheart firmly under one arm, Larajin took Rylith's hand, waiting for further instructions. The druid mimed a descending count, folding fingers and thumb one by one against her palm as she counted down from five to one, then "walked" two fingers in the air, as if they were stepping over something. Larajin nodded, and lifted her foot, moving it slightly toward the circle of powdered tree sap to show that she understood.

Outside the tent, one of the elves called out to another. It sounded as though the guard was being changed. As the owl stirred in its sleep, ruffling its feathers, both women froze, but after a few tense moments it settled again without opening its eyes.

Rylith gave Larajin a purposeful look and began the count. As her thumb joined her fingers against her palm, both women stepped into the circle, and Rylith spoke a single word.

The owl's enormous golden eyes flashed open, and the ground lurched sideways beneath Larajin's feet as tent and owl disappeared in a spinning blur. For an instant that stretched impossibly long between two heartbeats, a dark void surrounded her, and she thought she was going to be sick. Goldheart wriggled frantically, scratching Larajin's arm, then leaped away with an eerie, echoing howl. Larajin was too disoriented to try to catch her. All sense of up and down vanished as forward folded into backward and right into left. For one terrifying instant, she felt as though her body was turning itself inside out and upside down—but then it righted itself as Rylith gave her hand a hard squeeze. Then, with a thud that jarred Larajin's teeth together, they were on solid ground once more. Rylith released her hand.

Looking around, Larajin saw that she was in a forest. Rylith stood beside her, and Goldheart was perched on the branches of a tree above, intent upon grooming herself, apparently none the worse for wear save for some ruffled fur. Wherever they were, the place didn't look familiar. Unlike the strong, shady oaks of the Tangled Trees, the trees all around them were leafless and mottled with blight, and several were leaning or had already fallen. The ground under Larajin's feet was spongy with a putrid-smelling layer of what looked like decayed ferns and moss, and the once-thick underbrush had died back, leaving only skeletal twigs. Through them, Larajin could see a road.

"Where are we?" she asked Rylith.

The druid remained silent, with her lips pressed tightly together. Her only answer was to nod at the long, rectangular shadow that fell across the spot where they stood.

Larajin turned around and saw an enormous slab of gray granite, its front and sides covered in flowing Elvish script. The bottom of the stone looked as though it had been damaged by frost. Bending over, she found she could peer right through the monument's base, which had a crack in it more than a handspan wide. The fissure narrowed rapidly, but the crack continued all the way to the top of the monument, dividing it in two. It looked as though the two halves were about to topple to either side at any moment.

When she turned back to Rylith, Larajin saw a tear trickle down the druid's tattooed cheek. She didn't need to ask what was wrong. As a novice cleric of two goddesses who valued natural beauty above all else, she too was struck by the *wrongness* of this blighted wood. She whispered prayers to Sune and Hanali Celanil, asking the goddesses to take pity upon this place.

"This monument," Rylith said in a sad voice, "was erected to commemorate a pact of friendship between human and elf. For centuries, nothing has marred its surface. It has withstood frost and fire and healed itself of the willful damage of blade and hammer. Now it is a cracked mirror, a sad reflection of our current troubles."

Larajin laid a fingertip against the monument—gently, lest the slight touch topple it. Despite the heat of the sun that glared down through the bare branches overhead, the granite was as cold as ice. She shivered, and withdrew her hand.

"The Standing Stone," she said, remembering it from a book she'd read.

"You know its history?" Rylith asked. "The story of when it was erected and what it signifies?"

Larajin nodded. "Why did you bring me here?" she asked. "Why did we have to use magic to sneak away? Why wouldn't the elves let me leave the tent?"

Rylith sighed. "These are difficult times. Not only do the humans march against the forest, but the war has also pitted the council members against each other. There are many on the High Council who ignore the true threat to the forest, who refuse to heed our advice. One would think they had fallen victim to—"

She stopped abruptly, then shook her head, as if to dispel some disturbing thought.

"I have much work yet to do," she continued. "I can interrupt it for only a short time, and that time would be better spent speaking about your part in all of this than about mine." She extended a hand to Larajin. "Come. Walk with me. This is not a pleasant spot, and there is more I need to show you."

They walked for some time through the woods, Goldheart following above, until they had left the monument and the blighted forest behind. Up ahead, Larajin heard the sound of flowing water. It turned out to be a small creek, pebbled with rocks and surrounded by lush greenery. Rylith squatted on a sun-warmed stone, and motioned for Larajin to join her. When Larajin had settled, she pointed at a pool, on which a twig was floating. The twig drifted in a slow, lazy circle, framing their reflections. Rylith's face, with gray hair and dark tree-branch tattoos; and Larajin's, with unwrinkled skin and rust-colored hair hanging loose about her shoulders.

"Hazel eyes are very rare among our people," Rylith said. "Less than ten children in an entire generation have eyes like yours. Twins born with hazel eyes are rarer still."

Larajin wondered what this had to do with anything but told herself to be patient. Druids were never known to rush anything. Rylith would come to the point in time.

"There is a belief among our people that twins with hazel eyes are an omen of great good fortune, that the twins themselves are specially blessed by the gods—and that they will use this blessing to aid their race."

"My brother Leifander has hazel eyes?" Larajin asked.

"See for yourself." Rylith swept a hand over the pool of water, and the twig suddenly halted in place. For the space of several heartbeats, the pool became utterly still. Within it, Larajin could see a third face, that of a wood elf with braided bangs hung with feathers, and sharply pointed ears and almond-shaped eyes that were a hazel color just a shade darker than Larajin's own. His face was tattooed, but lacked the narrowness of a full-blooded elf. It was also strikingly handsome.

The image was frozen, the eyes unblinking—an illusion then, and not a glimpse of Leifander in that moment.

Larajin stared at her brother's face, trying to see a resemblance to her own, but could not. As Doriantha had observed, they were as different as day and night. Leifander looked like a full-blood elf, and Larajin a human.

Rylith moved her hand again, and the twig resumed its journey around the pool, making one last circuit, then escaping into the current of the stream. As it slipped away, Leifander's face rippled and faded from sight.

"Until quite recently, the truth—that Trisdea bore twins—was known only to a handful of people," the druid said. "Most of the elves in the Tangled Trees believed that she had borne only Leifander—being half human, he was such a large infant that it was easy to persuade people he'd made such a big bulge in Trisdea's stomach on his own. That fiction became even more credible when Thamalon Uskevren took you with him, away from the Tangled Trees."

"Was he supposed to have done that?" Larajin asked.

Rylith ignored the question. "That which is necessary has a way of happening," she said. "All things come full circle, given enough time."

She sighed, and continued, "There are some, however, who believe that the hand of the gods can be forced—that you and your brother should be reunited at any cost. When they first found out where you were living, they tried to force you to return to the Tangled Trees. They—"

"The elves who defended me in the Hunting Garden!" Larajin exclaimed, suddenly understanding.

Rylith nodded sadly. "Theirs was a great sacrifice, but they believed in you and in the power of the goddess that flows through you. As do I."

Larajin shivered, despite the heat of the sun. She had been chosen by two goddesses, it was true, and with their aid had worked magic. That alone made her special, but Rylith was saying that she was more than that. She was a person whom three elves had willingly sacrificed themselves to protect. A person of whom great things were expected—by an entire race. Larajin wondered how she could ever live up to such expectations.

She thought of her twin brother. At least she wouldn't have to do it alone.

"When I tried to leave the tent, an elf told me I had to wait for Leifander," she said. "He was worried that I would run away, wasn't he?"

"He was."

"But I wanted to meet Leifander. I would have given my word to wait until he came to the Tangled Trees—and kept it. Why didn't the elves trust me? Is it because of the war? Because I look . . . too human?"

"No," Rylith answered. "When I gave the gift of foresight to you at the Turning of the Seldanqith, you did not receive it as I had hoped. You seemed . . . alarmed and agitated by what you heard. Instead of conveying a message of hope to the people, you—"

"I panicked," Larajin whispered.

Rylith paused, and shook her head. "It caused great concern—and it was something I should have anticipated. I should have realized that you were not prepared—that the experience might frighten you. Being raised among humans . . ." She shrugged, and made a circle in the air before bowing her head and touching fingers to her forehead. "What is done is done. Everything is but a spoke in the wheel."

"I saw my brother's death," Larajin said in a pained whisper.

"Leifander's?" Rylith asked in alarm.

"No, Tal's—my half-brother."

"Ah." The druid made a dismissive gesture.

Larajin felt a rush of anger at the realization that Tal's death—the death of a mere human—meant nothing to the forest elves, but she forced it down in the hope that Rylith might be able to tell her what to do.

"What were the gods trying to tell me?" she asked. "What message should I have heard?"

"We may never know—but we may conjecture," Rylith said. "What remains of Cormanthor—of the great wood—is faced with a terrible prospect. A war could decimate our people and destroy the forest itself. The war is also sure to claim the lives of many humans."

Like Tal, Larajin thought grimly.

"This bloodshed was not meant to be," Rylith continued. "Someone has tipped the balance. Now the scales must be set level again. That task rests upon you and your brother, who share a great gift. Together, you can put a halt to the slaughter before it begins."

Larajin frowned, wondering if she was interpreting the druid's words correctly. "You expect Leifander and I to stop the war?"

Rylith stared into the trees, as if looking past them into a great distance. "Years before you and your brother were born, your sister Somnilthra prophesied that two children born to Trisdea would end her life but would save many more. That they would 'heal a great rift, and end a great strife.' That rift can be no other than the one between elf and human. That strife is this war.

"You and your brother are in balance—male and female, human and elf. Who better to balance the scales of fate?"

Larajin felt a tangle of conflicting emotions: relief that the war could still be halted and Tal's life saved—and dread.

"But . . . I wouldn't know where to begin. I couldn't—"

Not alone.

Startled, Larajin looked around. The voice was achingly beautiful and had come from everywhere at once, its syllables formed from the sighing of wind through branches, from the distant trill of birdsong in the wood, from the gurgle of the stream that flowed past the rock on which Larajin sat. A fragrance filled the air—heady and sweet, the smell of flowers—and not just any blossoms, but those of Hanali's Heart. Larajin looked down, and saw floating on the pool a single red petal, flecked with gold. For a moment, she thought the locket at her wrist had fallen open, but a quick glance told her that it was still securely fastened. She reached for the floating petal—

And jerked her hand back in alarm as Leifander's face appeared once more in the pool. This time, the image was moving, not still. Leifander lay on his back on a stone floor, his eyes wide and his mouth opened in a scream. He wrenched his head to the side as a squirming rat landed on the floor beside him. The rat lunged at Leifander's face, drawing blood. Leifander shook his head violently, dislodging the rat, but three more scurried in to lap at the hot, dark blood that trickled down his cheek.

"Why doesn't he throw them off?" she shouted, leaping to her feet in alarm as one of the rats ran across the vision in the pool, seemingly toward her own foot. "He's just lying there!"

Rylith glanced up at Larajin in alarm. "What is it? What do you see?"

Larajin was transfixed by the image in the pool. Standing up had somehow shifted it, giving a view of more than just Leifander's face. She could see manacles on each of his wrists and ankles, holding him spread-eagled on the floor—and more than a dozen rats, swarming around his body. They didn't look like ordinary rats.

Larajin dropped to her knees, lowering her face almost to

the surface of the water. The result was as she'd hoped—one of the rats loomed larger. Now that she could peer at it closely, she saw that its front legs were hairless and pink, and ended in tiny human hands.

"I recognize that creature!" she cried. "It's a rat from the sewers under the Hunting Gardens. Leifander must be in the Hulorn's dungeon."

Rylith's face paled.

Larajin stared in horror at the pond. She reached out for Leifander, but as her fingers touched the surface of the pool his image rippled, then was lost among the pebbles at the bottom of the pond. All that remained was the speckled red petal, bobbing amid sparkling reflections of the sun.

A different voice, equally melodic, but pitched in a different key, said, *Go to him.*

This time, Larajin didn't look around. She knew where the voice was coming from. It was Sune this time. Scooping the petal from the pond, she turned to the druid.

"That spell you used—the one that brought us here. Can you use it to send me back to Selgaunt?"

"I could, if I had visited Selgaunt, but I have never been to that city. The spell can only deliver me to somewhere I can recall well—to a place I can visualize as clearly as the palm of my own hand."

"What if I was the one who visualized where we were going? Would the spell work then?"

Rylith shook her head. "It would have to be a place of refuge, a place in which you felt utterly safe, and you would have to be the one to cast the spell."

"I see." Larajin scooped the petal from the stream. "Teach me."

Rylith shook her head. "Impossible! Only a druid of the inner circle can cast that spell."

"Could a cleric do it?"

"One who had studied for many years, certainly."

"I don't have years," Larajin gritted. "Tell me what to do."

"You will never succeed."

"I've got to at least try."

Rylith opened her mouth to protest, then set her lips in a grim line. "Yes, I suppose you do." She took a deep breath. "First, you'll need something sacred to your goddess."

"Which one?"

"Whichever favors you more."

Larajin considered, uncertain of the answer. Would it be Sune or Hanali Celanil? Both had blessed her in the past. Should she use Sune's red scarf or the locket that symbolized Hanali Celanil? Then she realized that she didn't need to choose. There was one thing sacred to both goddesses. She held up the red petal.

"That will do. Now use it to draw a circle."

Larajin frowned. How was she supposed to do that? With several dozen petals, she might construct a circle on the ground, as Rylith had done with her powder. With a lump of coal or a stick of chalk, she might draw a circle on the stone on which she squatted, but this petal was neither.

Then she realized the answer. Carefully, she lowered the petal to the pond, and dropped it so the eddying current would catch it. As before, the petal began to drift in a circle.

Larajin looked up. "What comes next?"

"Visualize a place of refuge—a place where you feel secure and safe. A place you know intimately. Close your eyes, if that helps."

Larajin did. She could only think of one place, in all of Selgaunt, that fit the description: her bedroom in Stormweather Towers. She concentrated on it, fixing every detail of the room in her mind. The narrow bed, the table her adoptive father had made her, the three-legged stool near the window, the simple trunk that held her clothes, and the shelf on the wall that held her collection of treasures—snail shells, pretty stones, an eagle's feather, and a jar of perfume given to her by her friend Kremlar—all came to her mind's eye.

The sounds of the stream and the forest boughs creaking faded, until all Larajin heard was Rylith's voice.

"Now, if you knew how to cast the spell, you would speak the word that activates it and step into the circle."

Larajin's concentration faltered. "What word?"

"Therein lies the problem. The word is unique to each individual casting the spell. I cannot teach it to you—it comes from the gods. After years of study, as I have said."

Rylith's voice had a finality to it that made Larajin's heart sink. Even so, she kept her eyes closed, keeping the image of her bedroom foremost in her thoughts. There had to be a way. Surely one of the goddesses would take pity on her and whisper the answer.

Larajin waited, but no more whispers came. She began to pray.

"Lady of the Heart of Gold, hear my prayer. Lady Firehair, hear my prayer. Place on my lips the words that will return me to Selgaunt, that will help me to save my brother's life. Help me to . . ."

Larajin felt the whisper enter her, felt it make its way to her heart and resonate there. It rushed from her chest to her neck to her cheeks, suffusing them with a hot warmth. It flowed to her lips, making them tingle. She spoke a word that was half in the common tongue, half in the language of the wood elves. Her ears heard it as two separate words, sung by two voices that were in perfect harmony.

"*Relthwin*. Refuge."

As floral scent rose into the air, Larajin opened her eyes. Beside her, Rylith was staring at the water, her eyes wide with surprise. Larajin looked down and saw a glowing circle on the surface of the pool. She stepped forward, placing her foot in the center of it. The water was only ankle deep, but her foot found no bottom. Instead she plunged downward, into water as clear and cold as ice.

Opening her eyes at the last moment, she saw a rippled surface above her, and Rylith's face. The druid had a hand raised, as if bidding her farewell, then something dived toward the water and hit it with a splash.

After an instant of disorientation that sent her perceptions folding in upon themselves, Larajin's foot struck something solid. Landing heavily, as if from a height, she sprawled onto a hard wooden floor beside a bed. Dripping wet, she lifted her head and peered around. She saw that she had indeed returned to her bedroom, and her heart was filled with a fierce joy.

An instant later, Goldheart landed with a wet thud on the floor beside her. On all four feet—instead of in the sprawling heap in which Larajin had landed. The tressym looked up at Larajin with the indignant expression that only a wet feline can muster, then ruffled its feathered wings and shook itself like a bird.

A moment later, the door opened, and Tal strode in, clad in the mail shirt and surcoat Larajin had seen him wearing in her vision, his sword at his hip. He didn't see Larajin and the tressym at first—he was on the opposite side of the bed, and his attention seemed to be fixed on the shelf on the far wall, which held Larajin's collection of treasures.

"Tal!" she exclaimed. "Thank the goddess—you're alive!"

Tal spun around, scabbard whirling. "Larajin!" he exclaimed, staring at her with a mixture of guilt and astonishment on his face. "Where did you come from?" He frowned. "Why are you dripping wet?"

Instead of answering, Larajin stood, gaping at her half-brother. This wasn't the Tal she remembered. His fingernails were elongated, almost like claws, and there was a heavy growth of beard on his face. His mouth and nose seemed distorted somehow, as if they'd been pulled forward by an unseen hand. His ears were slightly pointed and had tufts of hair growing out of their tips. A terrible thought occurred to Larajin. Had the Hulorn worked his dark magic upon her beloved half-brother? He smelled musky, almost like a dog.

Beside her, Goldheart hissed, her tail fluffed as big as

a bottle brush. The tressym's gold eyes were wide, pupils dilated, as if she was ready to attack.

"Tal . . . what's happened to you?"

Blushing furiously, Tal raised an arm to hide his face. "I . . . can explain this, Larajin. It's nothing, really. Just a . . . spell that went awry. I'm fine, really. I'll be back to normal soon enough."

Larajin wanted to demand a proper explanation, but already time was slipping away. If she didn't hurry, Leifander would be dead.

"I've got to get to the Hulorn's palace, and quickly," she told him. "There's someone in his dungeon I need to rescue—someone who is very . . . important to me. He'll die if I don't reach him in time. Will you help me?"

Instantly, Tal was all business. "Of course. What do you want me to do?"

"I'll explain on the way. And you can tell me what happened to you."

Tal nodded grimly, and rubbed the heavy beard on his cheeks. He eyed the tressym, which had backed into a corner and seemed disinclined to get near him.

"Let's go," he said. "But first, I need to find a scarf to hide my face."

CHAPTER 8

With one last, desperate heave, Leifander yanked at the bolt that held his left wrist to the floor. At last the rusted bolt cracked, then pulled free. Nearly weeping with relief, Leifander wrenched himself up off the floor—as much as he could, with his right wrist and both ankles still manacled—and flailed at the rats that had been worrying his flesh. The manacle around his wrist connected with a dull thud, slamming down like a hammer onto one of the rats. Leifander had the satisfaction of hearing a squeal as the injured rat scurried away.

Another rat took its place a moment later—and met the same fate. With a fury born of pent-up frustration, Leifander thrashed this way and that, killing five or six of the foul creatures.

Finally sensing their danger, the remaining rats

paused in their attack and hunkered just outside his reach, watching and waiting. It was as if they knew that the elf would tire soon enough—then they would feed.

The oil lamps had burned out some time ago, leaving Leifander in near darkness. A faint, gray circle of light came from the hole in the ceiling above—the ventilation pipe that the rats had come through. Now that the lamps were no longer filling the air with nose-clogging soot, Leifander could smell leaves and blooming flowers on the faint breeze that blew down through it.

The other end of the pipe must be above ground, he thought, in a garden, perhaps.

That gave him hope.

Still keeping a wary eye on the rats, he resumed his prayer to the Winged Mother. He'd repeated it dozens of times already. The goddess must surely hear it soon.

"Lady of the Skies, hear my plea. Send me the means to work my—"

The words tangled into a cry of pain as a rat sank filthy fangs into a tender spot on the bottom of his foot. His left foot—the one spot he couldn't reach, with his right wrist still manacled to the floor. He tried to kick the rat off, but the manacle around that ankle allowed little movement. The rat clung to his foot, eyes gleaming in the darkness. Leifander heard a chewing sound as it began to feed.

A fresh wave of pain lanced into him as a second rat, made bold by the success of the first, sank its fangs into his heel. A third rat scurried up onto his ankle and bit him there. Straining, Leifander was just able to reach it and knock it off, but the other rats were rushing forward. Leifander felt tiny human hands pulling at his toes, as if his foot were a cow's udder, being milked of its blood.

Gritting his teeth, Leifander resumed his prayer as best he could while the rats worried and gnawed at his left foot.

"Aerdrie Faenya, hear your priest in his torment!" he shouted at the hole in the ceiling. "Enfold me in your protecting wings, I beg of you!"

Nothing. The only sounds were the gnashing teeth of the rats and a scraping sound in the ventilation pipe above that was probably more of their foul brethren, come to join the feast. It felt as though the rats were flaying his foot, peeling back the callused skin to expose the soft and bloody tissue beneath.

He tried again. "Lady of Air and—"

He gasped at a fresh wave of pain and heard a cracking, grating sound. The rats had gnawed one toe down to the bone. He gulped back a cry.

"Lady of Air and Wind, send me aid."

A tear squeezed out of one eye. Down in this foul, close place, would his pleas even be heard?

Above him, a creature squeezed out of the ventilation pipe and began to fall toward him. For a moment, Leifander thought it was another rat. He raised his free hand and balled his fist, preparing to punch it out of the air, but an instant later the creature spread its wings, breaking its fall. It flew in a tight circle around the room. As it let out a loud caw, Leifander burst into relieved laughter. His prayers had been answered! There was no way a crow—even a young one like this—would have pushed itself through that narrow ventilation pipe without the hand of the goddess guiding it.

The crow hovered just above Leifander, wings fanning his face with a welcome breeze. Leifander spotted a loose feather in its tail and blessed the goddess for her gift. In another instant, he'd be able to transform, to slip wings and tiny crow's feet out of the manacles and fly away. Ignoring the pain of the rats still gnawing at his foot, he strained up for the feather.

Before he could pluck it from the crow's tail, the door leading to the cells crashed open, and light flooded into the room. The crow, startled by the noise, flew up toward the ceiling. Cursing his ill luck, Leifander wrenched around to look at the door, ready to pummel the wizard's feet with the manacle around his wrist in one last, futile act of defiance.

He stopped short, fist raised, gaping at what he saw. Two humans, both of them strangers. One was a dark-haired male, wearing a chain-mail shirt stretched across broad shoulders and a scarf that hid much of his face. The other was female, almost as slender as an elf, all but a few wisps of her amber-colored hair bound up in a bright red scarf. Both wore high boots that were splattered with mud and stank of sewage. The woman held a silver dagger that glowed with a bluish light reminiscent of moonlight but bright enough that it made Leifander wince. The man—who seemed to be shying away from the dagger's light, as if it pained him—held a set of keys in one hand and a sword that dripped with blood in the other.

"Leifander!" the woman cried. "You're alive."

Leifander wondered how this woman knew his name. For a confused moment, he thought that the wizard must have told her, but by the way the pair looked nervously around the room, it was clear they didn't belong there.

The man strode into the room and kicked at the rats, which scuttled away through the open door. He bent and began trying keys in the lock that held Leifander's wrist to the bolt in the floor. The woman, meanwhile, kneeled at Leifander's feet. He saw her wince, then swallow, as if bile had risen in her throat. His foot throbbed all the harder, as he realized how terrible his wounds must be. He shuddered when her fingers brushed his lacerated flesh.

"Be still," the woman said. "We're here to help you."

She began to pray.

It was a strange prayer, spoken mostly in the human tongue, but with the odd word of poorly pronounced Elvish mixed in. Leifander heard her invoke the name of the human goddess Sune, then blinked in surprise as Hanali Celanil's name followed.

The man fumbled with the keys, trying to find one that fit the manacle on Leifander's wrist.

"What's wrong with your fingers?" he asked, poking at the lock.

For a moment, Leifander wondered what he was talking about—it was his foot that was injured. Then he realized what the human meant.

"They're tattoos," he said through gritted teeth.

The man at last found the right key, and the wrist manacle sprung open. Leifander painfully sat up, rubbing his chafed wrist, then gestured at his ankles.

"The other manacles," he said. "They should open with the same key."

Above them, the crow continued to wing its way in a tight circle around the tiny room. The unnatural brightness of the dagger was frightening it. More than once, it swerved away from the glowing blade, narrowly avoiding crashing into a wall or the ceiling.

Down by Leifander's ankle, the woman was still praying. She'd set the glowing dagger down. Its light was gradually dimming as it lay untended on the cold stone floor. A ruddy red glow, however, was replacing it. The glow seemed to be flowing from the hand that was touching Leifander's savaged foot, and with it came a warmth that numbed the agony of the lacerations like a draught of bitterberry wine. An instant later, his foot felt whole again. Looking down, he saw that his wounds had fully closed. The only reminder of the injuries the rats had inflicted was a faint tingling.

The woman looked up, an expectant expression on her face. Realizing what is was she wanted, Leifander whispered his thanks. Her companion, meanwhile, fumbled open the manacle around one of Leifander's ankles.

As Leifander withdrew his foot, his woodland-keen hearing picked up the sound of footsteps approaching from behind the closed door.

"Someone's coming," he hissed. "Be quick."

Forcing himself up into a half squat on his freed foot—the second manacle was still tight around the ankle of the foot the woman had just healed—Leifander strained to reach the crow, but as it swooped down to meet him, it got in the way of the human, blocking his view of the manacle lock. The human swatted at the crow, backhanding it away from him.

"No!" Leifander cried, as the crow was sent tumbling.

An instant later the creature gave up and flew back up into the ventilation pipe and disappeared. Cursing, Leifander staggered to his feet as soon as the second manacle fell away from his ankle. He turned toward the two newcomers. However bold they might have been in this rescue attempt, they'd just cost him what might have been his only chance to reclaim his magic. With the crow gone, he'd be forced to rely on the two humans.

"Come on," the woman whispered, picking up her magic dagger again. "There's a way out, back through the cells. The guard's station—the jakes. We can use them to reach the sewers."

She slipped out of the room and hurried down the hallway between the cells. Leifander ran after her, jumping nimbly over the body of the guard his male rescuer must have killed, which lay in a spreading pool of blood, and skirting a second body without a mark on it that had probably been felled by the cleric's magic. The male paused just long enough to close the door behind them, then brought up the rear, his sword ready.

The woman led them through the maze of hallways to a small room with a filth-crusted hole in the floor. From the darkness below that opening came a terrible stench. The two humans exchanged glances, and some unspoken communication passed between them. The man kneeled, hooked his arm through the hole, and levered up the flooring stone into which the hole had been cut, creating a larger opening. With a nod, the female sat down and slipped through it, feet first. Leifander heard a splashing noise, and a muffled word, and the light from her dagger flared up through the opening like a beacon.

The man stood guard with his sword, staring back up the hallway, and motioned urgently toward the hole.

"You next," he ordered. "It's only a short drop."

Leifander took one look back down the hallway—he could hear shouts of alarm coming from the room in which the wizard had interrogated him—and made up his mind. Shivering, he forced down his fear of tight, dark spaces and concentrated on the magical blue light filling the space below the opening in the floor. Grimacing at the filth, he sat on the lip of the hole, then slid in, feet-first.

He landed with a splash in knee-deep sewage and was immediately overwhelmed by a smell that made him gag. The walls were close and tight on either side, barely wider than his shoulders, and the curved ceiling was just a hand-span above his head. He felt crushed by the weight of stone around him, unable to breathe. Dizzy, short of breath—unable to move. The woman yanked him aside, and an instant later her larger companion wedged himself down through the hole. He splashed into the sewage beside them, bending at the waist to keep his head from banging the ceiling. His sword scraped against the stone wall as he turned. He reached up and dragged the flooring stone back into place, sealing them inside the tunnel.

The shouts coming from above grew louder and were joined by the sound of running footsteps. The woman whispered something, and the light from her dagger blinked out.

Somehow the darkness made the walls seem even tighter, more confining, than they had before. Leifander's breath came quick and fast as he felt the stone all around him, walling him in on every side. Putting a hand on the wall beside him in an effort to steady himself didn't help—it only reminded him how close the walls were. Head spinning, stomach heaving, he fought for air and found none. Bright sparkles floated before his eyes.

The woman took Leifander's hand. Steadied by her touch, he fought his way back from the brink of panic. Forcing his eyes open, he met hers in the gloom, and nodded. In response, she tugged his hand. Leifander needed no further instruction. Wading through the stinking water as quietly as he could, he set off after the woman, while her companion followed close behind. As they rounded a bend, the shouts of the guards above slowly faded into the distance.

Leifander waited in the sewer, squatting on a ledge just below a grate that gave a view of the street above. Sunlight streamed down through the grate, forming a barred square on the ledge beside where he crouched in the shadows. The man who had rescued him—Tal, his name was—had climbed up through the grate while a wagon was parked above, using it to cover his emergence from the sewer. He'd gone to find Leifander some clothes to cover his nakedness and had left the woman to wait with him.

The woman stood in ankle-deep sewage farther back in the shadows. She looked as though she'd like to be out of the muck, but there wasn't room on the ledge for both of them, unless she wanted to risk being seen by those passing above. At least she had boots to keep her feet dry. She alternated looking up at the grate with sideways glances at Leifander, but didn't stare at him directly. After a moment, he realized why. Humans were uncomfortable with nakedness. Several times she seemed on the verge of speaking, only to hesitate and say nothing.

Leifander's bare feet were slimed with sewage that felt as though it had crept into every pore. He wriggled his toes and grimaced at the slippery feeling. He wished for a cool, cleansing rain, but the sky above was a flat, hot blue.

Ignoring the woman, he began to pray in his own language. The Winged Mother had sent one crow to him already. Perhaps she would send another. All he needed was one feather, then he wouldn't have to worry about clothes or creeping about in an enemy city. He could just fly away.

"What's that you're chanting, Leifander?" the woman asked suddenly. "Is it an elven prayer? I'm a cleric, as well. I worship one of the elf goddesses, Hanali Celanil."

Leifander snorted at her foolish prattle. A human claiming devotion to an elf deity? Ridiculous. He ran a hand in frustration through the tufts where his braids had been, concentrating on his prayer.

The woman didn't take the hint. "Are you praying to Aerdrie Faenya?" she persisted. "Are you casting a spell?"

Angry, Leifander switched to the common tongue. "You're interrupting," he told her bluntly, then he realized what she'd just said.

This woman not only knew his name, she knew which goddess he worshiped. A suspicion suddenly dawned.

"Who are you?" he asked.

"Your sister," the woman said, finally turning to meet his eye. "Your twin sister, Larajin."

He stared at her a moment. So it was all true. He did have a twin sister. Yet she looked nothing like him, and her mannerisms were as crass and fumbling as any human's. How could two people who shared the same womb have turned out to be such opposites? The gods must be laughing at the joke they had played.

"You don't look like an elf," he told her. "Or even like a half-elf."

Her eyes flicked to his ears and the tattoos on his face and hands. "You don't look like a half-elf either. I'd have sworn you were a full-blooded forest elf."

"How did you know where I was?" he asked, changing the subject. "Why did that other human—Tal—come to rescue me?"

Her face colored. "I was the one who rescued you, with Tal's help—and with Rylith's. We were beside a stream, near the Standing Stone, and when I looked into one of its pools I saw—"

Leifander's mouth dropped open. "You were with Rylith? Rylith of the Circle of the Emerald Leaves?"

"Why does that surprise you?"

Leifander shook his head. "Your father said you knew nothing of the forest elves—nothing about our people—until a few months ago. Why would one of the high druids of the sacred circle take you under her wing?"

"*Our* father, you mean," she corrected him.

Leifander dismissed that with an impatient wave.

"Rylith says that twins with hazel eyes are favored of the gods," she continued, "and that their birth is an omen of good fortune to come. You and I have a . . . a special destiny."

Leifander merely nodded. Any child could have told him that. Who did this human think she was, to parrot back to him his own people's lore? He frowned at the wall, not looking at her. Yet despite himself, he listened.

"Rylith says our half-sister Somnilthra prophesied that we would heal a great rift. Rylith says this rift is the one between human and elf—the one that led to this war."

Leifander quickly turned his head. "The High Council has declared war?"

"Yes, but Rylith says there's still time to stop it—some action that you and I can take that will prevent the war from happening. I must confess, I haven't a clue what it might be."

Leifander shook his head. "Why would we want to stop the war?"

That seemed to surprise her. It took Larajin a moment to find her voice. When she did, her tone was incredulous.

"Because . . . people will die." When he shrugged, she quickly added, "And not just humans. The war could wipe out the forest elves and raze the forest."

"Nonsense," Leifander retorted. "The humans will never defeat us. They can't even see in the dark. Some of us may fall, but the forest will remain ours forever."

Above them, a wagon rumbled over the grate, then stopped, blocking the sunlight.

"Why don't you care if there's a war?" Larajin asked, her voice rising in exasperation. "There must be someone you love, someone you don't want to see killed."

Leifander lowered his eyes. "She's already dead."

It had been said in a whisper, more to himself than to Larajin, but she'd heard him nonetheless. Her expression changed in an instant.

"What happened?" she asked softly.

He glared at her. "Humans killed her. Red Plumes, from Hillsfar. She ventured too close to their city, and they tried to capture her for their 'games.' I'm told she died bravely, killing two of them before she herself was slain."

Pride should have flared in his heart, but the pain was still too new. Chandrell had been his first love—worshiped from afar since she was a woman of fifty-eight years, and he a mere boy of twenty-one. Officially, he had yet to reach maturity, though the blood of a man already flowed hot in his veins. When she'd kissed him on the cheek after he'd done her a slight favor, he'd vowed to ask her to leap the bough with him, once he was at last old enough. He had prayed to his goddess that she would find no other lover before then.

Chandrell had been killed more than two years ago, but thinking of her still made his eyes sting. He'd succeeded in damping down his emotions all that time, but they squeezed out in the form of a single tear.

"I'm sorry," Larajin said softly, "but it would seem your quarrel is with Hillsfar, not with Sembia."

"It's with *humans*!" Leifander snapped, angrily wiping the tear away. "They should all be put to the sword."

"Then you might as well start with yourself," she spat back. "Or at least, half of yourself." She thrust a hand out, offering the magic dagger. "Here. Be my guest."

Leifander knocked her hand aside. This stupid woman was missing the point. Humans—Sembians, specifically—started the war with their magical depredations upon the forest. They had been the ones to break the ancient pact, and now they had to pay. If it meant a war, so be it. The elves would give a good accounting of themselves. Even if they were outnumbered, they would be fighting in the forest, on their own terms. The forest would protect them—and they would protect it, in turn.

"Your people understand nothing of pride, of honor," he told her. "That's what this war is about. Our dignity!"

"This talk about 'your people' and 'my people' is nonsense," she shouted back at him. "I'm a half-elf—and so are you!"

Leifander's rebuke was cut short by a grating noise overhead. Looking up, he noticed that Tal had returned.

"By the gods, keep quiet!" he hissed down at them. "I could hear you halfway down the street."

He lay prone on the road under the wagon and was reaching for something beside him. He found it, and passed a sack down to Larajin, who sheathed her dagger and waded forward to grab it. She opened it and began thrusting clothes at Leifander, not bothering to wait until he took them, just piling them on the ledge at his feet, together with a waterskin.

"Here," she said tersely. "Wash the worst of the sewage off, and disguise yourself with these. Unless you'd rather let a mob drag you through the streets."

Leifander picked up the nearest piece of clothing, a pair of white hose. Larajin was right, of course. If he was going to try to summon one of his feathered kin, he'd have a better chance of it away from the stinking sewer, and that meant going up onto the street. He had to pass as human, at least temporarily. He poured water over his legs and calves, rinsing off as much of the sewage as he could, then grudgingly yanked the hose over his wet feet. He put on a matching white doublet with sleeves slashed in gold and royal blue. There were leather gloves to cover his tattooed hands and black velvet slippers for his feet, and a gold turban set with tinkling silver bells, that sat awkwardly on his ears. In order to get it to fit, he had to tuck the points of his ears inside it. He grimaced, feeling foolish, then picked up the last item of clothing—a scarf similar to the one that Tal had worn and obviously intended to serve the same purpose—and wrapped it around his face, hiding his tattoos. It smelled strongly of perfume—a welcome change from the sewer.

Tal grinned down from above. He was no longer wearing the scarf that had covered his own face. He looked like any other human, which made Leifander wonder what he'd been hiding.

"Not bad," Tal said. "You look just like one of our—"

The wagon he was hiding under creaked as someone got into it, interrupting whatever he'd been about to say. Tal glanced back over his shoulder. From that direction came the sound of restless hooves against cobblestones.

"Let's get moving," he hissed, extending a hand down through the hole where the grate had been.

Leifander took it and allowed Tal to help him climb out of the sewer. He wriggled out onto his belly—soiling the fresh white clothes on the dirty cobblestones—and a moment later was joined by Larajin. The wagon above rolled away just as Tal slid the grate back into place. Suddenly exposed, the three lay at one edge of a crowded street.

There were humans everywhere—nobles strutting along with parasols to shade themselves from the late afternoon sun, peddlers pushing carts filled with rattling wares, gilded carriages rattling past, and throngs of humans carrying packages, boxes, and sacks, winding their way through the crowd. No one seemed to pay the slightest attention to the three "humans" who had appeared on the road after the wagon pulled away, though one or two did wrinkle their noses as they passed, no doubt smelling Larajin's filthy boots. As Tal, Larajin, and Leifander stood, brushing themselves off, only one or two heads turned. After a few brief, puzzled frowns they turned away, more concerned with going about their own business than satisfying idle curiosity.

"Come on," Larajin said, taking Leifander's arm. "My friend has a perfume shop, just a little down the road. We can hide there until we figure out how to get out of the city."

Leifander shook off her hand. Remembering his manners, he pressed a hand to his heart and gave her a brief bow.

"I thank you for helping me escape," he said, "despite the fact that had you arrived a moment later, I would have accomplished an escape on my own."

Ignoring Larajin's skeptical look and Tal's snort of disbelief, he continued, "I do not require any further assistance. We may share the same parents—" At this, Tal's eyebrows rose—"but that puts you under no obligation. Good-bye."

He turned to go, but Larajin caught his arm a second time.

"Th-the prophecy!" she sputtered. "The war." She glanced at Tal with troubled eyes, as if expecting him to lend his voice. "Rylith says we're the only ones who can stop it. She's a druid—a fellow elf. If you won't believe me, surely you'll believe her."

Beside her, Tal was looking increasingly nervous.

"Uh, Larajin," he whispered. "People are listening."

It was true. At the mention of the word "elf," more than one head had turned. Their argument was starting to attract attention, but Leifander didn't care. Exhausted from his long battle with the rats, itching in the hot clothes, still smelling of the sewer, and with the gods-cursed bells on the turban tinkling in his pinched ears, he'd had enough. He wanted to be rid of the two humans, to get away on his own somewhere where he could summon a crow, skinwalk, and launch himself into the clean blue sky and be quit of the stinking city.

"Larajin," Tal whispered again. "If we stand here and argue, the guards might see us. If he wants to leave, let him."

"Tal, it's not that simple," Larajin pleaded. "I have to make Leifander understand. If there's war, you'll . . ." She hesitated, blinking back tears. "The elves will kill you."

Now people were stopping and staring. "Elves?" one noble-woman asked in a fluttering voice.

"Should we call the guard?" a man asked, looking nervously around.

"They're just talking about the war," another muttered, shaking his head and walking on.

"That's right," Tal said quickly. "Nothing to get alarmed about. We're just—" Whatever else he had to say was drowned out by the rumble of a passing carriage.

Leifander was feeling claustrophobic again, hemmed in by the crush of people in the street. Tal and Larajin might have been trying to help, but they were only drawing unwanted attention.

"Black Archer pierce you both!" he hissed, yanking his arm out of Larajin's grasp.

Larajin's face paled. "Take it back!" she cried. "You've cursed him—take it back."

Leifander touched his forefinger to his lips through the fabric of the scarf, then flicked the curse up toward the heavens. "No."

"Take it back!" Larajin said again, in a high, tight voice.

Stubbornly, Leifander shook his head.

"Gods curse you!" she screamed, lunging at him and slamming both palms into his shoulders.

Taken by surprise, Leifander tripped backward over the curb. He fell heavily but sprang to his feet a moment later. Only when he heard the gasps of the crowd that had formed a circle around them did he realize what was wrong. His turban had been jostled off when he fell. The crowd was staring at his ears, their faces frozen in horror.

The silence broke. "An elf!" one man howled. "A spy! Call the guard!"

Pandemonium broke out all around them. People collided with one another, some scrambling to get away, others struggling to draw daggers or swords and lunge forward.

Still others turned with gallant concern as the noblewoman who had spoken earlier fainted, crumpling slowly to the ground in a heap amid her skirts.

Leifander spun, looking for an exit, but found none. He thrust out his hands, tattooed fingers splayed, then remembered at the last moment that he was unable to skinwalk. Nearly weeping with frustration, he wished for a feather—just one tiny black feather—so that he could fly.

Then Larajin spoke, in a tone he had not heard her use before. She sang out a single word in a voice as sweet as song, vibrant and pure. "*Calm*. Be calm, everyone!"

Amazingly, it worked. All around them, the crowd jerked to a sudden halt, and slowly limbs and faces relaxed. Leifander felt his own body relax as a feeling of peace settled upon him like the sweet languor found at the bottom of a bottle of wine. At the same time, a wonderful fragrance filled the air. After a moment, he recognized it as the scent that accompanied the winter-blossoming Hanali's Heart. He noticed the heart-shaped locket hanging from a red cord around Larajin's wrist. It was glowing a dusky amber color.

Maybe she really did draw her magic from an elf goddess.

Tal seemed unaffected by the spell—or perhaps he was merely quick witted. He stepped forward and laid a hand on Leifander's shoulder. With only the slightest of winks, he turned to the crowd.

"This man *is* a spy," he told them. "He serves Sembia." He thumped a hand against the House Uskevren emblem on his surcoat. "He's half human and part of my company. Anyone who wants to challenge him will have to take it up with my commander, Master Ferrick."

The name seemed to carry some weight. More than one sword slid back into its scabbard, but one man, a portly noble in a maroon doublet and hose, wasn't satisfied.

"What about the woman?" he asked. "She's awfully slender. Is she a halfie, too?"

Fear caused Larajin's eyes to widen, but otherwise she kept

her composure. "I'm as human as you are," she told the noble, then she yanked the scarf from her head, shaking her hair back from her ears. "Look here—do you see any points?"

Grudgingly the noble shook his head. His was the last challenge. The crowd seemed to believe Tal's bluff. People were already starting to disperse.

The glow surrounding Larajin's locket faded, and the scent of flowers vanished from the air.

"Come on," Tal muttered. "Let's get out of here."

Leifander, seeing the wisdom in this suggestion, scooped up his turban and pulled it back on, making ready to follow. Once he was away from the crowd, on a quiet street, he could try again to summon a crow.

Larajin, however, was slower to react. She stood in place, eyes glistening, whispering what sounded like a prayer.

"Hanali Celanil, forgive me," she said. "I did not mean to deny my heritage."

With a heavy sigh, she turned to follow them.

CHAPTER 9

"So that's it, then," Larajin said. "You're leaving. You're not even going to try to help."

Leifander squatted on the second-story balcony of Kremlar's perfume shop, stroking the glossy black feathers of a crow. The bird had come to his whispered prayer as faithfully as a hound to a horn, then it had plucked a downy feather from its breast and offered it to Leifander.

"There's nothing we can do," he answered as he took the feather from the crow.

"Not separately, no," Larajin conceded, "but Rylith said that together—"

"You are a Sembian," Leifander said, "and I belong to the Tangled Trees."

That seemed to be all that he was going to say. Leifander dismissed the crow, which took off into the dusk with a loud caw. He undid a strand of the braid that hung down his back, and lashed the feather securely to it with a length of fine embroidery thread Kremlar had given him.

Larajin turned to Tal, but he only shrugged. "I don't see how the pair of you could stop the war," he said. "It's inevitable. The armies are mobilizing; the militia from Ordulin is already on the march to—"

He stopped abruptly, remembering there was an elf present. Deliberately turning his back on Leifander, he strode to the far end of the balcony and stared up at the evening sky. Sunset painted the western sky a dusky yellow-red; the clouds looked as though they contained a smoldering fire.

Inside, Kremlar fussed with an oil lamp, trimming its wick. The dwarf had invited them up to his personal quarters above the shop and had listened with rapt attention as Larajin told Tal and Leifander about her journey north to the Tangled Trees, repeating what the druid had told her about the twins' destiny. Now he seemed embarrassed to be listening, like a host who finds his guests in the middle of a quarrel. When the wick was at last trimmed he stood nervously, fiddling with the rings that adorned each of his fingers.

On the balcony, Leifander spread his arms. A flutter ran through his tattooed fingers. He turned to Larajin, and gave her a long look.

"Good-bye, sister. May your goddesses protect you. I pray we never have to face each other as enemies."

A shudder coursed through him, long black feathers sprouted at his fingertips, and his body hunched in upon itself and shrank. In no more than a few heartbeats, he had transformed into a crow. He sprang into the air and flew up the street.

Larajin ran to the balcony and watched Leifander go. He headed northwest, toward the city walls and the River Arkhen. From there, she assumed, he would wing his way north toward the ancient woods, leaving her back where she'd started, in Selgaunt.

On the street below, she heard one of the city guard call out the All's Well. Hurriedly, she drew back from the balcony and retreated into Kremlar's rooms.

After a glance down at the guard in the street, Tal followed her inside.

"What will you do now?" he asked. "I'd advise that you not go home. The streets around Stormweather Towers have been thick with the guard, and Drakkar has come calling twice. He's still looking for you."

Kremlar walked nervously to the balcony doors and shut them, turning the key in the deadbolt. Lifting the tip of his neatly braided beard to his lips, he absently chewed on it—a habit that surfaced only when he was extremely nervous.

"You could . . . stay here with me," Kremlar said hesitantly.

Larajin was touched by the offer. Kremlar was desperately afraid of wizards. Years before, one had turned him to stone, after an exotic herb Kremlar had provided him proved stale. He'd stood in the wizard's garden for three long, desperate years, sentient but unable to move, before friends found him and prevailed upon a cleric to reverse the spell.

"Thank you, Kremlar," she said, then attempted a joke, "but your guest bed is far too small. My feet would hang out the end."

Kremlar merely nodded.

"Wherever Leifander's gone," Larajin continued, "I have to try to follow him. It's a matter of life or death."

She stared intently at a painting on the wall without really seeing it, not wanting to even glance in Tal's direction. If she did, the prickling in her eyes would almost certainly turn into a flood of tears.

"Master Ferrick says our company will be riding tomorrow," Tal said. "That's why I was in your room when you . . . reappeared. I was hoping to carry some token of yours with me into battle."

"You're leaving tomorrow?" Larajin rounded on him. "Why didn't you tell me?"

"You were concerned with rescuing your twin brother," he said in a voice bordering on annoyance. "I didn't want to ... distract you from what seemed to be your primary concern."

Larajin bit back her reply: that Tal *was* her primary concern. And tomorrow he would be riding to war. On fast horses, his company could reach the edge of the elven wood in as little as a tenday. Having witnessed the swift and silent attack by the elves on the Foxmantle caravan, Larajin knew what kind of reception awaited Master Ferrick's troops, once they reached the forest. Even if the rest of the company survived the attack, Tal would not.

"I didn't have a chance to tell you before now," Tal continued. "Especially with . . ." He shrugged. "Master Ferrick ordered us not to tell anyone when we'd ride—'A careless word is oft o'erheard' is his motto."

Larajin was only half listening. Her mind was entirely on the immediate problem. Leifander was gone, and she was trapped, once again, in Selgaunt. She could guess where Leifander was headed—back home to the Tangled Trees—but in order for her to follow him, she'd somehow have to get out of the city.

Suddenly, she realized the answer. "Tal—how large is Master Ferrick's company?"

Tal frowned. "Nearly two hundred riders. Why?"

"Do you think one more would be noticed?"

Tal was quick to guess her plan. He thought a moment, then answered, "You'd need armor and a surcoat and a horse."

"Could you get them for me? Would you?"

He nodded. "You can ride with us to Ordulin and take refuge there until Drakkar has at last given up his search for you. Ordulin should be a safe place to wait this war out."

"Thanks, Tal." Larajin gave her half-brother a grateful hug, then she turned to Kremlar and said, "I will take you up on that offer of a guest bed, after all, Kremlar, but just for one night."

Kremlar nodded.

The scratching of claws against glass drew Larajin's eyes to the balcony door.

"Goldheart!" she exclaimed. "What are you doing?"

The answer was obvious enough. The tressym was trying to get inside. She stood on her hind legs, wings folded against her back and forepaws scratching at the leaded glass. Over and over she pawed at it, then, when the people inside failed to promptly open the doors, she launched herself onto the rail of the balcony and perched there, wings flapping urgently.

"Gods protect us," Larajin exclaimed. "Let her in, Kremlar, before one of the guard sees her!"

It was Tal, however, who grabbed the key from Kremlar, sprinted for the doors, and opened them. As the tressym leaped down from the rail and padded inside, Kremlar trotted beside her, trying to herd her along by waving his hands in shooing motions.

"Don't let her near the furniture," he said in an anxious voice. "That chair cost me a hundred and twenty ravens."

Seemingly in response, Goldheart paused to knead the carpet. As her long white claws hooked its plush weave, tearing little tufts in the wool, Kremlar made a strangled noise and fluttered his hands more urgently. Goldheart looked up at the dwarf with wide, innocent eyes, then turned her back on him and walked straight up to Larajin and sat at her feet.

Yrrow?

Larajin stared down at the tressym. Was it just her imagination, or had Goldheart just spoken to her? Her ears heard a meow, but her heart heard a word: "Yes?"

A second meow, and again the echo of words in Larajin's mind: "You called for me?"

The air was thick with a flowery scent. Kremlar, who had fallen to his knees to pat the damaged carpet threads back into place, looked up and sniffed.

"That fragrance," he said, brows furrowed with the concentration of a connoisseur. "Sune's Kisses, if I don't miss my guess."

Larajin heard all of this in a strange echo, as if Kremlar's voice was coming from the bottom of a deep well. The only thing she heard with clarity was the voice of the tressym, who stood like a soldier at attention, wings neatly folded and forelegs stiff and straight.

"Yes, Lady?" she asked. "How may I be of service?"

This had to be Hanali Celanil's work. Larajin could think of no other reason why the tressym would suddenly develop human speech. She dropped to her knees and mirrored the tressym's pose, leaning forward on her hands.

"Goldheart, I need to find out where Leifander went—can you help?" As she spoke, a part of her mind registered the fact that her throat and mouth were making sounds like the meowing of a cat. Yet she could hear her words—and Goldheart's reply—as plainly as if they were speaking in the common tongue.

"He turned into a bi*rrrr*d," Goldheart answered with the faintest of growls. "A strange-smelling bird." A pink tongue darted out to wet thin lips. "He flew away."

"Could you follow him?" Larajin asked.

Goldheart's pupils dilated. "Chase!" she said excitedly. Her claws flexed into the carpet.

"Yes, chase," Larajin said, "but don't hurt him. Just follow—see where he goes, then come and find me, and tell me where he is. Can you do that?"

Larajin had no doubt the tressym could accomplish the task. No matter where Larajin had gone, in the past two tendays, Goldheart had been able to follow her—somehow even managing to include herself in the spell Larajin had cast to transport herself back to Selgaunt. The question really was, *would* Goldheart do it?

The tressym considered the request, then closed her eyes for an instant. It was the feline equivalent of a smile.

"I'll do it."

She rose, stretched, and rubbed her cheek affectionately against Larajin's arm, then turned and padded out onto the balcony. With a bright flutter of colorful wings, she launched herself into the air and was gone.

Tal, looking down at Larajin, uttered some garbled words. After a moment—when Larajin's ears had stopped tingling—she was able to grasp their meaning.

"That creature spoke to you?" he'd asked, a perplexed frown on his face. "What did it say?"

"She's going to follow Leifander and tell me where he's flown to," Larajin explained. "I'm going after him."

Tal's face clouded. "Why bother?" he grumbled. "He already said he wouldn't help you."

"He's my twin brother, Tal," she said. "It's important that we're together—the gods themselves are working to bring that about. Somehow, we've got to try to stop this war. I don't know how—I just know that we must."

She reached up and brushed an unruly strand of dark hair away from Tal's eyes.

"You've got to believe me, Tal. This is important. For everyone. Especially for you."

Tal's face paled. "Let's get ready, then," he said brusquely. "I'll fetch you a uniform, and ready a horse. In the morning, we'll ride."

Disguised as a soldier of Master Ferrick's company, Larajin slipped out of Selgaunt without incident. Guards in the gatehouse that opened onto the High Bridge gave the riders only a bored glance as they rode from the city. Larajin, clad in a mail shirt and surcoat, her hair tucked under a wide-brimmed cap, was no more to them than another soldier.

The company rode north throughout the morning, making good progress. When the sun reached its zenith, they stopped to water the horses and eat a quick meal. As she dismounted, Larajin spotted a familiar flash of color in the distance. Goldheart had returned and had landed behind a clump of bushes not far from the road.

Taking her leave of the other soldiers—pretending she was going to relieve herself behind the bushes—Larajin sought the tressym out. She cast the spell that would allow them to communicate and quickly learned that Goldheart had indeed been able to follow Leifander. The route he'd taken, however, was a surprise. Instead of winging due north, as Larajin had expected, he'd followed the River Arkhen. He'd flown upriver for several miles, continuing to follow the river almost until dawn, then at last shifted back into elf form to enter the Reverie.

"You did well, Goldheart," Larajin said, stroking the tressym. Goldheart gave a rumbling purr of pride, closing her eyes in a catlike smile. "Now I want you to return to where you last saw Leifander, find him again if you can, and continue to follow him until he ends his journey—until he spends more than a single night in one place. Can you do that?"

Goldheart nodded, then nudged Larajin's hand again, demanding another pat on the back. Larajin obliged her, then heard the sound of footsteps coming around the bushes.

"Go," she whispered to the tressym. "Quickly."

Goldheart flew away just as Tal strode into sight. He glanced up at the departing tressym and said something unintelligible. After a moment, Larajin's spell wore off. She could guess what he'd asked.

"I'm heading in the wrong direction," she told him. "Leifander flew northwest. He seems to be following the River Arkhen. When the company sets out again, I'm going to slip away and head upriver. If Master Ferrick notices me going, will you speak to him—explain why one of his 'soldiers' is leaving?"

Tal stared at her a long moment before nodding. "I don't like you setting out on your own," he said, "but I can see your mind is made up. Just promise me you'll be careful. That river path is a dangerous one—especially these days."

Larajin caught his hand and gave it a squeeze. "Thanks, Tal. Promise me that you'll be careful, too."

He grunted and gave a soldier's offhand shrug.

Larajin peered around the bushes and said, "It looks as if the others are getting ready to mount up again. We'd better get back, or they'll think we're both trying to slip away."

Then, seeing the thoughtful gleam in Tal's eye, she quickly added, "You could, you know . . . come with me. It would be safer."

Tal shook his head. "I'm no coward. It's my duty to fight, and I'm not shirking it. Even if—"

Larajin pressed fingers to his lips, silencing him. "Don't say it, Tal," she pleaded. "You'll survive this war, gods willing."

"Gods willing," Tal echoed grimly.

Larajin rode northwest, following a trail that was little more than a footpath bordered by thick forest on the right and a sheer drop to the river below on the left. Despite the slow pace it enforced, the path beside the river offered achingly beautiful scenery—too beautiful to be anything but the work of the goddess. Tufts of feathery fern and stunted maples with dark red foliage grew out of clefts of rock in the canyon below, their leaves and branches jeweled with river mist. More mist hung in the air above the river, sparkling with tiny rainbows. Trees shaded the path itself, filtering the afternoon sun to a pleasant warmth and rustling in the breeze.

In places, the path switchbacked down to the river, allowing Larajin a chance to splash ice-cold water onto her face while her horse drank. The pools offered darting silver fish and freshwater crabs, some of which Larajin had caught and cooked over a fire the night before.

As she rode, she kept watching for the flash of color that would announce Goldheart's return, but there was no sign of the tressym. Did that mean Leifander was traveling still? Had he veered north, already flown all the way back to the Tangled Trees? Or had he flown off in some other direction? There was no way of knowing.

Larajin was starting to wonder if doubling back to follow the River Arkhen had been the right decision. It might have been more sensible to have continued with Master Ferrick's company to Ordulin, then ridden the Dawnpost trail west. She would have reached Archenbridge—the town where the trail she did take ended—in about the same amount of time.

Instead she'd been on the river trail for six days with no sign of Leifander and no reports from Goldheart to let her know if she was still headed in the right direction. Tal and his company would have ridden as far as Featherdale. Just three more days riding would put them at the southern edge of the forest of Cormanthor.

Larajin gasped as her horse stumbled on a loose rock at the cliff's edge, sending her rocking backward in the saddle. For several agonizing moments her heart hammered in her chest as the horse's hind foot scrabbled for purchase, sending a scatter of rocks and dirt into the river below. Clinging to the pommel of her saddle, she prayed for deliverance, then the horse found its footing. With a second lurch it was upright and walking again.

Glancing back over her shoulder, Larajin stared at the spot where the horse had faltered. Far below the scuffed trail, the River Arkhen dashed itself against jagged rocks in its haste to reach the sea. Larajin and her horse had nearly joined it. Breathing a prayer of thanks to the goddesses for protecting her, she vowed to pay more attention to the trail.

Ahead the path leveled and widened, turning away from the edge of the canyon, into the trees. Larajin at last relaxed, lowering the reins and letting the horse find its own way. In the distance ahead she could hear the thunder of a waterfall. Archendale must be closer than she thought.

Then she realized that the noise was coming from the east,

away from the river. The waterfall at Archendale would be more to the north. . . .

Suddenly a running figure—a woman, with a strangely hunched back—appeared on the trail ahead. She was clad in dusty trousers and a shirt several times too large for her slender frame. She had a narrow face, hair so blonde it was almost white, and an elf's ears and eyes. She stumbled as she ran, wincing with each step of her bare feet. Her arms were thrown out ahead of her, as if she expected to fall at any moment, and her mouth was open wide, her chest heaving as she gasped for breath.

Startled, Larajin reined her horse to a stop. In the same moment the running woman saw her. The woman skidded to a halt several paces away and stared, wide-eyed. She glanced back over her shoulder in the direction of the rumbling sound, at Larajin again, then she darted off into the woods at the side of the trail.

A moment later, three riders burst into view. Seeing Larajin, they halted their horses. One of them—a man who looked like a half-orc, with hair that was receding above a bulging forehead and a muscular neck as thick as a tree trunk—glared at her, while the other two turned this way and that, peering into the woods. All three were clad in chain mail and carried shields emblazoned with a red sword. Larajin recognized them by that emblem as soldiers of Archendale.

"The elf!" the man with the thick neck shouted. "Did you see an elf run past just now?"

His horse pranced under him and snorted its impatience, as if eager to resume the chase.

Larajin felt her eyes narrow slightly, but she kept her face composed. She recognized the hand of the goddess when she saw it. After failing to intervene on behalf of the Harper agent who was beaten by the mob in his shop in Ordulin, Larajin was being given a chance to redeem herself.

"Oh, dear," she exclaimed, casting her face into a worried expression. "That must have been what I heard just a moment ago. A scream. It was just before I passed a spot near a cliff, where the trail had crumbled away. This elf of yours must have gone over the edge!"

She turned to stare behind her, toward the section of trail she'd just ridden.

"Right. Let's take a look, lads."

Spurring his horse forward, the leader of the soldiers rode past Larajin. Her own horse shied away, pinching her leg against the trunk of a tree. The other two soldiers followed in his wake. Larajin heard the hoofbeats abruptly slow—they must have come to the bend where the trail turned to follow the cliff edge—and she nudged her own horse forward. As she rode past the spot where the elf had darted into the woods, she glanced neither right nor left, in case the soldiers were looking.

She'd ridden no more than a hundred paces before the soldiers returned, this time riding at a trot. As they passed, forcing her horse to the side of the trail, Muscle Neck waved his thanks. The back of his right hand had a strange scar on it; a pattern of raised lines that looked like a brand.

Larajin waited until the hoofbeats of their horses had receded into the distance, then she turned her horse and rode back down the trail, stopping in the place where she'd last seen the elf. After a moment, a narrow face peeked out of a crack in a hollow stump a few paces into the forest. The elf squeezed out from inside the stump with difficulty, wincing as her misshapen back brushed against its trunk. She turned to Larajin and gave a peculiar bow, thrusting her arms behind her as she bent at the waist.

As the elf bowed, Larajin could see that the deformity on the woman's back seemed to be centered upon her shoulders. Just below each was a large hump, its exact shape hidden by the baggy shirt she wore.

"You I thank, lady," the elf said, though it took Larajin a moment or two to understand the words, which were spoken in a strange accent. It was almost as if the woman trilled her words. Her speech had the inflection of a song.

"Why were those men chasing you?" Larajin asked.

"I . . . came to Arch Dale after many miles journey," the woman said, watching Larajin's face all the while for her reaction. "Soldier with mark on hand, he recognize. He know I come from Hillsfar, by this mark."

She held up her left hand. On the back of it was a brand identical to the one on Muscle Neck's hand. Except that the elf's brand was fresher, still pink.

"I didn't think elves were allowed in Hillsfar," Larajin said.

A bitter look crossed the woman's face. "In arena, only. In games."

Larajin understood. She'd heard of the arena in Hillsfar—it was known far and wide in Faerûn. The Hillsfar Arena was the scene of fabled contests in which gladiators pitted themselves against fearsome monsters. Ogres, trolls, minotaurs . . . all had soaked the arena's sand with their blood.

Muscle Neck must have been one of the gladiators who fought there, and so must this elf, though with her fine bones and deformed shoulders she looked too frail to be a fighter.

"Were you a gladiator?" Larajin asked.

The woman frowned. "I am *elf.*"

She seemed to think this explanation enough, but it left Larajin unenlightened.

"I thought you said that elves fight in the arena," Larajin said.

"Elves *die* in arena," the woman said. "They are put in, with long chain at ankle. No escape can be make. It makes the crowd to laugh."

The words were spoken softly, but they made Larajin's blood turn cold. This woman might have spoken in the third person, but it was clear from the ache in her eyes that she was relating a horror that she herself had experienced. Larajin pictured her unarmed, chained to the center of the arena, frantically trying to escape the sword slashes of a burly gladiator like Muscle Neck while the crowd laughed and jeered.

"You escaped from the Hillsfar Arena, didn't you?" Larajin said in a grim voice. "That soldier—the one that looked like a half-orc—he was trying to capture you and sell you back."

The woman nodded, a quick bob of the head.

"What's your name?"

The elf hesitated, as if trying to decide whether to trust her. At last she answered. "Kith. You?"

Larajin gave truth for truth, answering with her real name, instead of Thazienne's. "Where are you headed?" she asked.

"To Evermeet."

Larajin frowned. "That's a long way from here. Why Evermeet?"

Kith's eyes brightened. "I be told it is place of all elves, of great magic. I go to . . . seek a great healing. Then I may follow wind home."

Healing? The woman must have been talking about her deformity.

"Where is home?" Larajin asked.

Kith answered with a sharp, sweet trill. After a moment, Larajin realized that this must have been the name of the place she came from.

"I've never heard of it," she told Kith, then she added, "If you're journeying to Evermeet, shouldn't you be headed west? You must have followed the Moonsea Ride out of Hillsfar. Why didn't you just stay on that road?"

Kith shrugged and immediately winced. Her deformed shoulders must have pained her.

"Red Plumes would follow," she answered. "Instead I come through trees, to Highmoon."

Larajin nodded. Journeying through the great forest made sense. Kith had probably been aided by the wood elves. It also explained how she had come so far with so little. The woman didn't seem to have a pack or provisions. Having reached

Highmoon, however, Kith should have continued west along the road that led through Thunder Gap and into Cormyr.

"You turned south, into Archendale," Larajin prompted. "Why?"

"Giants," Kith answered. She said no more, as if that one word was explanation enough. Then, seeing the blank look in Larajin's eyes, she added, "I am told giants be in mountains through which pierces road. They are enemy to my people. Without my . . ." She paused, then continued. "I would have no chance against them. I am told of southern road, one that passes south of mountains without piercing. Way of the Manticore. Do you know it?"

Larajin nodded. "That road is a long way from here—at least six days' journey to the south. There's no way to cross the river until you reach Selgaunt, and that means entering Sembia, which isn't exactly welcoming elves at the moment. You wouldn't be safe in the south. You'd do better to take your chances crossing the mountains. Maybe you could join a caravan. That should offer some protection from the—"

Kith balled her fist and all but shook it at Larajin. "They will see the mark!" she trilled. "They will think of Red Plumes' coin, and greed fill their hearts."

"That is a problem, it's true," Larajin acknowledged. "Even so, I would recommend the mountains as a better option. You can't travel any farther south. If you do, you'll be mistaken for a spy and killed."

Slowly, with a defeated look on her face, Kith lowered her hand. "All winds blow against I, it does seem," she said sadly.

"Not all the winds," Larajin said, trying to sound encouraging. "They blew me your way, didn't they? And those soldiers aren't looking for you any more. They'll be back in Archendale before dark and will soon forget all about you."

An idea struck her, and she added, "Why don't you travel with me a while—at least for the rest of today—and camp with me tonight? Here, climb up on the horse behind me."

She leaned over in the saddle and extended a hand down to Kith. After a moment, the elf took it. Placing a foot in the stirrup that Larajin had just removed her foot from, she swung lightly up behind her, and settled into place, her legs tucked against the saddlebags. She clutched nervously at the sides of Larajin's shirt as the horse began to walk. Kith had obviously never been on horseback before.

"Where we are travel?" Kith asked.

"I won't know that until Goldheart returns," Larajin said over her shoulder.

"Gold Heart?" Kith repeated. She thought about it a moment. "This be companion to you?"

"A companion, yes," Larajin answered with a smile. "One whose value I only recently realized." For the hundredth time that day, she glanced up at the sky through the trees, hoping to see the familiar flash of colorful wings. "I just hope nothing's happened to her."

That evening they made camp in the woods—well away from the trail, since by dusk the enormous stone arches of the bridge at Archendale had come into sight. Larajin fed and brushed the horse first—remembering what her adoptive father had taught her about always caring for your animals before attending to your own comforts—then she shared with Kith a simple meal of dried fruit and soldier's biscuit. It seemed to matter little to Kith that the latter was stale. The elf consumed it ravenously, as if she hadn't eaten in days. Perhaps that was why she was so thin.

Darkness fell swiftly as the sun sank behind the southernmost tip of the Thunder Peaks, just west of Archendale. Exhausted after her flight from the soldiers, Kith sank into a curious squatting position, her arms curled around her knees, and seemed to fall into a deep trance—the Reverie. Larajin made sure the horse hadn't slipped its hobbles—it was munching contentedly on some shoots of grass in the tiny clearing where she'd left it—then she lay down near Kith. She whispered her evening prayers, staring up through the branches at the bright pinpoints of the stars above, then she watched the moon slowly rise into view above the treetops. Its pale light flooded the forest.

Was Tal also staring up at the moon from his soldiers' camp? If her calculations were correct, in just a few more days his company would reach the forest of Cormanthor. She wondered if his last glance at the sky would be framed by the branches of trees, as was hers.

And what of Leifander—where was he? As to that, Larajin could not even hazard a guess. She whispered a prayer to Hanali Celanil, praising her for the beauty of the sky above and pleading with her to send word through her chosen messenger, as soon as she was able.

Larajin must have drifted off to sleep. She fell into a vivid dream in which she was soaring up through the air, rising toward the vivid stars above. All the world lay below her, a vast crazy-quilt of forest, lake, field, and town. Somewhere down below, there was something she was searching for, but when she tried to think of where it might be, her thoughts became hazy and confused. She realized she was not flying herself but was being carried by a giant eagle. Its wingtips brushed against her bare feet with each downstroke.

Larajin rolled over in her sleep, and the tickling against her foot stopped.

The dream resumed, but this time the eagle was gripping her in its feet. They completely enclosed her head. One of its talons was piercing the soft flesh of her—

With a start, Larajin awoke. Something was poking her cheek. It felt like the point of a dagger. Fumbling for her own dagger, she yanked it out of its scabbard.

"*Illunathros!*" she shouted, scrambling to her feet.

The trees all around her were bathed in the brilliant blue light of her enchanted dagger.

Sitting at her feet, wincing at the sudden glare, was Gold-heart. One paw was still raised. She had been kneading Larajin's cheek. Lowering her paw, she butted her head against Larajin's leg and began to purr.

A pace or two away, Kith sprang out of her crouch. She cried out as she spotted the tressym. A moment later, her alarm turned to a sigh of wonder as Goldheart unfolded her wings, shook them once delicately to smooth the feathers, then settled them against her back once more.

"This is Goldheart," Larajin explained. "The companion I mentioned earlier."

Kith fell to her knees in front of Goldheart and tentatively held out a hand. The tressym, after a quick sniff, lowered her head, indicating that the elf had permission to pat her. Kith stroked the tressym's head, hesitated, then ran her hand the length of Goldheart's back, fingers lingering upon the wings. The expression on her face, at first rapturous, soon turned to equal parts anguish and longing. She jerked her hand back and turned away, as if the very sight of the tressym pained her.

"What's wrong?" Larajin asked.

Words choked their way out of Kith's mouth. "I . . . had wings once. Gone, now."

"Wings?"

Kith fumbled at the ties that held her shirt closed, then yanked it down to her elbows, exposing her back. Under that baggy shirt lay the source of Kith's pain: two crudely hacked stubs where wings had once been. The severed limbs were healed over, but only just. The scars were still raw and red, the skin puckered and dotted with crude stitch marks. It looked as though muscle and bone had been severed with an axe, one brutal chop at a time. Larajin wondered how anyone could survive the agony that must have caused.

Kith's shoulders shook as she struggled to suppress her sobs. Goldheart, also staring at the elf's back, growled low in her throat, then, deliberately, she walked up to Kith and gave the elf's bare leg a gentle nudge with her cheek.

Kith yanked the shirt back up over her shoulders, wincing at its touch as she turned back to Larajin.

"You ask why I go Evermeet," she said. She jerked a thumb at her shoulder. "This be why. My shame. After I escape first time, arena let wizard take my wings, for his spells. How can I return to flock now? I must seek great healing, before return."

"Goddess grant it to you," Larajin whispered.

She realized what Kith was: an avariel elf—a breed of elf so rare that the books in Stormweather Towers had referred to them as mere legend. And here that "legend" stood in front of Larajin, broken and dejected. She wished she knew a healing spell that would regrow Kith's wings, but such powerful magic was beyond her. Her spells could close a wound, or slow bleeding, or even splice a shattered bone, but they could not regrow flesh and feather from air.

Kith's eyes dropped to Goldheart, who was still rubbing against her leg.

"Companion-to-Larajin, I know you mean comfort, but beautiful wings make sadness."

Turning away, Kith strode out of the circle of light cast by the dagger, into the moonlight-dappled forest. Larajin was about to run after her but paused as she heard Kith settle again, a short distance away in the woods. From that spot came the soft sound of a woman weeping.

Torn between her desire to comfort Kith and the certain knowledge that Goldheart must be bearing urgent news, Larajin hesitated. A familiar tingle began in her ears and lips. As it grew, she heard the tressym's meows turn into intelligible speech.

"She aches like a wounded bird," Goldheart observed, peering off into the darkness where Kith had disappeared. "Someone should give her a swift death."

"She needs healing," Larajin answered curtly, "and I can't give it to her."

Frustrated, she dropped to her knees in front of the tressym.

"I am glad to see that you are safe, Goldheart" she said. "Did you follow Leifander? Where is he now?"

"He nested for one night in a place not far from here, and another night in a place that lies a day's flight in that direction," Goldheart said, nodding toward the northwest as she spoke. "The place was at the edge of a great wood and had many trees heaped in piles. The humans and elves there busy themselves day and night building walls and practicing with their long-claws."

Larajin nodded. Goldheart must be describing a town in Deepingdale, known for its timber trade. She guessed that the "long-claws" were swords or daggers.

"He then flew toward the forest, stopping here and there to meet with groups of elves—but only nesting for one night in a single place. For the last two nights he has nested in the same spot: on a hill with no trees, only stones on top. I left him there this morning, and flew back to find you. I have been a day and most of this night returning."

Larajin mulled that over. "Can you describe the stones on the hill?" she asked.

Goldheart thought a moment, then scratched at the ground with a paw, leaving a half-circle mark. "They formed a bent line, like this."

"How many stones?"

"Many."

Larajin held up one hand, fingers splayed. "This many?"

"More."

She laid the dagger down, and held up her other hand. "This many?"

Goldheart studied her hands as the dagger's light waned. "Perhaps."

Larajin sat thinking as the dagger's light gradually went out. The moonlight was bright enough that she could still see the tressym clearly. Thanks to the elf blood that flowed in her veins, she could even see the colors of her wings.

"To get to this hill, how would you travel?" she asked.

"What would you see below as you flew?"

Goldheart thought a moment. "The place with the walls and piled-up trees, the edge of the forest, a river ... then the hill."

Larajin fell silent, considering this information. She had spent many long hours in the library at Stormweather Towers, reading every book she could find that described the history and geography of ancient Cormanthor, but none of the information she'd gleaned on the former elven kingdom mentioned a hill like the one Goldheart had just described.

Larajin did remember a map that showed the river Goldheart was probably talking about. It was called the Glaemril. It was reputed to be easy to cross. With Goldheart scouting from above and giving directions, Larajin could make her way to the hill where Leifander had camped, but she couldn't ride as fast as the tressym could fly—especially through thick forest. By the time she reached the hill, Leifander would probably be long gone.

The alternative was, of course, to have Goldheart return alone to the hill as soon as she was rested, and continue to follow Leifander, but that would leave Larajin blundering around in the forest on her own, searching in vain for a hill that might not even be visible from within the trees.

Remembering the dream she'd just awakened from, Larajin wished she had wings to fly—or that there was someone to carry her through the skies. If only the avariel elf still had her ...

A thought occurred to her then. Had the goddesses been trying to tell her something? Was it they who placed that dream in her mind?

If so, Larajin could see little use in it. Kith's wings were gone. She wasn't about to fly anywhere.

Goldheart rubbed against her, reminding Larajin of her presence. Larajin looked down at the tressym, remembering how Goldheart had looked when Larajin had found her in the Hunting Garden. Goldheart's wing had been broken and trailing behind her, feathers bedraggled and torn. Larajin had healed the wing, using the goddess's blessing to straighten bone, smooth scar tissue, and mend torn flesh and feather. When she'd finished, the wing was as good as new. Feathers that had been broken far short of their tips were whole again.

She shouldn't have been able to do that. According to the clerics in Sune's temple, it took many long years of prayer and study to develop the skills needed to use magic to regrow a body part, even something as small as a finger—or a feather.

Yet Larajin had done it. How?

As Larajin crouched, stroking Goldheart's silky fur with her free hand, she pondered. As recently as a few days before, she had managed what also should have been an impossible spell. With just the briefest bit of instruction from Rylith, she'd instantly transported herself over many miles, to a place of refuge.

Again, she had no idea how.

She sat, staring at the heart-shaped locket that hung from her wrist. After a long moment, she realized the answer. Normally, when she cast a spell, it was with the blessing of one goddess or the other. The spell was accompanied either by a red glow or by the scent of Hanali's Heart, but both times when she had cast a spell that should have been well beyond her, both the aura and the scent had manifested at once. Both goddesses had bestowed their blessings upon Larajin in the same instant, enhancing her power to cast spells.

Larajin still had no idea what she had done differently on those occasions. Had her prayers been more fervent—or had Sune and Hanali Celanil simply both been watching over her in the same instant? If she tried to cast a spell to regrow Kith's wings, would the goddesses respond to her prayer?

Larajin stared into the moonlight-dappled woods, toward the spot where she could hear the sound of Kith crying.

For Kith's sake, Larajin would at least try.

Giving Goldheart a final pat, she instructed the tressym to

wait where she was. Larajin didn't need the distraction of a feline rubbing against her leg as she tried to work her magic. She sheathed her dagger and strode into the woods.

Kith squatted near the base of a tree, hands clasped around her knees. Her tears had stopped, but she refused to look up as Larajin approached. Her eyes were locked on the ground as she rocked back and forth.

Larajin kneeled beside Kith and touched her arm.

"Kith?"

Kith flinched away.

"Kith, I'm a cleric. I know healing magic. I don't know if I am able, but I'd like to try to restore your wings."

Kith was instantly attentive. She rubbed an arm roughly across her face to wipe away her tears.

"You know a great healing? Why you not offer before?"

Larajin felt a guilty blush rise to her cheeks. "I . . . wasn't sure it would work," she said.

She bit her tongue, resolving not to tell Kith the real reason—that she needed the avariel elf's help to get to the hill Goldheart had described.

Larajin touched the locket at her wrist. "Shall I try?" she asked.

"Yes," Kith whispered.

"I need to touch you—to lay hands upon what remains of your wings. I'll try not to press too hard."

Kith nodded and pulled her shirt down, exposing the raw stumps where her wings had been.

"I be ready," she whispered.

"Then I'll begin."

Softly, Larajin began chanting a prayer. She started with the one she knew best: an invocation to Sune, a plea to set her worshipers' footsteps on the path to beauty, and to give their hands the power to restore beauty that had been lost. She followed it with a prayer to Hanali Celanil, one that praised the goddess for creating all of the brightly feathered creatures of the world. The prayer was imperfect, a rough translation in the common tongue, but as Larajin chanted it, a familiar fragrance arose around her. At the same time, a warm amber glow began to tingle her fingertips.

The scar tissue under her fingers smoothed, and Kith sighed in relief, but then the fragrance of flowers lessened, and the glow beneath her fingertips dimmed. Larajin's spell had smoothed the scars and was easing Kith's pain—but it was not enough. Unless she could restore Kith's wings entirely, she would never catch up to Leifander, Tal would die, and . . .

Kith gasped in pain. With a guilty start, Larajin realized that her fingers had been digging into the wing stubs. That was when she realized her mistake.

Gentling her touch, she whispered an apology. At the same time she resolved, in that instant, to merely heal Kith. If her spell was successful and Kith's wings were restored, she would not demand that Kith fly her to the hill where Leifander was camped. She would not even ask. If the goddesses willed it, Kith would offer of her own accord. If not . . .

Firmly, Larajin pushed any thought of the consequences out of her mind. Instead she began to pray once more. This time, the spell was entirely of her own devising. A name sprung to her lips unbidden: Lady Fireheart. Chanting it, Larajin felt a warmth rise in her heart and course down her arms toward her hands. It burst from her fingertips in a bright ruby glow. At the same time the scent of Hanali's Heart filled the air, a scent so strong that Larajin and Kith might have been crouching in an entire field of blossoms.

In that moment, Larajin felt something move under her hands. Kith must have felt it too. She gave a trilling cry that was half surprise, half joy, and shuddered. Her wings started to grow.

Flesh and muscle extended under Larajin's hands, and bone rushed outward to support them. A joint formed, then another length of wing, and all along it feathers sprouted and grew. Muscles twitched, skin rippled—and Larajin's hands were cast from the wings as they slowly unfurled, then burst into full extension as Kith sprang to her feet.

Larajin stared in wonder at Kith, who stood with a delighted look on her face, her wings fluttering gently. They were longer from shoulder to wingtip than the elf was tall, and their color was a shimmering white, each feather tipped at its end with a deep, glossy black. Kith stood confident and strong. Gone was the cringing, stooped posture she'd had earlier.

Trilling her delight, she burst into the air.

Larajin craned her head back, watching as Kith rose smoothly into the sky. Her white wings glowing in the moonlight, Kith circled once over the spot in the forest where Larajin stood. A moment later she was joined by Goldheart, who rose through the treetops to chase after her. Laughing, she tumbled with the tressym above the treetops, first letting Goldheart chase her, then sliding into a swooping turn or loop that put her in pursuit of the tressym.

On the ground below, Larajin watched the avariel elf and tressym at play. They shot overhead, Kith's wings making a whooshing sound loud enough for Larajin to hear, then disappeared behind the treetops. A moment later they soared back in a sweeping turn, disappeared from view again, then rose in a climb that saw both pairs of wings beating furiously, in what was seemingly a race to touch the moon. At the peak of their climb, each looped, one after the other, and dived toward the trees. So steep and rapid were their dives that Larajin winced, thinking they were about to dash themselves against the ground, but at the last instant each swooped just short of the treetops and disappeared from sight once more.

For several long moments Larajin stood alone in the forest, wondering if Goldheart and Kith had flown away and forgotten her, then she heard the beating of wings. First Kith then Goldheart descended between the trees, landing gently where Larajin stood.

Kith bowed deeply to Larajin, throwing her hands out behind her. Now that the elf had her wings back, what had at first appeared a peculiar motion made sense to Larajin. As the hands swept back, the wings unfurled, adding a sweeping grace to the bow, then the wings folded tight against Kith's back as the elf straightened.

"Larajin, great thanks," Kith said in a quiet trill. "From deep of my heart to tip of wing. I want return thanks to you. May I help for you, before winds carry home?"

Beside her, Goldheart folded her own wings and began washing a paw. Despite the tressym's seeming indifference, however, Larajin saw Goldheart glance coyly in her direction, as if sharing a secret.

"There is something you could help me with, but only if you truly wish to do so," Larajin answered.

"Please," Kith said. "Ask."

"There is a hill within the wood, a little over a day's flight northwest of here. Are your wings strong enough to carry me to it?"

Kith gave a trilling laugh, and unfurled her wings. Wedging one foot against a fallen log to brace herself, she flapped them with such vigor that the resulting wind buffeted Larajin, blowing her hair back over her shoulders.

"Strong?" Kith said, her eyes sparkling with delight. "More than before. Your goddess be most great." She folded her wings, chuckling. "When go?"

"As soon as possible," Larajin answered. "Tonight. I'll set the horse free—this close to Archenbridge, someone is sure to find it—and we can leave."

Kith nodded her agreement, and looked up at the sky.

"Moon is bright," she observed. "Good night for fly."

CHAPTER 10

The windriders flew in from the west, their nine mounts aligned in a V-shaped formation. Leifander shaded his eyes and peered into the setting sun, watching as the griffons and their riders drew nearer. Gradually they changed from distant silhouettes to individuals he could recognize.

At the point of the formation was Lord Kierin, resplendent in a red surcoat over chain mail and a burnished bronze helm, carrying a lance that sported several cream-colored ribbons that fluttered behind him. His griffon was a tawny giant with wings that shaded from pale brown to black at their tips. With the white head of a bald eagle and the body of a powerful lion, the griffon's forelegs ended in powerful talons, its hind legs in a lion's paws. Its tail streamed out behind it as it flew, lashing from side to side.

The other windriders rode similar mounts and were also armored in chain and helms. Each carried a lance, but these were primarily for show. Any real fighting was done with the powerful recurved bows and brightly fletched arrows that hung in quivers behind their saddles.

They circled once around the hilltop where Leifander stood, then landed gracefully next to its half-circle crown of upright stones. Lord Kierin housed his lance in a sling next to his stirrup, then swung out of the saddle. He was tall for an elf, with long white hair that matched the color of the ribbons on his lance. His eyes were the color of a summer sky. A deep vertical line creased his forehead, and his brows were drawn together in what had become a habitual frown. He was well beyond his middle years, in his third century of life, but Leifander had never seen a warrior with such poise and grace.

"Is it you, Leifander?" Lord Kierin said. He spoke the dialect of the Gold elves, but Leifander knew enough of it to reply in kind.

"I am he who bears that name." Leifander placed both hands upon his heart and bowed so low that his braid swung over his shoulder and touched the ground with its tip. "I beg your mercy for my transgression."

The other windriders had dismounted and gathered around the spot where Leifander and Lord Kierin stood. Five were male, three female, and all were moon elves with pale hair and amber eyes. They stood with legs slightly bowed from long years of riding, and seemed to stare through Leifander into the middle distance, as if still scanning the horizon.

Lord Kierin gave a deep, melancholy sigh. "Your words have placed me in great danger, it is true, but your transgression was no fault of your own. It was magic that moved your tongue and caused you to tell my true name, and so I forgive you."

Relief washed through Leifander in an icy shiver. It was Lord Kierin's right, should he so choose, to end Leifander's life. He had been generous.

"I hardly recognized you, my boy," Lord Kierin said,

switching into the forest elf dialect and dropping the formal tone he'd been using a moment earlier. "You have grown to an enormous size since last I saw you. Tell me, how is your father faring?"

He was referring, of course, to Leifander's adoptive father. Leifander had yet to summon the courage to tell others about the human blood that flowed in his veins.

"He is well, thank you, Lord Kierin," he answered, "as is my mother."

Lord Kierin switched back to the dialect that the other windriders spoke. "I hear that your eyes were also busy while you were in Selgaunt—with results much more to our favor." A rare smile twitched the corners of his mouth. "Did Lord Ulath send the rings with you?"

"He did." Leifander reached into the leather bag that was slung across his shoulder. Inside was an intricately carved wooden box the size of a loaf of bread. He handed it to Lord Kierin.

The windrider held it in his hands a moment, studying the floral patterns carved on its lid and sides, then he pressed a sequence of hidden catches—each the center of a flower—and the box sprang open with a soft click.

The other windriders gathered around as its contents were revealed. There were four pairs of rings, each pair consisting of a simple gold band for a human finger, and a larger gold band that was nearly the size of a bracelet with a hinge on one side that allowed it to open and a pin to close it on the other. The smaller ring of each pair was nested inside the larger, in a depression in the box's black velvet lining. The slanting rays of the setting sun gave the gold a ruddy glow, throwing into relief the delicate tracery of runes engraved on the rings.

One of the windriders—a woman with a shiny patch of puckered skin running from her cheek to her right ear, the tip of which had been burned away by whatever attack had left that burn scar—glanced at the rings, then up at Lord Kierin.

"Only four?" she asked. "Lord Ulath is stingy."

Lord Kierin gave her a look that made Leifander quail, even though he was not the recipient of it.

"Lord Ulath has a city to protect, Valatta," Lord Kierin reprimanded. "He has been most generous. Four rings will suit our purposes admirably. When the humans drop their disguise and open their wagons, we can attack from four directions at once. The humans won't know which way to turn. Once the first four have revealed themselves, the rest can join in the fray."

Valatta gave a curt nod, in deference to her commander, but her eyes were blazing. "By virtue of my loss, I demand the right to be among the first four."

Leifander, seeing the ache that lay deep within her fierce glare, felt an echoing pang in his own heart. Just as he had, Valatta had lost someone dear to her.

Lord Kierin laid a hand upon the shorter elf's shoulder.

"Valatta," he said, "I know you yearn to be the first to feather the enemy with your arrows, but we will let the beasts decide the question. Whichever of them most calmly accepts the ring will be among the first four."

He pulled one of the larger rings from the box, and turned toward the spot where the griffons crouched, unhaltered and waiting with perfect obedience for their masters.

"We'll test your mount first, Valatta."

Without another glance at Leifander—by elven standards he was a mere youth, not even as old as one of their squires— the windriders followed Valatta to her griffon. Only Lord Kierin remained where Leifander stood, arms folded as he watched his riders.

Valatta greeted her mount, gentling the griffon by working her fingers into its feathers to give its neck a good scratch. She took its reins in one hand and kneeled beside it, uttering a sharp command. Obediently, the griffon placed a taloned foot on her leg.

Valatta opened the golden ring and fastened it around the

griffon's ankle. As it closed, the griffon disappeared from sight. Leifander, despite having known what was going to happen, blinked in surprise at the suddenness of the transformation. One moment the griffon was there, the next it was not. He could see right through the spot where it must be to the tall slab of granite that a moment before had been blocked by the griffon's body. But the griffon was still there; under it was a flattened spot in the breeze-blown grass.

Valatta nodded, a satisfied smile on her lips. "That was easy enough," she said. "She seems to—"

Suddenly the hand that held the reins was wrenched upward. Her eyes widened in pain and three slashes of red sprang into being on her thigh. A loud cry—like the *scree* of an eagle but somehow also containing the snarl of a roaring lion—pealed across the hilltop. Hearing its cry, two of the other griffons responded in kind, fur rising in a line along their backs.

Jerked to her feet, Valatta staggered this way and that as she fought to control her invisible mount. Leifander heard the rushing beat of its powerful wings and saw Valatta's arm jerk back and forth as the griffon shook its head. Blood streamed down her leg, soaking her trousers above the spot where the griffon's talons had raked her flesh.

"Elsanna, no!" she cried, bracing her feet and gripping the invisible reins with both hands in an effort to prevent her mount from launching itself into the air. "Drop, Elsanna! Drop!"

One of the elves closest to Valatta grabbed at an invisible wing but was shaken loose a moment later. Another added his voice to Valatta's, also shouting for the griffon to drop to the ground. Others scrambled for their own mounts, grabbing their reins and yanking the creatures' heads down to the ground to keep them submissive.

Leifander glanced nervously at Lord Kierin. The Gold elf remained calm, save for a slight deepening of his frown. He raised his hands and briefly touched his fingertips to his eyes, then flicked his hands forward and spoke a single word.

A heartbeat later, Valatta's arms drooped. Swiftly, she kneeled down and removed the ring from her mount's ankle, revealing the sleeping form of her griffon. Chagrined, she handed the ring to another of the windriders, then limped to one of the standing stones and leaned on it, clenching her teeth against the pain of the scratches on her leg.

One of the other windriders caught Lord Kierin's eye, glanced in Valatta's direction, and raised his eyebrows in a silent question. Lord Kierin gave a slight shake of his head.

"Continue the tests," he ordered.

As Valatta's mount lay sleeping on the ground, a second griffon was fitted with the ring. This one displayed none of the high spirits that Elsanna had, instead accepting the ring without fuss. It crouched quietly, wings folded, until the ring was removed again. The windrider whose mount it was beamed proudly and passed the ring to the next.

Then came an interruption. "Lord Kierin, someone approaches," one of the elves said. He pointed to the southeast.

The sun had sunk below the horizon, painting the western sky a vivid red, but there was still enough light to clearly see the figure that winged its way toward Moonrise Hill. It had an unusual shape, and it took Leifander several moments to figure out that the creature was a winged elf—very rare, even in the lands to the north—supporting another, who clung to her chest.

As the avariel elf drew closer still, a second, smaller shape became visible in the air beside it, one that winged its way along strongly and without hindrance. It looked like a large bird, but with a body that had a strange silhouette, almost like that of a griffon.

With a sinking heart, Leifander recognized it as a tressym. It was the one he'd seen more than once in the past few days. He'd suspected that it was following him and had taken great pains to lose it, but now the creature had found him again, and it had brought company. If word of the windriders' ability to render themselves and their mounts invisible became common knowledge . . .

Lord Kieran glanced at Leifander and asked, "Were you expecting someone else to meet us here today?"

Leifander shook his head.

Lord Keirin gave a brisk, decisive nod. "Riders!" he shouted. "To your mounts!"

He strode toward the man who held the ring, thrusting the open box at him. With a slight bow, the fellow popped the magical ring back inside. The others swung up into their saddles—all except Valatta, who stared in frustration at her sleeping mount.

Lord Kieran snapped the box shut and tucked it into a bag at his hip. He mounted his own griffon and jerked the lance free from its holder.

"I want that avariel forced down," he ordered. "I would prefer we cause no wounds, but if arrows are the only thing that will convince the elf to land, so be it."

He glanced at Valatta, who was tugging at the reins of her mount in a futile effort to wake it. He flicked a hand in the sleeping griffon's direction and spoke a word to awaken it. An instant later, the griffon was on its feet, head twisting as it scanned the windriders all around it, who were rising into the air on their mounts.

As the winged elf drew closer to Moonrise Hill, Leifander's mouth gaped open as he saw who the person she was carrying was.

"By the Trickster's ears," Leifander swore, "what is *she* doing here?"

A moment later, he realized Larajin's danger. Half-elf his twin sister might be, but she looked fully human. As soon as the windriders got a close look at her, they'd assume she was an enemy spy and feather her with arrows.

"Lord Kierin, wait!" he cried, running toward the griffon as it leaped into the air. "The woman being carried by the winged elf is my sister. Call off your riders!"

For a terrible moment, Leifander didn't think Lord Kierin had heard. His griffon continued to soar upward after the others, then Lord Kierin's voice rang out, "Riders! Hold your arrows."

Leifander craned his head, watching anxiously as the windriders caught up to the winged elf, wheeled their mounts in a tight circle, and fell in on either side of her as she continued toward Moonrise Hill. Belatedly Leifander realized his arms were out to the side, his fingers splayed. So tense was the moment that he'd nearly skinwalked and launched himself into the air. Lowering his arms, he watched as the winged elf landed, depositing Larajin on the grassy hilltop. The tressym settled gracefully atop one of the stones behind them.

As the windriders landed their mounts on the hill, Larajin's first action was to place both hands upon her heart and bow deeply in the winged elf's direction. It was obviously a gesture of thanks. Her eyes ranged over the windriders, and she repeated the bow, this time for Lord Kierin.

Beside her, the winged elf was panting, bent over with hands on thighs. Her wings were only half folded. Their tips drooped against the ground.

"Leifander," Larajin said, turning to him. "Thanks be to the goddess that I've caught up with you at last. Hopefully this time you'll listen to me."

Lord Kierin, having dismounted from his griffon, strode up to where Larajin and Leifander stood. He spoke the common tongue fluently and had understood what Larajin said. He stared at her for a long moment, then glanced pointedly at Leifander.

"Your 'sister'?" he asked quietly.

Instantly, Leifander regretted his loose tongue. "She's only a half-elf," he answered quickly. "Her father was human."

At Lord Kierin's sharp look, Leifander realized that he had just compounded his error. Trisdea had given birth only twice in her lifetime. Not knowing that the second birth had produced twins, Lord Kierin would assume some other woman had borne Larajin, and would conclude that she and Leifander therefore had a father in common—and Leifander had just blurted out that this father was human.

"That's odd," Lord Kierin said in a soft voice, staring at Leifander. "You don't look—" He closed his lips abruptly, as if thinking better of what he'd been about to say.

Leifander noticed that Lord Kierin was staring at his ears, and he felt them flush to their very tips.

"I . . ." Leifander fumbled. "She . . ."

"I full sister to Leifander," Larajin blurted out in halting forest Elvish. "Trisdea birth us twins."

A mutter swept through the windriders who had gathered around them. They obviously knew enough of the forest elf tongue to understand her simple words.

"Is it true?" one of them whispered to another.

Afraid to look up, Leifander kept his eyes focused firmly on the ground. "It's true."

A callused hand—Lord Kierin's—reached out and caught Leifander under the chin, forcing his head up. Leifander expected to see hatred and disgust in Lord Kierin's eyes, but instead they glowed with compassion.

"Even I did not know this," he told his riders, "and I am one of his father's closest friends. Dalbrannil always maintained there was something special about his boy and hinted that the druids were keeping a deep secret about his birth. I had heard rumors in recent days, but I didn't believe them. Now I realize the whispers that were flying through the forest were true. Half-elves this pair of younglings might be, but they will be our salvation."

He gestured at Larajin, who stood frowning in confusion, obviously unable to follow Elvish when it was spoken at full speed.

"You see?" Lord Kierin continued. "She appears fully human, but elf blood flows true in her veins. She has come to join our side of the conflict. Look at her hazel eyes, and remember that she and Leifander are twins. With them marching beside our troops, lending us the blessing of the gods, we might yet win this war!"

As a cheer went up among the riders, Leifander frowned.

"*Might* win?" he whispered, shaking his head at Lord Kierin's choice of words. "Of course we'll win it."

Larajin, meanwhile, seemed to have grasped the general content of Lord Kierin's words. She rounded on him, berating him in Common.

"You've got it all wrong!" she cried. "Leifander and I aren't meant to *win* the war; we're meant to *stop* it. Rylith told me that this was Somnilthra's prophecy. She said we would heal a great rift and end a great strife. Elves and humans aren't meant to be going to war with one another. It's contrary to the will of the gods."

The riders—all of whom spoke the common tongue, at least in part—glanced at one another, clearly uneasy. Lord Kierin, however, appeared thoughtful.

"I do not share these heresies," Leifander told the riders in a nervous voice. "I am a warrior—a scout for the patrols of the Tangled Trees. My commander, Doriantha, can vouch for my loyalty. I want to fight in this war, not engage in some futile effort to stop it. I want revenge against the humans as much as anyone. I—"

Lord Kierin's hand upon his arm startled him into abrupt silence.

"As a warrior," Kierin told the other windriders, "I am as ready to fight as any of you, but as an elf who has lived many years and seen many good elves die in battle, I know the value of peace. A war averted is always better than a war fought—especially when it is doubtful that it can be fought to victory."

Leifander's mouth gaped at what he'd just heard. Could it be true? He'd expected Lord Kierin to be confident, as certain of victory as Leifander himself was. If so magnificent a warrior had doubts . . .

Lord Kierin turned to his riders with a grave look. "Somnilthra was a great seer. If what this girl says is correct— if Somnilthra herself prophesied that these two are to heal the rift between elf and human and stop this war, then we must accept that as their role." His eyes sought out Leifander's and he added, "And so must they."

Leifander started to shake his head, then looked around at those who stood on the hilltop. Some of the windriders looked hopeful, others, skeptical. Valatta was shaking her head in disgust.

But both Larajin and Kierin were looking at Leifander expectantly, as if waiting for him to say something. Even the winged elf was listening, her wings now folded and her head cocked to one side. Only the griffons and the tressym were oblivious to the tableaux, the latter having curled itself in a ball atop one of the standing stones and fallen soundly asleep.

"All right!" Leifander exploded at last. "I'll do it." He shook his head and added, in a low mutter, "But by the Winged Mother's mercy, I just wish someone would tell me what it is I'm supposed to do."

Later that night, Leifander was aroused from Reverie by the sound of beating wings. Sitting up, he saw the avariel elf—Kith, her name was—climbing into the sky. She hovered for a moment, waving farewell to someone below, then she turned and headed north.

Leifander sighed, wishing Kith had tarried longer before winging her way home. Avariel elves also worshiped the Winged Mother. He and Kith could have found much to talk about.

All around him on the hilltop were the seated forms of eight windriders, their heads bowed in Reverie. Their griffons slept nearby, with heads tucked under their wings. A shadow passed across the hilltop, though no other form, save

Kith's, was visible in the moonlit sky above. It was the ninth windrider keeping watch above, cloaked by the invisibility of a pair of rings.

Moonrise Hill was living up to its name. The standing stones cast long shadows that met at its central point: a moondial on which one could read the season. The moon was just short of full, a glowing white orb that filled the air with a soft blue-white light.

A figure that had been standing at the edge of the hill detached itself from the shadow of a stone and walked back in his direction. It was Larajin. She must have been the one who had bade Kith farewell. Halfway back to the spot where she'd spread her blanket, she noticed Leifander staring at her. She hesitated, then joined him.

"Thank you for agreeing to help me," she said. "I'm glad you finally changed your mind."

Leifander grunted and nodded in Lord Kierin's direction. "I do as I am bid."

"I've been lying awake most of the night, trying to think what we could do," she continued, "but I can't come up with any answers. I just wish Somnilthra was still alive so we could ask her what she meant."

Leifander stared at Larajin, confused. "You're speaking as though she was dead."

Larajin blinked. "Isn't she? Doriantha said she had passed on to Arvanaith."

"Elves do not 'die,' " he explained, "unless they are the victims of violence or accident. When they have reached a venerable age and are in decline, as Somnilthra was, they travel to Arvanaith."

"You mean Arvanaith is a place, here on Toril?" Larajin asked. "Like Evermeet?"

Leifander sighed, feeling as if he was talking to a very young child. "Their bodies remain here on the world of Toril but their souls journey to Arvanaith, where they await rebirth."

"So Somnilthra *is* dead," Larajin said, a twinge of uncertainty in her voice.

Leifander shook his head, trying to remain patient. "No, she is—" he nodded at the windriders—"in a kind of Reverie."

"They buried her alive?"

"What?"

"Isn't that what forest elves do with their dead? Bury them in the Vale of Lost Voices, under the trunks of trees?"

"Somnilthra was a seer," Leifander reminded her, hoping that at last Larajin would understand.

Her blank look told him she didn't.

"Seers are laid to rest in the crystalline towers under Lake Sember."

"Oh!" Larajin exclaimed. "I've heard of them."

Now it was Leifander's turn to look skeptical. "You have?"

How could a human—no, a half-elf raised in Sembia, he reminded himself—know of the crystalline towers? The woods around Lake Sember were forbidden to humans. Any found there were killed without question or mercy.

Larajin nodded eagerly. "Several months ago, a priest from Selgaunt—Diurgo Karn is his name—set out on a pilgrimage. The goddess Sune bid him travel to Lake Sember, a lake whose sacred waters she shares with the elf goddess Hanali Celanil. He had heard that crystalline towers within the lake rose to the surface on the night of the full moon and that their beauty surpassed all other—"

"How did he know of this?" Leifander asked harshly.

Larajin shrugged. "Diurgo didn't tell me. Nor did he make it to the lake. He abandoned his pilgrimage before he even got close."

Leifander shook his head in silent wonder, amazed that humans would know so much about a secret the elves had striven so diligently to preserve.

Larajin continued to prattle on. It seemed her foolish questions weren't finished yet.

"If Somnilthra is in Reverie, could we awaken her?"

"Only if the gods will it."

Larajin glanced up at the moon. "How far is it from here to Lake Sember?"

Leifander could see where this was headed, but he answered. "On foot, it would be a full day's journey to the southern shore of the lake."

"Could we see the crystalline towers from there?" Larajin asked.

Leifander decided to nip this idea in the bud. "Lake Sember is sacred. Only elves may look upon its waters. Any humans found on its shores are slain—and half-elves are just as unwelcome. We would be killed on sight."

That, of course, was a partial lie. Leifander could easily pass for a full-blooded elf, but he doubted if the gods would be so easily fooled, and he had no wish to anger them.

"Besides," he added, "even if we somehow avoided the elf patrols and managed to see the crystalline towers rise, they are in the middle of the lake. There would be no way to reach them."

Larajin sat a moment, thinking. "How are the bodies transported to the towers?"

"By the pallbearers—the clerics who lay them to rest." Leifander answered. "The gods give them the ability to walk upon the lake's surface."

"Ah."

"Do you know a spell that would allow you to do that?" he prodded.

Larajin shook her head. "I don't—and I know what you're going to say—that learning a new spell without a more experienced cleric to guide you in your prayers is impossible—but I've been doing a lot of impossible things these last few days."

Leifander gave a long, heavy sigh. "Why do you care so much about stopping the war? You're not a soldier."

"No, I'm not, but Tal is. If this war continues, he will die. I saw his death in a vision. He'll be shot . . ." Her voice caught, but she steeled herself. "He'll be killed by an elven arrow. Your curse has condemned him."

"*My* curse?" It took Leifander a moment to realize what she was talking about, but then he remembered the angry words he'd uttered shortly after their escape through the sewers. "'Black Archer pierce you' is a common expression," he protested. "Everyone uses it. It doesn't mean the god will actually listen."

Larajin's eyes blazed. "Then why wouldn't you take it back?"

"I will," he assured her. "Right now." He touched a forefinger to his lips, then smacked it against his open palm, withdrawing the curse. "There. It is done."

Larajin stared at him a moment, as if gauging his sincerity, then she nodded.

"Thank you, but even if the gods are placated, the elves aren't. Nor are the humans. More lives than just Tal's hang in the balance—thousands more. Once again, will you help me try to stop this war?"

Leifander glanced at the form of Lord Kierin in Reverie. He knew how the windrider would answer his protests. A soldier did his duty, no matter how hopeless the battle seemed.

"We should get some rest, if we're going to set out in the morning," Leifander said at last. "We'll need our wits about us to make it as far as the lakeshore."

Larajin's smile was as bright as the moonlight.

"Thanks," she whispered, and squeezed Leifander's hand.

Leifander squatted, studying the faint footprint on the rock beside the stream. It had been made by a bare foot, like his own and was fresh. The faint smudge of mud was still drying in the hot sun. Considering the way the person had been careful to step around the ferns, leaving them unbent, the print was no doubt left by a forest elf—part of a patrol, probably, and moving fast through the forest. That was fortunate, since it meant the patrol was well ahead of them and rapidly increasing the distance.

Larajin finished drinking from the stream and splashed noisily through the water, stumbling on a stone and overturning it, leaving an obvious sign of her passage. For the hundredth time that day, Leifander winced in silent annoyance. Did the Sembians teach their people nothing about stealth? She was as noisy as a moose shouldering its way through the woods.

"What were you looking at?" she asked.

He pointed at the footprint, but she glanced into the stream instead.

"The fish?" she guessed. "They look too small to eat."

Her stomach growled. They'd had nothing since morning, when they shared the windriders' breakfast, and it was late afternoon.

"Never mind," Leifander said, dropping his hand.

Even if he warned her that a patrol was nearby, he doubted she would be able to move quietly. The three or four times he'd scolded her already, she'd pouted and said she was trying.

Trying his patience, was more like it.

The tressym landed beside them and began lapping from the stream. The creature—whom Larajin insisted was called Goldheart, though Leifander had never heard of a tressym naming itself before—seemed intent upon following wherever Larajin went. It had been pursuing them since they set out, wings brilliantly flashing as it flew above the trees. Leifander hoped the patrol wouldn't spot it and send a scout back to learn what a magical creature was doing in this part of the woods.

"We'll follow the stream," he told her. "It flows to the north, and it's our quickest route to the lake."

Following it was also, he thought, one way to cover the noise Larajin was making. Unfortunately, it meant they wouldn't be able to hear anyone approaching through the forest either, but Larajin didn't need to know that.

"When we reach the shore, we'll travel along it to the west. There's a headland at the lake's midpoint that juts out some distance. That should give us the best view, come moonrise."

Larajin nodded, and wiggled her fingers for the tressym. It came to her as obediently as a lynx and arched its neck as she stroked its sleek fur.

"I'm going to shift into crow form, and scout ahead," Leifander told her. "If there are any patrols in the area, I'll see them better from the air."

Larajin glanced up at the enormous trees that lined both sides of the stream and asked, "Won't the branches be too thick?"

She wasn't as gullible as he'd assumed.

"Larajin," he said. "There's an elf patrol close by." He pointed to the east. "They went in that direction only a short time ago. By the grace of the gods, we were a distance behind them and didn't stumble out into the open while they were still crossing the stream. They're close enough that I'm worried they'll spot the tressym. They might assume it's a wizard's familiar and double back. If they find you here, this close to Lake Sember, you're a dead woman."

Larajin nodded, her face pale.

"I'm going to try to find them and make sure they keep traveling away from the lake. They'll trust me. I look . . . like one of them."

"How will you find me again?" Larajin asked.

Leifander had to smile. "When you get to the lake, find the headland. You'll know it by the oak tree that grows out of the bluff at the end of it. The tree was struck by lightning years ago and now has a fork near its base, and two trunks."

Larajin gave him a wry smile. "Hardly a good omen."

"I'll meet you at the oak before moonrise," Leifander continued. "Hide yourself well, and wait for me there."

CHAPTER 11

The moon crested the trees, spilling a shimmering line of white across the lake's surface. Lake Sember was truly as beautiful as Diurgo had said it would be. A wide expanse of deep water, the lake was bright turquoise in sunlight, a darker blue by moonlight. Its water smelled fresh and clean, tempting Lara-jin to slake her thirst, but instead she'd honored the prohibition against any but full-blooded elves drinking from the lake. Hanali Celanil might favor her, but she didn't want to risk the wrath of the other elf gods.

For the hundredth time since she'd hidden herself in a clump of brambles near the lakeshore, she rose from her crouch and peered into the forest. Wind whispered through the trees, stirring branches into motion. The only other sounds were the deep croaking of the frogs that lived in the rushes farther down the lakeshore and the occasional distant splash of a fish feeding on the insects that hovered over the lake at night.

"Where are you, Leifander?" she whispered to herself. "What's happened to you?"

She was certain she was in the right spot. A few paces away was the oak tree Leifander had described, its twinned trunks growing at angles to one another. Just beyond it was a drop of a pace or two and the water's edge.

Beside her, Goldheart sniffed the breeze, then dropped her jaw and inhaled deeply, having caught a scent. She turned her head this way and that, as if trying to catch the direction from which it came.

"What is it?" Larajin asked.

An instant later, she heard a crackling sound that seemed to originate from somewhere out on the lake. The noise was very faint, but it seemed familiar. After a moment, she realized what it reminded her of: spring thaw, in the River Arkhen, when the ice was breaking up.

Goldheart dropped to a crouch and slunk away through the brambles. Once she was clear, she launched herself into the air and flew to the oak. She landed on one of its branches and folded her wings, staring fixedly out at the lake.

Curious, Larajin crawled out through the path she'd made through the brambles. She walked to the oak tree and crouched in the shadow of its trunk, keeping it between herself and the forest. Squinting, she tried to see what had captured Goldheart's attention.

She spotted it almost at once. It was a finger of what looked like an inverted icicle rising slowly out of the lake some distance from the shore. A second shimmering spire followed a moment later, then a third. They were too distant to make out clearly, but she could see that each was rising from below the water's surface, one after the other in a line as the moonbeam spread across the lake. There were four of them, each making the crackling noise as it rose, yet leaving the surface of the lake eerily still. Each had to be at least a hundred paces high.

Larajin breathed a prayer to Hanali Celanil and Sune both, thanking them for allowing her to witness this wonderful sight. She stared at the lake until the last of the crystalline towers had finished rising, then glanced at the moon. It seemed to pause for a moment, round and full, just above the tops of the trees, then it continued its ascent into the sky.

Larajin bit her lip, wondering how long the towers would remain above the lake. That part of the legend, Diurgo hadn't known. They might remain until the moon set again—or they might sink back under the surface after just a few brief moments.

Leifander might know the answer—but Leifander wasn't there.

Perhaps Larajin should just set out on her own for the crystalline towers. She could instruct Goldheart to wait for Leifander and guide him to the towers, once he finally arrived.

Yes. That seemed like the best idea. But first, to see if she could actually cast the necessary spell.

She glanced up at Goldheart, who once again was sniffing the breeze. The tressym stared down at Larajin, an intense expression on her face. She growled once, low in her throat, and glanced back at the forest. Briefly, Larajin considered asking the goddess to bless her with the spell that would allow her to ask Goldheart what she'd scented, then decided against it. Even if there was something threatening back in the woods, she would, if the goddesses were willing, soon be well beyond its reach.

Climbing down lower on the outcropping of rock on which the lightning-struck oak stood, Larajin kneeled and dipped her fingers in the lake. The water was deep along that section of the shore and as cool as a night breeze. To Larajin's surprise, her touch stirred ripples that glowed a faint red, like phosphorescence in the sea. She glanced around, and noticed that the fish breaking the surface weren't producing any such effect. The places where they leaped and landed rippled, but the water there remained a cool, dark blue. Sune was with her.

She heard a flutter of wings behind her as Goldheart flew away. Nervous, she listened for movement in the forest but heard nothing.

With the realization that she was out in the open where she might be spotted by an elf patrol, Larajin decided not to tarry any longer. Touching the locket that hung at her wrist with fingers that were still wet from the lake, she began to pray. First a prayer to Sune, to make her footsteps as light as a lover's sigh, then a prayer to Hanali Celanil, asking her to make the waters of the lake as firm as a marriage bed.

A nearby splash startled her, but when she looked up, she saw it had only been a fish breaking the surface near where she squatted. The smell of Hanali's Heart rose from the ripples. Encouraged by the thought that the elf goddess was also listening to her prayers, Larajin quickly pulled off her boots. She stood, and placed her bare foot tentatively on the surface of the lake, testing its resistance.

Before she could step out onto the surface, however, a tickling in her nose and throat made her cough. It felt as if Sune's warm glow was drying her throat and as if Hanali Celanil's fragrance was cloying her nostrils to the point where it made her eyes water. Frightened, Larajin found her breathing becoming fast and shallow. That definitely wasn't part of the spell she'd been trying to cast—what were the goddesses doing?

Telling herself to have faith—the signs of the goddesses' blessings were all around her—Larajin took a step out onto the lake, but instead of finding solid footing, her foot plunged beneath the surface. Unbalanced, she tumbled into the water.

The fall saved her life. In the same moment that she tumbled forward, an arrow whistled overhead, so close that it plucked at her hair, giving it a painful yank. Had her spell worked, allowing her to step out onto the water's surface, the arrow would have buried itself in her back. As it was, it cut into the water next to her with a vicious splash.

Breaking the surface, Larajin saw an elf standing next to the forked oak tree—a forest elf, his face shadowed with tattoos, with a powerful short bow in his hand. It must have been his scent that Goldheart had caught just before she growled and flew away.

All of these thoughts flashed through Larajin's mind in a heartbeat. Meanwhile the elf, in a motion nearly too swift to follow, swept a hand to his quiver and plucked an arrow from it, then nocked it against the bowstring. Seeing an easy target, he took his time, sighting down the length of the arrow.

Larajin did the only thing she could, forcing her body back under the water with a powerful stroke of her hands. The arrow *thwooshed* down into the water a mere palm's breadth from her as she turned and swam, keeping below the surface. Then another arrow, and another arrow cut the surface, questing for her.

Forcing herself deeper, she stroked away from the spot where the elf archer stood. As long as she stayed below the surface, the water would slow the arrows, preventing them from reaching her, but with bright moonlight illuminating the lake, the elf would have no trouble spotting her when she resurfaced. With only one meager gasp of air in her lungs, she knew she'd never be able to put enough distance between herself and the archer.

Even so, she resolved to try. She swam on, gradually releasing the air in her lungs, trying to conserve it for as long as possible. Sparkles appeared before her eyes, and a dizziness gripped her, but still she swam on. If she broke the surface at the last possible moment, then immediately dived again, perhaps the elf wouldn't spot her. But not yet—not just yet . . .

Larajin swam and swam—and continued to swim long past the moment she should have been gasping for air. That was when she noticed the glow around her nose and mouth and felt the cool trickle of water down her nose and throat.

At first she assumed that the pressure of the water was forcing lake water into her nostrils, but instead of the harsh burning that usually caused, she felt a cool, soothing relief. In wonder, she opened her mouth and swallowed some of the water—and was immediately rewarded with a burst of energy that strengthened her muscles and cleared away the sparkles in her head. With a growing sense of wonder, she blew the water out again—and inhaled.

She was breathing water!

With a laugh that released the few tiny bubbles of air that had been in her lungs, Larajin gave thanks to the goddesses for their blessing. She had prayed for a spell to walk on water, but they had responded instead with what she truly needed: a spell that would save her life.

Swimming was easier than walking, especially with the strength that breathing water gave her. With sure, clean strokes, Larajin headed toward the distant shimmer of moonlight on water—the spot where the bases of the crystalline towers broke the surface.

As she swam, she wondered where Leifander was. Had he said or done something after meeting the patrol that caused them to suspect he had human blood in his veins? Had the same archer who was just shooting at Larajin already taken Leifander's life?

Realizing that she did not have the answers, Larajin pushed these morbid thoughts firmly out of her mind. There had to be some other explanation for Leifander not having met her, she told herself. But when she thought of one, it was just as unpalatable.

Perhaps, she thought, Leifander had been lying when he said he'd help her try to fulfill Somnilthra's prophecy and end the war. Leifander could easily pass for a full-blooded elf. The patrol would have received him with open arms, not with a flight of arrows. Had he abandoned Larajin and their quest?

There was no use in thinking about that now. Instead, Larajin had to focus on the task at hand, locating Somnilthra and somehow awakening her.

With smooth, sure strokes, she swam toward the crystalline towers.

Soon the base of one of the towers loomed ahead in the water, shimmering like a crystal, its edges distorted by ripples. As Larajin swam nearer, the water grew colder, eventually reaching the chill temperature of glacial runoff. She shivered and felt her skin prickle with goosebumps.

The lake water was too dark for her to see any details, even with her excellent night vision; for that she would have to break the surface. She hesitated a moment just beneath the surface of the lake, wondering if the transition back to breathing air would be painful—if she would cough and sputter like a drowning person, with a fierce ache in her chest. She summoned her courage and thrust her head above the water.

Miraculously, the lake water she'd drawn into her lungs a moment before turned to air, and she was breathing again. With her first exhalation, she whispered a prayer to the goddesses. Still treading water, she craned her neck to stare up at the closest of the four towers.

Paddling closer, she touched its slippery, cold surface. She pressed a hand to it and felt it give slightly, as if melting back. The towers were just as they had appeared: cold spires of ice, as slippery as inverted icicles. Inside each of them, high above the surface of the lake, Larajin could see dark shapes entombed in the ice—the bodies of elves.

Fortunately, the towers were cracked and craggy, as rough as a freshly splintered rock face, with plenty of handholds and footholds. Climbing shouldn't be too difficult—but which tower to choose?

Shivering, Larajin realized she'd have to make up her mind soon, or she'd be too chilled to climb. Deciding at last, she chose the tower that had been the last to rise and swam to it.

This tower was the smallest of the four, with just four bodies entombed inside it, and thus probably the most recent. If it had indeed grown like an icicle, from base to point, Somnilthra would be lying in repose near its craggy tip. She would probably be the last dark figure, nearly two hundred paces above the surface of the lake.

Hauling herself out of the water, Larajin carefully began her climb. The summer air warmed her skin, but soon her hands and feet grew first cold, then numb. The going was slow. More than once she was forced to double back and find a new route, after reaching a spot where the ice became a sheer wall, too steep to climb without a pick and rope.

High above her, the moon climbed to its apex in the sky. Below, the shimmering trail it etched across the surface of the lake grew shorter.

Best not to look down, she thought. The water was more than a hundred paces below her, and the distance made Larajin dizzy. Resolutely, she continued her climb, searching out handholds and footholds in the craggy ice.

The towers continued to make cracking noises, just as they had done since they rose. Every now and then Larajin heard a deep groan then a loud snap as a piece of ice broke free. A few heartbeats later the shard hit the water below with a loud splash, making her cringe.

When Larajin was level with the third of the dark shapes inside the tower she paused to peer through the ice at it, just as she had done as she'd passed the first two. The third elf was a male, dressed in the formal garb of the Gold elves. Laid out in a reclining position, hands folded upon his breast, he looked as though he was sleeping, despite the frost on his skin and the ice that pressed tightly against him on every side.

Shivering, her hair and clothes still damp from her swim across the lake, Larajin pressed on. She followed a ridge in the ice that led up and to her right, where she could see a ledge near the spot where the last body lay. If she made it to that spot, she would be as close to the body as she could get.

As she worked her way closer to the ledge, Larajin caught glimpses of the figure entombed inside the ice. The body was female—a fact Larajin noted with relief—a slender woman with delicate features, long pointed ears and coppery-red hair in two braids that lay upon her shoulders. A forest elf, judging by her leather breeches and ornately beaded boots and vest. The ice that entombed her—Larajin was peering up through more than an arm's length of the stuff—distorted the woman's features, making it impossible to see whether or not she resembled Leifander. Larajin could see a dark crescent—a tattoo—on one of her cheeks.

Was it a stylized moon, the symbol of the goddess Somnilthra had worshiped? Larajin prayed it was—that she wouldn't be forced to climb another of the towers.

She needed to get closer, to reach a ledge she'd spotted that was level with the body. Unfortunately, as she drew nearer to it, she saw there was a gap nearly a pace wide between the ledge and the ridge she'd climbed along. She knew it was crazy to risk a jump—the ice was too slippery for a safe landing—but by stretching, she just might be able to reach it with one foot. Then it would simply be a matter of transferring her weight with a slight hop, and she would be across.

Leaning out as far as she dared, she extended her right foot and tested the ledge with it. The ice seemed solid enough. Gradually, she eased her weight onto it . . .

And the ice below her right foot gave a deep, groaning crack.

Larajin froze, poised over the gap. An instant later, the ledge she'd been trying to reach gave way. Gasping, Larajin threw her weight back, trying to reach the safety of the spot where she'd just been standing, but her left foot slipped. Thrown off-balance, she fell to her knees. She scrabbled at the ice, seeking a handhold—and found one—but then her knees slipped from the edge. Her full weight was supported only by her hands. Pain shot through her left wrist as it twisted, and that hand lost its grip.

Just as she thought she was about to go over the edge, one scrabbling foot at last found a toehold, then the other found a foothold. She heaved herself upward, waves of agony shooting through her sprained wrist. As she pulled herself to safety, she felt her dagger catch on a outcropping of ice and yank from its sheath. It fell onto the ice and began to slide away.

Larajin grabbed for it, but her position forced her to reach with the hand that had been twisted in the ice. Her fingers still weren't working properly. They brushed against the hilt but would not close upon it. Despite the bright moonlight, the shadows of the splintered ice made the dagger difficult to see. Was it slipping out from under her fingertips and going over the edge?

"Illunathros!" she cried.

With a bright flash of blue light, the dagger illuminated— then it slipped off into space. Despondent, Larajin watched it fall toward the lake below. It flashed brightly as it tumbled end over end.

A loud caw echoed across the lake as a small dark shape streaked through the night toward the ice tower. At the last moment before the dagger struck the surface, the weapon's fall slowed until it was drifting down as gently as a feather. Just before it reached the water, the crow swooped low over the lake and neatly plucked it from the air with its feet. The bird wheeled in a graceful curve and began climbing toward the spot where Larajin crouched, the dagger glowing brightly in its talons.

"Leifander!" Larajin exclaimed.

The crow cawed again in greeting, then hovered next to Larajin, wings beating furiously. One wing lagged slightly behind the other, as if he were exhausted from a long flight.

Larajin reached out and took the dagger from him, nodded her head in an abbreviated bow of heartfelt thanks, and secured the dagger in the sheath at her hip.

Leifander landed, hopped sideways along the ridge toward a flat spot, then spread his wings. A moment later a ripple passed through him as he shifted back into elf form. His bare feet slid a little on the ice, and he waved his arms for a moment like beating wings before finding his balance. One arm seemed stiff, as if it pained him, and his right eye and cheek were splotchy with the shadows of fresh bruises.

"You're injured," Larajin observed aloud. "What happened?"

He winced, as if something other than his injuries pained him. "It's nothing."

"Did the elf near the forked oak attack you?"

Leifander glanced up sharply. "What elf?"

"The one who shot an arrow at me. He spotted me as I entered the water."

Leifander looked grimly back at the shore. "He must have been one of those who patrol the lake. We'll have trouble getting back. Especially now. The entire shore will be watching for us."

"You were gone so long," Larajin continued. "I thought, for a moment there, that you'd joined that elf patrol and weren't coming back. I'm sorry I doubted—"

Leifander interrupted her with a bitter laugh. "You were right," he said. "I did join them—for a time. The patrol needed a messenger . . . a swift one, with wings. I couldn't refuse; the message was a vital one."

Larajin's mouth turned down in disapproval. "And so you abandoned me," she said. "You turned your back on your duty—and our destiny."

"Only for a short time," he said, a guilty look in his eye.

Combined with his injuries, the look told her that something had happened to change his mind. She waited, silently, for him to tell her what it was.

"I delivered their message," Leifander said at last. "The commander who received it knew me and had heard the rumors about me being the son of a human—and not just any human, but a powerful merchant of Sembia. She believes that hazel-eyed twins are blessed by the gods—but said half-human twins didn't count. Worse still, she announced that half-elves are not to be counted among our allies nor to be trusted, now that Lord Ulath has declared Deepingdale neutral."

His voice dropped to a pained whisper, and he glanced across the lake at its tree-lined shore.

"I was raised in this forest and am the son of a noble warrior. I'm as much an elf as any of them. I look like an elf, I dress and act like an elf—I *am* an elf—and yet all they see now is my human half."

"Did they attack you?" Larajin asked softly.

"They claimed I was a traitor. They didn't believe I had only gone to Selgaunt at the druids' request. They tried to hold me, but I escaped. In doing so, I condemned myself. As long as this war continues, I won't be welcome among my people. Neither there," he said, pointing at the forest, "nor in your realm."

He gave Larajin a determined, fierce look and added, "I'm committed to what you called 'our destiny' now. Fully. I want this war to end. Let's see if Somnilthra can tell us how to fulfill that destiny."

Larajin glanced at the woman entombed in the ice next to them. "This *is* her, then?" she asked.

"Of course." Leifander cocked his head. "You must have known that, or you wouldn't have chosen this tower to climb."

Larajin started to smile, but just then the spire of ice shuddered. There was a deep groan, and a crack appeared above them. Splinters of ice, sparkling in the moonlight like shards of glass, tumbled free and fell onto the twins.

Unsteady on the slippery ridge, Larajin grabbed for Leifander's hand. As she steadied herself, her legs cramped from the cold that was seeping up through her bare feet, and she shuddered.

Leifander glanced sharply at her. "You're freezing!" he exclaimed. "Your fingers are nearly blue. Don't you have a spell that can warm them?"

Larajin shook her head. "No more than you have a spell to heal your bruises, it would seem. I tried praying, but the goddesses didn't answer." She touched his injured shoulder gently. "I could heal you, however."

"No time," he said, glancing pointedly at a crack just above where they stood. "Besides, the bruises are only a minor inconvenience. I wish I had a spell that could help you, but the Lady of Air and Wind answers prayers for heat with violence; all she knows is the fury of the lightning strike, and the blazing heat of the wind-whipped forest fire."

He glanced pointedly at Larajin's magic dagger. "That blade produces a cold blue light," he said. "Will it also produce a warm one?"

"I don't know," Larajin answered—then an idea occurred to her. "If it did, we could use it to melt a hole in the ice and reach Somnilthra."

"I heard you shout a word as the dagger fell," Leifander continued. "What was it?"

"*Illunathros.*"

Leifander nodded, as if recognizing the word, then stared at the dagger.

"Why isn't it glowing now?" he asked.

"Its magic only activates if I'm holding it," Larajin said.

"Can I see it?"

Larajin pulled the dagger from its sheath and handed it to Leifander, who turned it over in his hands, peering closely at it.

"Ah," he said. "I thought so. You see here—the Uskevren crest? It's a later addition, welded onto the hilt. The blade itself is of elven make."

"How do you know?"

"The word that activates its magic—it's Espruar. Translated, it would be 'cold illumination of the moon.' " He paused, lost in thought, then snapped his fingers. "That's it." He held the dagger up, and looked into Larajin's eyes. "I'd like to try something . . . the word, in Espruar, for 'warm light of the sun.'"

Larajin nodded her consent.

Leifander held the dagger aloft and spoke a single word, "*Solicallor*!"

The blade glowed a dull orange, like metal freshly pulled from the forge. Though she stood a pace away from Leifander, a wave of heat washed over Larajin. Leifander drew his breath in with a hiss. The hilt itself must have been uncomfortably hot, but he clung to it with determination. He held the dagger toward Larajin, and she warmed her hands over its ruddy glow. Before its heat faded, he rose to his feet and thrust the blade into the ice next to them.

The ice melted away. Trickles of water flowed from the hole the dagger's heat bored in the tower, only to slow and freeze again into dripping icicles near their feet. Leifander methodically pushed the dagger deeper into the ice, forcing it in until his arm was inserted up to the shoulder and the blade was no more than a finger's width from Somnilthra's cheek. He withdrew the blade and handed it to Larajin. Even as she took it, the glow faded and the metal cooled. She tucked it away in its sheath.

"What do we do now?" she asked. "How do we awaken Somnilthra?"

Leifander gave her a startled look. "I thought you knew."

Larajin shook her head. "You're the elf!" she protested.

"Half-elf—as are you." His eyes grew thoughtful, then twinkled. "Do you suppose, if we put those two halves together, we might come up with the answer?"

The tower gave another shuddering rumble, and a piece on the far side broke free and fell to the lake below with a splash. Larajin stared at Somnilthra, but despite the cracking of the ice and the rumbles that coursed through her tower, the entombed elf lay silent and still.

"I know a spell that can be used to contact an elf in the Reverie," Leifander said at last, "but I don't know if it will reach all the way to Arvanaith." He glanced at Larajin. "Have you been blessed with any spells that magically alter speech?"

Larajin nodded eagerly. "Only one," she said. "It lets me speak to Goldheart."

"The tressym?" Leifander's eyes brightened. "That's good. It means you're touching the creature's mind. If the gods are willing, they might grant you the power to also touch the mind of someone so long in the Reverie. If we pray together, to our respective gods, we might be able to reach Somnilthra. I can locate her spirit in Arvanaith, and you can touch her mind and hear her whispered thoughts."

Larajin stared at the hole the dagger had melted in the ice. It almost reached Somnilthra, but not quite.

"Do you think she'll hear me?" she asked doubtfully.

Leifander shrugged. "We won't know until we try."

He kneeled and spread his hands behind him in a pose that reminded Larajin of Kith's bow. A loud rumble came from the crystalline tower next to them, reminding Larajin that they didn't have much time left. The moon was steadily slipping toward the horizon, and she could see that the towers were slowly descending toward the surface of the lake.

She bowed her head and cupped her hands over her midriff, gently pressing the locket at her wrist against the spot where the mark of Sune had been. She began to pray. Beside her, she heard Leifander doing the same in the melodious language of the forest elves.

Inside the ice, moonlight shifted on Somnilthra's face as the moon set. Or had that been her eyelids flickering? Larajin concentrated on Somnilthra's tattooed cheek and prayed even more fervently.

"Hanali Celanil hear me and bless me," she whispered. "Sune hear me and answer. Give me the power to speak to my sister, and be heard. Bless her with speech, and give me the power to hear her in return."

The locket grew warm and began to glow a dull red, and the

scent of Hanali's Heart rose around her. Encouraged by these signs, Larajin leaned closer to the hole in the ice and cupped her hands around it, as she would around someone's ear.

"Somnilthra," she said into the darkened tunnel. "Can you hear me?"

A part of her was startled to realize that she was speaking fluent Elvish. Another part of her, embraced by the love of the goddesses, remained serene and listened for the answer. When it came, it was little more than a sigh, one laden with the exhaustion of many long years in Reverie.

Yes?

Leifander glanced up, an exuberant look in his eye. Had he heard the voice too?

Who . . . ?

After that single word, the voice faded beyond hearing. Larajin tapped her brother's shoulder.

"Keep praying," she hissed.

Nodding grimly, Leifander bowed his head and resumed his chant.

At the same time Larajin spoke again—quickly—into the hole.

"Somnilthra, it is your half . . ." She paused, then amended her words. "It is your sister and brother, Larajin and Leifander, the twins. The rift you predicted between human and elf has come to pass. Sembia and what remains of Cormanthor are at war. You prophesied that we could end the strife between the two races, but we don't know how. Tell us what to do!"

Inside the ice, Somnilthra's head shifted ever so slightly, as if she were trying to turn her face in their direction. The skin above her eyebrows was creased, in what Larajin imagined to be a frown. Her voice, heavy from the Reverie, drifted gently into Larajin's ear, though her sister's lips did not move.

To heal the splinter in the stone, you must use a heart. Hate may win wars, but only love will conquer them. Harness love, and you will win everything. Unharness hate, and you will lose everything, even your very lives.

"But what does that mean?" Larajin asked, speaking louder now. "*How* do we use love to conquer war?"

Somnilthra sighed—a sigh deeper than any Larajin had ever heard before.

Your gods will show you the way. Once again, her voice was growing faint. *I must . . .*

And it was gone.

Leifander rose to his feet. Despite the fact that he was barefoot on the ice, he was sweating.

"I couldn't stay in contact with her any longer," he said, shaking his head. "She drifted away."

The spire of ice shuddered under Larajin's bare feet. She peered down at the surface of the lake—closer now than it had been when they started their prayers.

"Could you hear Somnilthra when she spoke?" Larajin asked.

Leifander nodded. "I heard her words, but I don't know what they meant. We need wisdom—a wisdom well beyond our twenty-five years. Someone older, wiser, and more versed in the ways of magic must answer the riddle we've just been given."

They glanced at each other and said the name at the same time: "Rylith."

"The last time I saw her was several days ago, at the Standing Stone," Larajin said. "The gods only know where she is now."

"The gods aren't the only ones who will know where she is," Leifander said. "The other members of the sacred circle will know where she is—or, at least, should be able to get a message to her."

"Where can we find them?" Larajin asked. "Are they far from here?"

Leifander pointed to the northeast. "The druids—at least one of them, at all times—maintain a constant vigil at Moon-touch Oak. It lies in that direction." Then he added with a chuckle, as if at a private joke, "It's not far, as the crow flies."

"How many days on foot?"

His mirth vanished. "At least eight . . . possibly ten or twelve. The forest is quite thick, and there's the River Ashaba to ford."

Larajin winced. "That's too long," she said grimly. "By then Tal might be—"

She caught sight of a familiar figure winging its way toward them across the lake. She waved to attract Goldheart's attention, and the tressym did a graceful loop. Larajin was relieved by the creature's playful antics. Whatever Goldheart had been up to, she at least hadn't gotten feathered by elven arrows.

Goldheart landed on the ridge beside them and rubbed against Larajin's leg. She filled the air with a loud purring, as if relieved to see that Larajin had survived her brush with the elf archer.

"Easy for you to say, Goldheart," Larajin chided. "You flew away when things got dangerous. By the time the elf shot that first arrow, I'll bet you were already halfway to . . ."

All at once, a thought occurred to her. Maybe it wouldn't take a tenday, after all, for them to reach Moontouch Oak. Maybe there was a quicker way.

"Leifander," she asked slowly. "Could you teach me how to skinwalk?"

"Impossible," he snorted. "It takes months of study and prayer. I fasted and prayed in the treetops for many days before I was able to call the Crow to me. You'd need to do the same to seek out your totem animal. Without it—"

Larajin glanced pointedly at Goldheart. "What if my 'totem animal' was already here?"

Slowly, Leifander's eyebrows raised. He glanced down at the tressym, which looked up at him with luminous yellow eyes.

"She is sacred to my goddess," Larajin reminded him, kneeling down to stroke Goldheart's silky fur. She peered up at Leifander. "Will you teach me what to do?"

"I can try," Leifander conceded at last. He glanced at the first of the crystalline towers, which already was visibly lower in the water. "Your lesson will be a quick one."

"Let's begin then."

Leifander gave a resigned sigh. "Start by assuming the same posture as the tress—as your totem. You see? Just as I assume the posture of the crow." He squatted, holding his arms to the side.

Larajin studied Goldheart, who was sitting with catlike grace on the slippery ledge, her wings neatly folded. Larajin kneeled beside her—aware that her legs were articulated in the wrong direction but trying for the same pose as best she could—and straightened her arms, placing her palms flat on the ice. She hunched her shoulders, imagining wings.

"Close your eyes."

She did. A moment later, she felt a tickle of fur. Goldheart was twining herself between Larajin's arms. Larajin allowed herself a smile—whether aware of it or not, Goldheart was helping. A floral scent rose to Larajin's nostrils, and she felt a warmth at her wrist.

"As you pray, imagine your body shifting," Leifander continued. "The feathers come, and your body twists, and you feel your bones shift . . ."

He continued, describing the sensations that preceded skin-walking. Larajin listened avidly, imagining herself becoming a tressym. All the while, the manifestations of the goddesses' presence grew stronger. Larajin could see the amber glow of her locket, even with her eyes closed.

Leifander switched the course of his instruction. "At the same time that you are imagining your body shifting, you pray. The words of the prayer are . . . They begin with . . ."

He paused, and Larajin opened her eyes a crack, to see him shaking his head in frustration.

"It won't work," he said. "I can't put the prayer into words. The common tongue is too coarse."

"Then speak it in Elvish," Larajin said, switching to that language as the power of the goddesses swept through her, filling the air with a floral scent as thick as perfume. "Say the words of the spell, and I'll repeat them."

Leifander sniffed, and nodded at the bright red glow that enveloped them both. He began his prayer. Larajin echoed him, substituting the salutations and names of the goddesses she worshiped.

As she did, she imagined herself inhabiting the body of a tressym, with whiskers and wings and fur. Something tickled like a shiver down her spine, running swift as water from the nape of her neck to the tip of her ... tail? Surprised, she sank—claws?—into the ice. Suddenly dizzy as she shrank to a fraction of her former size, she spread her—wings?—flapping them for balance.

She rose into the air.

As her eyes sprang open, she saw Leifander, still squatting on the ledge, but in crow form. He stared up at her for a moment with glossy black eyes, then let out a hoarse croak of amazement. Startled, Larajin began to think about the wonder of her transformation, instead of just feeling it, and for a moment she forgot how to fly. She tumbled through the air, gasping, but then instinct took over and her wings beat strong and sure.

As she rose to the level of the ledge once more, Goldheart launched herself into the air. The tressym shot past Larajin like an arrow, as if goading her into a chase. Laughing, Larajin obliged. Flying was wonderful, exhilarating—even more amazing than breathing water had been. She chased Goldheart through the sky, and they tumbled like two kittens, high above the moonlight-dappled surface of the lake. They flew, hard and fast, in a laughing race to the lightning-struck tree at the lake's edge.

A dark shape shot past them, cawing furiously, then made a sharp turn to the side. Only then did Larajin remember the danger. The elf who had tried to kill her earlier was down there still, somewhere on the shore, and there would probably be others scouring the edges of the lake, looking for her. She doubted they'd recognize her in tressym form, but it was best not to take any chances.

Nodding to show that she understood, she turned in a graceful arc and allowed Leifander to set their course.

CHAPTER 12

Had Leifander been in elf form, he would have wept at what he saw below. The forest looked as if giant slugs had crisscrossed it, leaving meandering trails of slimy destruction in their wake. Wide swaths of the woods lay in blighted ruin, streaked with mud brown and ash gray that stood out clearly against the surrounding green. Inside the blighted areas, sticklike trees leaned at angles or lay broken upon the ground, and what few leaves remained on them were a lifeless, mottled yellow-gray.

Patches of mist drifted here and there, spreading the blight in new directions with each shift of the breeze. It seemed never to dissipate but instead maintained its deadly potency long after the wands had created it.

To the south, thick plumes of smoke rose from the

edges of the great forest: the handiwork of Sembia's soldiers, whose encampments Leifander could see in the distance on the rolling hills of Battledale. They were burning the edges of the wood, trying to either flush the elves out or draw them into battle.

Glancing up at the flat blue sky, he offered a silent prayer to the Leaflord to send rain. The summer sun was hot, the woods below tinder-dry. If the fires spread. . . .

Leifander flew grimly on, every now and then glancing behind him to see how Larajin was faring. To his great surprise she'd mastered skinwalking in a fraction of the time it should have taken—moments, instead of days—and now was indistinguishable from the tressym that seemed to accompany her everywhere.

The speed with which she'd learned it made him jealous. As twins, they were both destined for greatness, but Larajin seemed far more favored by the gods than he. Magic came to her easily, without effort. Even the difficult balance she had chosen—giving equal reverence to two goddesses, one human, one elf—didn't seem to slow her down. Any spell she turned her mind to, she accomplished, whereas Leifander had learned his magic only through long periods of fasting and solitary prayer, perched high in a sacred oak.

It didn't seem fair. Why, if they were twins, had the gods apportioned out their blessings in such unequal measure?

Behind him, he heard a plaintive mewing. Glancing back, he saw that one of the tressym—Larajin—had once again dropped behind and was flying in a circle just above the treetops. It was a warning sign that Leifander recognized. Her spell was coming to an end—much sooner than he'd expected. She needed to land.

At least he had one advantage. Unlike Larajin, who could skinwalk for no more than a morning or afternoon at a stretch, he could maintain animal form for days on end, shifting endlessly back and forth between crow and elf. Larajin had to pray anew each time her spell began to falter and hope that one of her goddesses would answer.

Leifander swooped back to where Larajin circled, surveying the forest below for a place to land. They'd come far already. They'd left the crystalline towers two nights before, crossed the River Ashaba, and had come to a place above the Vale of Lost Voices. The slash in the forest below was the trail that linked Essembra and Ashabenford. Rauthauvyr's Road lay perhaps ten or fifteen miles to the east. If they paused only briefly then flew on through the afternoon and evening, they could reach Moontouch Oak by the next day's dawn—assuming Larajin's strength and magic held out.

As he drew nearer to the spot where Larajin and Goldheart circled, Leifander caught a glimpse of movement in the forest below. Several dark shapes were moving along the trail—two or three, maybe more. He cawed and banked sharply to the left, trying to direct Larajin to a clearing a safe distance from the moving figures, but with catlike perversity she ignored his warning. Instead she dived down and landed on the trail itself, in a spot that would place her directly in the path of whoever—or whatever—was moving along it. Even the tressym had better instincts than that. It circled above the spot where she'd landed, refusing to join her.

Angry, Leifander changed his course, flying toward Larajin. She ought to have more sense than to risk exposing herself to what might turn out to be an elf patrol. He swooped down to treetop level, angling toward the trail.

Leifander gave a strangled caw as he passed over the trail and got a good, close look at the figures moving along it. They were enormous spiders—four of them. Bloated and hairy, as large as dogs, they moved in a tight group like a pack of trained hounds. Even from treetop level, Leifander could smell the foul stench that clung to them like mold to a dead leaf.

What were they doing in this part of the wood? Had they been feeding on the corpses of the human caravan drivers along Rauthauvyr's Road? Or was there a more sinister reason? Leifander prayed it was not so. This part of the forest was supposedly free from drow.

The spiders glanced up at Leifander as he soared past them. More than one set of legs flailed in the air in his direction, as if the creatures wished they could climb into the sky. Leifander flew on, shuddering. One bite from those venomous creatures would cause a slow numbness to spread through the body until it was paralyzed, and the spiders would feed. . . .

Larajin had landed about a hundred paces up the trail, where the spiders couldn't see her, but they could see the tressym that fluttered nervously above the spot where she stood. They paused, questing Larajin's scent. A vile chuckling sound filled the air, and they broke into a skittering run.

Frightened, Leifander flew as quickly as he could to the spot where Larajin had landed. He saw her on the trail below, crouched on the ground with arms outstretched and head bent. She must have just completed shifting back to human form. Unable to do more than caw at her, Leifander was forced to land and shift. As he rose to his feet, the spiders came into sight.

Larajin, however, gave them no more than a quick glance.

"It's Dray!" she said, pointing into the trees at a spot where the mist had blighted the underbrush, opening up the forest to view. "Something's happened to him."

Leifander gave the briefest of glances in the direction she'd indicated and saw a human, either unconscious or dead, who appeared to have been hung by his doublet upon the broken branch of a massive oak tree like a coat upon a hook. The man's feet dangled a full pace above the ground, just above where drifting mist had discolored the trunk.

Leifander had no time to wonder who the fellow was or how he'd wound up hanging from the tree. The spiders were almost upon them.

"Pray to your goddess!" he shouted at Larajin. "Either

skinwalk or do something to help me fight the spiders."

He heeded his own advice. Touching the feather in his braid, he uttered a quick prayer to the Lady of Air and Wind, beseeching her for just a fraction of her power. At the same time he raised his right hand and fluttered it, as if fanning a breeze.

The spell came—swiftly, thank the goddess. Leifander's hand speeded to a blur, and a roaring wind sprang from it. He directed the wind at the spiders, no more than a dozen paces away. As it struck, they slowed and hunkered to the ground. Struggling like men in a gale, they at first were blown backward a step or two, but after a moment's confusion they bent low and used their claw-tipped legs to drag themselves slowly forward.

"We've got to shift," Leifander shouted at Larajin over the roar of wind. "These spiders can climb trees. Flying is the only way we'll escape them. You go first!"

Larajin shook her head and pointed stubbornly at the spot where the man was hanging. "We can't just leave Dray. The spiders will kill him."

"He's probably already dead."

"What if he's still alive?"

"Why do you care?"

"He tried to save my life," Larajin said. "I owe the same to him."

That, Leifander could understand, even if he didn't like it.

He nodded at Larajin and said, "Then we'll make a stand."

It didn't look hopeful, however. The spiders had taken advantage of the twins' exchange of words and were making headway against the wind. Even with it howling against them, so close were they now that the stink of them filled the air, making Leifander gag.

Larajin clasped the locket around her wrist and called, "Keep your spell going. I'm going to try something."

She began to pray.

Had he the time, Leifander would have told her that it was probably too late. His spell was already failing. The fluttering in his hand was slowing to the point where his fingers were no longer a blur, and the strength of the magical wind was starting to drop. Made bolder, the spiders forced their way closer—too close to keep them all within the blast of wind. With a triumphant chitter, one of them suddenly found itself unimpeded, and leaped forward. It bit down, grazing Leifander's forearm even as he jerked it back.

Leifander quickly shifted the aim of his spell and forced the spider back, but too late. A numbness seized his arm, and it felt as if he had banged his elbow against something hard. His fluttering hand slowed, nearly stopped, then one of Larajin's hands began to glow.

In that same moment, the air was filled with the sweet scent of blooming flowers. She grabbed for his wounded forearm, and the numbness disappeared. For a wild moment Leifander thought that negating the venom was all she intended—that it wouldn't be enough. In another instant they would be swarmed by the spiders. Already the foul things were crouching, preparing to leap.

The tressym dived from the sky, howling a challenge. Brilliant wings flashing, it hurled itself straight at the spider closest to Leifander and Larajin—then swerved at the last moment, just out of reach. Legs bunched and the spider leaped, trying for this new prey. The tressym, however, was too swift for it. The spider fell back to the ground, venom dripping from its mouth.

The distraction was only momentary, but it was enough. Larajin's hand slid down Leifander's arm, toward his hand.

"Sune and Hanali Celanil, lend me a little of the water of Evergold—add your holy waters to my brother's storm!" she shouted.

A rush of energy flowed through Leifander and pulsed from

his fingertips. His hand again blurred and seemed to fuse with Larajin's. A spray of rain erupted from their fingers.

The rain, blown horizontally by the wind, shimmered with a golden glow. It struck the closest spider as it was preparing to leap, pitting its hairy flesh like sling stones. Chattering with rage and pain, the spider turned and tried to run but only managed a step or two before collapsing into a tangled heap of broken legs.

With the closest spider down, Leifander was able to direct his magical wind full force at the remaining three. He drove the magical rain at them, and as it struck it created sizzling pits in their flesh. The spiders cowered, trying to protect their heads by lowering them to the ground—then as one they turned and bolted. Blown by the wind at their backs, they skidded down the trail, chattering in terror as they tried to outrun the deadly rain. They made it no more than a few dozen paces, however, before crumpling to the ground like the first. There they seemed to melt, like lumps of dark clay in the rain. Still the shimmering drops, blown by the relentless magic wind, drove into them.

When nothing was left but a few scraps of hair and broken bits of leg, Larajin let go of Leifander's hand, and the spells ceased. Her eyes closed in relief, and she whispered a prayer of thanks to her goddesses.

Leifander echoed it. "Our spells . . ." he said slowly, nodding down at the little that remained of the spider that had fallen closest to them. "They shouldn't have been able to do that."

Larajin gave him an exhausted smile. "Not on their own, but together . . ."

He nodded, understanding. "The gods joined forces—through us—just as Hanali Celanil and Sune come together in you to augment your magic."

He closed his eyes for a moment and offered a contrite word of thanks—not just to the Winged Mother, but to Larajin's goddesses as well—for this twist of fate. Thanks to Larajin's stubbornness, they'd come close to being killed, but as a result, he had learned an amazing truth. Their spells, when joined, could be as powerful as those of the mightiest cleric.

It was something worth thinking about.

But first, there was the matter of the man in the tree to deal with. Larajin was already hurrying through the woods toward him, feet slipping on the rotted vegetation underfoot. Leifander jogged after her, and as he drew nearer to the oak tree, he got a better look at the man hanging from it.

The fellow was in his early twenties—fully adult, when measured in terms of the human life span—and had a handsome face. His jaw, framed by a thin line of neatly trimmed beard, hung slack, and his eyes were closed.

Was he a friend that Larajin knew from Selgaunt, perhaps? He was certainly dressed like a Sembian, in a doublet of blue and purple, dark blue hose, and what remained of a lace-collared shirt, its sleeves torn off at the shoulders. One of the sleeves had been tied around his arm in a makeshift bandage that was dark with dried blood.

As he drew closer to the oak, Leifander could see that the fellow was indeed breathing. Eyes roved beneath the closed lids, as if he were dreaming. Not unconscious, then, but the victim of some sort of spell.

Goldheart, having followed Larajin and Leifander, landed on a branch just above the sleeping man. With catlike curiosity, she stalked along the branch, sniffed him, then pawed at his cheek. When he did not respond, she settled back onto her haunches, considered a moment, then began to groom herself, as if she'd lost all interest in the fellow.

Leifander, however, remained curious. The magic that had induced the man's slumber must have been powerful. Either the person who had left him hanging on the tree—or someone who had come along the trail later, after the blight had revealed the spot where he hung—had stripped the fellow of his valuables without managing to wake him. A scabbed-over crease in his earlobe showed that an earring had been torn from it, and the little finger of his left hand was twisted at an odd angle and swollen to twice its size, as if someone had wrenched a ring from it.

As Larajin reached up to grab the man's legs and lift him down, Leifander saw clumps of loose earth around the base of the tree, partially hidden by the blighted vegetation. Suddenly he realized the oak's significance.

"Don't!" Leifander shouted. He leaped forward and knocked Larajin's arms down. "You'll be caught up in the spell."

Irritation smoldered in Larajin's eyes. "It's only a sleep spell," she said. "It doesn't rub off on other people."

"It will if you touch the tree."

Larajin gestured up at the tressym. "It didn't affect Goldheart."

"Of course it didn't," Leifander answered, exasperated at Larajin for missing a simple explanation. "She's a magical creature."

Leifander pointed up at the trunk of the oak, just above the spot where Dray hung.

"Do you see that?"

Larajin squinted. "Those scratches in the bark?"

"Yes. It's a warning, in Espruar. This is holy ground. An elf lies buried beneath that oak. This man," he pointed up at Dray, "must have been trying to loot the grave. He triggered the ward on the tree, and the elves probably hung him on it as an example. If either of us touches the tree, the magic of that ward will send us into a magical slumber. We'll be as helpless as babes."

"I thought elves were immune to magical slumber," Larajin said.

"We're half-elves," Leifander reminded her. "We may resist the magic—or we may not. Do you really want to take that gamble?"

Larajin considered for a moment, then shook her head. "I can't believe that Dray was trying to rob this grave," she said. "He's a Foxmantle—a wealthy Sembian merchant who led the caravan that I traveled north with. He has no need to stoop to tomb robbing. In fact, when some sellswords he hired to protect his caravan turned out to be brigands and looted an elven tomb, Dray ordered them to stop. He's a decent man."

Leifander glanced down at the disturbed ground, then up at the sleeping man, and asked, "Then what happened here?"

"I don't know," Larajin answered, "but Dray might. Let's wake him up and find out. Will you help me lift him down—carefully, so we don't touch the tree?"

Leifander nodded, and together they grasped Dray by his legs and eased him off the branch he'd been hanging from. They carried him a short distance through the woods, away from the area blighted by the mist, and laid him on clean ground. After a few moments, he began to stir. His eyes opened, and he stared up at them—then he sat up quickly and looked wildly about, as if expecting something to jump out from behind a tree at any moment.

"What's happened?" he gasped. "Where's Klarsh?"

Larajin seemed to recognize the name. "He's not here," she told Dray.

She explained how they'd found him hanging in a tree—alone. Leifander added his own observation: the rotted vegetation that surrounded the oak had been devoid of footprints. Whoever had left Dray in the tree had done so before the mist drifted into that part of the forest.

"How long have I been here?" Dray asked. "What day is it, Thazienne?"

Larajin—who didn't seem to find it unusual to be addressed by her half-sister's name—gave him a date from the human calendar.

"By the gods . . . that long?" Dray said in a whisper. "I've been asleep for more than a tenday, then."

He rose to his feet unsteadily, like an invalid climbing from bed. Larajin reached out to help him, careful not to jostle his injured arm.

"Can I heal that for you?" she asked.

Dray nodded eagerly. "Please. If you could."

Larajin placed her hands gently above the makeshift dressing and whispered a quick prayer. A glow spread from her fingers into his arm, and Dray breathed a deep sigh of relief. Gingerly at first—then with increasing confidence—he unwrapped the dressing. The skin underneath was puckered but whole. He wiggled the fingers of his left hand. Thanks to Larajin's magic, the broken finger had straightened, and the swelling was gone. Flexing it, he smiled.

"Where are you headed?" he asked.

Larajin gestured east.

"Back to Rauthauvyr's Road?" Dray asked. "Can I travel at least that far with you?"

"Not unless you can fly," Leifander said bluntly.

"We're using magic," Larajin explained. "We'd soon leave you behind."

"Ah," Dray said. He glanced at the trail, looking uncomfortable. "Perhaps I should try to reach Ashabenford, then," he said nervously. Then he added, "Are you sure I can't persuade you to accompany me?"

"We haven't time," Larajin told him. "We're trying to find someone. We believe she's to the east, deeper in the woods. She—"

Thankfully, Larajin caught Leifander's curt head shake, and changed the subject.

"How did you escape the ambush?" she asked Dray. "I thought the elves had killed you."

Dray glanced nervously at Leifander and dropped his voice to a whisper. "Is he one of them?"

"Yes," Larajin answered, "and no. He's a half-elf. He's my . . . friend. You can trust him."

Leifander gave this no comment. Instead he merely waited, arms folded, for Dray to tell them what had happened.

"Ah," Dray said. He spoke to Larajin, but kept an eye on Leifander, heedful of his reaction. "My escape was a fortuitous one—and not at all due to my own merits, I'm ashamed to add. After I grabbed the sword, an arrow struck my arm. I thought I was going to faint from the pain, then suddenly everything was gone."

Leifander frowned, and saw the same expression on Larajin's face. "Gone?" he asked.

"I'd been transported to another spot in the woods," Dray explained. "Magically—by Klarsh, as it turned out. It seems, having lost his chance at the, ah . . . spoils . . . he was trying to salvage something of value from the caravan: me.

"I had nothing to fight Klarsh with—I'd dropped the sword after the arrow struck my arm—and I knew he had powerful magic. I had no choice but to accompany him through the woods. I expected him to head for Essembra and on to Hillsfar, which was where that lout Enik had said the brigands would lie low with their loot. I was surprised when we went west, instead. When I asked Klarsh why, he said the north was hardly the neutral haven that Enik had expected. He said he didn't want to be 'conscripted,' and that Enik had been a fool."

"Conscripted?" Larajin echoed. "By whom? Have the cities of the Moonsea also declared war on the elves?"

Dray shrugged.

Leifander stared at the human, his patience wearing thin. When would the fellow get to the point? "How did you come to be digging up an elf grave?" he asked, nodding in the direction of the oak.

Dray paled and glanced imploringly at Larajin but continued when she urged him on with a nod.

"I didn't want to do it. Klarsh forced me—with his magic. I was no more than a puppet, jerked by magic strings. It was terrible, being so helpless. The last thing I remember was grabbing one of the roots, to pull it free and suddenly feeling very tired. Then I woke up, here, with you."

The story sounded reasonable to Leifander, but Larajin had one more question.

"Why didn't Klarsh use a spell to move the earth aside, as he had before?"

Dray shrugged. "Maybe he thought it would attract too much attention. He thought there might be other elf patrols in the woods. Perhaps he just wanted to humiliate me by forcing me to do manual labor."

"Or perhaps," Larajin said, "Klarsh intended you to fall victim to the tree's magical ward. As a wizard, he should have recognized the glyph on the tree for what it was. He'd probably decided to abandon his treasure hunt and ransom you instead. I'll bet it was he who took your ring and earring, as proof that he held you captive. The sleeping spell made you easy to handle—and to store. I suppose he intended to leave you here in the woods, hanging on that tree, for your relatives to pick up after they had delivered the ransom."

She glanced at the mist-scarred oak, then at the trail, and the four spider bodies that lay on it, and shuddered.

"You could have been killed by the mist, had it been just a little higher—or by spiders. You're a lucky man, Dray."

"Lucky to have met you, Thazienne," Dray answered with a bow.

Leifander, aware that he might as well be invisible to the human, bristled. His magic had played an equal part in saving Dray's life, and yet it went unacknowledged. It was not in his nature to boast his valor or to seek acknowledgement from a human. Even so, it rankled.

Larajin was oblivious to this slight. Instead she seemed troubled by something. She glanced at the ground, as if collecting her thoughts, then up at Dray.

"I'm not actually Thazienne," she said. "I'm a . . . relative of hers. My name's Larajin."

Dray's eyebrows rose. "Indeed? A relative, you say? You're an Uskevren, then?"

"Yes, but my mother was from a . . . part of the family that's not well known."

"Ah," Dray nodded sagely, as if this explained everything. "A dalliance, then." He studied her a moment, his head tilted to one side. "You're too young to be one of the illegitimate brats Roel was so fond of siring. Was your father Perivel, then? But no, he died when the first Stormweather Towers burned to the ground, years before you would have been born. That would leave . . ."

Leifander, growing impatient, supplied the answer. "Her father was Thamalon Uskevren," he told Dray, ignoring Larajin's frantic motions for silence. "I am also Thamalon's son."

Dray glanced at Leifander's tattooed face, then burst into laughter. Only when Leifander glowered at him was he able to choke it back.

"Oh that's a good one," Dray sputtered at last. "I suppose you'll be laying claim to the family fortune, then, like that fellow who pretended to be Thamalon's long-lost brother. I heard about that—about the fake Perivel, and the magical chalice that proved him an imposter."

Leifander dismissed this foolish notion with a curt flick of his fingers. Why did every human he confessed his parentage to assume he'd want to live in a crowded, stinking pile of stone like Selgaunt?

"I'm not interested in Sembian gold," he told Dray.

"Perhaps not," Dray agreed as his eyes slid sideways to Larajin, "but she is. Or to be more specific, she's interested in Foxmantle gold."

Dray turned to Larajin and nodded at her dagger. "The weapon with the Uskevren crest was a nice touch. It had me fooled. No wonder you were so keen on joining my caravan. You hoped to seduce me!"

Anger blazed in Larajin's eyes. "Seduce *you*?" she echoed in an exasperated voice. "You were the one who practically proposed marriage. I never—"

Leifander, growing impatient, touched Larajin's arm.

"This discussion is pointless," he told her. "You've repaid this man by saving his life, but now time is wasting. Let's shift and be off, before more spiders find us."

Dray, obviously realizing that he was about to be left to

make his own way home alone from the middle of the spider-infested woods, caught at Larajin's arm.

"Larajin, please forgive me," he begged. "I'm sorry to have insulted you. Please, won't you at least loan me your dagger, so I at least have a fighting chance of getting home?"

"I can't," Larajin answered. "It's . . . an heirloom, but Leifander might be able to spare his dagger."

"What?" Leifander whirled around and glared at her. He gestured angrily at Dray. "He's a human. An enemy."

Amazingly, Larajin moved between Leifander and Dray, as if shielding the human.

"He's harmless, Leifander, just a merchant. I'd stake my life on it."

"You'd stake other people's lives on it, you mean," Leifander muttered to himself. Then, seeing that Larajin was not going to be swayed from this foolish notion, he added, "Do you think he'll agree to a magically binding oath?"

Instead of answering, Larajin looked at Dray. The human nodded.

Leifander drew his dagger—smiling inwardly as Dray flinched—then reversed the blade. He spoke a prayer in Elvish, activating the spell that would bind Dray to his oath.

"Touch the hilt," he instructed.

Dray hesitated only an instant before obeying.

"Now swear," Leifander intoned, "that you'll only use this dagger to defend yourself against forest creatures—that you won't wield it against my people, the elves."

Dray drew himself up and placed a hand on his heart.

"I swear it," he said. He blinked once, as Leifander's spell rooted the suggested course of action firmly in his heart, then he hefted the dagger and added, with a grin, "Truth be told, I'm more a man to avoid fights than prompt them."

He turned to Larajin. "Thank you for all that you've done. Back on the caravan, when I said you were pretty, I wasn't lying. You're quite beautiful. If you really were an Uskevren, I'd renew my proposals." He winked. "But business, unfortunately, must always come before pleasure, even for a Foxmantle."

Leifander tugged impatiently at Larajin's arm. "Come," he said. "Time to shift."

Leifander squatted and spread his arms, preparing to skin-walk. Larajin nodded, then sank to her knees on the ground, clutching the locket at her wrist. As she began the spell that would shift her into tressym form, however, she cast one last glance over her shoulder at Dray, then she closed her eyes, as if the sight of him was distracting her.

Leifander shook his head at her folly. Dray might be handsome but he had little else to recommend him, and yet he'd won Larajin over with nothing more than a few charming words. It was amazing, Leifander thought, what lengths someone would go to, given the promise of a little romance.

CHAPTER 13

Dusk descended as they winged their way east. Ahead
in the distance, Larajin could see a sprinkling of
lights straddling a dark slash across the forest that
could only be Essembra and Rauthauvyr's Road.
Leifander dipped a wing, indicating that they should
land there, but before they drew much closer,
Goldheart began acting in a peculiar fashion. She
meowed once, loudly and plaintively, and circled off
to the south. When Larajin didn't follow, Goldheart
beat her wings furiously to catch up, then repeated
her meow-and-turn. This time, she continued to fly
away to the south, her tail lashing furiously.

Leifander, oblivious to Goldheart's antics, flew
steadily on to the east. If Larajin turned and flew
after Goldheart, would he follow? The battle with
the spiders had taught them that their strength lay

in keeping together, but there was no guarantee he wouldn't ignore the tressym and continue the search for Rylith on his own.

Larajin did the only thing she could—she prayed silently, since her tressym vocal chords could not articulate words. She begged the goddess to give her the power of human speech, so she could talk to Leifander. She knew he could understand language, even in crow form. If she could just—

There. A familiar red glow started at the tips of her whiskers and traveled down them like a flame along a wick. Her lips and tongue were tingling, too. She opened her mouth to call out to Leifander, but what burst forth was the caw of a crow.

Leifander understood it, however. Wheeling up and over in a loop, he flew back to her.

"What?" he cawed back. "What's wrong?"

Larajin jerked her head in the direction of the rapidly departing tressym.

"It's Goldheart. She's spotted something and wants us to follow her."

Larajin started a wide turn toward the south, and Leifander did a loop that placed him beside her, flying in the same direction—for the moment.

"She's probably hunting," Leifander said. "We don't have time for games of cat and mouse."

"I don't think so," Larajin replied. "She deliberately got my attention before turning south. She wants us to follow. I've learned to trust her intuition. Goldheart is blessed by the goddess. Hanali Celanil herself may be guiding her."

Leifander gave a rattling croak that to Larajin's ears was clearly a grumble of frustration.

"All right," he said after a moment. "Let's see what it is."

Goldheart, seeing that Larajin and Leifander were at last following, allowed them to catch up to her. As they did, Larajin switched to the tressym's language, meowing a question.

Goldheart's answer was cryptic. "He comes," she yowled back in an excited voice.

The tressym sped up. Unable to further question the creature, Larajin translated for Leifander, who jerked his wings in a shrug.

Goldheart led them south, then turned east to cross Rauthauvyr's Road. Even in the gloom of dusk, Larajin could see that it was choked with the aftermath of war. Half a dozen wagons of peculiar construction had obviously fallen victim to an elf ambush. They were stopped at odd angles along the road with horses lying dead in their traces. Dozens of bodies—the wagon drivers and the archers who must have been escorting them—lay scattered around the wagons and on the road itself. Larajin grimaced, glad she wasn't flying low enough to see their terrible wounds.

The only sign of those who had attacked the caravan was a creature that hung, dead, in the broken branches of a tree next to the road. Its body was a mix of eagle and lion, and there was a saddle on its back, though no rider was to be seen. Leifander, when he saw it, gave a strangled caw and swooped down for a closer look.

Goldheart continued to the south, not even glancing at the carnage below. It seemed she had another objective in mind. Larajin hoped it wasn't far. Already she could feel the looseness of limb that was the first warning of her change back to human form. Soon, she would have to land and rest and pray to renew her spell.

She saw Goldheart descend toward the treetops as if she had spotted something. Larajin glanced over her shoulder, and saw to her relief that Leifander was still following—he hadn't landed at the caravan. She angled toward the trees to the spot where Goldheart had landed. As she did, she heard the thudding of hooves and the snorting of horses.

Cautious, she landed on a branch and peered down through the tangle of foliage. Her heart leaped to her throat as she recognized one of the riders below. It was Master Ferrick, leader of the company Tal had joined. There was no sign of Tal among the riders, who numbered less than a dozen. All of them rode as though exhausted, and one was injured, with a stained dressing wrapped around his shoulder.

Had Tal's company already been attacked by the elves, leaving these men the only survivors? Had Larajin's vision of Tal's death already come to pass?

The riders were talking together in low voices, but at this height she couldn't hear what they were saying. She stalked from branch to branch, trying to get closer to the ground. At last she could pick out a little of the hushed conversation.

". . . our other patrols?" one of the men below asked.

Most of Master Ferrick's answer was pitched too low for Larajin to hear, but she thought she made out the words, ". . . wait for them at . . ." before the horses thudded on, and the riders were lost from sight again.

A rush of hope filled Larajin. They were going to wait for someone? Did that mean the company had merely split up—that Tal might still be alive?

Launching herself from the branch, she flew through the forest to a tree that lay in the general direction the men were traveling—north—then landed and strained her ears and eyes. So intent was she on watching for the men to reappear that she only realized something had landed beside her when she felt it brush against her. She turned, expecting Goldheart, but saw Leifander instead. She glanced up and saw the tressym circling anxiously overhead.

Though the soldiers were still too far away to hear him, Leifander's croaking was low, the equivalent of a whisper. The goddesses' blessing must still have been upon Larajin, for she heard what he said as plainly as if he'd spoken in Common—"Sembians?"—as well as the tightly controlled anger in his voice.

"It's Tal's company," she answered.

Leifander cocked his head as the riders came into sight again, watching. This time, the men below kept silent. More than one was looking around, as if fearful of attack. One of them looked up, and both Leifander and Larajin instinctively froze.

Leifander waited until the riders had disappeared from sight before speaking again.

"Your half-brother is not with them."

"No," Larajin admitted, "but Goldheart said Tal was coming this way."

"What of it?"

"If I can find Tal, I can warn him that the elves—"

"That the elves *what*?" Leifander cawed angrily. "Have windriders guarding the forest ahead? I think not!"

Frustrated, Larajin dug her claws into the branch. She had no idea what Leifander was talking about, but his accusatory tone galled her.

"We're on the same side now, remember?" she cawed back. "We're trying to stop this war."

"By betraying the elves' secrets?" Leifander asked hotly. "How *human* of you."

"And what of when we reach the druids?" Larajin hissed back. "Will you betray the movements of the men below and get my brother killed?"

Her words had been plain enough, but Leifander was giving her a blank look, his head cocked and his glossy black eyes unblinking. Then Larajin realized why. For some reason, her last few words had come out in the form of a tressym's angry yowl. Before she had time to wonder why this might be, Leifander launched himself into the air. Larajin, still angry, hurled herself after him, wings beating furiously.

They chased each other through the sky for several moments, he furiously cawing and she howling like a cat.

The trembling looseness that she'd felt earlier returned. Realizing that she had to land—and soon, before her spell wore off—Larajin searched the forest below. She briefly debated trying to find the Sembian riders again, then decided against it. Master Ferrick would recognize her, but his men might not—and Larajin didn't relish the thought of dying at the edge of a "friendly" sword after startling them in the darkness.

Rauthauvyr's Road was an equally unappealing place to land—it was too open, too exposed—but she had to make up her mind quickly. Each wing beat was an effort, and the treetops below loomed ever closer.

She tried to get Leifander's attention, but he seemed unwilling to recognize her plight. Instead it was Goldheart who aided her. The tressym circled above what appeared to be a small opening in the forest. As Larajin drew nearer, she saw it was the circular rooftop of a slender stone tower. It looked long abandoned. The wrought-iron rail that surrounded the top of the tower was rusted and bent, and ivy grew thickly on its stonework, disappearing inside broken windows.

The tower itself, however, looked solid enough, its timbered roof still intact. Larajin felt her limbs lengthening and changing shape, and she realized it was her only option if she didn't want to fall headlong from the sky.

She was just able to land on the mossy rooftop before her magic left her, returning her with a wrenching jolt to human form. Rising to her feet, Larajin searched the sky for Leifander and Goldheart.

Leifander was a rapidly disappearing dot in the distance, winging his way north. Goldheart however, had remained close by. Larajin waved to her, and as the tressym descended to where she stood, quickly repeated the prayer that would allow them to communicate.

"Goldheart, I need to pray—to regrow my wings," she told the tressym. "While I do that, I need you to follow Leifander. See where he goes, then come back and find me. Tell me where he lands."

Goldheart nodded her head in agreement, then growled low in her throat as she sniffed the wind. Her tail fluffed to twice its size.

"Be watchful," she hissed softly. "He comes."

Larajin withdrew her hand in alarm. "Who? Is it Tal who . . . ?"

Before she could complete her question, Goldheart launched herself into the air. She winged away through the night, following Leifander.

A chill breeze whispered through the treetops, making Larajin shiver. Above her, the cold orb of the moon beamed down, throwing a dark puddle of shadow at her feet. Feeling exposed, she wondered for a moment if she shouldn't try to climb down inside the tower and find a more secluded place to pray. The tower was tall and thin, no more than a few paces wide. The decorative leaf pattern of its rusted railings hinted at elven construction, and Larajin wondered if the tower had been built back in the days when Gold elves ruled Cormanthor.

Remembering Goldheart's warning to be watchful, she crossed to a darker patch of shadow that was an open trap-door hanging from one rusted hinge. She kneeled beside it to peer down into the tower. As she'd expected, it was hollow, with a single metal staircase spiraling down the inner walls to ground level, more than a hundred paces below.

The inside of the tower was choked with spiderwebs that glinted silver-white in the moonlight. Larajin jerked back in alarm as a fist-sized spider scuttled across one of the strands of silk, a few paces below her. She forced herself to take another look, to make sure there weren't larger spiders moving around down there. After a moment, she sighed with relief—there weren't.

The staircase, she saw, was no longer whole. It ended at a distance of about five paces up from the floor. It was as if the bottom of it had been torn from its moorings by an invisible hand. Frayed bits of metal littered the stone floor.

There was no way Larajin could have descended that twisted mess, even if she'd wanted to brave the spiders. If it was indeed Tal whom Goldheart had said was coming to this lonely spot, she'd have to fly down to meet him.

Just as she was about to sit down and begin the prayer that would return her to tressym form, another movement in the tower below caught her eye. At first Larajin thought she was looking at a pair of spiders, but after a moment she realized they were dark hands, reaching out of a hole in the ground. With a growing sense of dread she watched as the hands grasped a piece of the broken staircase and pushed it aside, widening the hole.

Larajin watched, transfixed, as a woman with glossy black skin climbed from the hole. The woman's slender build, pointed ears, and bone-white hair marked her as one of the dark elves—the drow. As she climbed from the hole, a spider dropped onto her shoulder from above. She reached up and stroked it like a pet.

As the drow glanced around, Larajin drew quickly back from the broken trapdoor. Heart pounding, she crouched against the rooftop of the tower, not daring to move. Listening, she could hear what sounded like more drow climbing out of the hole, then a flurry of conversation, spoken in a language that reminded her of the chittering of spiders.

How many drow were down there? Larajin didn't want to risk a look. Two or twenty, it really didn't matter. Larajin had no first-hand knowledge of the drow, but the books she'd read described the underworld elves as a cruel and cunning race, even deadlier than the poisonous spiders they worshiped. The drow were said to hate all races that walked in sunlight with equal vigor—humans and their elf cousins alike. Those they killed outright were the lucky ones. The rest were fed to the spiders. Bound tightly in their webs, these unfortunates faced a slow, gruesome death.

Touching the locket at her wrist, Larajin began the prayers that would allow her to skinwalk away from there. As the locket began to glow, she cupped it tightly in her hand, wary lest the glow give her away. As she prayed, she tried to make sense of why Goldheart had led her there. Was Tal indeed headed this way? Was Larajin expected to use her magic to protect him from the drow below?

The voices stopped abruptly, causing Larajin to halt her prayer in mid-whisper. Had she been heard? The answer came a moment later, when another voice—lower than the others, and male—sounded from below. He was speaking the chittering drow tongue, but between sentences there came a familiar wheeze.

Larajin didn't dare look down into the tower. Not with the moon so bright overhead. Instead she channeled the energy Sune had just blessed her with into the spell that allowed her to comprehend other languages. Her ears tingled briefly, and the words below became as clear as Common.

The drow speaking was female, and Larajin's spell revealed her words in mid-sentence. ". . . thank you for that, Drakkar."

Larajin let out a strangled gasp of alarm. Drakkar! She'd gone through so much to flee the man, and now here he was, in the great forest! In her panic, she missed Drakkar's reply.

The drow who had spoken a moment before continued, "How much longer, then?" she asked.

"The war builds momentum, even as we speak," Drakkar answered. "My master has gained the elves' confidence and will make a show of fighting beside them for a tenday or two—just long enough to drive the humans back. Then, when victory seems assured, there will be a falling out over an incident that will appear to be a deliberate act of betrayal by the elves. His forces will withdraw then. Left to their own devices, the elves will lose the war, and the Sembians, their desire for revenge sated, will return home. The few elves that survive can easily be slain, and the great forest will be ours."

As a chorus of voices chattered below—some asking why it would take so long, others congratulating Drakkar for his cunning—Larajin seized on that last word. Not 'yours' but 'ours.' She realized the wizard's dirty little secret. He might look as human as Larajin did, but despite the absence of pointed ears and glowing red eyes, drow blood flowed in his veins. Now that she thought about it, Drakkar's ink-black hair seemed too dark for a man of his age. It should have at least been streaked with gray. Its natural shade was probably pure white—something he would be careful to disguise with dye, so none would suspect his true heritage.

She understood why Goldheart had led her to the tower with the cryptic message, "He comes." It had been Hanali Celanil, speaking through her favored creature, who had wanted Larajin to overhear this exchange and realize what the ultimate end of the war would be: not just death for her dear brother Tal, but the destruction of the elves of the great wood, and the invasion of the forest by drow.

There was only one piece of the puzzle missing. Who was this 'master' Drakkar had just spoken of? Larajin listened intently to the voices below, but heard nothing that would answer that question. The drow spoke greedily of how they would turn the forest into a dark haven for their kind, once the other elves—whom they snarlingly referred to as "sunspit"—were slain. And woe betide any human who dared venture within the tree-shaded wood.

With growing horror, Larajin realized the drow were describing the vision she'd had, back in the Tangled Trees. Dark hands reaching out of the earth, tearing open the flesh of human and elf alike, soaking the ground with blood.

All this would come to pass, if she and Leifander didn't do something to prevent it, but once again, Leifander had gone off on his own—all over a stupid misunderstanding. Larajin had only wanted to warn Tal to turn back, before an elf archer killed him, but Leifander's simmering hatred of humans— only partially suppressed and now reopened like a broken scab—had caused him to suspect the worst of her.

With a sinking heart, Larajin recalled Somnilthra's warning: "Unharness hate, and you will lose everything. Even your very lives."

She had to find Leifander, and fast—before he did something stupid and got himself killed.

Grasping her locket still tighter, she began to pray in a near-silent whisper.

"Sune and Hanali Celanil, grant me the power to skinwalk just once more. I must find my brother. I must fly."

The familiar scent of Hanali's Heart filled the air, and the red glow erupted through her clenched fingers. Larajin drew herself into position, kneeling on the mossy boards with hands clenched into fists to ease their transition into paws. She felt her body contort and contract, felt fur flow down her skin, wings grow from her shoulders, and her spine elongate into a lashing tail. Her whiskers quivered as she caught the buglike smell of the drow below, and she heard their shouts of confusion and alarm. They'd caught the floral scent that accompanied her spellcasting and were shouting questions at each other, asking what it might mean.

It didn't matter. The stairs leading up to her perch were broken. The drow had no way to reach her. Almost laughing, Larajin launched herself into the air, wings beating as she soared from the tower.

In her elation at skinwalking, she'd forgotten about Drakkar. She realized her mistake when the wizard rose through the opening in the roof of the tower, trailing strands of web behind him like a torn veil. Spotting her at once in the bright moonlight, his eyes widened in recognition. He pointed his thorn-studded staff and shouted a word that was unintelligible, even to Larajin's goddess-blessed ears.

Something streaked from the end of the staff in a trail of red sparks, buzzing toward Larajin like an angry hornet. She tucked in her wings and plunged into a steep dive, crashing down through tree branches in an effort to escape. A sharp sting in her right hind paw, however, told her the maneuver had been in vain. Distracted by the painful sting, she tumbled in mid-air, only managing to find her wings again at the last moment before striking the ground. She flew on, weaving between tree trunks in a frantic bid to escape.

Behind and above her, she heard Drakkar shouting at

the drow as they poured noisily from the tower. Could the wizard see her? Despite the screening of branches overhead, it would certainly seem so. Whichever direction Larajin flew, she heard the sound of running footsteps in the forest close behind her. A knife flashed through the air and buried itself in the trunk of an oak she'd just swerved to avoid, and to her right she could hear branches breaking as the drow circled around, trying to flank her. Always from above, came the shouts of the wizard, directing the drow to her.

Flying hard, Larajin twisted her hind foot up and under her belly, straining for a look at it. What she saw in that brief glimpse frightened her still further. A thorn was wedged between the pads of her paw. Even as she glanced at it, the thorn disappeared into her flesh like blood into desert sand.

She dropped her paw and continued flying, unable to do anything about it but worry. Was the thorn tainted with some foul poison? Would her wing beats soon slow, as the venom clutched at her heart?

But no, the sting of the thorn was gone, leaving behind no residue of ache, no creeping pain that worried its way up her limb. It felt as though the thorn had completely disappeared, and yet still the drow were pursuing her.

Drakkar must have used his staff to cast some sort of detection spell upon her, Larajin decided—one that made him cognizant of her every move. She might escape the drow, might even be able to fly fast enough to leave Drakkar himself behind, but guided by his thorn, how long would it be until he caught up to her again?

A second, less pressing question also puzzled her. Drakkar must have recognized her. Why hadn't he simply killed her when he had the chance?

There could be only one answer. He must have mistaken Larajin, in her tressym form, for Goldheart. He either wanted Goldheart for his own evil purposes, or he hoped the tressym would lead him to Larajin.

Either way, Larajin was in trouble. As the voices of the drow and Drakkar's shouts gradually diminished behind her, she headed in the only direction that made any sense: north, to Essembra.

Yet she couldn't help but wonder, now that Leifander's hatred had been unleashed, if Somnilthra's dire prophecy would be fulfilled. Was Larajin only bringing death, in the form of Drakkar and his evil magic, more swiftly to her brother and ultimately, to herself?

CHAPTER 14

As soon as he reached Essembra, Leifander could see
that something was amiss. Essembra was a human
settlement—the only one ever permitted to take
hold inside Cormanthor—but there were far too
many humans down there, especially when travel
should have been cut off by the war.

The stables beside the inn were choked with
horses, and a number of carriages were lined up in
front of the inn itself. Moving figures crisscrossed
Rauthauvyr's Road or stood in groups in the moonlight, talking. A number of tents had been erected
on the north side of town. They looked military in
nature, made from stiff, off-white fabric, and rectangular in shape. The way the people moved about
between the tents, in regular, orderly groups, suggested soldiers.

But whose soldiers? Even if Lord Ilmeth had summoned every knight from the abbey, there still shouldn't have been this many soldiers about. And why were they camped on the north side of town?

Leifander swooped down over the tents for a closer look. When he saw the red plumes on the helmets of the knights below, he nearly tumbled from the sky in surprise.

By the gods! he thought. Not soldiers of Hillsfar!

But it was true. They were unmistakably Lord Maalthiir's soldiers, wearing full splint mail and carrying long swords. It was unthinkable that they should be camped on the outskirts of Essembra. The only explanation could be that they had taken advantage of the war and invaded from the north while Lord Ilmeth's back was turned. Yet if that was so, how had they made it this far south through the great wood without being cut to pieces by the elves? Why had they stopped at the very gates of the town, leaving the folk of Essembra unmolested? So bloodthirsty were the Red Plumes that Leifander would have expected to see Essembra's dirt streets soaked with blood and its buildings burning.

He circled back over the town, taking stock. The wooden watchtowers that lined Rauthauvyr's Road held soldiers whose shields bore Lord Ilmeth's crest, and the gates across the road had not been forced. The wooden palisade that surrounded the town's most important buildings was likewise untouched. Even the cottages in the forest surrounding Essembra appeared unharmed, with lights glowing cheerily in their windows. Lord Ilmeth was still in control of Essembra—or so it seemed. Had he actually *welcomed* the Red Plumes to his town?

If so, they weren't his only guests. Circling wider over the forest, Leifander saw movement beneath the trees and was just able to make out the round, forest-brown tents of his people. For a moment he debated landing and asking the elves what was happening, but then, from the direction of town, he heard a high-pitched cry. It was the shriek of a griffon. Were the windriders there, too?

Wheeling, he flew toward the center of town and saw that he had been right. A griffon was indeed tethered, all by itself, in a corral near the center of town. The other windriders' steeds were nowhere in sight.

Leifander landed on the roof of the town's highest building, the House of Gond. Hopping along its soft lead gutter, he peered down from the temple's two-story height, past the heavy iron battlements that supported its walls. Smoke and the occasional bright red cinder drifted from the building's numerous chimneys. The blacksmith priests of Gond must have been working through the night, forging the weapons of war.

He saw more humans—residents of Essembra—on the streets below. Many of them had swords at their hips, having no doubt been pressed into service with the militia. There were also knights in full armor and a handful of elves. Some were forest elves, padding along in bare feet with bows in hand; others had the haughty bearing and pale skin of Silver elves and were clad in chain mail and helms. All seemed to be moving in the same direction, toward the sprawling, multi-halled building known as Ilmeth's Manor.

The massive iron doors at the front of the manor were open to the street. Elves and humans hurried up the front stairs and into its lantern-lit interior. Leifander hopped off the temple roof and flapped his way to the manor, landing atop one of the massive wooden pillars that fronted the building. By twisting his neck, he was able to peer under the rooftop and get a look inside the doors. What he saw there nearly froze his blood.

The hall had been trimmed with all of the trappings of war, including battle standards and ceremonial lances. It was filled with human soldiers—both Lord Ilmeth's and the Red Plumes. The latter stood across the room from where the elves had assembled, no doubt warily keeping their distance. Flanking a table at the far end of the room was a group of high-ranking elves and Red Plumes officers, standing so close to one another they were almost rubbing shoulders. Worse still was the sight of Lord Ilmeth and half a dozen members of the Elven Council—including Lord Kierin—standing around a table with none other than Maalthiir, first lord of Hillsfar.

Leifander nearly gagged at the sight of the man. Short and stocky, Maalthiir had dark red hair shaved close to his scalp and eyebrows that joined above his nose in a V-shape, giving him a perpetual scowl. His jaw was square and blocky, his nose a mere stub. Had Leifander not known better, he would have guessed the man to have some orc blood in him. Perhaps that guess was correct. Self-loathing could explain the disdain Maalthiir felt for any but "trueblood" humans.

With barely suppressed hatred, Leifander stared at the man whose edicts had caused Chandrell's death. The man's hands might appear clean, but they were stained with the blood of countless innocent elves.

Regardless of this terrible fact, Maalthiir seemed welcome in Lord Ilmeth's manor. He stood quietly with the group at the table, watching as each person in turn took up a quill and signed a piece of parchment that had been spread on the table-top. He smiled pleasantly as he took the pen from Lord Kierin's hand—an elf's hand—to sign the document himself.

The ceremony reached its conclusion, and Lord Ilmeth picked up the parchment and held it out before him. The assembled crowd immediately fell into a respectful hush, broken only by the faint clink of armor as soldiers shifted for a better look.

"By this document," Lord Ilmeth's voice rang out, "Lord Maalthiir of Hillsfar pledges his soldiers—ten thousand swords—to the elven cause."

"Madness!" Leifander cawed, but his protest was lost in the cheer that echoed through the hall. Had the High Council lost their minds? How could they trust these humans?

Judging from the wary looks on some of the elves' faces, Leifander was not the only one with doubts. Lord Kierin turned to Maalthiir and placed both hands over his heart, bowing low. Maalthiir, a smug look on his face, clasped the windrider's shoulders in what had to be a false show of friendship.

It seemed to satisfy the assembled elves, however. Heads began to nod and a murmur of approval filled the room. Leifander knew what they must have been thinking. If so mighty a hero as Lord Kierin could bow to Maalthiir, the human must have renounced his evil ways.

Leifander, however, saw something they did not: the frozen smile on Lord Kierin's normally scowling face. He realized, with a sudden terrible clarity, that there could only be one explanation. Leifander had betrayed Lord Kierin's true name to that wizard, Drakkar. He, in turn, must have confided it to someone, who in turn conveyed the information to Maalthiir. The lord of Hillsfar had used that secret in a foul manner, to bend Lord Kierin to his will.

Nearly ill with guilt, Leifander vowed he would make Maalthiir pay for this evil deed—that he would, at the very least, kill the man and set Lord Kierin free. But how? It would be suicide to attack Maalthiir in a hall filled with Red Plumes. He decided instead to wait until the man was alone—or nearly so, with as few of his guards around him as possible—then he would strike.

In the hall below, the assembly was already breaking up.

"We march in the morning!" Lord Ilmeth shouted. "Pray to your gods for victory on the morrow!"

Leifander drew back from the edge of the rooftop as the soldiers began spilling out down the stairs, into the street. Among the elves, he saw a face he recognized. Surely Doriantha, of all elves, did not support this alliance? He leaned out and cawed softly down to her. She started, then glanced up and gave her head the slightest of shakes. At the same time, her fingers moved, conveying a swift and silent message: "Meet. Tent. Forest."

She stopped signing and hurried down the street. An instant later, Maalthiir emerged from the manor and strode down the stairs, flanked by his officers. Leifander crouched atop the column, hoping he hadn't been seen. He watched Maalthiir climb into a carriage. After a moment it rumbled up the street.

Springing into flight, Leifander followed the carriage. As he'd suspected, it drove out through the town's northern gate and rumbled toward the Red Plumes's camp.

Doriantha had left the walled portion of Essembra, and was walking toward the tents of the forest elves. She was careful not to glance up at the sky, even though she must have been curious as to whether or not Leifander was following her. Leifander wheeled in a circle, uncertain. Should he meet her at her tent first? If he did, he might miss a chance at Maalthiir.

Climbing higher into the sky, he circled over the Red Plume camp, watching, until the carriage at last drew up in front of a large tent hung with red pennants. Maalthiir stepped out of the carriage and strode inside.

Gliding through the humid night air high above the camp, Leifander thought. Maalthiir's tent was guarded not only by the Red Plumes who stood at attention outside but also, almost certainly, with magical wards that would announce an enemy's approach in an instant. How then, to get inside?

Leifander dipped into a faint current of air that ruffled his feathers, and he let it blow him along for a moment or two, savoring its coolness. If only he could render himself invisible, he might have a chance, but that was not in the repertoire of spells granted by the Lady of Air and Wind. No, the spells she blessed the faithful with dealt with the creatures of wing and feather or with harnessing the power of the stormy winds.

That was it. The winds . . .

Leifander began to pray. From his beak came the harsh cawing of a crow, but in his mind he heard his prayer as distinct words.

"Winged Mother, come to my aid. Transform my body into one of your gentle breezes. Turn feather, flesh, and bone to air!"

It started at his wingtips. His long black flight feathers disappeared. Losing stability, he tumbled, but the progression swiftly continued. He felt his legs disappear, then the rest of his wings, then his beak, then his hips, breast, throat and . . .

His body was gone, and yet his momentum through the sky continued. He slowed gradually, until he was no more than a breath of breeze in the sky. He had no weight, but somehow he still had a sense of up and down. He had no eyes or ears, but he could still see and hear. There, on the ground that drifted lazily below him, were the tents of the Red Plumes. And there, in the sky just above and behind, was the hurtling streak of a tressym, flying hard.

Larajin?

The thought drifted into his mind, then was gone. The tressym shot past, a downbeat of its wings scattering Leifander like smoke when a wick is blown out.

After a moment, he found cohesion again, and remembered his purpose. The tent—the big one, below. Maalthiir. But somehow, the passion that had enflamed him a few short moments ago was gone.

Drifting toward the ground, he floated gently past one of the Red Plumes who stood at rigid attention outside the tent, then drifted for a moment in front of the tent flap, seeking an opening. The soldier whirled, suddenly alert, as the ties that held the flap shut fluttered with Leifander's passing—and Leifander was inside.

The interior of the tent was lit with a profusion of candles mounted in rows on black iron candelabras that had been driven into the earth. Thick rugs, once beautiful but now tracked with mud, were strewn haphazardly across the floor of the tent. Strongboxes had been stacked atop them to form a long, low table around which three of Maalthiir's officers clustered. One of them was pouring red wine for the others.

Maalthiir himself was seated in a folding chair with thick pads of leather cushioning its seat and arms, drinking from a gold goblet. He lowered it, and made a show of smacking his lips.

"Sembian wine is sweet, but tomorrow you'll see if Sembian blood is even sweeter, eh, General Guff?"

The officer he'd addressed—a human with dark hair and a heavy growth of beard slashed by an scar that puckered forehead, eye, and cheek in a vertical line—chuckled. Lifting his own goblet, he drew his sword from its scabbard and poured wine along its gleaming blade.

"To victory," he toasted, then thrust the sword into the air.

The other two officers—a bald fellow with a barrel chest, and a lean, fair-haired man with whipcord muscles—joined the toast.

The bald officer rumbled a toast of his own. "To our allies."

The slender officer arched an eyebrow. "Which ones?" he asked. "I need to know whether to wish them victory or defeat."

Maalthiir guffawed at this apparent witticism while the two lesser officers roared with laughter, but Leifander could see nothing funny in the words. Neither could General Guff, it seemed. He growled low in his throat like a dog about to bare its fangs, and the other two officers immediately fell silent.

Maalthiir continued chuckling, his wine slopping onto his fingers as he made a dismissive gesture. "Ah, Guff. Always so serious. Nadire was just making a joke."

"He should be wary of those who listen," the general growled.

Leifander, who had been gently drifting up to this point, shrank in upon himself like a sharply indrawn breath.

"What do you mean?" Maalthiir asked, sitting forward suddenly in his chair and looking warily around. "Who's listening?"

Solemnly, Guff pointed at the ceiling of the tent. "The gods. Lord Tempus, specifically. His favor can be fickle."

"Ah." Maalthiir relaxed back into his chair, transferred his goblet to his other hand, and flicked the spilled wine from his fingers. "Let us pray to him then, for success." He raised his goblet. "May Tempus grant victory and defeat to the appropriate parties, so that our road-building venture may be a success."

The two lesser officers chuckled along with their lord at these last few words, which must have been a shared joke of some kind. Guff, however, turned his sword point-uppermost and bowed his head in prayer, his eyes closed and forehead touching the blade. A dribble of the wine he'd poured on the sword trickled down the steel onto his face, making it look as though he had been baptized with blood. His lips moved in silent prayer.

Leifander, as he drifted around the tent, noted the symbol of Tempus—a silver sword in flames on a blood-red field—on Guff's surcoat. He was glad for the languor his spell had caused. Had he tried to assume material form and attack Maalthiir in his tent, Guff would have killed him in a trice with the war god's powerful magic.

Instead Leifander floated, watching and waiting. He took care not to come too close to any of the men, in case they were sensitive to the unseen. Instead he hovered above them, circling on the roiling currents of hot air thrown off by the multitude of candles. Once, he drifted too close to one of the candelabras and found that open flame still had the power to burn him, even in this form. With a silent hiss of pain, he pulled his body away, leaving the candles guttering in his wake.

The slender officer—Nadire—had turned back to the makeshift table to pour himself more wine and happened to be looking in Leifander's direction at the time. He frowned at the sudden breeze, but he returned his attention to the wine soon enough, and Leifander relaxed once more.

When Guff was finished with his prayer, Maalthiir began discussing plans for the morning's march. None of it was of interest to Leifander, save for the fact that Maalthiir would be returning to Hillsfar the next day, leaving General Guff to command the Red Plumes. The news gave Leifander cause for hope. With the bulk of his soldiers there, Maalthiir would take only a bodyguard back to Hillsfar with him. There might be a chance yet to—

What was that Maalthiir had just said, in answer to one of Guff's questions? Leifander's attention, like what remained of his body, had been drifting. If he had heard correctly, Guff had asked a question about the poisonous mist that was blighting the forest and how his men might be protected against it. Maalthiir had told him not to worry.

"It has served its purpose," Maalthiir added. "I'll have Drakkar dispel it."

Drakkar? The name caused Leifander to swirl in confusion. The evil wizard had given every impression that he was in the service of the mayor of Selgaunt, yet Maalthiir was speaking of him like an old and trusted friend. Was Drakkar one of the "allies" mentioned earlier?

Nadire, meanwhile, opened one of the crates and rummaged inside it. He drew out a long tube of rolled parchment, then interrupted the discussion of tactics with a faint cough.

"Excuse me, Lord Maalthiir, but has the terminus of the new road been fixed yet?"

Maalthiir gave him an annoyed look. "You know as well as I that it hasn't."

Nadire moved two of the candelabras closer to where Maalthiir sat, then opened the parchment—which turned out to be a map—and spread it at Maalthiir's feet. Leifander, his curiosity piqued, drifted closer and recognized it as a map of the great forest by the names of the Dales that were written around the forest's outskirts.

"Will it be here?" Nadire asked, pointing at a spot at the western edge of the great forest.

Leifander drifted closer. What was this road they were talking about? Were the humans of Hillsfar—supposed allies of the elves—actually talking about hacking yet another open wound through the ancient forest? Anger swirled within him.

Maalthiir made no answer, only stared at Nadire with a strange expression on his face. Guff, having drained his goblet, squinted at the map.

"You know as well as I do, Nadire, that the best place for a port is—"

The barrel-chested officer started to jab a thick finger into the map, but Nadire's hand darted out fast as a striking snake, blocking him.

Nadire's attention wasn't on the officer, however, but on the candelabras. His gaze darted from one to another—and suddenly fixed on the candles directly behind Leifander. Too late, Leifander realized that their flickering—and his own curiosity—had betrayed him. He swept to the side but wasn't quick enough. Nadire spoke a word in an ancient human tongue, and a bolt of crackling energy flew from his outstretched fingertips.

Leifander found himself in crow form once more, tumbling to the floor.

"A spy!" Maalthiir shouted, leaping to his feet. "A gods-cursed Sembian spy!"

In that same instant Guff whipped out his sword. The barrel-chested officer leaped between Leifander and Maalthiir, protecting his lord. Nadire, having expended one spell, began chanting the words of a second.

Terrified though he was at having been discovered, Leifander still had one thing in his favor. Nadire had dispelled only one of the spells Leifander had cast upon himself. Still in crow form, he could at least beat a hasty retreat on the wing—if he lived long enough to get out of the tent.

General Guff charged, sword whistling through the air, but somehow Leifander managed to dodge the slash, wheeling in a tight circle inside the tent. Nadire, trying to track him with one hand, held back his spell as Guff got in the way. Maalthiir continued shouting, urging his officers to capture the spy.

Salvation came a heartbeat later, when one of the guards outside threw open the tent flap to look inside. Quick as a blink, Leifander shot through the opening, wings beating so furiously they felt like a hummingbird's. He climbed with powerful strokes up into the sky—then dived to gain speed and present a more difficult target for Nadire's spell.

Behind him, he heard Maalthiir howling orders. "Archers! Shoot that damned bird!" he shouted. "Bring down anything that flies."

One arrow, two—and a flurry whistled into the air, but already Leifander had flown out of range. Silently praising the goddess for maintaining his skinwalking abilities even in the face of Nadire's spell, he flew far to the south, to reinforce Maalthiir's false impression that he was a Sembian spy. Only when he was certain he could no longer be seen did he dive to treetop level and turn back in the direction of the forest elves' camp.

CHAPTER 15

As the tent flap rustled, Larajin jumped in alarm and raised her hand to cast a spell. Beside her, Doriantha drew a dagger with a slither of steel and Goldheart fluffed in alarm. But instead of the person Larajin most feared—Drakkar—pushing his way into the tent, it was Rylith, the person she most wanted to see.

The druid blinked once in surprise to see Larajin inside Doriantha's tent, then immediately nodded as if finding Larajin there was something she'd half expected.

She looked around the tent and asked, "Where is Leifander?"

"We don't know," Larajin said in a tense voice. "Doriantha saw him perched on Lord Ilreth's manor, and told him to meet her here, but he never arrived.

Goldheart spotted him flying over the Red Plumes's camp a short time later, but then he just . . . disappeared."

Rylith's eyebrows furrowed. "Disappeared?"

Instead of questioning Larajin further, however, she turned to the tressym and uttered a series of *mrrows* and *yrrows*, then finally, a soft growl.

Rylith switched back to the common tongue. "His disappearance doesn't appear to be the Red Plumes's work. I think it was some spell he cast upon himself—that he somehow managed to render his crow form invisible. As for his safety now . . ."

Her voice trailed off as a sudden commotion erupted, far from Doriantha's tent. Larajin could hear the shouts of men, and the faint but unmistakable *thrum-thrum-thrum* of a volley of arrows being loosed. It sounded as though the noise was coming from the northeast.

"The Red Plumes!" Larajin said, stiffening. "Do you think it's Leifander they're shooting at?"

Doriantha joined Larajin in giving Rylith a tense, expectant look, but the druid merely sat quietly, listening. After a moment, the sound of bows stopped, and there were more distant shouts.

"If Leifander is the cause of that commotion, we can only hope he has escaped," Rylith said. "As to that—we shall see."

Doriantha nodded in acceptance, but Larajin jumped to her feet. "What? You mean we're just going to sit here and wait? We should—"

Rylith silenced her with a gesture, then she pulled something out of a pouch that hung at her hip. She began to chant the words of a spell. The object was a fist-sized chunk of amber of a clear, yellow color. Within it was a single speck—an insect, Larajin assumed at first, but then the speck began to move. Larajin and Doriantha leaned closer, and Larajin's breath caught in her throat as she recognized the moving shape for what it was: a tiny black crow.

"Leifander!" she exclaimed. "But where is he?"

She peered deeper into the chunk of amber. Its base was stippled and seemed to be moving—a pattern she recognized easily, after long days of flying over it: the treetops of the great forest.

"You see these lights?" Rylith asked, pointing out a faint sparkle at one edge of the amber. "That's Essembra. He is coming back this way."

Larajin sighed in relief and was surprised to hear Doriantha sigh, too. She'd thought the elf woman a battle-hardened veteran, not one to be overly sentimental about the welfare of individual members of her command. It looked as though Larajin had been wrong about her.

"Rylith," Larajin said, "I have a problem. Someone else may also be headed this way. Earlier this evening, Drakkar—the wizard who was the cause of my fleeing Selgaunt—cast a spell on me. The spell embedded a magic thorn in my paw. I think it was some sort of tracking spell."

Rylith's eyebrows rose at the word paw. "Show me."

Larajin pulled off her boot and extended her foot to the druid. Rylith peered at it, her tattooed cheeks puckering as she pursed her lips. Placing her amber in her lap, she held Larajin's foot in one hand and prodded at the sole with a forefinger, as if feeling for something under the skin. She placed the flat of her hand against the bottom of Larajin's foot and chanted the words to a spell.

A foul, burning smell filled the air, and the spot on Larajin's foot where the thorn had embedded itself became an intense point of heat and pain. Involuntarily, she jerked her foot back.

"What's happening?" she gasped.

Beside her, Goldheart sniffed at the foot, then growled.

Rylith shook her head grimly. "The wizard's magic is too strong. I can't dispel it."

Disappointment swept over Larajin as she cradled her aching foot. She'd been certain Rylith could help her.

"Drakkar will come for me, then," she whispered. "He'll find me."

Outside the tent, a stick cracked, and Larajin jumped.

Rylith placed a hand on Larajin's shoulder. "If he does, may the goddesses protect you. May they grant that you won't have to face Drakkar alone."

As if on cue, the tent flap whipped open. Leifander rushed inside, an urgent look on his face.

"Doriantha! Maalthiir is planning to—"

Noticing Larajin and Rylith, he halted in mid-sentence.

"Rylith," he breathed, placing both hands over his heart and giving a quick bow. "It's good to see you." He glanced at Larajin. "And you, Larajin," he added, though his words were strained. "I'm . . . going to need your help."

"You were spying on Maalthiir?" Rylith asked.

Leifander nodded, his eyes sparkling.

"Sit," Rylith commanded. "Tell us what you've seen and heard."

Leifander did as he was told and began telling the others something about Maalthiir planning to carve a road through the forest to the upper reaches of the Sea of Fallen Stars.

"It must be the reason behind the alliance," Leifander added. "Maalthiir knew the High Council would never agree to another road being built—especially not now. He probably hoped to gain the council's favor by sending his soldiers to fight with us. Do you think they'll grant him permission?"

Larajin, listening while she pulled her boot back on, now knew the name of the "master" Drakkar had spoken of earlier.

"Maalthiir isn't planning to ask the council's permission for anything," she said grimly. "He won't have to. Not once the drow control the forest."

Leifander and Doriantha both gave her startled looks. Rylith's eyes merely widened.

"The drow?" Leifander blurted. "What do they have to do with any of this?"

Quickly, Larajin related the story of what she'd seen and heard at the tower.

"Gods curse Maalthiir—and his wizard Drakkar!" Doriantha exclaimed. "*That's* why they're insisting all of the elf forces march toward Essembra. They hope we'll leave the rest of the forest unguarded."

Leifander's eyes had a thoughtful look. "Drakkar," he said slowly. "Maalthiir mentioned him."

"What did he say?" Rylith prompted.

"Something about the mist that caused the blight. He said Drakkar could dispel it."

"All of it?" Doriantha asked. "Impossible. It's spread throughout the forest, over an area of many miles."

Leifander shrugged. "Maalthiir made it sound as though Drakkar could dispel all of it at once with a wave of his hand."

It was Rylith who made the connection. "The poisonous mist," she said slowly. "It must be Drakkar's doing."

Leifander shook his head. "It's no mere spell," he said. "The mist came from wands—like the one I captured."

"Wands that must have been made by Drakkar," Rylith said, "and imbued with a spell that made their effects permanent." As she said the latter, she glanced at Larajin's foot, then away again.

"Drakkar is at the root of this war," Larajin said grimly. "He wormed his way into the Hulorn's confidence, and got him to persuade Sembia's Merchant Council to use the wands. He knew it would provoke the elves."

"I suspected as much," Rylith said, "but there's more. The choke creeper 'infestation' that prompted the use of the wands—it too was deliberate."

"You mean, someone planted the stuff?" Larajin asked.

She shuddered, remembering how the creeper had nearly strangled her.

As Rylith nodded, Leifander's eyes widened.

"The Sembians!" he exclaimed. "It must have been them.

When I carried the druids' message to Thamalon Uskevren, in Selgaunt, I saw choke creeper sprouting in his garden. I thought it was a weed he'd foolishly overlooked, but now I see the truth. He must be involved in all of this." His lips curved in a sneer. "It makes me feel dirty, to have this man's blood in my veins."

Larajin's cheeks flushed with anger as Leifander talked about Thamalon Uskevren—her father—like a common criminal, but it was Rylith who reprimanded him.

"Leifander! I will not have you speak this way. You are not thinking. The Sembians have nothing to gain from this war. It has cut off their trade with the cities of the north. You are wrong about your father. Thamalon Uskevren is a friend to the elves. The choke creeper was in his garden because he was trying to help us—he was trying to find a way to exterminate it *without* using the wands."

Leifander's mouth opened. "You knew this all along? Why didn't you tell me?"

"I wanted you to draw your own conclusions about your father," Rylith answered.

In the uncomfortable silence that followed, Leifander's face colored. He stared into the distance, then slowly nodded.

"You're right," he said at last. "I wasn't thinking. There is only one person who has anything to gain in all of this."

"Maalthiir," Doriantha spat. "All of the strands of the web lead back to him."

A brief silence followed, broken only by the sound of Goldheart's wings rustling as she worried a frayed feather with her teeth. Doriantha held up her dagger. Her eyes glittered as brightly as its polished steel.

"I say we kill the spider," she said. "Maalthiir must die."

She started to rise, but Leifander caught her arm.

"Don't!" he exclaimed. "You'll only be playing into his hands. Make an attempt on his life, and he'll have an excuse to turn on us." He gestured in the direction of the Red Plumes's camp. "Maalthiir has already tricked us into permitting hundreds of his soldiers to march into the heart of Corman-thor. He's hoping for a falling out—maybe not so soon as this, but eventually. If an incident doesn't occur on its own, he's planning to cause one."

Grudgingly, Doriantha sank back down again.

"Something has to be done," Rylith added, "but Leifander is right, Doriantha. Even if you succeed in killing Maalthiir, it will not stop this war. It will only throw tinder on the flames and force us to fight on three fronts: the Sembians, the drow, and the Red Plumes. We will be defeated—and the great forest will be lost."

Though the discussion was animated, Larajin was only half listening. Instead she pondered Somnilthra's prophecy. Somnilthra had said that, together Leifander and Larajin could heal the rift between human and elf and end the war. She'd told them to make use of a heart and to use love rather than hate.

A heart in love . . .

Larajin realized the answer. Love, she reflected, could make people do things they would not ordinarily do—foolish things, things contrary to their nature. Larajin herself had played love's fool less than a year before. Smitten with love for Diurgo—a noble who barely acknowledged her existence—she'd tried to follow him on his pilgrimage to Lake Sember. She hadn't cared about the consequences. The furor caused by her leaving Stormweather Towers without telling anyone where she was going, the anxious moments she'd caused her family, the possible dangers she'd face. It hadn't even mattered that Diurgo felt nothing for her. She'd ignored all of this and run after him, driven on by the beating of a love-smitten heart.

Her eyes fell on Doriantha. At first she saw only the tattoos, rough clothing, and feathered braid, then she looked deeper and saw a woman whose keen intelligence and fiery spirit would cause any man to fall in love with her, even a city-bred human.

Perhaps, if the goddesses were willing, even a human

with a pathological hatred of elves. If Maalthiir were in love with an elf, Larajin realized, he might abandon his plans to backstab her people, but could it be done? Could the two goddesses work together through Larajin to fill his heart with a love that went beyond the foolish, into the realm of the foolhardy?

If they could—if Maalthiir's love was strong and foolish enough—he might even be persuaded to work at brokering a peace between his elf allies and Sembia—or even to use his army against the drow . . .

Then Larajin realized the flaw in her plan. Thanks to Leifander spying on Maalthiir, the Red Plumes were as stirred up as a nest of hornets. There was no way she was going to get close enough to cast a spell on him, even in tressym form. Yet the attempt would have to be made that night—before Drakkar found her.

Larajin's gaze fell on Leifander, and in that moment she remembered that the prophesy was not hers alone to fulfill. Her brother had a role in all of this, too. That was what the goddesses had been trying to tell them, all along. The twins must combine their magic. Together, they could do anything.

The thought filled Larajin with a sudden rush of hope, leaving her giddy. Breathless, she interrupted the discussion.

"I know how we can do stop this war," she cried, "how we can mend the rift between human and elf. It was just as Somnilthra said, we have to use love to conquer war."

She turned to Doriantha, and saw open skepticism in the elf's eyes. The hardest part would be persuading Doriantha to play along with what would sound like a ridiculous plan, but if the spell Larajin cast on Maalthiir was strong enough, Doriantha could even slap him across the face without dampening his feelings for her. She needn't even pretend to care for Maalthiir. She just might relish the thought of tricking him into using his Red Plumes to rid the forest of drow.

"Doriantha," Larajin said, "I'm going to tell you something

I know will sound crazy, but please hear me out. Leifander and I will need your help."

Before Doriantha could reply, Larajin turned to the druid and said, "Rylith, we'll need your help, too. Would you be able to use your amber to locate Maalthiir?"

Rylith nodded.

Larajin turned to her brother and asked, "Leifander, could you summon up a breeze and use it to carry a small, light object in a precise path over a distance of several hundred paces?"

He made a dismissive gesture. "Child's play."

"Could you do it if you could only see the object in Rylith's amber?"

"I suppose," he said, frowning, "but to what end? And what object?"

Larajin picked up a downy feather that Goldheart had preened from her wing, noting with satisfaction that it was predominantly red—Sune's sacred color.

"This feather," she said.

Leifander and Doriantha stared at her blankly, but on Rylith's face Larajin saw the dawning of a smile. Quickly, Larajin began to speak.

Larajin completed her prayer and held up the tressym feather. Small and downy, it was perhaps the most unusual "weapon" of war ever wielded. Tiny though it might be, it vibrated with magical power. Its color had deepened to a vivid crimson that almost seemed to glow in the darkness, and the scent of Hanali's Heart wafted from it as though it had been soaked in perfume.

"It's ready," she told Doriantha. "Now it's time for you to kiss it."

Doriantha hesitated, her lip curling, then leaned forward. She gave the feather the briefest of kisses, and stared skeptically at it.

"Are you sure this will work? Isn't the enchantment on it too obvious?"

"Only up close," Larajin said. "It'll be Leifander's job to blow the feather up against Maalthiir in such a way that he doesn't see it coming until it's too late."

Overhead, a thickly leafed duskwood tree swayed in the wind, throwing a patter of shadows across the moonlit forest floor. The breeze—cool and refreshing, and carrying rich woodland scents—had been summoned by Leifander. He sat cross-legged on a mossy boulder, eyes closed and arms extended. His hands drifted in lazy circles, fanning the breeze that fluttered the glossy black feathers in the end of his braid.

Rylith, standing next to him, peered intently into her amber. "I see him," she said softly. "Maalthiir is at the center of a group of soldiers. He has just passed through the northern gate and is walking in the direction of the manor house."

Larajin nodded. "We'd better hurry. Once he's indoors, it will be more difficult."

She strode to where Leifander sat and held the feather up in front of him. "Ready?" she asked.

He drew a deep breath, opened his eyes, then nodded. Larajin let go of the feather, which started to drift to the ground. Leifander exhaled. Caught by his breath, the feather at first tumbled through the air, then seemed to find its bearings. It floated away through the forest, weaving its way through the trees.

"Quickly," Larajin told Rylith. "The amber." Then, to Doriantha, "Go now. The feather will reach him before you do."

As Doriantha slipped away into the night, the druid raised the fist-sized chunk of amber so Leifander could peer into it. The image inside, which a moment ago had shown a group of Red Plumes striding up Rauthauvyr's Road, suddenly shifted. Something rushed into view from a distant point, deep within the amber's yellow depths. It drew close enough for Larajin to recognize it as the tressym feather—and it was gone.

"What's happened?" Larajin asked, alarmed.

"Watch," Rylith said.

Larajin did, and saw that the image inside the amber had changed yet again. Instead of the view being fixed at a single point, like a watcher looking down from above, the objects inside the amber seemed to lunge wildly past while the viewpoint constantly changed. A tree appeared, loomed close for a moment, then was gone. A clump of ferns raced up from below—then tumbled away as the view soared up toward the sky like a bird. The angle shifted wildly to avoid a tree branch that suddenly came into view, then a level course once more.

Watching, Larajin realized that the amber was showing the world from the perspective of the feather. Blown by the breeze, tumbling this way and that, it floated out of the forest and into a clearing, then drifted above an expanse of trampled earth that Larajin recognized as Rauthauvyr's Road. A palisaded wall loomed ahead—and a moving carriage, the passage of which sent the feather spiraling—and the open gates approached, and passed by.

Dizzy, Larajin had to look away for a moment to clear her head. She watched Leifander instead, marveling at his control. He was drawing air in through his nostrils and blowing it out through pursed lips in a constant stream, like a trained musician. Eyes locked on the amber, he shifted his head ever so slightly this way and that, altering the flow and direction of his magical breeze. His brow was furrowed in a look of intense concentration, and a trickle of sweat rolled down his temple and tattooed cheek, eventually dripping from his jaw. He ignored it, his chest rising and falling slowly, hands still fanning the air.

Larajin turned her attention back to the amber. The feather moved through the town, drifting over rooftops and corrals, seeking the road Maalthiir and his men were walking. As it passed over the chimneys of the temple of Gond, the image inside the amber tumbled wildly as a current of hot air from a chimney caught it, and for several heart-stopping moments Larajin thought Leifander had lost control of the feather. When the view steadied, the street zoomed up from below.

Walking along it were six men. Their figures enlarged inside the amber as the feather drifted down toward them. One of the figures—an officer with a scar running in a vertical line down one cheek—looked up as if sensing something was wrong, and Larajin held her breath. Maalthiir, walking beside him, noticed his officer looking up and glanced in the same direction, a look of bloodthirsty anticipation on his face, as if he was expecting the return of the crow that had spied on him earlier.

As Leifander blew out the last of his breath in a rush Maalthiir's face enlarged, filling the amber completely. Closer still—a square, stubbled jaw—and closer still—tight, cruel lips—and—

Nothing. The amber was empty.

Leifander slumped, closing his eyes. His breathing became rapid and shallow, and his skin paled. Larajin reached for his shoulder, thinking he was going to fall, but then his eyes opened and his back straightened.

"I did it," he said in a proud voice. "The feather struck Maalthiir full on the lips. It was amazing. Never have I felt so close to the Lady of Air and Wind. I felt like a nestling, enfolded in her powerful wings."

"And now it's up to Doriantha," Larajin said. "May Hanali Celanil and Sune watch over her, and protect her."

That brought Leifander down to earth.

He gave Rylith a worried look and asked, "Can you see her in the amber?"

The druid spoke a flowing phrase in Elvish. A figure appeared within the amber. It was Doriantha, walking along Rauthauvyr's Road. Anxiously, Larajin peered over Rylith's shoulder, watching as Doriantha was challenged at the gate, then allowed to pass through. Doriantha hurried up the road, toward the manor, then up its steps. The view shifted then, showing her entering the great hall. Figures were clustered at the end of it. Maalthiir, his officers, and Lord Ilmeth of Essembra were there. They were involved in an animated discussion, heads close together, but when Doriantha entered, Maalthiir glanced up and the scowl on his face softened. When Doriantha placed a hand above her heart and gave a graceful bow, the scowl melted from his face. A moment later, after beckoning Doriantha forward and listening to her speak, his expression changed to a dreamy smile.

"The spell worked!" Larajin exclaimed with relief.

"It did indeed," Leifander added a moment later. He too was staring into the amber, watching Larajin's plan unfold. "You see? Maalthiir's drawn away from his men and has led Doriantha to a quiet corner to talk. Just look at the desire, burning in his ugly eyes. He'll be asking her to lay with him in another moment. Yes, there! They're leaving the hall together."

With that last comment, Leifander's voice had dropped to a low growl. Tearing his eyes away from the amber, he leaped from the boulder and began pacing back and forth across the clearing.

Watching him, Larajin suddenly realized something. Her brother had feelings for Doriantha. The elf warrior, in turn, cared for Leifander. Hanali Celanil had blessed them both, though their love had yet to fully blossom.

Larajin offered up a prayer for Doriantha's safety, imploring the goddesses to give the archer's budding romance with Leifander time and tranquility in which to blossom. It would be a grim thing indeed if Maalthiir or his officers were to discover Larajin's plot and Leifander were to lose a second woman he adored to the Red Plumes's wrath.

Intent upon her prayer, Larajin at first didn't pay any attention to Rylith's quick intake of breath, but then the druid spoke in a strangled whisper.

"No—what was Doriantha thinking? She has stabbed him!"

"Who's been stabbed?"

A glance into the amber gave Larajin the answer. She saw Maalthiir staggering into the great hall, hands clasped to a stomach that was leaking red. The officer with the scarred face sprang immediately to his side, easing him to the ground and laying hands upon his wound, probably invoking a healing spell. In that same instant, Doriantha came into view.

Leifander, who had joined Larajin and Rylith in peering into the amber, let out an anguished cry.

"What is she doing—why doesn't she flee? She'll be killed!"

Doriantha was pointing behind her, at the hallway she'd just emerged from. Two of Maalthiir's men seized her—strangely, Doriantha did nothing to resist them—while the remaining three ran in the direction she'd been pointing. After a few moments they reappeared, forcing two captives ahead of them at sword point.

Rylith let out a relieved sigh as the two men holding Doriantha released her and gave quick, apologetic bows.

"All is well. It appears that it was not Doriantha who attacked Maalthiir, but someone else—two humans. My guess is they are Sembian spies."

"Sembians?" Larajin asked in a tense, low voice.

A sense of premonition gripping her, she peered more intently at the amber in Rylith's hands. The two captives were on their knees, one with blood running from a gash in his leg, the other holding his head as if he'd been struck. As Larajin watched, their hands were forced behind their backs, and bound.

Maalthiir, his bloody wound stanched by magic, sat up groggily and said something. The officer who had been tending him nodded, then strode over and slapped the captive with the wounded leg. He barked an order over his shoulder, obviously relaying Maalthiir's orders. One of the Red Plumes bent his bow, stringing it.

The second captive—the one who had been holding his head—turned to see what was happening. As he did, Larajin recognized his face. Suddenly, she knew what would come next—she'd seen it in her vision.

"Goddess, no!" she said in a high, tight voice. "That captive—it's Tal. They're about to execute him!"

Heart pounding, Larajin winged her way toward the town as fast as she could fly. Fear lent an urgency to each stroke of her wings, and determination made her ignore the oldiers in the streets below who were pointing up at her and shouting. An arrow sang past her, barely a pace away, but she only realized the soldiers below were shooting at her when a second arrow, closer than the first, snagged her wing and sent her tumbling. Furiously, she beat her wing to loosen it from her feathers, then recovered and flew on.

A short distance behind her, a small black shape trailed in her wake. Leifander had skinwalked only a heartbeat or two after Larajin did, but whether he meant to help her or to try to stop her was unclear. Nor did it matter. The only thing Larajin could think of was Tal.

Swooping down to street level, she flew toward Ilmeth's Manor. With a rush of relief, she saw that Tal was still alive. Two Red Plumes had dragged him out onto the street, and were trying to force the struggling Tal to his knees. The archer—one of the Red Plumes—stood a few paces away, an arrow nocked but the bow held loosely at his side. The other captive lay on his face in the street in a pool of blood, the point of an arrow protruding from his back. The soldiers threw Tal face-first onto the ground beside the body, then took a quick pace back. The archer raised his bow as Tal struggled to rise.

Howling her fury, Larajin dived at the archer. She raked him with all four feet, claws tearing at his face. Above her, she heard a hoarse caw, and from behind her came a stranger sound—the snarl of an angry dog. She risked a glance back, and saw Tal rising to his feet, getting ready to run. There was no time to see if he made it, however. She had to avoid the archer, who flailed at her, cursing.

Larajin scratched his arm, but her claws slid harmlessly off the thick leather bracer that protected it. His fist connected with her head, knocking her spinning through the air. She crashed into a wooden rail in front of the building opposite Ilmeth's Manor, and felt something crack in one wing, then she fell heavily to the ground. Shaky, unable to rise, she looked up and saw the archer aiming his arrow at her.

So this is how I'm going to die, she thought, vision blurring from the pain of her injured wing. Silently, she began to pray. Goddess enfold my soul in your love, I—

A heartbeat before the archer loosed his arrow, a large dark shape streaked up the street. Leaping into the air, it struck the archer full in the chest, knocking him down.

The other two soldiers—Ilmeth's men—were also in trouble. Leifander, still in crow form, had landed on the rooftop above Larajin and was flapping his wings furiously. The blast of magical wind he summoned caught the two full on, tumbling them backward like blown leaves against the steps of Ilmeth's Manor. Inside the manor, Red Plumes officers shouted orders, drew steel, and tried to join the fight. The wind howled in through the open doorway, driving them back.

At last able to rise to her feet but still unable to straighten her injured wing, Larajin looked around. She saw no sign of Tal—she prayed that meant he'd escaped—but she did finally get a good look at her savior. It was an enormous wolf that stared back at her with bright green eyes. Amazingly, the wolf reared up and walked like a man on its two hind legs. Bending at the waist, he reached down with paws that looked like elongated, hairy hands, picked her up, and gently cradled her to his chest, then he ran.

The pain of her injured wing nearly made Larajin faint. Gentle though he was, the wolf-creature couldn't help but jostle her as he ran. Larajin had a dim sense of buildings flashing past, then a gate, and shouting soldiers, and arrows singing past. Head lolling, she happened to look up and saw Leifander flying low and hard after them, then trees were on either side and the wolf-creature's run became a series of leaps and zigzags as he made his way deeper into the forest.

The pain in her wing was intense, all consuming. Larajin tried to cast a healing spell, but the prayer would not come to her lips. She found herself unable to maintain concentration, and she began slipping out of tressym form. Her torso and limbs elongated, fur and feathers shrank back into her skin, and her injured wing became an injured left arm. The wolf-creature, suddenly finding his burden increased tenfold, staggered under the increased weight and nearly dropped her. Sagging to his knees, he lowered her to the forest floor.

Behind him, Leifander settled onto a branch, then hopped along it, his head cocked.

The wolf-creature crouched for a moment in silence, still panting from his run. Then, in a voice that was part growl, part yip, he barked out a single word.

"Larajin?"

Larajin peered up at the creature, whose face was thrown into shadow by the moonlight that streamed down from above. The wolf lifted his head to glance up at Leifander, and she got a better look at his features. They were those of a wolf indeed, with pointed ears and a mouth filled with sharp white fangs, but there was something about those green eyes, the way they sparkled with intelligence—and recognition. Larajin suddenly realized that she was looking not at some strange forest creature but at a product of a magical contagion that had shifted an ordinary man into a werewolf—and not just any man.

"Tal?" she asked.

The werewolf nodded.

Behind him, Leifander had shifted back to elf form. He hopped lightly down from the branch.

"I didn't know your brother could skinwalk," he said.

Tal spun in place and snarled, exposing teeth and claws. Larajin reached out to stop him with her good arm—then gasped as a fresh wave of pain wracked her body. Tal, however, must have recognized Leifander, for his hands relaxed, then dropped to his side. He grinned, tongue lolling.

"Leifander," Tal said. "I see my sister found you."

Leifander dipped his head in a slight bow.

Dizzy with pain, Larajin was also reeling from having learned Tal's secret. Suddenly, all of Tal's strange ways made sense: his constant obsession with shaving, his monthly bouts with the "flu" that supposedly confined him to bed, his wolfish appetite, and his reluctance to handle the silver dagger he'd given her—all were explained by the fact that he was infected with lycanthropy.

Larajin hadn't been the only one in the Uskevren household with a secret. Maybe it was time to share hers.

"Tal," she began. "There's something I . . ."

Moving sent a shock of pain through her injured arm. Before she did anything else, she needed to heal it. Cradling the arm against her chest, she touched her locket and began to pray to both goddesses. Healing a cracked bone wasn't easy.

"Sune and Hanali Celanil, grant me your blessing. Lend me a little of your healing magic." The locket began to warm under her fingers, and a hint of floral scent rose from it. "Heal my—"

She gasped as a sharp pain lanced through her foot. It felt as though something sharp had gotten inside the boot, and Larajin had trod upon it. She recognized it as the sharp sting of the thorn.

Tal kneeled by her side, his wide green eyes brimming with concern. "What's wrong, Larajin? Your face has gone ashen."

Leifander was a heartbeat behind him. He too kneeled at Larajin's side. "Isn't it obvious? Her arm's injured. Larajin, do you want me to try to—"

"Get away from me, both of you," Larajin gasped, looking wildly around the forest and groping for the magic dagger in its sheath at her hip. "It's Drakkar. He's coming for—"

Before she could complete her warning, a bolt of magical energy hissed through the night. Streaking a line of silvery sparks, it wound its way in a tight spiral around Tal's torso, solidifying into a sparkling coil that pinned his arms against his sides. Howling, he leaped to his feet, but the coil of energy had rooted itself in the ground like a vine. It tightened around his body, creasing his skin, and the smell of burning flesh filled the air. Crashing to the ground, Tal lay, panting, eyes wide.

"It's . . . silver." he gasped. "It burns like . . . poison."

Leifander had reacted swiftly, braid flying out behind as he whipped around to face the spot from which the magical attack had originated. In a voice tight with urgency, he began chanting the words to a spell in the flowing language of the forest elves.

Speedy though his reaction had been, it wasn't fast enough. A voice in the woods barked three quick, chittering words, and Leifander's prayer suddenly stopped. His eyes glazed and his tattooed face fell into a slack-jawed expression. A moment later, he started to drool. He stared stupidly around, a confused look on his face. His lips moved, trying to form words, but all that came out was a soft grunt.

As soon as she had seen the magic energy streaking toward Tal, Larajin began to pray. The glow around the locket intensified, and the smell of Hanali's Heart filled the air. Larajin abandoned her healing spell. Instead she beseeched her goddesses for one of the first spells they'd ever bestowed upon her.

As Drakkar stepped out of the forest, she shouted at him with all of the power she could muster: "Flee!"

Though the floral smell intensified and the glow from the locket became as bright as a small campfire, nothing happened. Drakkar stared down at her, unperturbed, then flicked his fingers in her direction. She found herself unable to move, save for blinking and breathing. She resisted his spell with all of her willpower, but though sweat broke out on her brow and her fingers trembled, her body remained rigid. Her jaw was locked shut and her lips wouldn't even twitch. There would be no more prayers. She looked wildly around, heart hammering in her chest, silently hoping that Rylith, Doriantha—or even Goldheart—would appear to rescue her.

They didn't.

Blinking back tears of frustration, Larajin stared up at Drakkar. Was his resistance to magic really so strong that he had resisted the combined power of two goddesses? Had her spells failed her?

No, she told herself. The floral scent of Hanali's Heart still hung in the air, and though the glow from the locket was dimming, Larajin could still feel the warmth of Sune's magic pulsing from it. The goddesses hadn't denied Larajin their blessing—they'd just altered the form she'd expected it to take, just as they had at Lake Sember, when they'd granted Larajin a spell that enabled her to breathe water instead of to walk upon it.

They wanted her to cast a different spell, but which?

Drakkar leaned on his thorn-studded staff, staring at Larajin, his posture one of pure malice. A strand of cobweb still clung to his jet-black hair. Absently, he brushed it away.

"Well now, if it isn't the serving girl from Selgaunt who likes tressym so much she became one," he wheezed, sarcasm dripping from his voice. "What are you doing, so far from home? Spying, I'll warrant. Let's find out what you learned."

Studying his staff, he plucked a thorn from it. He circled around Leifander, who stared dully at the wizard as he walked by, then bent over Larajin.

He paused, sniffing the air. The floral fragrance hung heavily around Larajin. Did he realize what it signified?

He glanced at the red glow that shone between the fingers

of Larajin's right hand—the one clasping the locket—and spoke a word in the drow tongue. A moment later, the glow faded altogether, but though the visible manifestation of Sune's magic was gone, the magic itself remained. Larajin felt its warmth flow out of the locket and up her arm to coalesce deep within her, around her heart.

Picking up a stick, Drakkar used it to pry Larajin's lower lip down but could not force open her clenched jaw. He struggled a moment, then wheezed a warning at her.

"I'm going to release your jaw," he said, "but no tricks—and no spellcasting. Utter one word, and you're a dead woman. Understand?"

He laughed at Larajin as she lay frozen on the ground, perhaps savoring her anguish at being unable even to nod. His fingers moved in a spiderlike dance across her jaw. Suddenly able to open her mouth, Larajin spoke the only words that wouldn't cause her immediate doom.

"Drakkar, please," she whispered. "I'll tell you whatever you want to know."

"Of course you will." With that brief comment, he forced open her mouth, and jammed the thorn into her tongue.

Grimacing at the bitter taste, Larajin tried to spit the thorn from her mouth, but instead it wormed its way ever deeper into her tongue. Drakkar stared down at her, waiting for whatever foul magic he'd just worked on her to take effect.

She glared up at him. Drakkar had blasted Leifander's mind, had bound Tal in silver knowing it was poisonous to him, and now was about to subject her to some equally foul magic, then kill her. She strained her eyes, glancing at Leifander's drooling face, at Tal's struggling form. Two brothers whom she'd do anything to be able to save—even sacrifice herself, so strong was her love for them . . .

. . . and Larajin realized the spell the goddesses wanted her to cast. It was the most powerful one in their arsenal—the one that had already turned Maalthiir into a lovesick fool. All Larajin had to do was get Drakkar to lower his lips to hers.

The thorn wriggled deeper into her tongue. Then, all at once, the pain of it disappeared. Drakkar, as if sensing his magic had come to fruition, straightened.

"Now then," he wheezed. "What were you doing at the tower in the forest? What did you see and hear?"

"I saw you meeting with . . . the drow," she answered, keeping her voice deliberately faint and weak. "You were . . . talking about . . . the plan to . . ."

Drakkar leaned closer. "To what?"

Larajin whispered. "I heard you say . . ."

As Drakkar cocked his head, Larajin offered up one last, silent prayer to Sune and Hanali Celanil. As she completed it, magical energy flowed through her, causing her entire body to flush a deep red and the floral scent to rush from her pores. For one brief instant, the paralysis left her—but that instant was enough. Jerking her head upward, she kissed Drakkar full on the lips. Then her body stiffened and became rigid once more.

The wizard staggered back, angrily wiping the back of his hand against his lips. His face twisted in an angry sneer, and he raised his staff, clearly about to discharge the full force of its magical energies upon her—but a heartbeat later, his expression slowly began to change. The sneer softened, then left his face entirely. His eyes widened, and his lips parted in a soft smile.

"Larajin," he sighed.

Larajin closed her eyes, breathing a sigh of thanks to her goddesses. She gave Drakkar an imploring look.

"Free me?"

"Of course, Larajin, dear. Of course." With a wave of one dark hand, he released her.

Larajin sat up and immediately kneeled over Tal, who was still struggling against his bonds, albeit feebly. He seemed too weak to speak or even to acknowledge Larajin as she whispered encouragement to him and stroked his brow. Out of the corner of her eye, Larajin saw a dark glint in Drakkar's eyes. She instantly understood the look for what it was.

"You needn't be jealous," she told the wizard. "He's only a . . . my brother." She blinked. Why had she said that? She'd intended to say that Tal was a friend, yet something had compelled her to blurt out the truth instead.

The thorn. Like the one that had pierced her foot earlier that evening, it had vanished, but its magic was still strong.

Drakkar's eyes narrowed with suspicion. "This werewolf is your brother? Who is he?"

Finding herself unable to lie, Larajin let the truth tumble out. "He's the youngest son of the Uskevren household, Talbot."

"How is he the brother of a serving girl?"

"His father Thamalon had a—dalliance—with my mother. Tal is my half-brother."

"Ah." The explanation seemed to satisfy Drakkar. He glanced at the slack-jawed Leifander, who starred dully back at him. "And the elf? He claims to be Thamalon Uskevren's son. Is he your brother, too?"

Larajin blinked in surprise. Drakkar already knew about Leifander's parentage? The spell compelled her to answer.

"Yes. He's my brother too."

The wizard merely grunted.

"Drakkar," she continued. "You know I can't lie to you. If I promise to prevent either of my brothers from harming you, will you reverse the spells you cast on them? Please . . . for my sake?"

Drakkar glanced briefly at Tal, then stared at Larajin, a look of intense longing on his face. "Answer one question for me, first."

Larajin braced herself.

"Do you love me?"

"No."

He winced.

Larajin had to speak quickly, or all would be lost. "Can't you understand how it pains me to see my brothers like this?"

she asked Drakkar. "Imagine how you felt, just now, when I admitted I didn't love you. My anguish is equal to what you just felt, but at least you have hope, that one day, if you redeem yourself . . ."

She let her voice trail off, wary about saying too much. She wanted to give Drakkar the illusion that she might love him, one day. If she continued speaking, however, the truth would come out. She didn't even trust herself to look at Drakkar, lest the thorn compel her expression to show what she truly felt. Fear. Disgust. Hatred.

"Very well!" Drakkar cried.

He made a quick hand gesture and spoke a word in the drow tongue. With a faint hissing sound, the magical coils vanished. Tal groaned and rolled over onto his back, staring at the sky. Dark singe lines crisscrossed his flesh, but at least he was alive.

"And Leifander?" Larajin asked.

Drakkar beckoned for Leifander to approach him. Leifander blinked in confusion a moment, then at last grasped what the wizard wanted. He walked to Drakkar, obedient and docile, and gave the wizard an innocent, trusting look as Drakkar's questing fingers moved across his scalp.

"Ah!" Drakkar grunted after a moment or two. "There."

He plucked something out of Leifander's scalp, and held it up for Larajin to see. It was another thorn. Drakkar flicked it away into the forest.

Leifander's eyes cleared instantly. With a harsh caw, he leaped for the wizard's throat. Larajin, however, had anticipated this, and shouted a single command: "Stop!"

Once again, the fragrance of Hanali's Heart filled the air as the locket at Larajin's wrist pulsed red. Suddenly rigid, Leifander strained against Larajin's spell a moment or two, then, finding himself unable to attack Drakkar, he whirled on her.

"Why?" he asked in a strangled voice.

"I made a promise to Drakkar," Larajin said, "that if he

restored your mind, I wouldn't let you harm him."

"My ... mind?" Leifander rubbed a temple and looked around like a sleeper who had suddenly awakened. He saw Tal groaning on the ground, and added, "What happened here?"

Drakkar continued to eye Leifander warily. His fingers hovered over on his staff, ready to pluck a thorn at the first sign of trouble.

"I'm having a talk with Drakkar," Larajin answered. "Just like Doriantha is talking to Maalthiir."

Understanding bloomed instantly in Leifander's eyes.

"I see." He glanced at Drakkar, then feigned disgust. "Fine. Talk to him, then." Deliberately, he turned his back on her.

Larajin turned her attention back to Drakkar, whose posture was still tense and ready. Infatuated with her he might be, but he was still cautious.

"Drakkar, like you, I'm half human and half elf," Larajin continued. "I've faced a lack of acceptance because of it, but I'm not a traitor to my people."

"Nor am I!" Drakkar wheezed. "My people—"

"You've turned your back on your human side," Larajin said, "and that saddens me." She let the words hang in the air a moment, then added, "Do you know what would make me very happy?"

Drakkar's face brightened. "What?"

"If this war had never begun."

Drakkar shook his head. "But it has. It can't be stopped."

Larajin looked him square in the eye. "Yes it can. You can stop it by returning to Selgaunt and using your influence with the Hulorn to persuade him to petition against the war."

Out of the corner of her eye, Larajin could see Leifander begin to smile.

"It would also please me if you would speak to Lord Maalthiir and try to make him realize that the forest elves are too strong and that his plans to carve a road through the forest will never succeed."

"But they will!" Drakkar said. "We'll use the wands I created—using the mist, we can clear a road in a tenday." He was obviously trying to impress her.

Larajin shook her head slowly. "Causing further destruction to the forest would make me very sad. And very unhappy with you, Drakkar."

The wizard's face fell.

"Finally, you could speak to the drow and convince them that they're better off in their lairs below ground—that the forest is no place for them."

"I would do anything for you, Larajin, but I cannot accomplish the impossible," Drakkar said. "The drow aren't likely to—"

"Very well," Larajin interrupted, "but my first two requests—you will speak to the Hulorn, and to Maalthiir, won't you?"

For a moment, defiance flickered in Drakkar's eyes, and Larajin thought she had lost him. He gave a great sigh, like a lovesick youth.

"For you, Larajin . . . I'll do it."

Beside Larajin, Leifander had to pretend to cough, to cover his wide grin. Tal had risen feebly to a sitting position and was gaping at what he heard.

Larajin ignored him.

"There is one thing more you could do for me, if you would," she told Drakkar.

Drakkar's eyebrows lifted. "What is it, my dear?"

She lifted her foot slightly. "This thorn hurts," she said simply. "Could you please remove it?"

"Of course!" Kneeling at her side like a Sembian gallant, Drakkar removed her boot and plucked the thorn from the sole of her foot.

"And this one, too?" Larajin asked, pointing at her tongue.

"Yes. Immediately."

Somehow she kept her face neutral while Drakkar's fingers probed inside her mouth. When the thorn was gone, relief washed through her.

"Thank you," she said, then she let a touch of haughtiness creep into her voice. Deliberately she adopted the same tone Thazienne used to such good effect on her hordes of lovesick suitors. "Well, Drakkar, what are you waiting for? The Hulorn is going to be the toughest to convince. You'd better start back for Selgaunt at once."

"I . . ." Once again resistance flickered in Drakkar's eyes— then was gone, as a rush of floral scent filled the air. "At once, my dear," he said, bowing. "At once."

He disappeared with a soft *pop*.

Leifander turned to Larajin, no longer trying to hide his grin, and asked, "Do you think he'll do it?"

Larajin nodded. "I've never felt the power of the goddesses so keenly as when I cast that spell upon him. He'll do it." She shrugged. "As to whether it's enough to put an end to this war, well, we'll see."

She groaned, at last acknowledging the pain of her injured arm. During the exhilaration of working her magic upon Drakkar, she'd been able to ignore it, but the pain was washing over her in waves, making her feel faint and queasy.

"Now," she told him, "I have to mend this arm of mine."

EPILOGUE

Two figures stood in the forest, watching through a gap in the trees as soldiers with red plumes on their helms trooped past along the road. Riding beside them in an open carriage were four men. Three were officers—one with a vertical scar across his face, another burly and bald, the third a wiry, thin man with fair hair. They stared at the soldiers under their command and shook their heads, as if mightily displeased. The fourth man—who had close-cropped red hair and eyebrows that met in a V—kept turning to look south, back the way they had come, a lovesick look on his face.

The two figures surreptitiously watching the soldiers from the woods—a wild elf with tattooed cheeks and hands and glossy black feathers in his braid; and a woman wearing a red scarf in her hair and a heart-shaped locket at her wrist—turned to each other and grinned, as if sharing a great secret, then they glanced at the woman next to them.

This woman was older than the other two, with gray hair and a face creased with wrinkles and tattooed in a tree-branch pattern. She crouched near the base of an enormous standing stone whose glossy gray surface was carved with Elvish script. She ran a hand across the surface of the stone, then peered closely at it, and smiled.

"It is done," she told the other two. "The prophesy is fulfilled. The rift is healed, and the crack has vanished."

She lifted her wrinkled face to catch the sun, and savored a moment of birdsong that echoed through the wood.

"The gods themselves are singing," she added, standing. "What will you do now?"

The man's eyes ranged over the trees, and the new vegetation that was growing in a blighted patch of wood. As he considered his answer, a wren burst out of a clump of undergrowth, winging its way toward him. It landed on the man's shoulder, tail flicking, as a winged cat padded out of the bush. The tressym glanced around the clearing and spotted the bird on the man's shoulder. It crouched, tail lashing, about to spring—but then a sharp word from the woman in red brought it to heel. Obediently it padded over to her and wove itself in and out through her ankles, then settled at her feet—only occasionally glancing slyly up at the bird.

The man lifted the wren gently from his shoulder and lifted it to his lips.

"Take more care," he whispered in its ear. "The war may be over, but for a nestling like you, the woods still hold many dangers."

The bird cocked its head, as if listening to the advice, then it sprang into flight. The tressym, still lying at the woman's feet, lifted its head sharply, then glanced up at its mistress and decided against pursuit.

The man at last answered the gray-haired woman's question. "I'm a creature of the great forest," he told her, "and the forest needs our protection, still. The drow are growing in boldness and number—" his eye fell on the carving on the standing stone—"and someone has to ensure that the ancient pact is honored."

The gray-haired woman nodded. "And you?" she asked the younger woman.

"I'm returning to Selgaunt," the woman answered. "I want to see my family again and study in Sune's temple. Perhaps," she added, a mischievous smile on her face, "I may ask my father to donate a little of the family fortune toward setting up a place of worship dedicated to the goddesses: Sune and Hanali Celanil both. I've already decided on the vestments the clerics will wear. They'll be made from a cloth dyed Sune's crimson, and embroidered in gold with Hanali Celanil's hearts."

The older woman nodded, a pleased look in her eye.

"May the goddess grant you your every wish," the man said. He gave her a formal bow, both hands on his heart.

The younger woman smiled and started to place her hands on her own heart—then impulsively, she gave him a hug instead. As she broke away, laughing, the tressym at her feet *brrowed*, and looked up at her questioningly.

"Yes, Goldheart, it's time we were off." She turned to the older woman. "Good-bye, Rylith."

"Farewell. We'll see you again, soon enough. There's much you've yet to learn about the elf goddess."

"That's true," the woman said.

She kneeled beside the tressym, hands braced on the ground in front of her, and spoke the words of a prayer. Swiftly, a transformation came over her. She shrank, sprouted whiskers and fur, and wings grew from her shoulders. In another moment, she was indistinguishable from the tressym beside her, aside from the fact that her wings were a uniform crimson color, rather than a peacock's rainbow.

Launching herself into the air, she flew away, the tressym following close behind.

On the ground below, the man and woman closed their eyes, savoring the floral scent she left in her wake.

LISA SMEDMAN

The New York Times best-selling author of *Extinction* follows up
on the War of the Spider Queen with a new trilogy that brings
the Chosen of Lolth out of the Demonweb Pits and on a bloody
rampage across Faerûn.

THE LADY PENITENT

BOOK I
SACRIFICE OF THE WIDOW

Halisstra Melarn has been a priestess of Lolth, a repentant follower of Eilistraee, and
a would-be killer of gods, but now she's been transformed into the monstrous Lady
Penitent, and those she once called friends will feel the sting of her venom.

BOOK II
STORM OF THE DEAD

As the followers of Eilistraee fall one by one to Halisstra's wrath, Lolth turns her
attention to the other gods.

September 2007

BOOK III
ASCENDANCY OF THE LAST

The dark elves of Faerûn must finally choose between a goddess that offers
redemption and peace, or a goddess that demands sacrifice and blood. We know
what a human would choose, but what about a drow?

June 2008

RICHARD LEE BYERS

The author of *Dissolution* and The Year of Rogue Dragons sets his
sights on the realm of Thay in a new trilogy that no
FORGOTTEN REALMS® fan can afford to miss.

THE HAUNTED LAND

BOOK I
UNCLEAN

Many powerful wizards hold Thay in their control, but when one of them
grows weary of being one of many, and goes to war, it will be at the head of
an army of undead.

BOOK II
UNDEAD

The dead walk in Thay, and as the rest of Faerûn looks on in stunned horror, the very
nature of this mysterious, dangerous realm begins to change.

March 2008

BOOK III
UNHOLY

Forces undreamed of even by Szass Tam have brought havoc and death to Thay, but
the lich's true intentions remain a mystery—a mystery that could spell doom for the
entire world.

Early 2009

ANTHOLOGY
REALMS OF THE DEAD

A collection of new short stories by some of the Realms' most popular authors sheds
new light on the horrible nature of the undead of Faerûn. Prepare yourself for the
terror of the *Realms of the Dead*.

Early 2010

THOMAS M. REID

The author of *Insurrection* and The Scions of Arrabar Trilogy
rescues Aliisza and Kaanyr Vhok from the tattered remnants
of their assault on Menzoberranzan, and sends them off on
a quest across the multiverse that will leave
FORGOTTEN REALMS® fans reeling!

THE EMPYREAN ODYSSEY

BOOK I
THE GOSSAMER PLAIN

Kaanyr Vhok, fresh from his defeat against the drow, turns to hated Sundabar for the
victory his demonic forces demand, but there's more to his ambitions than just one
human city. In his quest for arcane power, he sends the alu-fiend Aliisza on a mission
that will challenge her in ways she never dreamed of.

BOOK II
THE FRACTURED SKY

A demon surrounded by angels in a universe of righteousness? How did that
become Aliisza's life?

November 2008

BOOK III
THE CRYSTAL MOUNTAIN

What Aliisza has witnessed has changed her forever, but that's nothing compared
to what has happened to the multiverse itself. The startling climax will change the
nature of the cosmos forever.

Mid-2009

*"Reid is proving himself to be one of the best up and coming authors
in the FORGOTTEN REALMS universe."*
—fantasy-fan.org

PAUL S. KEMP

"I would rank Kemp among WotC's most talented authors, past and present, such as R. A. Salvatore, Elaine Cunningham, and Troy Denning."
—Fantasy Hotlist

The New York Times best-selling author of *Resurrection* and The Erevis Cale Trilogy plunges ever deeper into the shadows that surround the FORGOTTEN REALMS® world in this Realms-shaking new trilogy.

THE TWILIGHT WAR

BOOK I
SHADOWBRED
It takes a shade to know a shade, but will take more than a shade to stand against the Twelve Princes of Shade Enclave. All of the realm of Sembia may not be enough.

BOOK II
SHADOWSTORM
Civil war rends Sembia, and the ancient archwizards of Shade offer to help. But with friends like these . . .

September 2007

BOOK III
SHADOWREALM
No longer content to stay within the bounds of their magnificent floating city, the Shadovar promise a new era, and a new empire, for the future of Faerûn.

May 2008

Anthology
REALMS OF WAR
A collection of all new stories by your favorite FORGOTTEN REALMS authors digs deep into the bloody history of Faerûn.

January 2008